UNBOUND.

Carn turned to Brandt, still puzzled. "You're giving me . . ."

"Giving nothing," Solan interrupted with pedantic precision. "This is a matter of control, not ownership. You merely run all of Mr. Karrelian's concerns until his return."

"His return," Carn echoed. He drew in a breath, cool and damp. In the gathering darkness, he could almost believe himself back in the Atahr Vin. "The Binding. You're going after him."

"To hell with the Binding," Brandt growled in return. "To hell with Aston and to hell with Imbress and to hell with the entire Ministry of Intelligence." As he spoke, he could feel the boiling surge of rage, just as he had in the Atahr Vin, but his voice remained low and cold. "Damn them all, and damn all of Chaldus and Yndor besides. I'm going after *him*."

And the image hung in Brandt's mind, as clear as Carn's own: the bald skull beaded with sweat, the pupils dilated so the irises seemed only thin, dark bands. That leering smile.

Galatine Hazard was going to find an assassin named Hain.

And, when he did, he was going to cut his legs off. . . .

THE CHRONICLES OF THE UNBINDING

HAZARD'S PRICE

Robert S. Stone

ACE BOOKS, NEW YORK

HAZARD'S PRICE

An Ace Book / published by arrangement with
the author

PRINTING HISTORY
Ace mass-market edition / August 2001

All rights reserved.
Copyright © 2001 by Robert S. Stone
Cover art by Keith Birdsong

This book, or parts thereof, may not be reproduced in any form
without permission.
For information address: The Berkley Publishing Group,
a division of Penguin Putnam Inc.,
375 Hudson Street, New York, New York 10014.

Visit our website at
www.penguinputnam.com

Check out the ACE Science Fiction & Fantasy newsletter
and much more on the Internet at Club PPI!

ISBN: 0-441-00837-2

ACE®
Ace Books are published by The Berkley Publishing Group,
a division of Penguin Putnam Inc.,
375 Hudson Street, New York, New York 10014.
ACE and the "A" design
are trademarks belonging to Penguin Putnam Inc.

PRINTED IN THE UNITED STATES OF AMERICA

10 9 8 7 6 5 4 3 2 1

In memory of my father, who once predicted I'd be the first man on Mars and wasn't far off the mark.

With deep gratitude to Deb, whose love and encouragement helped bring this to fruition; and to Bennett Lovett-Graff, John Lockhart, and Matt Payne for their sparkling humor and intelligent commentary.

For that which is bound to be freed,
That which is strong must be broken.

—FRAGMENT OF AN ANCIENT KHRINE BALLAD

PROLOGUE

From his quiet vantage in the shadow of the gates, Madh watched the carriages thunder by and clatter to a stop before the mansion's marble steps. Liveried footmen helped the guests down to the cobbled plaza and ushered them through the mansion's broad doors. There, they joined the joyous assembly that had gathered to celebrate the wake of the world.

Of course, none of these champagne-swiggers knew the true meaning of their festivities. No one, that is, except Madh. The rest of the throng—an aging collection of parts suppliers, retailers, foggy-eyed philanthropists, and minor bureaucrats—supposed they were attending one of that ceaseless cycle of parties that greased the wheels of commerce, the turnings of which they found more reliable than the progress of the seasons. Tonight's extravaganza was the production of Brandt Karrelian, a man whom no one particularly liked but who, as the largest manufacturer of electrical generators in eastern Chaldus, threw parties that few could afford to miss. With a casual word spoken between sips of wine, Brandt Karrelian could seal deals that would dictate a year's tide of fortunes. But tonight, Madh knew, a more portentous covenant would be sealed than even Karrelian could dream of.

Karrelian's estate was an odd place for a celebration, Madh thought, and an odd place for the end of the world to begin. Even from this distance, he could feel the hum of huge generators housed beneath the ground—generators whose capacity far exceeded the ostentatious brilliance of the mansion's lighting. There could be only one purpose for such machines: to disrupt any exercise of magic in the vicinity. And yet Madh could sense deeply laid wards that protected the house in subtle, lethal ways—wards that seemed undisturbed by the electrical fields. It was rare to find powerful generators and equally potent sorcery working in the same vicinity without interfering with each other. Such elaborate protection Brandt Karrelian had paid for dearly, although it would not help him a whit when the end came.

But the end would never come if Madh remained in the shadows of Karrelian's elms all evening. As two more carriages rattled along the cobblestone drive, Madh decided sourly that it was time to join the gathering. He strolled toward the pool of light that splashed through the mansion's doors, making an effort to look as happily vapid as the other revelers. He feared that even if he succeeded in erasing the contempt from his face, he would still be noticed for his olive skin and his foreign manners. But as he passed into the mansion's marble antechamber, he drew no more attention from Karrelian's doormen than a polite greeting.

Once inside the house, there was no mistaking the scene of the party. Through a nearby set of open doors lay a vast ballroom, brilliantly lit and packed with partygoers whose fevered conversations mounted to a roar. Madh hesitated upon the threshold, loath to step into the ballroom. There were few things he hated more than crowds, save crowds of Chaldeans—and nothing worse except rich, jaded Chaldeans. If there were such a place as hell, Madh suspected the devil would model it after one of Brandt Karrelian's parties. But, thinking of his master and his task, Madh sighed and stepped inside. A soberly clad waiter approached him, bearing a silver tray of champagne glasses, but Madh declined and, with a crooked smile, melted into the crowd.

"Court him, *court him*," a middle-aged brunette was whispering urgently into her husband's ear. The woman's figure was skeletal, the product of self-induced starvation, and it had been crammed into a black crepe evening gown of yet more diminutive proportions, by what marvel of magic or engineering, Madh could not guess.

Her husband, a rotund man of vanishing gray hair and stern countenance, was dressed in the current mode: a crisp black jacket that terminated at the waist, fastened by two close-set buttons; a black silken bow tie over a dazzling white shirt; and a pair of black woolen trousers that flared wide at the thighs but tapered to a close fit above his gleaming shoes. The broad, immaculate surfaces of his outfit played counterpoint to the deep-set lines of his face— a face that was struggling as fruitlessly as Madh's to manufacture a smile.

"I've lasted three decades in this business on the strength of my wits. I'll be damned before I go begging on my knees to an upstart—"

"And," his wife responded, "will your unbent knees be a comfort in debtor's prison? Will you see your children thrown into the streets simply to spite Karrelian?"

Tonight, it appeared, everyone's mind was on their gracious host. Madh's piercing black eyes swept across the great ballroom, but Brandt Karrelian was not to be found.

Madh settled for a scrutiny of the man's house instead. The elaborate wainscoting and the rich, dark parquet—evidently, Karrelian had imported the mansion's lumber from the exotic hardwood forests of Brindis. More impressive still was the massive crystal chandelier, suspended from the ceiling thirty feet above like a galaxy of piercing stars. The cost of the crystal was staggering enough, but more significant was the fact that electric bulbs, not gas or candles, gave the ballroom its merciless radiance.

Madh pondered the excessive brilliance of the room for a moment. Was it simply the vanity of a man who had made his fortune—at least, his *legal* fortune—by investing in the newly burgeoning industry of electricity, or was there another reason? Did Karrelian somehow prefer this surgical light, this glare that exposed every wrinkle beneath cunning makeup and turned every smile into a leer?

Madh shook his head, afraid he had been letting his imagination run unchecked. The grotesque atmosphere of the ball was no doubt imparted by his own prejudice, not by some quality of the light. Nevertheless, his speculations had been tending in a crucial direction: there was no denying that Brandt Karrelian was an obscenely wealthy man . . . and a man whose temper was as notoriously capricious as his holdings were vast.

How does one buy such a man? Such was the nature of Madh's task. Surely, not with gold.

For the first time that night, Madh's brow furrowed in the contemplation of failure. Failure, among the many things his master did not tolerate, ranked supreme. He pushed past a knot of city officials who were loudly regaling each other with thrice-told jokes and found himself by one of the room's narrow windows. Madh had noticed these windows before—indeed, in Madh's profession, windows were one of the first things one noticed. From a distance, they seemed like broad arches of leaded glass, almost ten feet in height. A closer look revealed that the individual panes were divided by iron bars as stout as you'd find in a cage at the zoo. And

Madh suspected that the ends of those bars sank deep
into the mansion's limestone walls. In the event of a fire,
Karrelian's guests would be stampeded to death, for not
even a boy could wriggle out the slim apertures of the
mansion's windows. And, more to the point, not even a
boy could wriggle in.

Perhaps gold could not buy Brandt Karrelian, but
Madh relaxed in the knowledge that there were things
Karrelian feared. And where there was fear, Madh's experience told him, there was desire. The two were bound
more intimately than a heated pair of lovers.

He turned at the sound of a gasp behind him. A few
feet away stood one of the younger women at the party,
barely out of her teens. Every line of her lithe body was
proudly defined beneath the silken embrace of a sheer
red dress, the back of which was a deep V that teasingly
hinted at the cleft of her buttocks. Her long blond hair
had been braided into a sinuous rope that swayed playfully around that fleshy valley, obscuring or exposing it
at whim. Madh frowned at the display. Among his people, a woman would be shunned for dressing this way
in public. These decadent Chaldeans. . . .

At her side stood an older man, in his middle or late
thirties, it would seem, although the sprinkling of gray
in his black hair made him look more severe than his
years. Or perhaps that was the work of his cold hazel
eyes. He was more simply dressed than the other revelers, wearing neither jacket nor tie. Instead, only a crisp
white shirt covered a frame that was mostly lean, although Madh could see the beginnings of a soft curve
gathering above the waist of the man's black pants.

"The problem with spring," the blond said in a light
tone, "is how quickly the insects return to Chaldus. They
sting clear through a woman's dress."

"Come off it," the man replied in an accent that hinted
more of alleys than estates. "You can tell the difference
between a mosquito and a pinch. That was a pinch."

The blond's face hardened with displeasure.

"And you, Brandt, should be able to recognize a polite hint. But it seems I must be direct. Your attentions are unwanted; my husband is here tonight."

Brandt Karrelian smiled and leaned close to her ear. Even Madh's preternaturally sharp hearing could barely make out his reply.

"He won't miss you. It would only take us five minutes—"

"More's the pity," the woman responded, and whirling gracefully, she retreated past Madh toward the center of the room.

The rejection touched but lightly on Karrelian's mood. Straightening to his full height, a few inches shy of six feet, he surveyed the crowd for more likely game.

But he had been targeted himself, he realized, as a hand slipped firmly beneath his elbow.

Brandt looked up at a man whom he did not recognize, perhaps two inches taller than himself and dressed impeccably in the current fashion, though his tie was askew. His skin was swarthy—not like the tans of the idle rich who cluttered the ballroom, but with a redder hue beneath it, like one who has long been burned by sun and wind. The newcomer's sable hair, swept back in an arch as it receded from a point in the center of his brow, and his equally dark eyes, the long lines of his jaw, the sparkling teeth, and the sharp, narrow nose all made him seem a beast of prey.

"Do I know you?" Brandt began amiably, as if the man's startling features had not caught his attention.

"No. I wasn't invited," Madh replied in a smooth, soft voice that none but Brandt could hear, "but when I learned that Galatine Hazard was throwing a ball, I could not deny myself the pleasure of attending."

In the instant that Madh uttered that long-forgotten name, Brandt's smile dissolved. With a swiftness that even Madh could not follow, Brandt disengaged his arm from his visitor's grasp and returned the favor, wrapping his fingers around Madh's elbow. Although it seemed a casual gesture, the strength of the grip was already deadening the nerves of Madh's forearm.

Brandt's face remained tranquil, but his words came clipped short as he began to steer Madh through the crowd.

"Sorry, friend, but this is a private party. No uninvited guests—especially fools and madmen. Hell, I've got enough of those here under legitimate pretenses."

Madh did not resist, but allowed himself to be led toward the ballroom's open doors while Brandt had his say. Then, with an unruffled, almost pleasant smile, he replied.

"I can announce that name you so fear to the entire assembly—or we can speak in private."

Brandt stopped short and reappraised his unwanted guest. The man's small, dark eyes met his readily, unwavering. No doubt he was willing to carry out his threat. The thought of it made Brandt want to laugh. After all, not a day went by that he didn't consider doing the same thing himself—shout out to the world, *I've been right here, under your bloody noses!* And tonight, of all nights, ending the charade would be a blessing. At the least, it would spare him the remainder of this damned party.

But what of tomorrow? Who would he be then?

When Brandt began walking again, Madh was pleased to note a change of course, toward a small door that led to the interior of the mansion. Out of the corner of his eye, Madh saw another man walking with urgency along a parallel route. Dressed in a simple black suit, he nevertheless stood out in the crowd. Although only an inch or two taller than six feet, he possessed that sort of rare breadth and solidity that indicated prodigious strength, despite his fifty years. Madh recognized him easily from his description: Carn, now Karrelian's "personal secre-

tary," but in truth the man who had taught Karrelian his-
trade. And when, a dozen years ago, the pupil had
eclipsed his master, Carn had remained loyal to Brandt
in a way that Madh could appreciate. Loyalty, in Madh's
view, was the virtue most lacking in the Chaldean republic, where every man imagined himself his own master. Better, Madh believed, to recognize your superiors
and pledge them unswerving fealty. It was a truer way
to live.

The three men filed into a dimly lit corridor and proceeded into a small, elegant sitting room. Carn locked
the door behind them and, as if this were not sufficient,
placed his sturdy body against the well-polished wood.

Calmly, Madh picked out a plushly upholstered armchair and lowered himself into its yielding cushions. He
crossed his legs and, smiling faintly, looked up at his
audience.

Brandt Karrelian stood by the window, arms akimbo,
as he glowered at Madh.

"I have traveled far," Madh began, "in search of the
man known as Galatine Hazard."

"This is the residence of Brandt Karrelian," Carn interrupted gruffly, his deep voice little removed from a
growl. "You will find no one else here."

Again, that faint smile flickered over Madh's features.
"As I said, Galatine Hazard."

Carn's eyes narrowed and he shifted his weight subtly
onto the balls of his feet, ready to spring forward. In
Madh's profession, one noticed these things; one's life
depended on it. But Carn did not move. A subtle gesture
of Brandt's hand forestalled him.

"I've heard of this . . . Galatine Hazard," Brandt said
slowly, as if he were still trying to place the name. "A
sneak thief, wasn't he? Or some type of spy? That's
assuming he existed at all, judging by the foolish stories
people tell about him. As foolish as the name itself. Anyway, it's lucky for you that you haven't found him. A

ruthless criminal like that—well, he'd probably kill anyone who threatened to expose him. Me, though, I'm just
a harmless businessman. So, if you're in the market for
an electrical generator, you can chew my ear all night.
Otherwise, clear out so I can enjoy my damned party."

Madh sighed. He had been hoping to avoid exchang-
ing threats—even veiled ones. And Karrelian was not to
be taken lightly. No doubt he had made many a man
regret speaking the name of Galatine Hazard in his presence.

But his master had warned him of this, too, and Madh
would not be so easily dismissed.

"Now that we have gotten past your obligatory de-
nial—and I do hope you feel better for it—perhaps we
can proceed to a concrete proposition."

"Look around you," Karrelian interrupted, sweeping
his hands in an arc that embraced the room's antique
mahogany furnishings and intricate Brindisian rug.
"Does it look as if I have much to gain from any proposition?"

Curiously, however, Madh noticed the gleam of interest, of *hunger*, in Karrelian's eyes. As if Karrelian's
question were not merely rhetorical. And, instantly,
Madh saw what he had been searching for all evening:
the only lure that would suit Galatine Hazard's long-
jaded palate.

"An interesting question," Madh said, spreading his
hands as if weighing unspoken offers. "If such a man as
Galatine Hazard were to disappear, to assume the identity of a respected industrialist, what might be left wanting in his life? Not money, certainly, or fame.
Adventure, perhaps?" Here, Madh allowed a trace of a
smile to twitch upon his lips. "Ah, but there is the adventure of selling generators, of building market share.
Yes, Mr. Karrelian, I'm sure your guests—busy cringing
with fear and envy—offer challenge enough for a man
like yourself. You can look forward to decades of rolling

in profits until you're too old to chew your own food."

Brandt ground his teeth, but said nothing. It was bad enough that he had to suffer through this ball and the innumerable morons whom he'd been obliged to invite. That this intruder should rub his nose in the fact was unpardonable.

Madh flashed a toothy smile and leaned forward.

"Mine, Mr. Karrelian, is a business that offers true challenges, and I ask only that you hear my proposition before you judge it. If you decline after hearing me, I will honor your word and bother you no more, never again to speak the name of Galatine Hazard."

Sensing that the quickest method to rid himself of the intruder was simply to listen, Brandt leaned against the arm of a nearby chair and nodded warily for Madh to proceed. The stranger's dark eyes glittered as he warmed to his task.

"I represent a man—a great man—whose name I must withhold, although it is not unknown to the world. He suffers, as do we all in our wretched and fallen state, from a certain lack of knowledge. There are those who could remedy this defect in his learning, but man, as we know, is a covetous creature. No one, alas, is disposed to share what all should freely possess. Consequently, my master requires that some research be done—and in this age, across the whole breadth of the land, there is no man so adept at uncovering secrets as Galatine Hazard."

Madh paused for a moment, giving time for his words to take hold. When he continued, his voice dropped to a whisper that hinted of untold rewards.

"But these, Mr. Karrelian, these are more than the secrets of a lifetime. They are the secrets of an entire age! And, although you may name your own price—and name it freely, whether it is money or land or magic— your real reward will simply be the triumph of having accomplished what no one, for centuries, has considered within a single man's grasp."

In response, Brandt sneered. "If there's one thing I get more than my fill of, it's salesmen. And what I just heard, for all its sugar coating, was a sales pitch. Better than most, sure. But no different than any other: full of vague and glorious promises, yet curiously lacking in details."

Madh shrugged and spread his palms, as if such matters were beyond his control.

"I can say only so much until you swear yourself to the task. I cannot yet name my master, nor can I tell you more about the information he requires. I can say, however, that the task is not without danger. There will be blood involved, and some of it you will be required to spill—"

Before Madh could finish the thought, Karrelian jumped forward, his face twisting with rage. He grabbed Madh by the lapels and dragged him out of the chair, slamming him against the polished wainscoting.

"Galatine Hazard was a spy, a crook—not an assassin, damn you. Now, clear out before I call the city guard!"

Madh pulled free of Brandt's grasp and stepped away, locking Brandt's eyes in his own sad gaze.

"I urge you to reconsider," he advised. "Heed me, lest you forfeit a kingdom!"

"Heed *me*," Brandt replied darkly, "lest you forfeit your head."

Abruptly, Madh's composure broke and his features clouded with a sort of melancholy anger. He spoke bitterly, but quietly.

"There are others, Galatine Hazard, and you shall live to rue this day."

"Shall I?" Brandt cried. "Carn, fetch my sword!"

In an instant, Brandt's old friend vanished into the hallway. And just as swiftly, Madh, too, retreated through the door and disappeared into the night. Although his loyalty to his master was without flaw, Madh was no fool.

When Carn slipped back inside the room a moment later, his lined face was split by a broad grin.

"Your *sword*?" he repeated, laughing with deep peals that shook his chest. "Now *that*, my friend, was a good one." Carn broke into another fit of laughter, leaning against the wall as if he could barely hold himself upright. "Where did we pack your sword, anyway?"

Finally, Brandt broke into a grin. He shook his head and slapped his friend on the back.

"Somewhere in the attic," Brandt guessed, "gathering cobwebs and rust. Lucky for our guest that it wasn't at hand. The smallest cut would probably have meant death by lockjaw."

Carn laughed again, rubbing his eyes.

"I suppose we should have our blades polished one day," the older man observed, the mirth slowly leaving his voice. "And I should probably make sure that lunatic really left the grounds."

With an affectionate tap to Brandt's shoulder, Carn turned and departed.

Brandt remained rooted in place, reluctant to return to the party's ongoing charade of pleasantries. So much more inviting to stay here, alone, where no one called him by any name, present or past. What would it take, Brandt wondered, to rid himself thoroughly of his past, his storehouse of secrets? And what, he wondered, would he be without it? A signer of checks, a counter of inventories. . . .

A noise at the door recalled him to the present and he looked up, expecting to see Carn but finding only one of his more tiresome guests. If he did not return to the party, Brandt realized, the party would hunt him down.

"Brandt," the man cried, joyously stretching out the

name on his tongue as if to enjoy it longer. "I'd been hoping to catch you alone tonight."

"Of course you had, Garrett." Brandt wearily surveyed the man's fat, alcohol-flushed cheeks. Two tiny pink eyes sparkled above those cheeks, wary as a squirrel that coveted a nut in a man's hand. "You want to know whether I'll renew our wire contract after the way you gouged me last quarter."

Garrett's jaw dropped helplessly against his breast. Flustered, he tried to compose a response, but the sound that emerged was incomprehensible.

"That's all right," Brandt continued. "I'll sign it."

Tentatively, Garrett laughed, as if he'd been in on the joke all along.

"Well, Brandt—"

"Shut up, Garrett," Brandt interrupted as he passed the man and headed back toward the ballroom. "Consider your silence the price of renewal. Now, come along. It's time I made my speech."

Both men reentered the harsh light of the ballroom and Brandt made his way to the buffet tables at the front. He paused for a moment to survey the crowd, everyone working so hard for their laughter. Finally, he lifted an empty crystal goblet and rapped it sharply with a spoon. The roar of merriment died away, and Brandt found every face in the hall turned toward him expectantly, awaiting their host's words with composed smiles.

"Dear friends," Brandt announced. "Dear friends. I cannot conceive how to thank you for once again attending my annual festival, except with these two words: Go home."

And with that, Brandt released the goblet he was still holding and watched it tumble end over end until it shattered against the floor, glittering slivers skittering across the parquet.

Someone toward the back hooted with outrage, but most merrymakers settled for a gasp or a discreetly nervous chuckle. For a moment, no one seemed to know what to do, until Carn appeared in their midst and efficiently, irresistibly, began to hasten the exodus. A few guests who thought themselves more privileged, more dear, inquired after Brandt's health and met, as a reply, those same two words.

Go home. If only, Brandt thought, it were that easy.

Brandt leaned heavily against the buffet table and watched the bejeweled and bedizened horde file out through the gaping twin doors, glancing anxiously over their shoulders, until the last one dissolved into the night.

The evening, Brandt thought, had finally come to a satisfactory end.

But Brandt little realized that this evening was only the beginning of an end—an end he had not begun to imagine.

CHAPTER 1

Two weeks later and a hundred miles away, Madh crouched noiselessly behind the red sandstone wall of a different estate. Through the dark of a moonless midnight, he studied the man next to him, idly reflecting that he would have preferred working with Hazard. Although Madh could not say that Hain was less skilled than Hazard—he had no true way to judge—there was something distasteful about the young assassin.

"Why this delay?" Madh whispered. "You assured me you would handle things easily . . . and quickly."

Hain grinned and ran a hand over his recently shaved scalp. At the most delicate times, he had found, hair could get in the way.

"Success is a matter of proper preparation, my friend," he replied, noting the way Madh's nose wrinkled at the words "my friend." Hain had always thought it ironic that his employers found him repulsive . . . yet they returned to him unfailingly when they needed his peculiar brand of help. "Preparation," he concluded. "Preparation is everything."

"Well, be quick," Madh snapped, and turned away to

scan for guardsmen. He had spotted six of them already. Before long, he would know whether Hain was as good as he claimed or merely an arrogant braggart. And a dead braggart.

Hain grinned again and reached into a small pouch at his waist. He brought out a hypodermic needle and a small, corked vial of clear fluid. The assassin rolled up his sleeve, twisted it into place, and quickly located the median cubital vein in the crook of his arm. Then, with a surgeon's expertise, he inserted the needle through the cork and drew back on the plunger, half-filling the chamber of the hypodermic. He tapped the hypo twice, expelling a bubble of air from the needle, and brought the tip to his vein. Slowly, with relish, Hain applied pressure. He watched the needle stretch the skin of his arm and finally, wonderfully, break through. His nostrils flared at the familiar penetration of his flesh and, within moments, he felt the tingling rush of the drug.

As the veridine filtered into his brain, the night snapped into focus. Everything moved with infinite slowness, with seamless fluidity. Hain stretched wide his arms and suppressed an urge to shout. Yes, a shout would have annoyed Madh, that ignorant bastard, who turned his back, disdaining the drug. Let the clients sneer, Hain thought. They all returned; they all paid well.

Madh waited a moment longer and turned back toward the assassin. "Are you quite done?" he hissed, staring pointedly at the hypodermic in Hain's hand.

Fool, Hain thought. With lethal precision, he flicked the hypodermic at Madh's left eye. When the glistening, deadly dart was only inches away, Madh caught the missile casually.

"You wouldn't want to lose this, would you?" Madh asked quietly as he weighed the hypodermic in his hand. Scowling, he pocketed it. "I told you, there are to be no traces except for the coin."

Hain glared at the smaller man for a moment. Finally, he shrugged and turned to the wall. He measured three paces backward, vaulted, and disappeared over the carefully mortared stones into the estate.

Pernom Ell reclined on a plush loveseat in his bedroom, sipping brandy and idly fondling the prostitute at his side. As the old man ran his shriveled, yellow hand along her fragrant thigh, he considered privilege. She, no doubt, would prefer a different hand than his invading the soft hollow beneath her knee, but it wasn't hers to choose. It was a matter of privilege—and privilege, Pernom Ell knew, was his. His career in the government had been long and toilsome, but it had made possible the ease of these twilight years. The world had not troubled him now for more than a decade. So, when the tip of the stiletto touched the base of his throat, Pernom Ell was quite surprised.

"Good evening, old man," whispered a gravelly voice.

"*What?*" Ell rasped, dropping his glass and thrashing against the strong arm that pinned him to the loveseat. The prostitute began to turn at the sound of Ell's distress but, before she saw Hain, the assassin whipped his hand around and smashed the hilt of the stiletto against her forehead. The girl collapsed unconscious onto the ornate rug, a bloody bruise welling up against the skin of her brow.

"A bit young for you, I should think," Hain observed as he returned the blade to Ell's neck.

"What is this?" Ell shouted, writhing desperately. The tip of the knife bit into the old man's flesh as he struggled, and a dark bead of blood rose around the steel. "If you mean to rob me—"

"Shut up, you fool, and quit struggling, or you'll do my job for me."

Those were sobering words. "You . . . you mean to

kill me?" Ell asked, sinking back into the cushions.

Hain smiled, leaning forward until his lips almost brushed the old man's ear, as if he meant to kiss him. Ell smelled of mothballs and brandy and fear. The last was an aroma with which Hain held intimate acquaintance. A connoisseur, he relished it.

"Kill you? Not immediately, but yes."

It was then that the screaming began, Ell calling for his guards, struggling helplessly against Hain's grip. The assassin merely laughed.

"Guards? Scream all you want, old man, but your 'guards' have been dealt with: six on the outer perimeter by the wall, four around the inner courtyard, two in the antechamber, two at the top of the stairs, and two crossbowmen on the roof. Those last two were smoking and playing cards, by the way. Quite a waste of money, don't you agree?"

Ell felt his throat tighten. Sixteen men. *Sixteen*. And this one braggart. . . . "You killed them all *yourself*?"

Hain grinned again. "They're merely incapacitated. I would rather have killed them, but my employer insists on one death only this night."

The frank answer seemed to rouse the old minister's spirits. Ell twisted his head around to face his attacker and felt the knife prick deeper into his skin. No matter: Ell paid blood willingly for his first glimpse of Hain's sneering features. With his twisted face and shaven head, the assassin resembled less a man than one of the demons in Ell's antique books of myth.

"Then be done with it!" Ell hissed. "I've heard enough!"

"But I have not heard enough from you, Minister. There are certain words. . . . You know the ones I mean."

It took the old man a moment to fathom Hain's intention, but when he did, he laughed harshly. Ell was no fool. Any minister of Chaldus knew that, for any of a thousand things he had done, there were men who would happily take his life. But this, of all things. . . .

"If the Phrase is what you're after, then you're sorely misinformed. Do you think they would allow us to *remember* after we retire? What you seek has been utterly removed from our minds."

"Not removed, old man," Hain replied as he drew a small, dark gem from a pouch at his side. He put his index finger to Ell's temple, grinding his fingernail into the old man's flesh. "It's all still in there, every jot of it—just buried. But I've got certain tricks for making people remember. For your own sake, don't try to resist me. I know many ways to cause pain and, believe me, I rather enjoy using them."

Miranda awoke as the sun broke over the crest of the hill and poured strong, morning light into the bedroom. She stretched for a moment, got out of bed, and slipped on a long, silk robe. Roland was already gone. Miranda smiled slightly to herself, wondering what her crazy old man could be doing up so early in the morning. She stopped at the mirror for a moment to arrange her hair (still black, she thought happily, despite her wrinkles) and wash her face in the porcelain basin. Then she pulled aside the sheer white drapes and threw open the glass doors that led to the balcony. The warm spring air rolled over her, bringing with it the scent of plums that would soon be ripe for picking. Leaning against the wrought-iron handrail, she arched her back and absorbed the vista, better each morning than any breakfast: the bright, ordered colors of the garden and the blooming trees of the groves beyond. It looked to be a marvelous day.

Of course, that would depend mostly on Roland. He had been acting oddly for the past week, ever since word of Pernom Ell's death. Granted, the two men had worked together for years on the Council—but at their age you were no longer shocked when your friends died. No, it was the idea of *murder* that was so disturbing.

Thinking about it made Miranda nervous. Perhaps, she thought, it would be best to discuss the incident with Roland. She walked through the bedroom to the hall, where Anissa, one of the maids, was dusting a small cherry table by the stairs.

"Anissa, have you seen Lord Calador?"

The maid looked up from her work. "I believe I saw him going to the basement, my lady."

Miranda took an involuntary step backward at the news. The basement was primarily used for storage, so only the servants went down there. Except for one room. And whatever reason had prompted Roland to go to that room did not augur good to come.

Miranda hurried down the wide oak staircase to the main floor and passed through the kitchen to a stairway that led to the basement. At the bottom of the stairs there was a fieldstone corridor lined with doors on each side: wine cellar, larder, miscellaneous storerooms. And there was one more door at the end of the hallway: a stout, oaken door bound with iron bolts and braces. Two strong locks usually secured it. Now it was ajar. Miranda rushed toward the chamber.

The room held no furniture, only a dozen huge iron chests. Leaning against a chest in the far corner was Roland, busily honing a long, broad sword. Miranda hadn't seen him hold that sword for sixteen years, and now it recalled vivid images of their past. She saw the Roland of her youth, a tremendous man—almost a giant. Broad of chest, stout of limb, sharp-eyed, and prone to laughter. Back then he had worn his golden hair like a thick mane and, though it was now more white than blond, he wore it thus still, accompanied by a beard. Nor had he suffered the passage of decades as most men did. He had lost a couple of inches, true, but Roland's height

remained closer to seven feet than six. And though he
was no longer as strong as he had been, he still lifted
heavy iron weights each morning, still rode hard to keep
his thighs firm, and hunted to preserve the sharpness of
his senses.

The only important difference between the Roland of
her youth and the one before her now, Miranda knew,
was that he had not for sixteen years been called upon
to slay enemies of the state on the field of battle. It was
a pleasant difference, one she cherished. And to see him
hold that sword again shook her.

"What happened?" she asked quietly.

At the sound of her voice, he looked up and smiled
at her mournfully. Once more, Roland ran a gray stone
along the edge of the blade. Then he carefully laid both
upon the lid of the chest and reached into his shirt
pocket.

"This arrived by messenger early this morning," he
explained in his rumbling bass, offering her the letter.
"I didn't want to wake you. It may well have been your
last peaceful night's sleep for a long while."

Apprehensive, she searched his eyes. They were the
same cold blue disks that he wore when he returned from
a battle—eyes that saw past her, past basement walls
and spring orchards to bloody fields and fields yet to be
bloodied. She took the letter from his hand, the letter
that had stolen sixteen years in a blow.

The message was simple: "Abrinius Loft murdered.
As Ell: signs of torture, coin in mouth. Take appropriate
action." It was signed "Aston."

Miranda put her hand to her mouth. "Heaven above.
Another."

Roland stepped toward her and rested his massive
hands on her shoulders. "Nine days between them, dear.
Only nine days."

She looked up at him, her brow furrowed. "You
should have woken me right away. We have a lot to

do." More sharply, she added: "And I expect to contribute to any decision you've been planning."

He smiled a little. "Of course. I just couldn't bear to wake you. As I said, I doubt we'll have much peaceful sleep for a while. All the murders have been committed at night—"

"The letter didn't mention that."

Roland swept a stray white lock from his brow and sighed.

"The messenger had a few details to add. Apparently, this time there had been quite a struggle. Loft had given his all, pulled out every stop. Destroyed half the bloody house with those fireballs of his. Apparently, whoever killed him was a more competent mage than the old dodderer."

"Dodderer?" Miranda protested. "Loft was once the nation's premier sorcerer."

"In rank alone, my dear, not in power. I don't mean to speak ill of the dead, but it doesn't pay to deceive ourselves. Abrinius was more a politician and intriguer than sorcerer, and that, perhaps, is our sole encouragement. Although Loft could not stop whoever is behind these crimes, perhaps a more powerful man can."

"Tarem Selod?" Miranda said quietly, naming another of the men who had sat with Roland as ministers of the nation. "Then you think they will come after everyone."

"I have no reason to think otherwise," Roland replied, his voice low and grave. "And there is no denying that Selod is a better mage than a dozen Lofts."

Miranda frowned but let the issue drop. Something else was bothering her. "A coin again? That was the trademark of some spy, years ago. What was that man's name . . . ?" She let the memory rouse itself, tumble from her brain to her tongue. "Hazard, it was Hazard. You don't think he's behind this, do you?"

Roland scowled and shook his head.

"It makes no sense—not that any other explanation

makes more sense. Hazard hasn't done anything in years, as far as I know. But, then again, neither had Abrinius Loft or Pernom Ell." Roland ran a massive hand through his mane of hair and shrugged. "I once knew a field marshal who was being blackmailed by Hazard. The old boy had an immoderate fondness for his younger troops that Hazard had somehow discovered. On the basis of that annual income alone, a man could have lived in luxury. I don't see why Hazard would abandon retirement now, but who can tell?" Roland paused and sighed. "And it doesn't really matter. What matters is that two retired ministers have been murdered. More than murdered: tortured as well. Someone wants something from my colleagues—wants it badly enough to go to great risk to get it. That tells me we're in danger, too. Or I should say, I'm in danger. Everyone else in both Pernom's and Abrinius's households was incapacitated, but not otherwise harmed."

"Well, what about Ravenwood?" Miranda asked, hugging herself. "You did your bit for the government. Now let the government help you."

"That's what Kermane told me this morning," Roland said, remembering that particular conversation with a frown. Kermane Ash had once been the Prime Minister of Chaldus, and retirement had done nothing to lessen his ministerial demeanor.

"You've seen Kermane already?"

"He's been at his Dacwith house all season. The messenger stopped there first, and Kermane accompanied him here."

"He wanted your opinion?"

Roland shook his head, half-grinning. "Has Kermane ever been interested in anyone's opinion but his own? No, he plans to insist that Ravenwood grant us official protection. But since I'm closer to our dear Prime Minister than he, Kermane wanted me to draft the letter. He thought it might gain us a few precious extra troops."

"And you think . . . ?" But from his tone, Miranda could already guess.

Roland glanced again at the letter and frowned. "I don't know whom we ought to fear more: this mysterious assassin or Andus Ravenwood."

"Isn't it worth talking to him?"

"He's a friend, but he's still the Prime Minister. Do you think there will be a real decision for him to make?"

Miranda paused for a moment, a chill creeping through her. "You think this is about the Phrases," she said very quietly.

"I don't *know* what it's about; neither, I guess, does Ravenwood. But he can't afford to take any chances."

She reached up gently to touch his cheek. "I liked this place, Roland."

Finally, the ice in his blue eyes melted as the old man smiled.

"We'll return. I promise."

CHAPTER 2

More than the stacks of reports to be read and laws to be signed, more than the latest estimates of Yndlian military strength, more even than a chronic lack of sleep, Andus Ravenwood's recent ulcer attacks reminded him that he was not a happy man. Upon his election as Prime Minister six years ago, he had known he was abandoning himself to a series of worries that no sane human being ought willingly to accept, much less seek out. But now, he reflected as he waited for the last High Council members to file into the conference room, things had reached a pitch that even he had never foreseen. And his innards were writhing in equal rhythm.

He leaned back into the leather armchair and told himself that perhaps he was not to blame for his stomach pains and chronic insomnia. Forty years ago, he had been little more than a society rake with a sharp mind and a talent for languages. When he had entered the Ministry of Foreign Affairs, he had envisioned a pampered life in some well-appointed embassy in a very, very quiet part of the world. State dinners, discreet philandering, the occasional report. . . . Andus tried to determine when those goals had gone awry—how a seemingly innocent chain of promotions had led him to the High Council and, finally, to the Prime Minister's seat. Somehow, Andus couldn't avoid the feeling that all of Chaldus had played him for a fool.

Andus glanced again at the quiet, dimly lit council chamber and wondered what was keeping Taylor Ash. The other four chief ministers were there and, although that constituted a quorum, the problem at hand was one that no one understood better than the Chief Minister of Intelligence. Not that Andus particularly cared where a solution came from. The present dilemma was ruining his health and, worse, what little remained of his sex life. He fervently hoped—almost prayed, though he was not a religious man—that the assembled wisdom of Chaldus's chief ministers would force him into a decision that he was loath to make alone.

Jame Kordor, the Minister of Finance, seemed to notice Andus's tension and winked at him. Andus smiled. Jame had a knack for reading his mood and helping to lighten it. He seemed to Andus almost a stereotype of the jolly fat man. And Kordor was more than fat; he was downright corpulent. Kordor himself used the word, good-naturedly of course, in reference to his famous stomach; he refused to admit that any other adjective could do justice to sixty-six years of determined dining.

But Ravenwood's cheer was only momentary. Of what use, ultimately, was a wink? And that, he feared, was all Jame Kordor would provide. A competent financier, but hardly a visionary. In the end, Ravenwood wondered how much he could rely on any of his assembled ministers. Across the broad mahogany table from Kordor sat Landa Wells, Minister of the Interior. Clearly, the crisis did not weigh too heavily on her, for she was deep into a budgetary debate with Amet Pale, the Minister of War. Pale complained that he needed more funds to maintain a mobile, invasion-repulsing militia along the Cirran River. Wells, with her typical dry wit, noted that his militia would be none too mobile without well-maintained roads to travel.

Nor could Andus rely on Pale for reasoned insight. The current minister was in every way an antithesis of the man who had preceded him. Unlike Roland, Duke Calador, Amet Pale did not physically resemble a warrior. His features were so pretty, so delicate, that Ravenwood suspected the general of paying a wizard to maintain his good looks. Either way, Pale was the last man Ravenwood could imagine in battle. And worse still, Andus reflected, Amet Pale was nothing like his predecessor in demeanor. As well as a good friend, Roland had been an excellent minister—thoroughly professional when there was a war to be fought, but in no great rush to fight one. Roland had seen little glory in his job, only a commitment to the safety of his nation. Pale, however, teetered on the edge of jingoism. Given the subject of their meeting, Andus knew in advance what Pale's position would be. It made him wish all the more fervently that Roland could be sitting at the table as Minister of War and that, instead, it was Amet Pale's life that hung by a thread.

Nor could Ravenwood count on his Minister of Magic, who served simultaneously as the governmental representative of the National Arcane Authority. Ravenwood could not be sure whether Orbis Thale represented the good of the country as much as he did that of his sorcerous brethren. In most cases, those concerns coincided, but in this present business. . . . Ravenwood glanced at the mage but, as usual, Thale's features were hidden within the deep crimson cowl that he wore. Andus despised the theatricality of that cowl. He could only hope that, beneath it, the man was made of more honest stuff.

The door opened, disrupting Andus's reverie, and

Taylor Ash entered the room. On most days, Andus could count on the young man as his most reliable ally, but today he wondered. They were gathered to discuss the lives and deaths of the country's ex-ministers, including Kermane Ash, the former Prime Minister . . . and Taylor's father. Andus studied the young man carefully. The thick shock of black hair, sparkling gray eyes, and disarming smile weren't the typical features of a Minister of Intelligence. Nor was it at all usual for a thirty-two-year-old to occupy a seat on the High Council; in fact, Ash was the youngest ever to achieve the distinction. And there would have been many more rumblings that Taylor's position was due only to his father's influence, except that Taylor had shunned his father's Ministry of Finance and devoted himself to Intelligence instead. There, Barr Aston, one of the shrewdest and most fiercely independent men ever to occupy a minister's seat, could not help but recognize Taylor's talent, despite a distinct distaste for the young man's father. That Aston had not sent the young Ash to the farthest, coldest intelligence post on the continent had surprised the Chaldean cognoscenti. When it became apparent that Aston was grooming the boy to replace him, no one was fool enough to charge nepotism.

At Taylor's arrival, everyone sat up, sensing the meeting would begin. Several ministers opened pads to take notes, but Taylor, who always had the most information to disseminate and assimilate, never wrote anything down. He casually swept his hair away from his eyes and glanced at Andus. Taylor's look was grim, but for reasons Ravenwood could not divine. Of course, Taylor knew what a bloody topic they had assembled to discuss. Literally bloody, Ravenwood reflected, and it was the same blood that ran in Taylor's veins. But was the young man grim because he was ready to bow before a cruel and inevitable decision or because he was set on opposing it?

The Prime Minister cleared his throat. "This meeting of the High Council, on the fourth day of the third month of the one hundred and seventy-eighth year of the republic, is called to order," Ravenwood said, reciting the formula wearily. "Why don't we just get on with this, Taylor?"

The young man nodded and leaned forward.

"Okay, we all know the basics. Two dead. Not merely dead, of course, or we wouldn't be here. Two *murdered*. It's a bit premature to conclude that someone is killing all our ex-ministers, but we lack the luxury of time. If we wait for four more to die, we can be pretty sure that the ministers are indeed the target, but then there won't be any left to save. Under these circumstances, I've taken standard precautions. As soon as Ell's body was found, I assigned my best operatives to the remaining ex-Council members."

"And did you inform our predecessors that they are being observed?" Pale asked.

Ash shot the Minister of War an annoyed look. "Naturally not. I don't think any of them are aware of my agents except Tarem Selod. For some reason, whenever one of the operatives trespasses on Selod's grounds, he seems to fall asleep."

A low chuckle issued from Orbis Thale.

Taylor smiled. "I agree with your assessment of your colleague's skill, Thale. I withdrew my men to a strictly observational distance. If Selod can't take care of himself, we certainly can't take care of him."

"Obviously," Andus interrupted, "the same can't be said of Abrinius Loft."

At that, a troubled look crossed Taylor's face. "We sometimes make light of Loft's arcane abilities. Certainly, he wasn't in the same league as the titans of the NAA, but he was no slouch either. He destroyed his entire estate in his struggles."

Thale snorted. "Parlor tricks."

"Perhaps for you and a very few of your peers," Taylor argued, "but be honest: though Loft was not a preeminent power, he was not far removed from that rank. If we underestimate Loft, we also underestimate his murderer, and that's a mistake I'd rather avoid. Whoever killed Loft was not only able to protect himself from a fairly potent wizard, but he also located and disabled two of my best men before doing so. That indicates an individual or individuals of varied and dangerous skills."

"A good wizard could do all these things," Thale suggested.

Taylor frowned. "But a good wizard *did not*. My men awoke with some very physical lumps on their heads. Naturally, I've increased the size of my observation teams since then."

Amet Pale drew himself up at this, thrusting out his uniformed chest. "I believe my young friend is quite right. We should not underestimate our unknown foe. Whoever is behind this has proved that he's better than either a wizard or the Ministry of Intelligence can handle. Which means we must consider. . . . alternatives."

Andus was about to protest such a turn in the conversation—not because he believed there were any other solutions, but because of the cold-hearted haste with which Pale suggested it—but Taylor beat him to it. The young man had leaned forward, his knuckles white as he gripped the arms of his chair.

"I think we have more 'alternatives' at this stage than the one you prefer, General Pale. I admit that my response should have been more thorough. At the moment of the first murder, we should have blanketed each of these ex-ministers. Not only me, but all of us. We should have surrounded them with the best intelligence operatives, some damned potent wizards, and half a platoon apiece."

"Much as I hate to put it this way," Jame Kordor broke in, "that's hardly economical. What I mean to say is, surrounding these men is no solution, but only a temporary measure. None of them will consent to live the remainder of their lives in virtual imprisonment, yet once we remove that protection, we're left in this same, vulnerable situation."

Pale and Landa Wells nodded at this logic, finding themselves in rare agreement.

"My agents can deal with this," Taylor protested, "if you just give us time."

"We can afford no time," Amet Palc protested, striking the desk sharply with his open palm. "Already, Mallioch may possess two of our Phrases. That would give him eight of the twelve, you realize."

"We can all perform the arithmetic," Taylor countered, an edge creeping into his voice.

Of course, Taylor thought, Pale would assume that Mallioch had ordered the murders. Just because the nations of Yndor and Chaldus had fought one another for centuries, that did not mean Yndor was responsible for each of Chaldus's ills . . . although simple-minded nationalists always insisted it was so. War had ended almost two decades ago, though soldiers like Pale could not seem to get the fact through their skulls. Under Mallioch, Yndor had proved a temperate neighbor. Taylor prayed that it remained so, that there was another explanation for the murders, however unlikely.

"But have you added up the *implications*?" Pale asked. "Give the Emperor of Yndor all twelve Phrases, and he need never go to war with us. He can simply dictate his terms and we will be in no position to resist. Four more Phrases—four more tired old men—and this nation falls to its knees. Or we willingly consign our world back into barbarity."

"Four Phrases give us a lot of room to maneuver," Taylor argued. "If we keep even one Phrase out of Mallioch's reach, the rest are useless. And aren't you jumping to a conclusion about who is behind this?"

Andus Ravenwood sighed, reluctant to support Pale's logic. "Unless we assume the murders are Mallioch's doing, our only other possibility is that some psychopath has a compulsion to kill retired civil servants. Taylor, only those Phrases make these men valuable enough to kill, and there are precious few people who would be interested in doing so. There are precious few people who even know the Phrases exist."

"Even if we presume that Mallioch is after the Phrases," Taylor argued, "every minister is protected against this sort of thing. Although two men are dead, there's no reason to assume they surrendered their Phrases. We remove all memory of those words upon retirement. Hell, that's the same protection *we're* counting on when we retire." Taylor paused for a moment and looked hard at each of his colleagues. "General Pale is proposing that we set a precedent for our own eventual death sentences."

Orbis Thale shook his cowled head. "Unfortunately, I can agree only with the latter conclusion. The fact that Loft was murdered at all indicates that the murderer got what he wanted from Ell. Without that first Phrase, the rest would be useless. Second, you are quite right about Loft. He was no true power, but he was more than competent. Anyone able to survive Loft's attempts to save his life could possibly hold the power to circumvent the memory blocks we installed."

Again, Pale slapped the table. "That's all the information we need for a vote. No matter how distasteful the circumstances, we cannot ignore this one central fact: the future of our nation rests on the wisdom of our actions. I am not without compassion, but can we gamble millions of lives for the sake of four? For the sake of four men who certainly knew what they were risking when they took the vows of their ministry? For the sake of four men who devoted their entire careers to the preservation of this nation's safety? Gentlemen, do you not

believe that our ex-colleagues would sacrifice themselves gladly for the welfare of their country?"

Ravenwood pursed his lips. "We'll find out when the
knock comes at their door."

Yet, when the vote came around to the Prime Minister, always the last to vote, Andus Ravenwood made
it unanimous.

All the ministers had filed out except for Ravenwood, who slouched in his chair in a defeated attitude,
and a pensive Taylor Ash. Andus could not bring himself to meet his younger colleague's eyes.

"Taylor, I know that one of the four men we just
condemned was your father," Andus began, feeling as
awkward as a schoolboy.

"*Is* my father," Taylor corrected blackly.

"Is," Andus agreed. "I'm truly sorry."

For a moment, the two men sat in silence. Finally,
Ravenwood spoke again. "To weigh the good of a nation
against the love of a father. . . ."

"Two fathers," Taylor said between tightly clenched
teeth. "Barr Aston has been as much my father as anyone. And to show my gratitude, I've ordered both their
deaths."

Andus shifted uncomfortably in his chair. He had
known it would be necessary to speak privately with
Taylor. No one could ask such a price of a man without
at least offering consolation. But the young Ash certainly wasn't making it easy.

"You know," Ravenwood said softly, "I've been self-
pitying about my role in all of this lately, but I feel petty
now. No one, Taylor, has been asked for such sacrifices
as yours. All along, however, I had confidence that you
would hold to your supreme duty—your obligation to
ministry and motherland. And you voted, as I did, for

the painful remedy. As always, you are a credit to your office."

"Not only the Council's youngest chief minister," Taylor observed sourly, "but its first parricide as well. Quite a distinction, eh?"

Taylor slowly turned to face Ravenwood, and the tired Prime Minister saw a terrible look in those gray eyes, a look that he shuddered to apprehend in one still so young.

"I'm afraid I haven't spoken well," Andus replied. "Of course I knew you would uphold your duty. But, most of all, I feared what this meeting would produce. Taylor, you were the only one who tried to stop us in our headlong dash toward bloodshed. Only you spoke for mercy, if not for reason. And I'm grateful."

"Don't be," Taylor replied as he stood up and looked out into the night over the city of Prandis. "I knew what the results of the meeting would be. As we all did, Andus. I played the devil's advocate, hoping that it would stir up some discussion, that it would somehow inspire an unexpected alternative. But I never believed for a minute that it would work. You see, I had already signed the orders before I walked through the door."

CHAPTER 3

"**I** will not wait for you tonight," Madh said near the end of the street.

Hain suppressed a chuckle. "Why not?"

"I've shown you where the house is. You know the rest. Why need I wait?"

Why, indeed? Madh thought. He remembered their last task, only four days ago, when Hain had triumphantly burst from Abrinius Loft's burning house—born, it seemed, of the very flames. There had been blood that night on Hain's mouth, and the blood had not been Hain's. It was bad enough that Madh had to deal with such a beast at all; he need not wait to see Hain's results.

"What if I run into trouble?" Hain asked, smirking.

"You are paid not to run into trouble. And be assured, if you did, I would not lift a hand to help."

At that, Madh kicked his heels into his horse's side and galloped away.

"Sleep well," Hain called as he watched Madh's figure dwindle into the night. He began to laugh as he reached for the hypodermic in his pouch.

•   •   •

Something troubled Hain about the house. It was a sprawling three-story with a big, wraparound porch and plenty of windows. The whole place was as still as the night, but something disturbed him. Everything was *too* still, *too* open. There was no fence, the windows were large, and many of them stood half-open. Either it was a house that invited intruders or it was the house of an arrogantly self-assured man. Knowing a little of Tarem Selod's history, Hain felt sure that the latter hypothesis was correct.

He grinned. The arrogant ones were more satisfying to break.

Although the front door did not appear locked, Hain opted to seek another entrance: appearances were often deceiving in his business, and at times, the most inviting doorway was also the deadliest. A window on the second floor would better suit his purposes. Hain circled quietly to the back of the house and selected his window: it was barely cracked open, and the room beyond was dark.

The foundation of the house was constructed of large, rounded stones which, after four feet, gave way to courses of bricks. There was something of a ledge—no more than an inch wide—at the meeting of stone and brick. It would be enough. Hain measured off eight paces, took a few deep breaths, and sprinted toward the house. As he approached it, he hurtled into the air, his right foot hitting the small ledge. Instantly, he pushed off with all his strength, jumping just high enough to wrap his fingers around the window sill. It was but a moment's work to steady himself and quietly coax the window half-open. Then he pulled himself up and slid into the house of Tarem Selod.

As always, the first thing Hain did after overt movement was freeze. He crouched in the darkness under the window, held his breath, and listened for the telltale signs that someone had heard him. There was nothing at first, then the slight rustle of paper, a page being turned. So, the mage was reading. He suspected nothing.

Hain turned his attention back to his surroundings. He was in a small guest bedroom which, luckily, had no rug. Too often, rugs hid creaky floorboards. Hain scanned the floor, looking for the boards that were raised above the rest, the ones which would creak. Finally satisfied, with the care of a tightrope walker, the assassin picked his way to the door. He slid his bare fingers over the hinges: there was little dust. Again, a good sign. If the room was often used, there was less chance of the door squeaking. He turned the handle cautiously and began to inch the door open. It took the better part of a minute, but Hain opened the door without noise and slid into the upstairs hallway.

Again he heard the rustling of paper. It was coming from downstairs and, from the hallway, the sound was clear. There were no doors between them. The mage was most likely in a sitting room just off the stairway. Hain had to be most careful now: if he could hear the mage clearly, the opposite would be true as well. In Selod's case, it was most important that Hain take the victim by surprise.

There was a rug in the hallway, but it was only a runner. On each side, Hain could see the bare floorboards. Again, he picked the safest route and navigated noiselessly to the stairs. He was in luck: from his vantage at the top of the stairs he could see the back of Selod's white-haired head. The mage was sitting in a high-back chair and reading a book. In a moment, Hain thought, the danger would be over. From a leather pouch at his belt, he retrieved a delicate crystal egg within which swirled fine tendrils of yellow gas.

"Don't you find it tedious to move so slowly?" the mage asked offhandedly as he flipped another page of his book.

Hain almost choked on his astonishment. How . . . ?

"I left the door open for you, but of course you young people always have to do things the hard way. Oh, don't look so infernally surprised. I've known of your presence since you set foot on my property. You see, I have a somewhat more intimate relationship with my possessions than the average homeowner. Well, don't just stand there gaping. Come downstairs . . . and you needn't bother being quiet about it." Selod put down his book on a nearby end table, carefully marking his place with a red ribbon. "Let's hurry up with this, shall we? I'm in the middle of the last chapter, and I so dreadfully do wish to know, as they say, who done it."

Hain shook his head incredulously and quickly descended a half-dozen steps. Selod rose and turned to face him. The mage was a small man, perhaps five-seven, and beginning to put on weight about his middle. For a man of such age, he possessed a remarkably full head of hair, albeit white. With his wrinkled face and spindly limbs, Selod looked to be about seventy. But there were those who swore that he had looked seventy when their grandfathers were young. Hain had never believed the tales before but, looking into Selod's eyes, he began to wonder. Those were ancient eyes, those pale blue circles, and they looked as if they could destroy him by merely wishing him dead.

Such thoughts were ridiculous superstition, Hain told himself. He was simply unnerved by being discovered. Perhaps he had taken too much veridine. With a toss of his head, Hain shook off his doubts. Selod was a man—more powerful than most, but a man nonetheless. And as such, Hain could master him. With a sure snap of his wrist, the assassin launched the crystal egg across the room. His aim was true: the glass shattered against the center of Selod's chest.

"What?" the mage cried, staggering backward. Yellowish smoke billowed from the broken egg and enveloped the old man's figure. "What?"

Each time the wizard opened his mouth, he seemed to suck in the roiling vapors. After only a moment, the last wispy tendril of smoke had snaked its way inside Selod's mouth. The old man stumbled forward, touching his lips with confusion.

Lightly, contemptuously, Hain skipped down the remaining steps.

"I don't know what you think you're doing, you fool, but you'll regret it," Sclod threatened, but he sounded less sure of himself. The mage's brow, Hain noted with satisfaction, was creased with worry. "I'll blast you to the pits of hell, I'll—"

Hain yawned ostentatiously. It was exactly such arrogance that he hated most about mages.

"Never place your faith in magic, old man," Hain sneered. "Or did your mother never warn you about placing all your eggs in one basket? You see, with my one glass egg, I've knocked your basket to the ground."

"What was that?" Selod asked, stepping forward. "Don't toy with me, or I'll make you suffer as—"

"Try it," Hain suggested amiably. He could almost laugh, the old man was so pathetic. Were these the giants of the nation, these mages who ruled through superstition? "Come, bring down the lightning, the fire, the tempests. Have at it, you old fraud!"

Selod was gesticulating wildly, chanting spell after spell, desperately searching for one that would work. Hain noted the emaciated arms that emerged from the red satin sleeves. He smiled at the frail ankles that emerged beneath the mage's robe.

"You see, Selod, you're nothing without your magic. I despise you." Slowly, dramatically, Hain slipped a knife from the sheath at his belt. "And I shall show you what true power is."

Then the world buckled beneath him. Distantly, Hain

realized that there was a dagger protruding from his right thigh. Where had it come from? The world was speeding up, spinning into a frenzied jig. Where was his veridine . . . ?

Then Hain saw the other dagger in the mage's ancient hands and he forced himself to move, to drop to the floor and roll forward, finding cover behind Selod's couch. He felt no pain as he pulled the dagger from his leg but watched, fascinated, as his blood jetted from the wound. The dagger was slim, aerodynamic. The mage's? How?

Suddenly, the old man was upon him, feinting and thrusting with his other blade. Hain rolled out of the way instinctively but felt a line of pain sear his arm. He had to snap out of it, he realized suddenly, or he would die. Although he had underestimated Selod, he was not beaten yet. Selod was an old man, he reminded himself. Selod couldn't possibly win a knife fight. But unless he pulled himself together, Hain could *lose*.

Using the mage's own dagger, Hain parried the next slash and pulled himself to his feet. From the corner of his eye, he could see the blood flowing from his leg, but he would have to ignore that. He parried again with the mage's blade and thrust with his own dagger. At the last second he remembered that he couldn't kill the old man, that he must take him alive. The dagger pierced the skin of Selod's stomach, but Hain stopped the blow before it was fatal. Then, with speed born of years of practice, he reversed his grip on the other knife and whipped his arm up. The pommel caught the mage on the chin, snapping his head back. Tarem Selod fell to the floor, unconscious, blood trickling from the split flesh of his jaw.

Hain gulped air in ragged gasps as he tore off strips of his shirt and bound them around the wound in his thigh. Satisfied that the bleeding was slowing, he turned his attention toward his left arm. Luckily, it was only a superficial cut. He didn't bother with it further; he had to finish matters with the mage. There were words he had to learn. But as he reached toward the old man, he noticed that his hand was shaking. The mage would wait.

Yes, a few minutes was all it would take.

Hain opened the pouch at his belt and, trembling, found the needle.

"Wake up!"

Again Hain splashed water on the wizard's face. For a second, he feared that he had hit the old man too hard and killed him. But, no, the pulse was there and steady. In fact, Selod's eyelids had started to flutter. Hain showered the mage with more water. "Wake up, I say!"

Finally, Selod's eyes opened. He blinked and jerked his head, remembering what had happened.

"I was afraid for you, old man. I was afraid I had killed you too soon. You see, there are words you know, words I must know. You will tell them to me and you will tell the truth. I will know if you lie, believe me. And believe this: I hope you struggle, I hope you lie. I owe you a debt, old man, and I will pay you in pain."

"You're a melodramatic pig," Selod whispered.

"Your insults," Hain replied, laughing, "aren't half as sharp as my knife."

He began by wrapping his hand around Selod's wrist, holding it in place. Then he put the edge of his dagger to Selod's palm and slowly began to press. The old man's skin was pushed inward until finally, stretched to its limit, it split open. Inch by inch, Hain pulled the knife down, cutting open the wizard's hand.

The wizard offered no struggle, his eyes locking onto Hain with ferocious concentration.

"You actually enjoy this," Selod said hoarsely.

"But you won't." Hain reached into the pouch that had held the egg. It also held a gem that was more precious for its magical properties than for its mineral ones.

It was pear-shaped and colored a dusky blue. Hain wiped it against the blood on Selod's palm. "Now, I shall know if you lie."

"Who is behind this?" Selod asked sharply. "You're obviously not alone. You don't have the brains for this sort of thing. And you don't possess the power to fashion that glass ball you used. Only a few people on the entire continent do. *Who is it?*"

"I'll ask the questions," Hain replied curtly. "There are only twenty words I am interested in, and you know which they are."

"Never," Selod vowed softly.

"I can't say I'm surprised. Or disappointed." He applied the tip of the dagger to Selod's right cheek, just below the ear, and slowly broke the skin. With great care, he traced a bloody line down to the man's chin.

"The words."

After a moment, Hain repeated the process on the other side.

"The words," he repeated.

"You want words?" the mage gasped. "Try these: I curse you to hell."

Hain smiled. "If you haven't noticed, your magic has been nullified. Pity you won't live long enough to recover it."

Selod shut his mouth firmly.

Content, Hain shrugged and opened the mage's robe to the waist. Under his breath, he began to hum. No matter that the chest was sunken, the skin puckered and marked with age. There Hain beheld a fertile landscape upon which to exercise his rare and bloody arts. A small body, to be sure, and old, but containing infinite scope for the practice of his ingenuity. Hain had all night and all the anguish in the world to lavish on Tarem Selod, and he was never so happy as when he was at work.

• • •

Finally. the words had come and the small blue stone had changed to green: the mage had spoken truly. Hain devoted five minutes to memorizing what Selod had said. Like all the others, Selod's phrase was not in a language Hain had ever heard, and that made the task harder. Precision was paramount. Madh had stressed it time and again—the words were all that mattered.

Hain surveyed Selod's body. It was barely recognizable. The assassin had to give the old man credit for perseverance . . . and thanks. Rarely was Hain afforded such an opportunity to exercise the full extent of his talents. Indeed, ordinary methods had done little good, so Hain had improvised. He had begun by lighting a cheerful blaze in Selod's fireplace. Ultimately, most of the mage's skin had been consumed by it. So, the old man was yet alive, his ruined chest expanding weakly to inhale. Keeping them alive that long, Hain reflected, was a true talent.

His work done, Hain would rather let the mage die lingeringly, but there was the chance that someone would stumble upon him before the end. It wasn't likely, but it was possible that Selod could be revived long enough to describe his attacker. And that, Madh had emphasized, was to be avoided at all costs. Somewhat disappointed, Hain ran the blade of his dagger across the mage's throat, severing both veins and arteries. Finally, he opened the dead mouth and placed a large, gold coin upon the tongue.

Only a bit of tidying was in order before the evening was done. Hain replaced the poker by the fire and looked for something with which to clean his knife. Conveniently, there was a handkerchief on the end table.

Hadn't the mage's book been on the end table? Hain glanced behind the small wooden pedestal, assuming the book had been knocked off during the struggle. There was nothing. He shook his head and turned back toward Selod.

Hain gasped. The old man was whole. There was not a cut or a burn on the peaceful, recumbent body. Unbelievably, the mage stirred as if from sleep and winked, momentarily fixing Hain with a lucid, blue eye.

Hain dropped the knife and stumbled backward.

Abruptly, things returned to normal. The corpse was once again a corpse, lying in a vast pool of blood.

Perhaps his own blood loss . . . ?

Shaking, Hain bolted from the house.

"What?" Madh roared as he shot to his feet. upsetting his chair in the process.

"Just for a second, I swear. Then it was normal again."

"Corpses simply don't do that," Madh said quietly, regaining his composure.

"This one did."

Madh stared into the assassin's eyes, frowning, but saying nothing. Suddenly, it occurred to Hain what his employer was thinking.

"It wasn't the drug, I'm telling you. I know what veridine does, and it isn't a hallucinogen." But Hain's voice quavered. If he were forced to choose, he would rather that the drug be the explanation, considering the alternative. After all, if dead men could come again to life, there would be a legion of the dead clamoring for an hour or two with Hain.

Madh righted his chair and sat down again. He suppressed a sigh, not willing to let Hain see the depths of his weariness with this business. He yearned to be done with it all, to return home.

"Well, if it was the drug—or your imagination—then it's harmless. But if this happens again, your career will meet a premature end. You're careless, Hain, you know that? You're arrogant, and one day, that's going to get

you killed." He looked pointedly at the bandages around
Hain's thigh. "It almost did already."

Hain said nothing, but he glowered at his employer.
Where was Madh when there was work to be done?
Where was Madh when the dead came to life? When all
of this was over and Hain was paid, he vowed that Madh
would regret this conversation.

"If it were up to me," Madh went on, "I would be rid
of you right now. Tonight is proof that you aren't the
man for this task. My master, however, is pleased with
our progress. There are only three left. But, so help me,
if there is trouble like this again, you will pay for it.
Now, leave me."

Hain turned toward the door, and as he did so, Madh
noticed the assassin's left sheath. It was empty.

"What happened to your dagger?"

Hain turned around, remembering how he'd dropped
the blade. "I lost it."

"*Where?*"

Hain scowled. "At Selod's."

"Damn you," Madh said quietly. "Get out of here."

The house was as Hain had described it, but now
it was darkened for the night. By Madh's estimation,
there was only an hour left before dawn. But despite the
lateness of the hour, Madh did not hurry to dismount.
Even from this distance, the house reeked of magic—so
much so that he was surprised he couldn't smell it back
at the inn. Focusing his concentration, Madh could detect the lingering remnants of his master's scent. It was
distinctly the trace of the crystal egg. But there was as
well a unique and strong flavor that accompanied it, and
one he would not forget: the signature of Tarem Selod.
This was no surprise. For those who could discern such
things, a mage's true home always carried his mark.

Rather, it was the magnitude of the impression that dismayed Madh. To those who could see, the rafters of Tarem Selod's house fairly vibrated with evidence of his recent exertions. Something had happened here that transcended Madh's carefully laid plans.

Madh hitched his horse to a nearby tree and walked quickly onto the grounds, following the gravel path straight to Selod's porch and only stopping before the front door. Hesitantly, he tried the knob and swung the door open. Madh entered the mage's house cautiously. Of course, he had his master's assurances and protection, but Tarem Selod was apparently more resourceful than even his master had reckoned. This evening, Selod should have been as powerless as a babe. Unless Hain had missed with the egg. Yet, Madh was sure he had not lied about that; if Hain had missed, Madh could see no reason why Selod would have let him live.

Dismissing such unprofitable speculation, Madh moved quickly and silently through the mage's antechamber, down the hall, and into the sitting room. All that mattered now was that he retrieve the knife and make sure that Selod was dead. It was dark inside the house, but he did not bother with a lamp. Madh's black eyes devoured the lesser darkness of the house as if it were nothing. The problem was, there was only nothing to see.

There was no knife. There was no blood.

And Tarem Selod was gone.

Taylor Ash left Ravenwood's company feeling profoundly disturbed. He had not exactly lied to the Prime Minister and, on the strength of that, he hoped his performance had been convincing: the world-weary intelligence officer, forced by cruel circumstance to sign his own father's execution order. The world-weariness had been easy enough to convey; he felt it only too acutely. As for ordering his father's execution, however . . . Taylor merely said he had signed the orders— he hadn't said what they were. But Taylor's professional instincts nagged at him. He realized that, were his father and Barr Aston not involved, he might well have arranged the executions.

On the other hand, he argued to himself, killing never solved anything. That was precisely the problem with Amet Pale and his bloodthirsty lot. They couldn't understand that blood means less than knowledge. Kill the ex-ministers before the enemy gets them, and perhaps you've foiled the enemy's plan. But you have also left yourself an unknown enemy. The short-term solution merely compounded the long-term problem. Ash was convinced of a better alternative, one that might save lives and locate the true culprit. With renewed energy in his step, he arrived at the eighth floor of Council Tower and rushed to his office.

Jolah, his assistant, nearly knocked him over as he walked through the door.

"Thank heavens you're back," she gasped. Her soft brown hair was all awry and there were bags under her eyes. The stress of the crisis had begun to trickle down to everyone involved. "I was about to go looking for you."

"What's the matter?" Ash asked, although he instantly knew what the matter had to be: Roland Duke Calador, or Tarem Selod, or Barr Aston.

Or his father.

"Out with it!" he snapped. Immediately he regretted the outburst, and apologized. Jolah had been his chief administrative aide since the day he took office. A few months ago, before any of the current trouble had surfaced, she had made clear to him that she hoped he would become more than her boss. Taylor had put a quick stop to any thoughts of romance, but their relationship had been uncomfortable ever since. Worse still,

the events of the last few days had made him unchar-
acteristically curt. All he needed, he thought ruefully,
was to prompt Jolah to quit. Now, of all times, he needed
her professional acumen most.

Jolah let the incident pass without comment, more
concerned with imparting her news. "It's Tarem Selod."

"Dead?" he asked.

"We're not sure."

"Not sure?" he replied, feeling his temper rise again.
"The name of this department is supposed to be Intelligence. Have someone feel the old man's wrist. If
there's no damned pulse, then—"

He stopped short. He was losing it again. Slowly and
deliberately, he sat down on a nearby couch and began
to massage his pounding temples.

Control. Control, he reminded himself, is everything
right now.

"I'm sorry. Go on."

Jolah brushed back her long, dark hair and peered
intently at Taylor before continuing.

"The problem is that we don't have a body, live or
dead."

"Do you mean that Selod disappeared? Got wind of
the murders and fled?"

Jolah shook her head unhappily. "I wish it were that
simple. Our murderer got to Selod, we know that much.
Our surveillance men have the bruises to prove it."

Taylor pressed his palms against his eyes. His head
felt as if it would like nothing more than to split down
the middle. "I thought I increased the coverage to ten
operatives."

"Not all of them had arrived at the time of the incident. Two were still in transit."

"Even so, eight. . . ." Ash rubbed his forehead painfully. "Bloody damnation! So, when they came to, they
entered the house and . . . ?"

"No body and no signs of a struggle."

Taylor sighed but, bad as the news was, it still was valuable. As he began to mold the information into various patterns, testing to see which would fit best, he forgot his headache and even his meeting with Ravenwood.

"Does the break in the pattern mean that Selod killed the killers?" Taylor speculated. "If so, where are the assassins' bodies, and why did Selod disappear? Afraid of more? From what I know of him, that's not the old man's style. Were they unable to break him and forced to kidnap him? If that's the case, why no signs of a struggle? Judging by previous incidents, our culprit is no neat freak, and I would expect Selod to put up more of a fight than Loft or Ell." Ash sighed again, frustrated by the logical impasse. "What did our beautiful dreamers do when they regained consciousness?"

"Four needed immediate medical attention. One brought in the report to the main base in Leones. The other three stayed at the scene in case of further developments."

"At least someone's doing things right. Anything happen?"

Jolah winced. "That's the worst part. Soon afterward, a single man rode to Selod's house and walked right in. When he left a few minutes later, he looked agitated. Two of our three remaining agents followed him."

"And?"

"And it's been six hours. We haven't heard a word."

CHAPTER 4

One would have thought a plague was ravaging downtown Prandis, so quickly did the crowds hurry along the streets of the nation's capital. The city was laid out like a wagon wheel, with the stark granite monolith of Council Tower at the hub. From that hub, everyone was rushing along the major streets that led like spokes from the Tower to the city's circumference. But the cause of the exodus was far more prosaic than a plague. It was simply the close of another working week—more than cause enough to send thousands of civil service employees scurrying to their homes in the residential districts, jostling each other and jockeying for position as they went. It was as if the sentinels of the nation had vacated their posts, abandoned their vigilance and care, leaving only the stark granite monolith of the Council Tower as lonely watchguard for the nation.

But as workers spilled out of the blocky municipal buildings that crowded the center of the city, Brandt Karrelian fought the tide of traffic. Through the throngs of pedestrians and carriages and creaking wooden bicycles, he strolled stubbornly toward the city's rapidly emptying center. Council Tower seemed a long walk from Brandt's estate, especially during these brisk, early spring days, but he had made the trek a habit, a weekly pilgrimage. While everyone burst from their offices and hurried home—or to bars or plays, lovers or friends— Brandt was drawn to the deserted seat of power. He could never fully articulate why—just a vague sense that when everyone else had gone, then he belonged.

Of late, he had felt the need to wander more often. Something about the mansion, big as it was, induced claustrophobia. The place was built of secrets—secrets he had painstakingly gathered and guarded, the true mortar of the house—and, more than ever, those secrets seemed to suffocate him. He thought of the files in his subbasement vault, each color-coded to its family of sin like some chromatic taxonomy of hell, each clamoring for daylight. A sliver of daylight was all Brandt asked for upon the emptying streets.

Brandt seldom followed the same route to Prandis. Today he found himself in a quiet residential neighborhood. A moment's observation told him that the area was upper middle-class. It was obvious from the size of the houses and their carefully manicured lawns, but the true telltale shone through the windows: the light was often electrical. Because magical energy disrupted the flow of electricity with dismaying ease, central generators were impractical—and individual generators were expensive. Brandt had once dreamed of centralized plants that, like a remote heart of the city, would pump their power through subterranean arteries to each individual house. But building one would be folly. Any minor magical occurrence near a power line would disrupt electricity for miles in a centralized system, and in the city of Prandis there was not a second when someone was not working magic somewhere.

Centuries had passed since the first generators had been built, yet still the National Arcane Authority had found no solution to the interference problem. For those who wanted the convenience of electricity, the only solution was to buy an individual generator, but even those fortunate few had to endure blackouts whenever a spell was cast too close to their home. Ultimately, because generators were expensive, and so was fuel, those who could do without electricity, did. As Brandt looked at the windows in this neighborhood, he often saw the fitful, flickering light of lanterns. But in almost as many houses, he found the steady illumination of electricity. This was an uncommonly high ratio, indicating that these people were fairly well-to-do. And it all meant money in Brandt's pocket.

Years ago, after retiring from espionage, he had sought solace in the generator business. The venture had started as a front, as a token of legitimacy to explain the wealth he had illicitly built. Brandt had been fascinated for a time by the engineers who acted as if they were the new breed of wizard, making things happen through the manipulation of particles so impossibly small that magic seemed mundane by comparison. And there had been the challenge of nurturing an industry dependent on rare iron and magnets, which kept prices high. But, ultimately, these challenges called for reports and meetings, statistics compiled and dissected, each of which weighed like another anchor upon his chest. These days, it was all Brandt could do to summon the enthusiasm to act the happy figurehead and affix his signature to the documents that were shuffled across his desk.

A rather stout man passed Brandt and strolled happily up a brick-paved walk to his porch. In a singular display of ostentation, two electric bulbs flanked the front door. The man carried a shiny, well-made briefcase. Some midlevel bureaucrat, Brandt thought sourly. As the man wiped his shoes on a welcome mat, a once-pretty woman opened the door for her husband and threw her arms around him. The man's briefcase fell to the ground, but he didn't seem to mind. He kissed his wife as if he hadn't seen her for days.

Brandt accelerated his pace.

Before long, he reached the center of the city. The streets were almost deserted, save for the crews of cleaners who hurried by with their brooms and dustpans. The new mayor, who had campaigned for office largely on the issue of civic hygiene, was implementing his promised policies. Brandt, though, found that he missed the grime. After a fifteen-year acquaintance, it had somehow put him at ease.

A burst of laughter drew his attention. A couple was emerging from a nearby restaurant and, as the door opened, the alluring sound of a mirthful crowd wafted into the street. Morbidly fascinated by that gaiety, Brandt wandered almost unconsciously toward the place. Council House, it was called, ostensibly to appeal to government employees. Brandt had never eaten there, but he could tell it was expensive. In Prandis, restaurants were best judged by their lighting. The really cheap ones, of course, could afford no generator. The moderately priced ones, anxious to establish their respectability, made a conspicuous display of their electric bulbs. It was only in elite establishments that one voluntarily sacrificed electricity for the primitive ambience of dining by candlelight. Council House belonged to this last variety.

Brandt wasn't worried about the price—that was one thing he would never need to worry about again. But there might be a dress code. Unlike the couple that was retreating down the street, Brandt did not cut a fashionable figure. Unless there was good reason, he preferred to dress shabbily. Tonight he wore an old tweed jacket with brown pants and walking shoes, a plain blue shirt with no tie, and a red scarf to ward off the chill April wind. Nevertheless, there was something about the place that intrigued him, so he crossed the street and headed for the entrance.

A red-uniformed doorman frowned slightly, but he swung open the polished oak door and Brandt slipped inside, finding himself in a warm, dim vestibule. A tuxedoed maitre d' stood by a pair of glass doors, solemnly guarding the dining room behind him. The whole place was tastefully done, Brandt noted. Elegant wainscoting, crystal chandeliers, and fine mauve table linen—the season's color. Off to Brandt's left was a separate entrance to the bar, where a well-heeled crowd joked, sipped their drinks, and whispered confidentially while they awaited tables.

"Can I help you?" the host asked imperiously, casting a contemptuous look at Brandt's attire.

Both the question and the tone of voice were all too familiar. That sneering, moneyed superiority. . . . It was as if seventeen years had been suddenly wiped away, leaving Brandt once again an aspiring twenty-year-old burglar who, though poorly dressed and still more poorly behaved, had for the first time in his life accumulated enough cash in his pocket to walk into a fancy downtown restaurant. Now, hundreds of such meals later, he felt equally out of place.

And he responded much as he had that first time, marshaling a disingenuous bluntness calculated to worsen the brewing conflict. "I'm hungry. I'd like to eat."

The host smiled slyly. "Well, unless you have a reservation—"

"I don't," Brandt snapped, craning his neck for a better view of the dining room. "But I see you have empty tables."

"I'm sorry," the man explained without the slightest trace of sincerity, "but those are reserved. In fact, I'm afraid the earliest available reservations are next week."

"Right," Brandt replied. "I'll just have a drink at your bar, then."

The host scowled but said nothing.

"You don't need a reservation for the bar stools, do you?" Brandt asked. This time, sarcasm got the better of him and leaked into his voice. The host's scowl deepened, but he made no move to stop Brandt as he strode toward the bar, jostling more than a few patrons before he found a seat at the far end of the mahogany expanse. Everyone, it seemed, was here with a group of friends or a lover, and the whole place buzzed with a spirited geniality. Brandt felt buffeted by the chatter, drowned beneath fathoms of small talk. He cursed himself for continuing the charade, but he'd be damned before he was cowed by a puffed-up usher.

After a moment, the slick-haired bartender asked for his order.

"Moon Farm, white, please," Brandt growled. It was his favorite wine—a habit begun in boyhood, and one that he shared with the majority of bums and winos across the breadth of Chaldus. There was not a chance that the Council House would stock such a cheap brand. Brandt knew this—in fact, he had placed the order just to observe the gratifying drop of the bartender's jaw. "No? Crap. Just make it Mertouil," he amended, naming an expensive bottle before the bartender had time to recover. He would have preferred the Moon Farm. To hell with bouquet; both wines got you to the same place.

You can take the guttersnipe out of the streets, he thought grimly, *but. . . .*

While the bartender left to find the bottle, Brandt let his gaze wander across the bar again. It stopped this time on a woman he hadn't noticed before. She sat alone with a glass of white wine, but she was paying more attention to the crowd than to her drink. Neck craned ever so slightly, she seemed to be scanning the room, as if looking for someone she knew. In that posture, Brandt thought, her green silk dress showed off her figure to the best possible advantage, stopping just short of revealing too much. She had impeccably arranged shoulder-length auburn hair and a small, slightly upturned nose. It was the nose that made Brandt look twice. He had always liked that sort of puckish nose.

Brandt leaned forward in his seat and smiled, waiting for her to make eye contact. The woman recognized the invitation and her eyes flickered over Brandt, assessing him in an instant. Her lips puckered slightly with distaste and she turned away. Whatever she searched for in the crowd, she had not found it in Brandt.

The bartender returned with Brandt's Mertouil. Brandt fished into his pocket and brought out a roll of crisp bills, all hundreds. He tossed one onto the bar and turned his back.

"Do you have anything smaller, sir?" the bartender asked, not yet comprehending that Brandt was about to leave.

"Keep it," Brandt said dryly. For the second time that night the bartender's jaw dropped. The sum on the bar more than equaled his entire week's wage.

"But—" the bartender stammered as Brandt turned to leave. "But don't you even want the wine?"

"I'm not paying for the wine," Brandt muttered as he pushed through the happy throng toward the door. "I'm paying for the lesson."

Back in the streets. Brandt found that he knew no place he wanted to go. He wandered aimlessly for a time and, as always happens in downtown Prandis, found himself at Council Tower. Leaning against the wrought iron fence, he gazed across the vast garden of well-manicured plants and equally manicured guards, settling his gaze on the Tower. The slim granite spire rose two hundred feet into the air, culminating in a twenty-foot stylized sculpture of a hawk, the symbol of the Chaldean government. The statue was made of solid steel—a monumental display of wealth in Prandis, where steel was scarce and bronze was used most often in its stead.

A quiet night, and he alone with the Tower, was a time he relished. Darkness would fall, the government's ministers would be driven home in their carriages, and who would come to replace them? As a young man, just after he and Carn had moved to Prandis, Brandt used to walk to the Tower almost every night and watch the building shut down, light after lighting fading from the windows above. It was like some solemn changing of the guard. Tonight, though, the steady electric lights of the structure poured through many windows, even at the highest floors. Tonight, the ministers were busy. On a lark, Brandt thought of going inside. It could easily be done. Cross to the front gate and deliver a terse message to the guards. There were any number of people still likely to be inside—a dozen, at least—to whom two words would suffice to gain Brandt's admission. It would be oddly comforting, Brandt thought, to be within those walls tonight.

But it wouldn't be sporting of him to panic those poor civil servants, already made to work overtime into the weekend. They belonged there and he . . . he belonged. . . .

Brandt sighed, letting the equation expire uncompleted, and turned toward home.

By the flicker of candlelight. Masya admired the gray hair that quilted Carn's chest—a balance of virility and fragility that spoke so much of the man himself. Her fingers itched to wander through that hair, but she held them back, afraid to wake him. These were the times she cherished most, after they had dined and spoken quietly of their week, after they had made love upon her pallet, when he lay asleep, snoring softly, and she could imagine him sleeping through the night, finding him there in the morning beside her. But he never did wake up beside her in the morning, so she stole these moments while he slept, not knowing what he dreamed while she dreamed of another life.

Finally, she bowed to desire, letting her fingers fall softly onto his chest, just below the tuft of hair that often peeked above his shirt collar. Her hands did not look so old in the candlelight, Masya thought, though they still seemed ugly to her. Would he prefer long, painted fingernails, she wondered, rather than the short, plain nails that wandered toward his ribs? She laid her hand flat across his stomach, feeling the warmth there, and was happy.

A few moments later, Carn began to stir. He seldom slept more than an hour, and had never slept so long that the candle guttered out. Still semiconscious, he felt Masya's body pressed against his own, and he smiled. Through hooded eyes, he peered at her brown hair spilling onto his chest, at the white planes of her arms and legs below. She was not a conventionally beautiful woman, in the sense of the curved beauties that graced the mansion when Brandt entertained. Masya labored for a living—as a laundress or a maid or a seamstress; whatever the occasion warranted—and when she moved, Carn could follow the play of muscles beneath her skin. He craned his neck forward to kiss her softly atop her head, pausing a moment to savor the scent of henna in her hair. When he slipped free of her limbs a moment later, he moved as carefully as if she had been made of eggshells.

She said nothing, watching as he began methodically to dress. When he was done, he turned to the table and gathered the dishes, trying to move them quietly to the tin tub that sat upon the counter. Masya rolled over and sighed.

"Leave the dishes," she said softly.

Carn smiled at her, but proceeded to dip each plate into the water, scrub it clean, dry it, and stack it neatly into the cabinet above the counter. For him, it was a matter of showing respect. Masya had never found a way to persuade him to leave the dishes where they were, to leave an empty wine bottle overturned by the fireplace, or to let a sock lie abandoned beneath the chair. And so, like every other morning after one of his visits, she would awaken with no physical trace that he had ever been there. Except the ache beneath her ribs.

"Stay," she said, almost regretting the wounded look in his eyes.

"You know I can't. We've discussed this."

"Back to your feather bed and your mansion?" she asked archly.

"Back to Brandt," Carn emended. He looked about the shabby, one-room apartment. Here and there the brick lay exposed through wounds in the plaster. He yearned to fix the place, or move her entirely, but Masya refused to accept his "charity."

"You know I would trade the mansion to stay here, by your side—"

"Except that Brandt would wither and die without you?" she asked, a growing bite to her voice. "He would crawl beneath his bed and never come out again? Or waste away until a gust of wind scattered him to the poles?"

She rose and walked behind Carn, pressing herself to his back.

"I'll never understand what binds you to him," she murmured into his skin.

Carn was not sure he understood himself, not in the sense Masya meant. What bound him to Brandt was subterranean, the result of decades-long tectonic movements, not something that could be explained in a sentence.

"Masya, it's a matter of years. And lives. I'm more

times in debt to him for my life—and he to me—than all his accountants could reckon with their stacks of ledgers."

"So you stay with him out of some silly debt—"

"Not a debt," Carn gently corrected. "A friendship. We are friends, and he needs me."

Masya turned Carn around, placed her hands upon his cheeks. "*I* need you."

"Then come live with me," he replied, not for the first time. This conversation had become a ritual between them, something to be exorcised each night before he could leave.

She let go of him and pushed the tub of dirty dishwater farther down the counter.

"I'm a simple woman, my love. I don't belong in a mansion. I wouldn't know what to do there, unless I had a bucket in one hand and a brush in the other."

Carn smiled sadly, running his finger along the curve of her jaw.

"Then we need to wait a little longer."

But, as many times as he'd said so, Carn still didn't know what they were waiting for.

The weekend had begun and, like so many single women in Prandis, Elena Imbress was looking for a man. She took a long drag on the cigarette she had just rolled and contemplated the smoke as it rose toward the dark sky. In general, she supposed, men were about as substantial as smoke and, in her experience, tended to stick around about as long. But for this one night, Elena was content with her similarity to the other women in Prandis. Indeed, she thought with a smile, she was even on the hunt for a rich man. Now there was a pursuit very much in the classic Prandine tradition.

On the other hand, most of the night's huntresses weren't using crossbows.

Elena took another drag of her cigarette, frowned at it, and crushed it against the terra-cotta tiles of the roof. She had started smoking as a little girl, but tobacco did little for her, truth be told; cigarettes had merely been one of a dozen ways of rebelling against her father, who had been, while he lived, a successful cloth merchant in the northern town of Athon. Laman Imbress had counted his two daughters as ornaments of prosperity, about on a par with his better furnishings. While Elena's sister settled comfortably into that role, Elena had bent her efforts toward discomfiting her father—wearing men's clothes, hunting, swearing, and smoking. Now, fifteen years after leaving home, these were the only traces of childhood that remained with her.

The yellow brick walls of the building rose three feet above the flat, tiled roof, forming a low parapet. Elena peered over the top course of bricks. Directly beneath her ran the broad expanse of Exchange Street, a commercial boulevard that ran from Council Tower toward the western suburbs. Dominated by banks and office buildings, Exchange was typically deserted at night. Straining her eyes against the darkness, Elena could see no one save a single man in a tweed jacket sauntering slowly west. That was her man.

She dropped back behind the cover of the parapet and took a moment to examine her crossbows. She had brought two, because they took so long to reload. Two shots would be more than enough, she thought. In fact, two shots too many, as far as Elena was concerned. Brandt Karrelian was a dried-up old businessman, regardless of the whispers about his past. The man was of neither interest nor importance—and certainly no reason to spend half her night stalking through alleys and over rooftops. But orders were orders, and after the past two weeks' disasters, Elena had little taste for rebellion.

She released the safeties on each bow, placing one within easy reach and keeping hold of the second. With her back pressed against the cool bricks, hardly breathing, she let the sounds of the street rise toward her. Far-off strains of music wafted her way and an occasional burst of laughter, but nothing from Exchange. Karrelian either wore very soft-soled shoes or he walked like a cat. She was tempted to peek, but chided herself to be patient. The man was strolling, taking his time. She closed her eyes and waited, counting each pulse of her blood as it tolled through her ears.

Finally, Elena heard a soft step echo upward from the cobblestones. Rising cautiously above the parapet, she saw Karrelian almost directly below her. He *did* walk a little like a cat, she thought. If she hadn't been straining, she never would have heard him. But there he was, thirty feet below her without an ounce of cover. Elena had bagged stags bounding through dense woods at ten times this distance. By comparison, this was such an easy shot, it was hardly sporting. *With no more challenge than this,* Elena wondered, *how do snipers salvage a sense of self-worth?*

Another step brought Karrelian's back into view. Elena brought the butt of the crossbow to her shoulder and, taking careful aim down the shaft, squeezed the trigger gently. Now, the evening's entertainment would finally begin.

It was on the way home that it happened—an explosive clatter across the cobblestones of Exchange Street just behind him. Brandt whirled around to find the broken remnants of a crossbow bolt only a foot away. For an instant he stood frozen to the spot, but that would do no good except offer the archer an opportunity to improve his aim. Just as a high-pitched whistling sound reached his ears, Brandt dived away. Another explosive impact immediately followed.

There was an alley only a few yards down the street,

and Brandt sprinted toward it for all he was worth. If there was more than one sniper, he knew, he'd never make it. But if someone had to reload a crossbow. . . . A third bolt struck the bricks only a foot to his left as he rounded the corner and accelerated down the trash-strewn alley. He dodged heaps of rotting garbage and abandoned furniture, plunging into darkness. Finally, there were no more shots, nor could he hear pursuit. The archer had been on the rooftops—a good position for a sniper, as long as his shots were sure. But Brandt had been lucky: when a rooftop sniper missed, he had little chance of chasing the target afterward.

After a couple of blocks, Brandt ducked into a doorway to catch his breath. His heart was pounding and his entire body felt oddly light. It was a sensation he had not experienced for years—the keen physical edge of danger—and it was strangely exhilarating. Acting on instinct, Brandt continued through the alley, turned left at the next corner, and found another alley nearby that led back toward the scene of the attack. Keeping to the shadows, he loped along at an easy rate until he reached Exchange. Everything appeared to be deserted. Brandt crossed the street quickly and, taking to another back alley, cautiously approached the old brick building where he guessed the sniper had been hidden. A fairly sturdy drainpipe ran from the roof to the cobblestones. It was all Brandt needed. During his prime, there had been few second-story men better than he. A drainpipe offered a simple climb—almost as easy as a staircase. A slight grin had crept across his lips by the time he reached the top.

With exceeding caution, Brandt peered over the uppermost course of bricks, only to find the roof deserted. No great surprise. Once the target had fled, it would be foolish for an assassin to hang around. Brandt was almost disappointed to have been robbed of a fight. There was nothing to do now but look around, hoping for some sort of clue. He pulled himself softly up to the tiled surface of the roof. Careful to keep his footsteps quiet, he crossed to the side of the building that overlooked Exchange. It was a well-chosen location for an ambush. Brandt could see clearly down the boulevard for a hundred yards in either direction. The assassin had waited until Brandt was almost beneath him to try his first shot.

Brandt turned his attention back to the surface of the roof. Only a foot from the parapet lay a hand-rolled cigarette butt. Brandt knelt to feel it—still warm and moist. Indeed, the assassin had been here, but a cigarette butt told him very little that he needed to know. And there were two things that Brandt needed to know very badly indeed:

Who had tried to kill him, and why on earth had the man been such a poor shot?

After forty years of toil, Fikkis could now claim the indifferent title of slumlord. He owned nearly sixty buildings throughout the dilapidated cheapstreet and tenderloin districts of Prandis, not that he much profited by them, what with taxes and bribing building inspectors and making the occasional repairs. Unlike most of his slumlord brethren, Fikkis strove to keep his tenants happy. Contented tenants, Fikkis had found, didn't bother their landlords, and bother was the last thing Fikkis sought. He had entered the real estate business only because owning sixty buildings meant that, on any given night, he could be sleeping in any one of sixty places—or none of them at all, on occasion. It was one of Fikkis' quirks that no one must know where he slept. Fikkis cherished his quirks—they had kept him alive for decades in a city where he had much to fear. As his mother had told him half a century ago as she was hauled away to prison, nobody loves a snitch, mothers included.

It had been a worse night than usual. Wracked by

insomnia, Fikkis had been unable to sleep until long past midnight, by which time he had half-emptied the bottle of rye that sat on the rude wooden table by his cot. He had slept soundly for a few hours thereafter, but had now begun snoring with a violence that threatened to wake him.

He was woken instead by a foot that lashed out at one of the weak wooden legs of the cot, breaking it off entirely. Overbalanced by Fikkis' weight, the cot listed sharply to its side, spilling the informant out onto the rough wooden floor. He cried out as he came awake, struggling against a tangle of thin blankets that had twisted about his limbs.

"It's almost morning, Fikkis. Wake up."

Fikkis struggled against the blankets that ensnared him, not noticing the odd whining noise that rose from his diaphragm. His heart beat like a battering ram, threatening to break through the frail flesh and brittle ribs that sixty-three years of vicious life had left him. He was too old, he thought, for a fight. After all those decades of striving, he had hoped for an end with more dignity, but it seemed he would be disappointed. Inside his pocket was a clever knife whose blade swung open when a spring release was pressed. He had found the knife but couldn't seem to extricate his arm from the last of his blankets. Finally, he twisted free and triggered the blade, blinking at the darkness in search of the intruder.

A strong hand caught his wrist and, with one sure twist, wrenched the knife away. Fikkis strained against the darkness and his cataracts, hoping at least to see the man who had come to kill him.

"Who are you?" he wailed.

The response was a chuckle.

"Come now, Fikkis, has it been that long?"

Then the figure backed away. On the table, next to the rye, there was an oil lamp. The intruder struck a match and held it to the lamp's wick, waiting for the growing glow to steady itself before he blew out the match.

Fikkis gasped. The features were older and perhaps a little rounder, but largely unchanged: the piercing hazel eyes, that inscrutable, tight-lipped smile, the unkempt black hair only lightly touched by gray.

"Hazard!"

Brandt smiled. "So you do remember me. That's a comfort. I'd hate to think of myself as the type of man who leaves no impression."

Fikkis licked his lips nervously. Hazard had once been a valuable customer. No doubt, he had come as a customer again, so Fikkis needn't fear for his safety. But, despite Hazard's banter, there was an edge to his voice. . . .

"How did you find me?" Fikkis asked.

"Slowly," Brandt replied, easing into the cane-backed chair behind the table. He hoped he didn't look as tired as he felt. This was the twenty-seventh fleabag tenement he had searched that night . . . and he counted himself lucky to have found the old snitch this soon. "Seems like you've bought every rundown shack in Prandis since last we spoke. With the money I used to pay you, I know you can afford better." Brandt squirmed in his seat. "At least you might have bought more comfortable chairs, Fikkis. Your reputation as a host is at stake tonight."

Fikkis frowned sourly, gesturing at his cot. "I try to avoid guests. They have a tendency to break the furniture."

Brandt's smile widened by a hair.

The old man threw off the remaining blankets and pulled himself to his feet, smoothing the stained brown shirt and ill-fitting pants he had worn to bed.

"So, Hazard, now that you've become a big-time industrialist, what do you want with me? Not just here to look up an old friend, I presume."

Brandt did not reply directly. Instead, he measured the informant's emaciated frame, the nervous eyes. Once, he had been able to trust the man—so far as a man like Fikkis could be trusted.

"Still in business, Fikkis?"

"I hardly see why that should matter to you," the old man said as he ran his fingers through his few remaining strands of gray hair, pulling them across his scalp from one ear to the other.

"It matters to me," Brandt said quietly, "if someone is paying for information about me."

Fikkis frowned and reached for the bottle of rye. He had no glasses because, as he had said, he avoided guests. It was a household of two, just him and the bottle. He took a swig.

"We had a deal, Hazard, when you left the business. I never say a word about you and you leave me alone. I've held to the arrangement more than a decade. What makes you think I'd change now?"

"Someone tried to kill me tonight."

The simple statement registered visibly on Fikkis's face. His old brown eyes narrowed as he began calculating, and Brandt swore he could see the spin of profit whirling through Fikkis's brain.

"Why would anyone attempt such a thing?" the old man asked with a sardonic hint in his voice.

"I was hoping," Brandt responded dryly, "that you would tell me."

The old informant chuckled and took another swig of rye. "I never thought I'd hear such words from you, Hazard. The high life hasn't been good to you—made you soft. Losing touch in your mansion, eh?" The old man chuckled again. "Indeed, indeed. It's hard to keep track of the tides and eddies of Chaldean politics once you've left the street."

"That's hardly an answer," Brandt snapped. He had always hated dealing with Fikkis, but coming back to

the old man under these circumstances was almost in-
tolerable. "Have you been selling information about
me?"

That last question cut through the air, carried by a
cold and threatening tone, and it sobered Fikkis quickly.

"No," the old man answered, "not that I haven't been
approached. I have—many times—over the years. But
I've always kept my word to you, Hazard, I swear.
That's not to say there aren't others who know more
about you than you'd like, despite your caution."

Brandt sighed. He had to hand it to the old man—
Fikkis was still an expert at baiting a hook. "All right,
Fikkis, to whom *haven't* you sold what you know about
me?"

Fikkis smiled. The tide was shifting again. "So you're
asking me for information, Hazard?"

Brandt chuckled despite himself and reached into his
pocket. The roll of bills was still there, and he began to
peel them off, one by one, spreading them across Fikkis'
table. When he had laid down ten, he stopped.

"Come, now," Fikkis chided. "You said you were almost killed tonight."

"I said someone tried to kill me," Brandt corrected
sharply, but he counted off another ten bills. "I never
said whether he had a chance of succeeding."

The old man chortled. "Perhaps you haven't changed
so much as I thought. Well, for old times' sake, I'll tell
you this: There's been a rash of murders lately, not only
in Prandis, but throughout Chaldus. Retired government
men, all this month. First stiff was Pernom Ell, who held
the Ministry of the Interior for nearly thirty years. Ran
domestic policy like it was his toy." Fikkis's eyes narrowed. "But you must know all about Mr. Ell. I believe
he was one of the men with whom you once did *business*.

"Second came Abrinius Loft, half-wizard, half-bean
counter. He died eight days after Ell. Another . . . sub-

ject . . . of yours, I believe. And most recently, there was Tarem Selod, once Minister of Foreign Relations and, incidentally, a far more powerful wizard than Loft. He was found this morning."

Fikkis fell silent, intent on the way Hazard absorbed this information. He betrayed no visible reaction, but the way he concentrated on each word . . . Fikkis was willing to bet that Hazard had heard none of this before. Indeed, he had come a long way from the streets.

"Interesting," Brandt replied, "but what does that have to do with someone shooting crossbows at me? Are you saying some nutcase has launched a murder spree of retirees, and I'm next on the list?"

"Hardly," the old man said, beginning to enjoy himself. "You don't qualify for his kind of list."

"Can the games, Fikkis, and get to the point."

Fikkis glanced again at the money in Brandt's hand. After a moment, Brandt sighed and let another set of bills fall to the table.

"The word on the street is, in the mouth of each of the corpses, the killer had left a newly minted gold capital. Your signature, I believe."

Brandt leaned slowly back in the chair, a numbing chill spreading through his limbs. Someone was killing retired diplomats and making it seem as if Brandt was responsible. That might explain the sniper tonight. Someone—some scared old man who thought he might be next on the list—had tried to take preemptive action. Brandt's stomach lurched. He had built his life carefully, and its foundation relied on balance. For years, as Galatine Hazard, he had worked as the most skilled spy and industrial thief in the nation. If there was a secret to be had, it was Hazard that they turned to. And then, after he had had his fill of work, Hazard turned on them— blackmailed his own clients with their own secrets. A simple matter of balance, of give-and-take. And Brandt had been sure to take quite modestly, demanding such a reasonable annual fee that no one ever complained. The publication of his extensive files, Brandt knew, would hurt far more than the money he asked; if everything continued in the manner he had arranged, there was no reason he couldn't continue collecting his dues for decades. But if there was even a hint that he was now *killing* his former clients . . . all bets were off. They would try to kill him first, whatever he might do with his information.

"I've been set up," Brandt murmured, "very, very well."

"So it would seem," Fikkis answered, sounding positively cheerful. "You know, I've had my eye on an old tenement near the river. . . ."

Brandt glared at the old man as he dropped the rest of his money roll on the table. "There's more?"

"Just a couple of odd coincidences that stand out to a pair of eyes as old as mine. The first is this: if all our ex-ministers were being murdered, you'd think the government would try to clamp a lid on the matter as quickly as possible. It's not the type of information you publicize. It panics people."

"So?" Brandt growled.

"So, funny enough, while the names and positions of the victims have been kept strictly secret, the bit about the gold coins hasn't. More like the opposite: the Ministry of Intelligence seems to be going out of its way to trumpet the fact that you're killing off your old customers. Although no one knows it's ministers that have been murdered, this entire city is buzzing with rumors that Galatine Hazard has gone off his rocker."

Brandt scowled and jumped to his feet, knocking over his chair in the process.

"Careful of the furniture," Fikkis warned. "And there's one more thing before you go. As I said, I have been approached for information about you. The last time was about one week ago. A short man with blond hair. I don't think he realized that I knew him, but I know most everyone in this town."

"Well?" Brandt snapped.

"It was Jin Annard, the Deputy Minister of Intelligence." When the old man looked up at Brandt, there was an odd mixture of mockery and pity in his eyes. "You know, Karrelian, you can play hermit in that mansion of yours for all I care, but it might behoove you to visit me more often. I so enjoy your visits, after all."

Fikkis stepped forward to count the pile of bills that lay on his table. As Brandt disappeared into the cold hallway, he heard the old man call after him, "Good luck, Galatine Hazard."

Galatine Hazard. It was the name of the man he had been. It was a name that could destroy the man he had become.

What scared Brandt most was, he was not sure he would mind.

CHAPTER 5

Hain reined in and dismounted as Madh spurred his small roan mare toward a wooded hillock in the distance. The pair had been riding northeast for two hours, silent in their grim distaste for one another. Since the incident at Selod's house, Madh had grown more cryptic. He had been pushing their pace all morning without a hint of their eventual destination. Apparently, they had reached that destination now, although Hain could not imagine why they had bothered with this ride. The woods west of Chaldus were boring and damp—a place to catch a cold, not an old Chaldean minister.

Madh slowed his mare at the foot of the small hill and jumped to the green-brown turf. With an easy stride, as if he hadn't been riding all morning, he began to climb toward the peak. The slope was lightly scattered with black willows, the largest of which was rooted at the very crest of the hillock, spreading its gnarled boughs high above its brethren. A large black bird that had been resting on one of those ancient limbs launched itself into the air and made directly for the small, dark man. It alit on Madh's arm and hopped up to his shoulder.

A strange bird indeed, thought Hain. He squinted in the midmorning light, cursing the sun in his eyes. Was that a bird at all?

After a few moments, a speck appeared in the clear eastern sky and sped toward the hillock. It circled twice, spreading wide its black wings as it slowed, and landed on Madh's other shoulder. There, Madh and the birds remained in some silent, unmoving consultation. After several minutes, Hain found himself battling an urge to approach them. It was ultimately his reluctance to seem curious that held him to his spot, appearing idly to check his horse's shoes while, in truth, he strained his eyes toward the distant sight. Abruptly, the strange conference concluded. Both creatures launched themselves into the air and soon disappeared into the morning sky. Madh brushed off his clothes and descended the hill as leisurely as he had climbed. At the base, he remounted and spurred his horse into a mild trot toward Hain. The assassin disguised his sour look and leaped back into his saddle, awaiting Madh's arrival with a growing curiosity.

"Homunculi?" Hain asked softly as the other man drew near.

"Your eyes are sharp," Madh replied in an uninterested tone.

"I thought homunculi were legends. Peasant tales for stormy nights."

Madh's eyes narrowed thoughtfully. "No, not legend. Many of the creatures that peasants whisper of did indeed exist, and still do. After the Binding, they were merely . . . diminished. They retreated to the deep places, where some persist to this day, although often in a pitiable state. This makes them less useful to us, but more malleable. If they possessed their old power, I could never control as many as I do today."

"So they're your agents," Hain said, pleased with his conclusion. "That's how you gather information."

Madh smiled slyly. "That is part of it. What concerns us now, however, is Kermane Ash. He is fleeing to the capital, seeking sanctuary beneath Ravenwood's wing."

Hain laughed. "No matter. Let the old fool flee. I can reach him in the heart of the strongest Chaldean citadel if need be."

"But can you reach him in the grave?" Madh retorted, scowling. "One day, Hain, your conceit will be your ruin. The Chaldeans are not as stupid as you think. When Ash reaches Ravenwood, Ravenwood will kill him to keep the old man from us."

"Then we'll just have to reach Ash first," Hain replied, seemingly amused.

Taylor Ash arrived at the eighth floor groggy from his scant two hours' sleep. It had been at Jolah's request that he'd gone home at all, and now, returning to the office half-conscious, he appreciated the wisdom of her suggestion. He should have slept longer. He would be little good to anyone in his current condition.

When he opened the door to the executive suite and walked into the reception area, he was surprised to find Jolah there, looking fresh as could be. She was working longer and lonelier hours than he, Taylor realized, and without the least word of complaint. He remembered his snappishness of the day before and, repenting, wished there was some way he could apologize without letting things get personal. The last thing he needed was to rekindle her romantic inclinations. Some nice word, then, but not intimate. Her clothes? No, he'd seen that tan suit too many times. . . .

"Lovely ring," he told her, noticing the pearl and diamond jewel on her right forefinger. "Is it new?"

She fidgeted with the hem of her jacket, seeming at

once embarrassed and pleased that he had noticed.

"Sometimes," she said quietly, "when you've been working hard, you should treat yourself to a reward."

Taylor chuckled. "Is that a hint for a raise?"

"Not at all." She blushed. "Just a simple answer to a simple question."

That was enough small talk to ease his conscience, so Taylor returned to the business of Intelligence. "Listen, I want you to round up four or five agents and distribute them outside the Tower. Have them watch for my father."

"Your father? Don't you want to see him?"

"That's precisely it," Taylor answered gravely. "I do want to see him."

Jolah shook her head, puzzled. "Can't he make it upstairs without an escort?"

"Of course he can. But once he gets into the building, it won't be me he'll come to see."

"Why not?" Jolah asked, her confusion growing. Of all the people in the world to whom she would flee if she were in trouble, Taylor Ash was the first. She could not imagine anyone—especially Taylor's own father—thinking differently.

"Just send the men out," the young Ash answered. Feeling his lips curl into a scowl, he retreated toward his office.

My father will not come to see me, he thought, *because it would amount to asking a favor from his son. And favors are something the venerable Ash family does not indulge in. No, the old fool will bluster straight into Ravenwood's office, confront the P.M. face to face . . . and get himself killed in the process.*

Taylor sighed as he slipped into the dim interior of his office and swung the door closed behind him. Less than an hour old, he thought grimly, and already the day had soured, but at least it was hard to see how it could get any worse.

"Good morning, Minister."

Taylor snapped out of his reverie and stared at the visitor who sat comfortably in Taylor's leather chair, feet propped up on his desk. For a shadow of a second, he hoped it was his father settled in the chair, but a quick look told him otherwise. This was a much younger man than his father, though older than Taylor. And there was something familiar about those gray-green eyes . . .

"Mr. Karrelian, isn't it?" Taylor said, trying not to look surprised. Damn it, why hadn't Jolah warned him Karrelian was here? Taylor shot a withering glance over his shoulder, but the polished oak door had already swung shut.

"Oh, don't be mad at her," Brandt said amiably, divining the meaning of Taylor's bleak look. "No one knows I'm here but you. Filling out guest registers, wearing identification tags—it's too much of a bother."

Taylor roughly shoved thoughts of Jolah and his father to the back of his mind. Karrelian was trouble enough without distractions. For a moment, Taylor simply stood there, scowling at Karrelian's cocky smile. He had been expecting a visit from the former spy sooner or later: Karrelian was bound to discover the degree to which Intelligence was blaming him for the murders. In fact, Taylor had been counting on it. He had not, however, been counting on Karrelian to arrive unannounced and lay claim to his office. Heaven only knew how long the man had been there or what he'd read. The information stacked in neat piles on Taylor's desk was worth a fortune to the right people . . . and Karrelian was just the sort who'd be willing to sell it, no matter what the consequences.

Taylor itched to kick Karrelian out of his chair. Instead, he eased himself into an armchair on the visitor's side of the desk, studying Karrelian all the while. For all the forced buoyancy of the industrialist's tone, Taylor could see that the man had hardly spent a better night than himself. The skin beneath Karrelian's eyes was dark and puffy. His hair and clothes were disarrayed, as if he had gone far too long between looks in a mirror. Therein, Taylor thought, lay the cue for the tone he should take.

"Come to sell me a generator, I suppose?"

"Not hardly," Brandt answered crisply. Apparently, Karrelian's veneer of civility would not last long this morning, and Taylor smiled at the thought of getting to business.

Brandt pulled his feet from the desk and leaned forward, peering intently at Taylor Ash. He had known the man's father, but not Taylor himself. The young man had joined Intelligence only a few months before Brandt had abandoned the business of espionage. Brandt had had little to do with the Ministry of Intelligence since then, yet Taylor Ash recognized him. That in itself was interesting.

"You know why I'm here," Brandt said, his voice quiet but sharp. "That, or you don't deserve your job."

Ash nodded. "Something to do with a series of dead men and some newly minted coins."

At the mention of the coins, the corners of Karrelian's mouth twitched into a frown.

"I had nothing to do with those murders."

"Of course not," Ash chuckled. "But I hope you haven't come here to clear your name. That would be a waste of time. If we suspected you were the assassin, we would have eliminated you long ago."

"Then why," Brandt asked harshly, "are you advertising the fact that the killings are my work?"

"Advertising?" Taylor repeated, feigning indignation. "No, we've done nothing of the kind. We've told certain curious parties that the victims were found with coins in their mouths. And that's just the simple truth. The public is capable of drawing its own conclusions."

"Charmingly democratic," Brandt remarked.

"Tell me," Taylor asked, raising his brows as if concerned, "have there been any attempts on your life yet?"

Brandt couldn't decide whether the young man was a fool—for, if Brandt had not already been pretty certain that Taylor Ash was behind last night's halfhearted sniper attack, that last comment gave it away—or whether Ash was so sure of his own position that he *wanted* Brandt to know who was pulling the strings.

"Funny you should ask," Brandt replied, masking his annoyance. "The first 'attempt,' as you put it, was last night. Abysmal shot, by the way."

Taylor shrugged. "Good assassins cost so much these days."

The last trace of Brandt's smirk disappeared.

"Go to hell, Ash. You're every bit as treacherous as your father—"

Taylor rose from his seat and glowered darkly at Karrelian.

"My father," he snapped, "happens to be one of the men whose lives are at risk. Whatever his faults, he is a patriot, not some cheap spy and extortionist. I'll thank you not to speak of him."

Brandt paused a moment, staring at the minister. He had turned a bright red, and his lips were drawn back virtually in a snarl. Interestingly, the elder Ash was a sensitive topic—and because Taylor Ash was upset, he had perhaps let something slip, implying that the assassin had more ex-ministers on his list. Brandt made a mental note of it.

"A spy and extortionist? I suppose that's a fair description," he said, fixing a composed smile upon his lips. "But I was good at what I did. Speaking of work, I should leave you to yours. I hear you've got a growing pile of bodies to count."

But Brandt made no move to leave. Both men understood that the negotiations were just beginning.

Slowly, Taylor returned to his seat. "I want nothing

to do with you, Mr. Karrelian. But someone has chosen to implicate you in the current series of murders, no doubt to obscure his own trail. We know you're innocent, but we have very little incentive to waste our time convincing others of that fact. We might as well simply go about our business and let you collect your just desserts."

"If I die," Brandt replied, "a lot of very scandalous information will be released to the press. Information about a lot of people, Mr. Ash, and your father not least among them."

Again, Taylor wondered about the wisdom of dealing with such a distasteful man. But he had already set these events in motion; there was nothing left to do but play out his hand and hope that Imbress enjoyed dealing with Karrelian more than he did.

"It seems that it would be in everyone's best interest that the killings stop as quickly as possible. I hear that, once upon a time, you had something of a talent for discovering secrets. You might try to discover who is behind the current rash of crimes."

Brandt laughed. Was *this* the reason Ash had gone to so much trouble to subtly arrange this meeting? Brandt had known there was some dark reason for the misinformation Taylor Ash was spreading, but a recruiting effort . . . ? He could hardly believe it.

"So little faith in your own operatives, Ash?"

Taylor was appalled by the man's nerve—and yet Brandt was right. The vast machinery of the Ministry of Intelligence had discovered nothing valuable about the murders. The only thing they knew was that the assassin had chosen to frame Karrelian and, for that reason, Taylor had decided to draw the former spy into the equation. Perhaps Karrelian knew something. Or perhaps his presence would somehow disturb the assassin, make him sloppy. Yet it galled Taylor to have to resort to such alternatives, and it was doubly galling that Karrelian himself should call attention to it. When Taylor finally replied, it was in the most forbidding voice he could muster.

"I would suggest, Mr. Karrelian, that you begin working. I will devote my slight powers of persuasion to informing your former clientele of your innocence. But we are talking about a large number of vastly wealthy, vastly powerful, and vastly fearful old men. If the killings continue, my assurances will mean very little to them. They will eliminate you, Mr. Karrelian, just to be certain."

Brandt frowned. "And where am I supposed to start on this silly chase of yours?"

"You have the names, I assume: Pernom Ell, Abrinius Loft, Tarem Selod. Start there."

So Ash did not intend for him to know who the further targets were. More ex-ministers, likely as not. Brandt made a quick mental calculation. Besides Kermane Ash, there were only a pair of other retirees: some general, long since gone from government, whose name escaped him; and Taylor's predecessor, Barr Aston.

"I wonder why anyone would go to such trouble to kill a bunch of old men," Brandt said, arching an eyebrow at Ash.

The minister frowned and rose to his feet. "This meeting is over, Mr. Karrelian."

Brandt rose from Taylor's chair and strode wordlessly toward the door.

"And one last thing," Taylor said. "If you find whoever is responsible, I suggest that you kill them promptly, if it doesn't offend your precious scruples. You can be sure that they will not fail to show you the same consideration."

Then the door slammed and Brandt was gone. Wearily, Taylor levered himself to his feet and moved to his own chair, his mind already turning back to his father, wondering at the strange ways of fate. That the former

Prime Minister of the nation might depend for his life on the likes of Brandt Karrelian. . . .

Taylor stopped as he sat down behind his desk. Behind a pile of folders, standing out against the dark wood, lay a lone cigarette butt. Taylor was not a smoker; clearly, Karrelian had left it there. Taylor picked up the butt and found that it was cold. It had not been smoked in the office. But why in heaven would Karrelian have chosen to leave it there, for Taylor to find?

And then he realized he would have to tell Imbress to stop smoking on the job.

Shortly after dawn, a large black carriage pulled by two handsome roans rattled to a stop in front of a small house in the suburbs of Prandis. The black-liveried driver jumped lightly from his seat and pulled open the coach's leather-embossed door. A dignified elderly man stepped down to the cobbled street, leaning only slightly on a gold-handled cane.

"This will take only ten minutes, Carl."

The driver merely inclined his head, watching with amused admiration as the old man let himself through the wrought iron gate and walked confidently across the lawn toward the brick house beyond. *Three hard days of travel*, Carl mused, *and he still seems as fresh as ever. As if he owned the place. As if he owned the whole world*. Carl shook his head in wonder and went to fetch the feed bag for the team of horses that was not half so spirited as their owner, Kermane Ash.

Ash had hoped to reach Prandis during the night, but with the new moon and the poor roads (when would Ravenwood finally allocate sufficient funds for Landa Wells's poor Ministry of the Interior?), they had been considerably delayed. The best they had been able to manage was early morning, and the old minister was hard-pressed to contain his disappointment. He had wanted to burst in on Ravenwood during the middle of the night—the more effectively to display his outrage at the sluggishness of official response to the series of hideous murders. During the day, however, he would seem merely another item in the Prime Minister's busy agenda . . . and how well he knew what a weak impression that would leave. He almost considered waiting until the next nightfall to see Ravenwood, but Kermane Ash was not that patient a man.

On the other hand, because there wasn't any rush, he might as well stop by his son's house to see if "Intelligence" had learned anything about the crimes. After a lifetime of frustrating experience with the department, Ash always thought of it in quotes, even after his own son had taken charge.

It was not yet seven o'clock. Kermane Ash would have been in his office. But his son? Ash suspected that he would find Taylor still in bed.

Near the front door, a gardener was pruning a long-neglected azalea, snipping unwanted growth with a pair of curved, gleaming shears. Sweat already streaked his shirt and gathered on his brow beneath the brim of his old gray cap. Now there, thought Ash with some satisfaction, was a real working man.

"My son home?" Ash called out forcefully as he approached the door, not breaking stride.

The gardener turned to him, apparently seeing the old man for the first time. He wiped his brow and shrugged. "Don't know, sir. Haven't yet been here an hour and I haven't seen anyone leave."

Still in bed, Ash thought.

"You're the old P.M., aren't you, sir?" the gardener asked reverently, squinting up at him.

Ash nodded curtly, somewhat put off by the ambiguous "old." He must mean "former," Ash decided.

The gardener broke into a grin. "Well, I'm honored to meet you, sir. Me pappy always said you were the best thing to happen to Chaldus that he ever seen."

Just as he grasped the brass knob and opened the door, Ash turned to bestow a kindly smile on the young man. Now there was a youth who understood his place in the world. In fact, Ash noted with satisfaction, the young gardener had doffed his cap in respect.

A shame, he reflected, thinking about his own full head of distinguished silver hair, that such a young man as that had gone bald.

Despite the obvious need for haste, Roland and Miranda had found that it wasn't so simple to leave their home on the spur of the moment. Nobility in Chaldus had meant little for nearly two hundred years, but Roland remained Duke of Calador. When Chaldus had become a republic, his family had lost the rule of the vast wooded hill-lands that constituted the present province of Calador, and retained only those lands which belonged to the family estate proper. Over the centuries, those holdings had slowly dwindled, being sold steadily to pay for the growing nation's ever-increasing taxes. Two generations ago, the former duke had sold Castle Calador and moved to the more pleasant manor which Roland and Miranda had eventually made their home. It shared none of the gloom of the monolithic old castle and, because it was much smaller, it allowed the duke to dispense with all but a handful of a staff he could no longer afford. Moreover, it was located in the center of the few square miles of land that the Calador family still owned, where they could better supervise the daily business of their tenant farmers, the grain mill, and an old brewery. All told, nearly a thousand people still depended on the Caladors for their livelihood, and it took Roland and Miranda two full days to ensure that everything would run smoothly in their absence. Finally, they had returned to the house to pack and complete a few essential personal chores. Miranda was upstairs in her study, writing letters to their three children that would allay any fears arising from their planned disappearance. Roland was downstairs in the library, sorting through the boxes of papers he had brought with him when he'd retired from the ministry. The few indispensable documents he packed carefully in a sealskin bag to bring with him. The ones which were merely dangerous in the wrong hands, he fed to the crackling fire.

After consigning yet another file to the flames, Roland paused to stretch his aching shoulders. He had not parted with his armor and great sword for a moment during the last two days. The longer they waited, the more certain he was that an attempt would be made on their lives—whether by the mysterious assassin or the more prosaic killers from the Ministry of Intelligence, Roland could not be sure. He was almost tempted to stay, merely to see who would reach him first.

So, a few minutes later, when the attack finally came, he was not surprised; he was merely disappointed by the sound of breaking glass. He had expected them to arrive discreetly, not like Brindisian pachyderms stampeding through the verandah's glass doors. A man of his stature, Roland liked to think, at least deserved to be murdered respectfully. Well, then, he would simply wait in the library and let them come to him, the upstarts. He slid his sword free from its sheath and placed it on the nearby desk. There were a few dozen files left. He placed them calmly in the fire.

Only one thing troubled him. He had asked Miranda to flee in the event of an attack, and believed that she would be safe doing so. In the prior murders, no one had been killed but the ex-minister. If Miranda stayed away from the fight, she should be perfectly safe. But Roland had never been able to dictate his wife's actions—in fact, the reverse had more often held true. And, as he heard several pairs of feet running up the steps to the second floor, he began to fear for her. There were too many people in the house. From the sound of it, they appeared to be covering all the rooms. That meant the government men had beaten the original assassins here. For the first time, a chilling thought entered Roland's mind. Even if Intelligence needed only *him* dead, would it tolerate a grieving widow publicly protesting covert government death squads? The killers from Council Tower would spare no one. In a flood of rage, Roland lifted his sword.

At that moment, two armed men burst through the doorway. They were wearing nondescript black leather armor—light and mobile, assassins' garb—and carried short swords.

"We've found him," the one in the rear cried out. Roland smiled grimly. Let them converge on him. Perhaps Miranda would be overlooked.

"You might have knocked," the old warrior said mildly.

The man in front, a youngish blond, seemed slightly puzzled. His comrade, obviously a veteran of this sort of assignment, ignored the remark. He passed his younger partner and advanced warily around one side of the large desk. "Circle left," he ordered grimly.

The sound of hurried footsteps approached, and Roland realized he would have to act quickly or face an entire squad at once. It had been some time since he had indulged in such sport and, forced to acknowledge that he was a little rusty, he decided he would have to be less chivalrous than his wont. He feinted tentatively toward the veteran on his right, forcing the man to bring up his sword. Then, with a quick downward thrust, he caught the man's handguard with his blade, slamming the assassin's weapon down into the desk. The man tried desperately to pull the weapon free, but Roland's sword trapped it implacably against the antique wood. With reflexes astounding for a man of his years, the old duke lashed out with his other hand, catching the assassin's curly black hair. With a tremendous wrench, he sent the man hurtling headfirst into the wall. With a clatter of pokers and bellows, the would-be killer collapsed and lay still near the fireplace. His head lolled backward at an unnatural angle.

Forty years of experience tells in a deadly manner. While the young assassin's gaze lingered momentarily on his dead comrade, Roland, a veteran of a thousand such battles, turned to the next task at hand. Distracted by the violence of one death, the young man barely knew it before he suffered his own.

It was odd, Roland thought, that Intelligence would send such unseasoned operatives into the field. Usually, it took years of experience before one of Intelligence's spies was assigned to any task more complicated than simple information-gathering. But he had no time for mysteries, not while other killers roamed the house and Miranda remained in danger.

Roland burst out of the library and turned left down the hallway, headed toward the glass garden door that had been the killers' point of entry.

"I'm here," he bellowed, "for any that dare find me!"

As he passed the kitchen, he ran into two more. Apparently, they had been instructed to remain in pairs, perhaps because these men, too, were very young.

With one quick blow, Roland split open the head of the first one, but he had no time to draw back his sword before the second man was upon him. He twisted wildly out of the way, but the blow still caught him on the chest. His mail deflected the deadly edge, but pain shot through his ribs and Roland knew he would have a nasty bruise there for the next two weeks.

And worse, if he didn't get his old body into action.

His own sword was stubbornly stuck in the corpse's skull, and Roland could waste no time trying to pull it free. He released the hilt and sprang forward, grappling

with the remaining assassin. Old though he was, few
living men were Roland's size, and the old duke retained
the strength of a bear. Though his opponent was solidly
built and a determined fighter, the contest did not last
long. Calador crushed the man's body between his own
and the wall, and clamping a huge hand on each side of
the man's head, broke his neck with one sure twist.

As he let the body slip to the floor, the heavy sound
of footsteps came to him from upstairs. The duke's cry
was tortured.

"Miranda!"

Unwilling to waste a second, he stooped to pick up
one of the assassins' swords rather than retrieve his own.
As his hand slid around the hilt, the solution to one
puzzle flashed instantly into his mind. These blades were
rare Camnis steel, forged at the Deshi Metalworks. He
knew these swords as well as he knew his own. He had
helped negotiate the contract that brought them to Chaldus.

They were army issue.

Roland howled with rage at the insult. So Amet Pale
did not trust Ash to do the job, and he had sent his own
men to be sure. No wonder these killers were so young.
Pale must have had a hard time recruiting veterans willing to assassinate their own former minister. As he
dashed up the back steps to the second floor, he vowed
that it would not only be *former* ministers who would
die that year.

Roland paused at the door of the bedroom to look for
Miranda. She wasn't there, but a soldier lay supine on
the rug, his throat slit. The young man's feet were ensnared in a riot of fuchsia, and Roland smiled grimly as
he recognized the colorful tangle as a skein of Miranda's
yarn. She had been knitting a sweater for their youngest
grandson. In her outrage, Miranda's magic manifested
itself as a rebellion of the house itself against its violated
domesticity.

But there were sounds coming from down the hallway, and Roland spared no time in following them. Miranda was a competent magician, but no mage to be feared. Even one soldier could easily kill her if she had no time to prepare.

As he dashed to the front of the house, he reached the balustrade where the second floor overlooked the two-story marble atrium. He saw there what he had most dreaded. Miranda was in full flight, running down the spacious curved stairwell to the atrium, and only a few steps behind her followed a soldier with a bared blade. Even as Roland burst into pursuit, he realized he would never catch them in time. His heart pounding, he screamed unintelligibly, hoping to draw the assassin his way.

Instead, just as Miranda crossed the middle of the atrium, she stopped and looked up. Roland expected a parting smile but, no, she was not looking at him—

There was a tremendous snap as the crystal chandelier tore loose from its moorings and plummeted forty feet onto Amet Pale's murderous henchman. Crushed by the fixture's enormous weight, he lay still, the fractured crystals of the chandelier awash in the reflected crimson of his blood.

Roland rushed down the stairs, around the chaos of broken glass, and swept Miranda into his arms, spinning her around in a tremendous hug.

"You're more dangerous than they are," she scolded lightly, relieved to see him unharmed.

"You're right," Roland growled in agreement, letting her down. "And this is no time to celebrate. There may be more—"

"No," Miranda replied quietly. "They're all dead. I can feel it."

Roland dropped the borrowed sword to the floor and suddenly felt a tremendous weariness steal over him.

Tenderly, he brought his callused palm to his wife's soft cheek. "I was worried for you."

Miranda's blue eyes twinkled with mischief.

"Don't worry, old man. I can still take care of myself."

"Apparently so," Roland mused, turning to look at the last dead soldier and the ruin of glass and twisted metal around him. "That was my grandmother's chandelier. She brought it with her from the old ballroom when the duke sold the castle."

"I know," Miranda said, turning away to hide a smile.

"You always hated it."

"True," she replied, "but I let you keep it because I knew it would come in handy."

Roland laughed, realizing that there were years and years he still wanted to spend with this woman. A new energy infused him. "Gather your things quickly," he said, kissing her brow. "I think the time has finally come to leave."

The first thing Brandt did when he got home was visit his wine cellar. There, alongside hundreds of bottles of costly vintages that he reserved for guests, Brandt had stacked eight cases of Moon's Farm. He grabbed a bottle of the cheap wine and headed upstairs to the kitchen in order to find a corkscrew. Carn, dressed in his morning robe, walked into the room to find Brandt laboring over a crumbling cork.

"Hair of the dog that bit you?" Carn asked with a smile as he rubbed his tired eyes. "You were gone all night. Must have had a blast."

Late as Carn had returned from Masya, he had half expected Brandt to be home already. True, sometimes Brandt's nighttime ramblings in the city ended with a happenstance tryst: some girl met at a bar—or on a street corner. But Brandt never spent the night. Usually, no more than an hour after midnight, Brandt returned to the mansion, and always alone.

"A blast?" Brandt repeated as he continued to fight with the cork. Finally frustrated, he threw both the bottle and corkscrew into the trash. For the first time, Carn got a glimpse of his old friend's face, and he didn't like what he saw.

"Yeah," Brandt continued, "you could call it that. Three blasts, in fact, if you count one for each crossbow bolt."

"*What?*" Carn thundered, coming instantly awake. He rushed across the cold marble tile of the kitchen and grabbed Brandt by the arm, swinging him face-to-face. "You're not joking, are you?"

Brandt sighed and retreated to a nearby chair. "No," he replied, "no joke. No damned joke at all."

And then he proceeded to detail the night's events: the suspicious attempt on his life, his visit to Fikkis, his interview with Taylor Ash. As always, Carn absorbed the information with quiet, penetrating concentration. Only after Brandt was entirely finished did Carn ask the question that had so weighed on his friend's mind during the long walk back from Council Tower.

"So, what will you do now?"

Brandt smiled and pinched the small roll of fat that gathered above the waist of his pants. "I figure it's about time I started getting rid of this flab."

Carn's eyebrows arched. "Then you'll do what Ash asks?"

Brandt's smile widened. "Oh, I figure to do much more than he asks. But, one way or another, I'm already involved. Ash didn't leave much choice as far as that's concerned."

"I'm not so sure," Carn argued. "We still have sources we can check, see if we can find out what they're up to at Intelligence."

"Oh, we'll check, but I know what we'll find. Ell and Loft and Selod are dead, and a lot of old, rich bastards are very worried about Galatine Hazard. Whether it's true or not, if Taylor Ash decides to pin the blame on me, things will get uncomfortable around here. So we'll humor the upstart and start a little intelligence-gathering mission, just like the good old days. But we take no risks. When we figure out who's killing these old turds, we tell His Highness over in Council Tower. Let him take care of the sloppy details. And in the meantime, we get to learn exactly what makes a retired government official so important, and to whom." Brandt grinned. "A piece of potentially lucrative information."

Slowly, the fear that had gripped Carn melted away. Life had suddenly become more dangerous, but they had lived through treacherous times before. What mattered most was the unexpected gleam in Brandt's eye. This was the most spirited he had seen his old companion in months.

Brandt pressed his hands to the side of his head and ran his fingers through his thick black hair like a man coming awake after a long sleep.

"We're back in business, my friend."

"Taylor, you slugabed, where are you?" Kermane Ash bellowed again. The kitchen and dining room had proved empty, without even a trace of a breakfast having been prepared. It was galling to think he had raised a son this lazy, more galling still to think he'd have to climb the stairs himself to rouse Taylor from sleep. How many times had he told the boy to hire at least one servant? A certain frugality was to be commended, but there were appearances to keep up. The Ashes had not risen to the heights of Chaldean society to act like a bunch of mannerless johnny-come-latelies. Yet there was nothing for it; he would have to kick the boy from between the sheets.

But, no, when Kermane walked back into the hallway, there was his son by the base of the stairs, limned by the dazzling brightness of the morning sun.

"Thank goodness you've finally woken up."

"Sorry, your honor," the figure replied, "but it's only my humble self."

Kermane squinted against the light as the figure took a step forward. It was the gardener, but what was he doing inside the house?

"I don't mean to be forward," the gardener continued, "but I've brought you a little present. It's hardly worthy for a man of your stature, but I'd like you to have it."

When the gardener held out his hand, the flesh seemed made of pure light. After a moment, Ash realized that the man was offering a small mirror, the kind a woman might use to check her makeup. He had no use for such a thing, but the light that the glass reflected into his eyes was so irritating that he snatched the mirror from the gardener's fingers.

"Thank you," Ash said gruffly, looking for someplace to put down the thing. "I'm looking for my son."

The gardener grinned. "Surprising sometimes what you can find in a mirror."

This idiotic conversation had gone on long enough, Ash was thinking as he glanced down at the thing. Just a plain mirror—a small oval of glass framed in a simple curve of oak. His face filled the reflection, crowding out everything around it. The rest of Kermane's vision—the gardener, the hallway, even his own hand—faded from view, leaving only the image of his own face.

A handsome face, Ash thought, and more: a strong face. Surprising, really, how good he looked after such a long, difficult trip. Almost seven decades, yet still the model of authority. Andus Ravenwood would tremble when Kermane came calling later in the day. Ravenwood wasn't half the man he was, never would be. No, Ravenwood hardly merited the same chair that Kermane had occupied for so many years as Prime Minister. Certainly, Ravenwood wasn't capable of handling a crisis like the one at hand. If only Ash himself were still P.M. . . .

Now there was a thought. There was no precedent, Kermane conceded, yet he was certain that he could skirt around the constitutional issues. He need simply convince Ravenwood to step down . . .

"I could be Prime Minister again," Kermane said to himself, to the self that stared back at him from the mirror.

"Indeed, we could be," the mirror replied.

Such a handsome face, he thought again, only distantly noticing how unfamiliar the voice sounded—deep and commanding, with an accent that spoke of exotic lands. My true voice, Kermane thought. The voice that should be mine.

"But," the mirror continued, "do we remember all the things a Prime Minister needs to know?"

"Of course I do," Ash retorted. "My mind is as sharp as it was half a century ago—twice as sharp as the milk-fed babes that run the Tower today."

"No doubt," his reflection replied. "But there are some things they tried to make us forget. They wanted to take certain things from us when we left the Tower, because they didn't want us to be as strong now as we were then."

In the mirror, his lips curled at the edge with the taunting grin of a private joke.

"Nonsense. My mind is indomitable."

The lips curled further. "Then speak the words, the seven words Hamir gave us as the seal of our office."

The Phrase, of course. The Phrase was what made him unique, what only he knew in all the world—well, he and that upstart Ravenwood, assuming Ravenwood hadn't forgotten. But one mustn't forget the Phrase. It was the most grave responsibility they carried as ministers of the nation. Ash searched for it, but his tongue fumbled over the misty syllables.

"Surely," the mirror said, "a man as strong as we are could not forget."

But the words would not come. Absurd, because they were carved so deeply into his mind, ever since the day he took the oath of office. He could see the room in Council Tower where it had happened, just himself and Livins, his predecessor. Kermane Ash had shaped his entire life toward that day, toward the moment that Livins had laid a hand on Kermane's head and, without speaking them, the words had come.

The same words that now tumbled from Ash's tongue.

His face in the mirror smiled back broadly, even as his own lips rounded to form the final syllable.

And then a gloved hand obscured the reflection from Ash's view, wresting the mirror from his grip. Ash looked up to find the gardener, who also was smiling, the sun glinting from his teeth almost as brilliantly as it gleamed along the curved edge of the pruning shears in his hand.

Jame Kordor considered breakfast his safeguard against the day's woes. Each omelette, pastry, or fruit provided ballast against the trying winds of government that would, Kordor suspected, one day wreck him utterly. By any man's calculation, the portly Minister of Finance had laid up enough ballast for the worst tempest, but Kordor could already feel the gale stirring. And so it was that, early on this April morning, an unusually large collection of hand-painted Gathon china lay before him, freighted with his favorite delicacies.

There was one dish, however, that Kordor had not ordered. That was the elaborate silver platter upon which his butler delivered the calling cards of visitors. Its presence among those more welcome dishes was disturbing, for Kordor had expected no breakfast companions that morning. But, then again, there was no calling card on the tray.

Instead, like a single bright eye staring up at Kordor's miserable pair, there lay one newly minted gold capital.

"Sir?" the butler prompted for the second time. His master sat slumped as if dead in his huge velvet-upholstered armchair. A flake of almond croissant clung irreverently to the minister's lower lip.

Slowly, Kordor turned his eyes from the baleful disk on the platter. He pulled himself upright and gently wiped his mouth with a napkin. "Send him in," the minister said, barely audibly.

His butler nodded curtly, then paused to add: "I shall instruct your guards to attend in the alcoves."

"No!" Kordor snapped. Long ago, he had built secret nooks into the wood-paneled dining room to foster both his physical security and, equally important, his ability to eavesdrop on guests. But if Hazard had come to call . . .

"I will see the visitor alone," Kordor commanded, sounding decisive for the first time that day. This was now a matter of balancing costs, of measuring debits and credits—something the Minister of Finance understood intimately. Although he suspected a remote threat of violence if Hazard had come to speak with him personally, this risk was dwarfed by the danger that someone might overhear what the self-glorified thief had to say. "I shall see him alone," Kordor repeated. "Utterly alone."

Like several of the most highly placed officials in Chaldean government, Kordor knew that Brandt Karrelian was Galatine Hazard, but it was a fact that remained unvoiced. At the few ceremonies and parties that they had both attended, Kordor had even chatted amiably with Brandt, never alluding to the fact that here was the extortionist to whom Kordor paid annual tribute of eight thousand capitals.

But for Brandt to call on him *as* Galatine Hazard, that was unprecedented. Even dangerous. Best, Kordor decided, that he deal with the man as decisively as possible. Satisfy him and make him go away. If only, Kordor thought, he knew what could satisfy such a man . . .

When Brandt strode unaccompanied into the room, Kordor was struck by the simplicity of his black suit. As if he were in mourning. Disturbed, Kordor reached negligently toward an eclair, striving to act as if he were unruffled by Brandt's appearance. But for once his hunger had completely vanished.

"Good morning, Jame," Brandt began affably.

"And good morning to you, Mr. Karrelian. I wonder why you neglected to offer your more formal calling card."

Brandt smiled and seated himself on the edge of the long mahogany table. "Consider it a token of the gravity of my visit. And proper compensation for your time."

Kordor frowned, but said nothing, hoping that Brandt would come quickly to the subject of the conversation.

Casually, Brandt picked up an empty dish, tapped away the powdered sugar crumbs, and carefully appraised the hand-painted gold design. "Gathon china. Very nice."

"One should always dine on the best," Kordor replied, grateful that the preliminary business had been concluded so tactfully. What no one save Brandt in all of Chaldus knew was that Kordor's father had been an agent of the southern theocracy. And although Kordor's basic allegiance lay with Chaldus, his early reputation as Undersecretary of Finance had been based on negotiating a low-tariff bilateral trade agreement with Gathony—for which Kordor had been quite covertly and quite substantially rewarded by the Gathon thearch. Revelation of the impropriety would have ruined the minister utterly.

Brandt replaced the dish on the table and smiled without warmth.

"Someone," Brandt began softly, "holds a grudge against old men in your profession and, not incidentally, a grudge against me. As for me, well, I've never made many friends. But the old men . . . Frankly, I'm puzzled. Why would someone want to kill your predecessor, Jame? Why might they want to kill you when you retire?"

Kordor put down the eclair, untouched. Of course, Karrelian was here to discuss the *murders*, not Kordor's hidden past. Still, Jame felt not a whit of relief. That Karrelian was here at all meant that he wanted something—and if Karrelian did not get it, he possessed the power to bring the walls down about Jame's head.

"My advice," Kordor began carefully, "would be: forget what you know, take a vacation. The clime of Shorereach is delightful at this time of year. Every spring, they make a cider there from the immature flesh of southern peaches. A marvelous concoction. It could make you forget the cares of the whole world."

"I would love to forget," Brandt replied, "and in your case particularly, there are some things I would be willing to consign to oblivion. But this matter of the grudges . . ." Brandt sighed. "One of your colleagues keeps jogging my memory."

Kordor's eyes narrowed as he leaned back into the plush velvet cushions. Hazard had replaced the stick with the carrot, and now that danger no longer loomed so close, Kordor's acute mind began to work in earnest. He picked up the eclair again and took a thoughtful bite. One of his colleagues . . . The process of elimination took only a moment to complete. Only Ash would have brought Hazard into this affair. Probably as a distraction to the murderer, a random factor in the field that would increase Intelligence's ability to master the situation. Remarkably imprudent, Kordor decided. Ash was perhaps unacquainted with Hazard's investigative ability, but Kordor knew it with painful intimacy. Galatine Hazard possessed the irritating habit of discovering more than he should know and, in this case, that was greatly to be feared.

"The men who have died," Kordor said finally, "occupied very different terms of office. Ell retired a dozen years ago, whereas Loft only rose to minister four years before that. That leaves a very short time span in which all three men served concurrently—perhaps four or five years, just before you left Belfar, I suppose." Kordor smiled at the surprised frown that flitted across Karrelian's features. "Yes, I know a thing or two about you, as well. As for the ministers, they must have done something in those years, perhaps passed some legislation that earned them an enemy. Turn your eyes to the past, Hazard."

Brandt's lips twitched—neither a smile nor a frown; merely the transient record of an unrecognizable emotion. Small as it was, the gesture unnerved the Minister of Finance.

"Those would be the years 162 through 166," Brandt mused. "The ministerial business conducted in those years would fill a library. As I recall, Jame, in 162 you were a young attaché at Finance, jockeying to become the undersecretary. The draft for a trade agreement with Gathony won you that job. Perhaps that will jog your memory of the era. You can tell me when next I see you."

Brandt reached for a small apricot tart and took a hearty bite. Licking his lips, he bowed to the minister as he walked lightly from the room.

•   •   •

Brandt's visit to Kordor had yielded little fruit other than the small tart he finished as he reached the road. Kordor had supplied one possibility, but it reeked of subterfuge. No one kills politicians for legislation they passed a dozen years earlier. What Brandt couldn't decide was whether the minister knew nothing and was desperately fashioning a story in order to save his over-sized hide—or whether Kordor knew things that he would fight to conceal. Perhaps when he had time, Brandt would review in more detail Kordor's dealings with Gathony. There might be darker secrets there than a simple case of graft.

As Brandt replayed the interview in his mind, only one phrase rang true: *Turn your eyes to the past, Hazard.*

It was absurd to think that anyone was killing the retired ministers because of things they had done lately. These murders were somehow a by-product of the past—perhaps, as Kordor hinted, a by-product of the fleeting time they had served together. Well, Brandt decided as he nudged his horse toward home, that suited him fine. The past, as ever, was all he had.

It had been another spirit•crushing day for Taylor Ash. The men he had stationed around Council Tower had reported no sign of his father, although Taylor had been sure that Kermane Ash would arrive soon. It had now been four days since Kermane had left his home in the country, and Taylor knew his father was not the type of man to go into hiding. But if he had not come to the Council, flight seemed to be the only alternative. If the old man did try to hide, Taylor thought dispiritedly, he would do it so clumsily that the murderers would find him in an instant. Kermane Ash could never endure so much as an hour without announcing to the world that he was indeed Kermane Ash, lion of the realm.

Taylor realized with a chill that, with each minute that passed, the likelihood grew that his father was dead.

Moreover, he had been expecting word from his agents stationed at the Calador estate. Nothing had been heard all day, and he had been forced to send Imbress there to reconnoiter. He dreaded the news that would return on the morrow.

Then there was the problem of Barr Aston, the Minister of Intelligence whom Taylor had succeeded. He had hoped that at least Barr would trust him and seek his aid, but the wily old minister had too much of the operative left in him. He had vanished from the face of the earth, defying the ability of Taylor's best agents to track him.

Taylor grimaced and shook his head at the sheet of notes on the desk before him. The arithmetic was all too simple. Three ministers had already been taken. Three more were left, but the government couldn't seem to find any of them. Taylor would be able to suppress this information for a few days, perhaps, but Amet Pale would soon start clamoring for proof that the situation had been resolved. Once Pale uncovered the way of things, Taylor knew what course the Minister would insist on, the course that Pale's ministry had been named for.

War.

The last Chaldean military action of any size had been fought more than twenty years ago, under Calador's guidance. Since Pale had risen to the minister's post, he had lacked an opportunity to bloody the nation in the name of glorious battle. Ash suspected that the War Minister would relish the idea of a preemptive attack. And it fell on Taylor's shoulders to prevent that.

But there was nothing more he could do that night. Intelligence work depended quite obviously on intelligence and, infuriatingly, not a useful word had passed through his portal all day. Even Jolah had given up and gone home. It was the best course. With a good night's sleep, he would return fresh the next morning, when perhaps there would be something to do.

Taylor locked the office and descended to the stables at the base of the tower. His horse, Scry, neighed a spirited greeting and Taylor regretted that he had no carrots to feed him. Scry was a superb chestnut stallion, a gift from Barr Aston in recognition of Taylor's promotion. Until lately, Taylor had almost forgotten how much pleasure he derived from riding. Under normal circumstances, Taylor took his carriage to work so he could do some preliminary reading before he reached the office. But given the cruel hours he had been working of late, he disliked asking his driver to labor so early and late. Perhaps that was a good thing, Taylor decided. He'd been slipping out of shape lately, and riding was the only exercise he had time for. Perhaps he'd continue to ride Scry to work, even after this whole thing blew over. . . .

At this late hour, one lone attendant reclined in the musty tack room beneath the tower. Taylor peered inside to confirm what he'd already heard: the low, sonorous drone of the man's snoring. Content with the idea of saddling Scry himself, Taylor let the man sleep. Quietly, he turned to the soothing tasks of buckles and straps, to the familiar smell of wool and seasoned leather.

As Taylor approached, Scry snorted a greeting and pawed anxiously at the stall door. Those were sentiments the weary Minister of Intelligence could easily comprehend. Since this latest crisis had erupted, it seemed as if he had been living in Council Tower. Taylor yearned to free himself of the monolithic heap of stone and simply wander. His job had been fun, once upon a time, when he had been a field operative traveling the world.

He indulged his wanderlust as far as letting Scry choose the path home. The horse was well acquainted with the twisted roads of suburban Prandis and could find his way without prompting. So it was that Taylor crossed the River Mirth at the Sentinel Bridge and rode uphill toward his home from the north. Rather than taking the main road, Scry followed the path that ran alongside the river, leading to the back of the property. Taylor could see his house from the bottom of the hill, and he could see more. Limned against the young sliver of a moon, leaving his house through the back patio doors, were two black-clad men. Without quite understanding what this meant, Taylor spurred Scry with uncharacteristic intensity and the great stallion leapt into a headlong charge. Such speed was almost suicidal in the moon's fickle light, but Scry raced up the dirt trail without hesitation, eager to gallop after weeks of inactivity. Within seconds, they had reached the low stone wall that marked the extent of Ash's land, and the horse cleared the wall with a fluid leap that hardly broke his pace.

The first sounds of hooves on the path had alerted the intruders that Ash was approaching, and they darted into the thick woods that stood behind the house. As Taylor rode toward the trees, he noticed, in a far corner of his backyard, a team of horses casually grazing on his lawn. Oddly, the horses were hitched to a carriage and they had not, it seemed, been tethered.

Strange, Taylor thought, that a thief would ride in a cumbersome and conspicuous carriage. In fact, too strange to credit. The more likely explanation for the presence of the carriage flashed into his mind, and he once more dug his heels into Scry's ribs, urging even greater speed from the stallion.

Taylor's landholdings were far from extensive: merely five acres, and those spread out against the river. Less than two hundred feet lay between his house and the murmuring waters of the Mirth. And it was the river to which his quarry was flying.

Although Taylor possessed extensive field experience from his earlier days as an intelligence operative, the duties of minister were of a decidedly more cerebral bent. Physical danger was no longer a daily fact of his work and, consequently, Taylor carried no weapon. He would have to improvise. Scry had slowed to accommodate the increasing density of the trees, and Taylor hoped to renew a game he hadn't played since school days. It was one of the equestrian tricks he used to practice when he'd had nothing better to do than fritter away adolescent afternoons on horseback while his father ran the country. The game simply entailed easing one's body over the side of the horse and snatching something off the ground during full gallop. In this case, an old branch would do. A cudgel was not his weapon of choice, but it was the only one available.

Three years of desk work had tightened his muscles, though, and the ground sped by a few tantalizing inches beyond his fingertips. Perhaps if he hooked his leg around the saddlehorn—

The world spun out of control, and Taylor's breath exploded from his lungs as he hit the ground. Cursing, he rolled over and struggled to his feet. A few tottering steps brought him within view of the river, where he saw the two men drag a canoe into the current and paddle quickly downstream. Before Taylor could reach the sandy bank, they had disappeared into the treacherous night, and the sound of their paddling dissolved into the gurgling waters.

Mirth indeed.

Taylor felt hot breath on his neck as Scry nuzzled him from behind. For Scry, this had been a night of rare exercise, a welcome introduction of energy into a deadening routine. If only, Taylor thought, he himself knew no better.

A closer inspection of the carriage told him what he had already guessed. The Prime Minister's seal did not appear on the carriage door—it had probably been effaced by Kermane Ash's efficient factotum, Carl—but the carriage itself was a long, luxurious version of the barouche that Taylor knew his father preferred.

He entered the house through the patio doors that the killers had left open, heedlessly tracking mud onto the tile floor of the solarium and beyond onto the parquet of the sitting room. Arranged neatly in an antique armchair sat Carl's corpse, its slit throat grinning obscenely across the room. Taylor swallowed heavily, his last shred of hope destroyed.

Slowly, almost in a trance, Taylor turned toward the hallway and found, sprawled across the foot of the steps, his father's body. Taylor switched on that great luxury, the electric chandelier that hung high above the wainscoted atrium, wincing as light flooded down. The corpse was naked and networked with shallow cuts. And, in the electric glare, Taylor could see the golden glint between the teeth.

Worst of all, perhaps, was the look in his father's dead eyes, a look that Taylor could not remember having witnessed before. It was shock—the sheer amazement of having experienced something that, for once in his life, Kermane Ash had not himself planned.

A few feet away, bloody and rent, lay the remains of the old man's shirt. Taylor placed it gently over Kermane's face.

Then Taylor switched off the lights and sat beside his father on the cool wooden steps, contemplating a tattered shroud of foreclosed hopes.

CHAPTER 6

Taylor Ash sat up through the night beside the cold body of his father. It had been an ugly night, a night of silent, bitter recriminations that had come too late for both father and son. A night in which Taylor had succeeded only in compounding loss with shame. It was mad, he knew, to sit with a corpse and curse it—to parade through his mind his father's failures and his own humiliations, and to fling these sour reproaches at a man who would recognize them no more dead than he had when he was alive. It was mad, and it would drive him mad.

Yes, he thought, *the streak of foolishness runs strong in Ash blood, sire and son alike.*

And he might indeed have been lost that night if not for Barr Aston. It was the hour before dawn when Taylor remembered something the old chief of intelligence had told him. They had been talking just before Aston's retirement, only a few years ago, and Taylor had asked Aston how it felt.

"It feels good," Aston had replied. "For the past twenty years, I've been only a minister, not a man."

It was the only way to survive this job, he thought: to gather up every shred of humanity, every kernel of individuality, and pack it away in some box not to be opened as long as you remained a minister of Chaldus. His father had understood that—had, in fact, learned the lesson too well. Kermane Ash had retired, yet he had never ceased being a minister. It had been his single, vast failing.

And what, Taylor asked himself, was his own failing?

It was a question he did not dare answer. With a quiet desperation, Taylor closed his eyes and tried to imagine that the corpse beside him was just that: a corpse and no more. He had seen dozens of dead men in his professional life, and he had been painstakingly trained to discover how they became that way. Not a whit of difference now, he told himself. When he opened his eyes, it was the Minister of Intelligence who looked out on the carnage before him.

Slowly and carefully, Taylor concentrated on piecing together what had happened the day before. His father and Carl were nearly a day dead. They had been killed, without any possibility of doubt, early the previous morning. From the bloody tracks on the floor, Taylor could reconstruct events with some precision. The killer had surprised his father in the hallway, near the staircase, and had started torturing him there. Dried red-black prints on the floorboards showed that his father had crawled halfway down the hallway toward the library and had then been dragged back to the steps, where he was ultimately killed. How had Kermane Ash found this brief respite to attempt escape? Apparently, Carl had left the carriage and surprised the murderer in the midst of his bloody work. With characteristic fidelity, Carl had fought to the very end, and as a result, the assassin had finally been forced to break his pattern. The ferocity of Carl's attack had dictated that, for once, more than a minister be killed. Most of that struggle had taken place

near the front door. Afterward, the killer had carried
Carl's body into the sitting room and propped it up in
the chair as some sort of macabre joke.

There were two salient features of the episode that
weighed on Taylor's mind. First, only one set of bloody
tracks left the site of Carl's struggle and went down the
hall, where the murderer had caught the crawling Kermane Ash. Second, the murders had happened the previous morning. The inevitable conclusion was that the
men Taylor had chased the night before were not the
murderers. Another variable had entered the situation,
but Taylor suspected he knew how it fit in.

What remained a mystery was the identity of the assassin. That was the vital piece of information Taylor
yearned for. He gazed again at the body beside him. If
only he could see through those glazed yellowing eyes
and witness his father's last moments. But the corpse lay
mute at his feet. His father could tell him nothing he
needed to hear. Just like the thirty years before, Taylor
thought. Why should death change anything?

As Taylor continued to study his father's white, rigid
flesh, a strange calm began to settle upon him. It was
over, the curses and the recriminations. Kermane Ash
was dead, and one of his few legacies to his son was a
steadfast atheism. There would be no afterlife for Kermane Ash, no eternal rewards. The old man had arranged for his own rewards to be delivered upon earth.
He would have to remain content with them and hope
that history would prove kind.

Sunlight was now pouring strong through the circular
stained glass window above the front door, dyeing the
dried blood a deep purple. The handle of the door rotated, and the lithe figure of Jolah slipped inside the
house, buoyant in spirits, wearing a new spring dress.

"Hey, sleepyhead," she called out even before she'd
opened the door. "Why aren't you at the office? There's
news—"

And then she saw Taylor sitting by his father's body, and screamed.

"News indeed," Taylor whispered as his assistant slumped to the floor.

CHAPTER 7

Deep in the earth beneath his mansion, in a room protected by every ingenuity magic and engineering had to offer, Brandt could not tell that the sun had risen. It had been another sleepless night, unless he counted the catnaps that his body had forced upon him from time to time. It seemed like an eternity since he had returned from Kordor to this room, where his files were stored: every scrap of information he had learned during long years of espionage and theft—the taproot of his wealth. The majority were yellow files which detailed the personal failings of Brandt's flock: sexual peccadilloes, minor graft, capitulations to a thousand petty temptations. . . . Only slightly smaller in number were the red files, detailing criminal matters of a more serious nature: arsons, rapes, murders cold- and hot-blooded. And then there was the collection of black files, each of which harbored high crimes against the state—the kinds of acts that would bring low the mighty, that would lead a man to the scaffold. The kinds of political betrayals that might prove fodder for an assassin.

And, yet, no answer.

Brandt laid his head on the desk, wishing he could simply go to sleep. A long day of reading had taken its expected toll on his eyes, but there had been an unexpected toll as well. Brandt had never spent so much time immersing himself in his files at one sitting—and he had not anticipated that it would be such a dispiriting venture. Like drowning in a tide of sewage. He was father confessor to the damned, he realized, nodding quietly at each horror, then spitting out absolution for coin. . . .

Where had his good mood flown, he wondered. Returning from Kordor's house, he had been excited again at the thought of the chase. But to wade through all of this. . . .

He sighed and rearranged the collection of folders, as if placing them in a different order would lend sudden inspiration. Slim enough pickings, to be sure. Ell's career of graft and coercion, Loft's sexual perversities, the assorted villainies of a broad cast of characters who had once occupied Council Tower—each now long retired or dead. Brandt had read through enough evidence to ruin the careers of dozens of the ex-ministers' peers, but he had found nothing that could even begin to explain the murders. His files said little about Tarem Selod, and nothing that was useful.

By some coincidence, he noticed, there had been only one living ex-minister from each ministry when the killings had started: a complete set for the assassin to collect. A complete set in one sense, yet random in another. His files yielded few clues to what made these men important as a group. Never did their pasts point toward one shared enemy. As Kordor had observed, the three dead men had served on the High Council together for almost four years, but Taylor Ash implied that the murderer was after the remaining retirees as well. When Brandt factored their careers into the time line he had sketched, the intersections vanished. These six men had never been Council members all at one time. Indeed, as far as Brandt could determine, these six men had seldom stood in the same room together.

Which hinted that something deeper hid behind these killings. Something that transcended the normal motives for violence that he had observed during his long dalliance with the underside of government. Scandal, fear, greed, ambition, corruption: these were no motives to kill retired men. Not all of them. Not with such precision and effort. But what motives were left?

If the files proved fruitless, Brandt thought, the only alternative was to find the next victim before the killer did, and he wasn't about to risk his neck for the sake of a few old men. No. . . .

Why would a man kill another man? Brandt's mind wandered from this private library to the books in his library upstairs. For appearance's sake, he had stocked those shelves well, paying dearly for a set of Chaldean classics. He hadn't gotten far through those volumes, but one of the few philosophers he had read (the name had started with an A, so he'd gotten to that book early) had said this: Men act on two motives alone—to pursue something or to avoid it.

An absurdly simple way to put the matter, Brandt thought, but perhaps simplicity was what he needed. To avoid? This seemed the easier option to rule out. The old men were retired, not particularly doing much of anything, and therefore not much of a threat to be avoided. To pursue? There the possibilities lay. . . . The old ministers had something someone else wanted, but what? Nothing tangible—these were no simple thefts. And that left Brandt thinking about the one intangible commodity that he knew men would go to any lengths to obtain: information.

Information. The word stood out, reminded him of a night almost a month ago, a night he should not have forgotten. A tedious party with a dangerous guest. A man who knew the name Galatine Hazard. A man who had spoken of information to be gathered . . . and of the men who held that information as obstacles to be removed. A man who, when Brandt had thrown him out, had spoken of revenge. Finally, things were beginning to make sense. Brandt now knew what he was looking for: a man not much larger than himself, with a strangely dark complexion and black, deep-set eyes.

"Carn." Brandt called. blinking as he emerged from the basement into morning's light. Typically, Carn was sitting at the kitchen table—eschewing the formalities of the dining hall—as he sipped his coffee and sorted through the morning mail.

"Carn," Brandt repeated, taking a seat across from his friend, "we're making progress."

"So, it seems, are they." Carn sifted through the stack of mail, his broad, deep-lined face set in a frown. "This just came for you."

Brandt took the small ivory envelope that Carn proffered. No stamp, Brandt noted. It had been hand-delivered. He pulled out the short note inside and read it swiftly.

Calador attacked. Proceed to ducal manor. Imbress will be your control agent.

Brandt crumpled the note and thrust it into his pocket. "Not much on details, are the bastards? 'Attacked' doesn't say too much . . . although this business about a control agent does. They want to keep me on their damned leash."

"Wouldn't you do the same?" Carn asked.

Brandt looked surprised. "I have a hard time imagining myself as a government agent, but I suppose, if you put it that way. . . ."

Carn grinned and slapped his friend on the arm. "Naturally, you'd do the same. On the other hand, would you expect anyone to cooperate?"

Brandt laughed and shook his head, although he wasn't sure he agreed with Carn's assessment. Taylor Ash looked like the kind of man who expected *everyone* to cooperate. Except, of course, this meddlesome assassin. Brandt lapsed into silence as he performed ministerial roll call. Ell, Loft, Selod, Calador. That left only two: Aston and Ash. Brandt assumed that the elder Ash would be taken care of by his son. Meddling directly with the Ash family was something Brandt preferred to postpone . . . for now. Aston, though, was a different matter. The man must be in his late seventies, perhaps older.

"Carn," Brandt began slowly, "do you remember that swarthy partycrasher at our ball?"

"Of course," Carn replied. It wasn't so often that strangers came to speak to Galatine Hazard. "You're thinking he has something to do with this?"

Brandt nodded and explained his suspicions.

"Get his description to some of our old contacts," Brandt concluded. "Have them keep an eye out for him, though I doubt he'll prove easy to find. On the other hand, there are two men that he'll be looking for. The best we can do is get to them first. I want you to find Barr Aston. I doubt the old man's sitting at home, waiting to be killed, but he's also too old to have fled far. No one his age travels the trade roads. He'd stand out like a bullseye. No, more likely he's holed up somewhere in or around Prandis. He may have called in old Intelligence debts and be hiding in one of their safe houses."

Carn nodded, his eyes glittering. With difficulty, he suppressed a smile—for the first time in a year, Brandt seemed truly happy. Or at least purposeful. It amounted to the same thing, Carn thought, and he was glad to see it.

"I don't think it would take me too long to get a list

of government safe houses. We have our own debts to call in, you know."

"Good. While you're at it, get a list of all the property that Aston owns—even properties that his friends own. Check it all out and find him. Then bring him here, willing or not." Brandt smiled. "This game has been going on long enough without our dealing a hand."

At ten o'clock every night, the common room closed at the Four Marks Inn. Many of the transients, weary from their day's travel, were already long asleep; the few remaining had just filed out of the drafty hall and retired to their beds. After extinguishing all but two of the tallow candles, Orvin scrubbed the old wooden tables and swept the floor in the flickering, inadequate light. It was through such diligent economy that Orvin hoped one day to buy an electric generator and thus make his small hostel one of the more respectable establishments along the Prandis-Corwyn Road.

After cleaning the hall, Orvin collected the downstairs chamberpots to empty them in a ditch behind the stables. The air was chill and humid, and Orvin liked the blurry halo that the mist imparted to the moonlit woods. After emptying the pots, Orvin paused on his way back to the inn. The breeze was carrying an odd sound, the distinct beat of galloping hooves along the hard-packed road. Horses were common along the highway, of course, but no one traveled at a gallop. There were only a few large towns between the inn and Prandis, which stood more than thirty leagues to the south. Corwyn was twice that distance to the north. In the rural region that lay between those two cities, few people found themselves so pressed for time that they galloped . . . and there really was no place to gallop to.

And so it was that Orvin upended one of his buckets

and took a seat, curious to see who was in such a famous rush.

After a few minutes, the pounding drew near, and Orvin was startled to see a black-cloaked figure drawing his horse off the road, riding directly toward the inn. Orvin stood uncomfortably and wondered whether he had been foolish to indulge his curiosity. He had wanted to *see* the traveler, but nothing more. . . .

If he had made the wrong decision, it was already too late. The rider had seen him, and yanking hard on the reins, vaulted off the horse before it had fully come to a stop. Orvin looked at the poor creature: its chest heaved mightily and foam flecked the sides of its jaws. It was a handsome bay, white-socked—a fine animal if its owner hadn't already ruined it.

"You work here?"

Orvin turned his attention to the rider. The man was dressed completely in black, which Orvin found disturbing. On the other hand, he was a fairly small man and he appeared to be unarmed. Orvin's thoughts turned to his axe, embedded in the chopping block on the far side of the stables.

"You work here?" the rider repeated sharply.

Orvin nodded.

"Good." The rider was fishing for something beneath his cloak—his purse. "I want to buy a horse."

"A horse?"

The man gestured impatiently at the stable, only a few yards away. "Unless that's purely for show, I assume you own horses."

"Some are the guests'. . . . ," Orvin replied slowly.

"And some," the rider concluded, "are not. I'll buy one of those, and you can keep this horse as part of the bargain."

Orvin knelt by the bay and began to examine its hooves. "Could kill a horse riding it like that," he muttered. "You may've crippled this one."

But Orvin could tell that the bay was healthy, merely tired. She was a better horse than any in his stables, worth two hundred capitals at least.

The rider took a step closer, and Orvin got his first good look at the man's face. Chiseled, severe features. Harsh, impatient hazel eyes. . . .

"You can nurse her to health," the man replied sourly. "Now, how much for your best horse?"

Orvin's fingers twitched reflexively as he calculated a figure that, combined with his carefully husbanded savings, would make a nice down payment on a small generator.

"Done," Brandt snapped as he opened his purse. "And you can leave me one of those buckets while you go fetch the beast."

The ride from Prandis to Calador took a day and a half by a fast carriage or slightly less on horseback. Either mode was too slow for Brandt's purposes, so he chose to switch horses every two hours at roadside inns. This was a prohibitively expensive operation for most people, and despite his wealth, Brandt was irked by the exorbitant sums these two-bit roadside extortionists were charging him for their sway-backed nags. Nevertheless, to stop and dicker with them over the price of the horses would defeat the purpose of his weary ride: to arrive in the town of Calador under the cover of night. There was something in the sound of "control agent" that Brandt didn't like. It smacked of the manipulation that Ash had been practicing upon him from the very start. For a long time, he had considered ignoring the message entirely, but he realized there might be some benefit in witnessing the assassin's handiwork himself. That, however, would depend on avoiding this Agent Imbress's guided tour. Which meant a long, hard ride and an arrival late at night.

Thus, Brandt delivered three hundred capitals into Orvin's very sweaty hand and relieved himself while he waited for the horse. In a moment, the innkeeper returned with an aging sorrel, rather thin but at least recently shod. Wordlessly, Brandt leaped atop the beast and set off at a gallop on the last leg of his journey.

The sorrel gave out during the last three miles, and it was probably just as well. Brandt himself was almost at the point of collapsing. Exhausted and unspeakably saddle-sore, he let the mare walk at her own labored pace into the town of Calador. Calador—a village, really—was a tranquil, rustic place, typical of the farmland Brandt had galloped through for dozens of miles. Perhaps a thousand people lived there, most of them working at the duke's businesses. There was a large milling venture which operated out of the nearby woodlands and some agricultural concerns, including a vineyard that produced respectable wines—too respectable for Brandt's tastes. These ventures were supplemented by a variety of independent merchants who had moved to Calador to service the needs of the duke's workers. Judging by the neat rows of clapboard and shingle houses, the carefully tended gardens and proudly maintained thoroughfares, the occupants of Calador were a well-contented lot.

Bucolic enough to make Brandt gag.

The small ducal manor was located three miles out of town, in the midst of the estate's remaining few hundred acres. The way was clearly marked, and Brandt spurred his protesting horse into a few more minutes of labor. Before he could see the house in the distance, he directed the mare into a small thicket of trees and tethered her. From there, he would walk, intending to elude the Intelligence operatives that he suspected would be patrolling the area.

And operatives there were. As he glided stealthily from tree to tree, Brandt counted five men stationed around the quiet house. Two were having a chat on the front lawn, silhouetted clearly by the light of the crescent moon. If Brandt had brought a bow, they would have made absurdly easy shots. And Brandt considered himself a lousy archer.

Another agent was stationed behind the sculpted shrubbery to the left of the front door—the first place you would expect. Two more were seated on the patio out back. Where was the intelligence in Intelligence, Brandt wondered. Whoever this Imbress was, he couldn't manage his own local operatives. Yet Ash had asked him to manage Brandt?

With contemptuous ease, Brandt slid around to the side of the house and vaulted up to the sill of the kitchen window. A moment's work sufficed to open the latch and slide the sash open. Brandt smiled to himself as he dropped lightly to the tile floor. He hadn't done this sort of thing for ages, but it came back to him smoothly and completely. His fingers, his legs remembered what to do. Breaking into someone else's house, for the first time in years Brandt felt truly at home.

He closed the window quietly and commenced showing himself around by the silvery light of the young moon. Tomorrow, he expected a tour of the manor from Imbress, but the agent would doubtless show Brandt only what he wanted Brandt to see. Tonight, however, with no one around to interfere, Brandt hoped he would discover what had really happened to Roland, Duke Calador.

After a cursory examination, he concluded that the kitchen would yield no clues. Of all the rooms in a house, kitchens are the most antiseptic, leaving the least trace of violence. Brandt moved noiselessly into the hallway. Neat and dignified. The long corridor was decorated with oil portraits and bronze busts of ducal family members. An ornate runner followed the exact center of the corridor. Expensive. Brandt knew a little about rugs, having liberated his share from the mansions of Belfar as a teenager. Rugs were so cumbersome to steal that it paid to learn which ones were worth real money. After hauling a few worthless rugs to his fence long ago, Brandt had quickly learned the difference between quality and reproductions.

At the end of the corridor, Brandt reached the formal entrance chamber, with its marble floor and sweeping stairway. Through the enormous, arched windows that flanked the main door, enough moonlight poured in to read by. Another rug occupied the center of the ante-chamber, but this rug was markedly inferior in quality to the hall runner. It was odd, Brandt thought, that anyone would want to cover such a stunning marble pattern with a rug, and odder still that the rug chosen would be so drab. Suspicious, he began to roll the rug off the floor. At the exact center of the chamber he found the problem: three feet of marble tiles had been fractured. Someone, Brandt concluded, had dropped something a trifle heavier than a book.

He glanced up and smiled grimly upon finding the vacant space where surely a chandelier had hung. In better light, he would be able to see exactly where the fixture had been anchored. He would also be able to inspect the marble. Along the cracked edges, the color would tell him how long the fissures had been exposed to air. But Brandt was sure the exposed marble would gleam a virgin white. Without doubt, the chandelier had fallen during the attack.

Which led to a more important series of questions. Falling chandeliers seemed unlikely in a free-for-all, much less an assassination. What, exactly, had happened here? And why was the Ministry of Intelligence going to such trouble to obscure the truth?

Absorbed in thought, Brandt unrolled the rug and backtracked to the rear of the house, where he found the large glass doors that led to the patio. The patio was tiled with expensive, hand-painted terra-cotta, probably imported from Gathony. Very relaxing, Brandt thought, the way the house simply opened onto the large patio, and the patio onto the spacious gardens beyond. He felt a momentary pang for the contrast to his own home, so fortress-like by comparison.

But such frail delights as glass doors bred danger, and the casual ease of the comfortable patio whispered complacency. Such, at least, was the effect on the two agents from Intelligence who lounged on the patio steps, murmuring contentedly to one another in the cool night breeze. Had either bothered to turn around, he would see, framed in those glass doors like some unexpected portrait, a glowering Galatine Hazard.

Brandt was about to turn away when he noticed an incongruous detail. The glass panes of the left door were beveled, but those of the right were not. He bent down and began to examine the floor, letting his fingers run across the polished oak planks. There, glimmering slightly in a crack between two floorboards, Brandt found what he expected: a tiny sliver of glass. One of the doors had been shattered inward, then. Not a particularly stealthy means of entry. Things simply weren't adding up to a quick, quiet assassination.

There was a stairway nearby, and Brandt decided he might as well have a quick look at the upper floor. He found several bedrooms, a study, and a sewing room, each of which looked undisturbed. Brandt wandered about the darkened house, noting the profusion of lace and embroidery, the easy domesticity of the place. The walls of the master bedroom were filled with oil paintings—family portraits, but much more recent than the ones downstairs. There were children in many of them, depicted at a variety of ages. Three in all, Brandt decided after a moment. With a little work, he was able to trace each of the Calador children from infancy, through adolescence, into adulthood. And on the far wall he could dimly make out another portrait: a huge man and a delicate, beautiful woman. Unlike the classical poses that filled the portraiture Brandt knew in Prandis, here the two were holding hands and smiling warmly at one another.

Frowning, Brandt turned and left the room.

Despite what he had already discovered, Brandt felt oddly discontented as he descended to the first floor. It had been his intention simply to leave and return tomorrow. Let Intelligence think he had not been here and that, like some unthinking dupe, he accepted whatever flimsy story they offered. It was obvious that the operatives had done a lot of cleaning up around the house, and Brandt was curious to see how far Imbress's official story would vary from what he had discovered tonight.

But on his way out, Brandt passed the entrance to the antique-filled great room, where the Caladors had obviously spent much of their time. Despite its tremendous size and the six-foot-wide fireplace in the middle of the interior wall, they had managed to make this room seem intimate with warm mahogany wainscoting, rich rugs, and antique tapestries. Brandt prowled about the place for a moment, scowling. And then, without thinking, he fairly threw himself onto a deep-cushioned, floral-print sofa. The pillows caressed his aching limbs like some welcoming, feathery sea. He knew that it made absolutely no sense to relax now; he could find a room in town for that. But sense slipped away as the weariness of two sleepless days crept over him. Within seconds he was asleep.

Morning was just peering over the horizon and spreading a faint blush through the Caladors' great room when Brandt was awakened by the unfamiliar sound of a woman sighing. The sigh had issued from the main entrance to the room, directly behind him. Chances were, he figured, whoever was there had not seen him nestled in the high-backed sofa.

Silently, Brandt lifted his head and stole a look at his visitor. A woman was rearranging the position of a vase on a table by the door. She was fully Brandt's height, perhaps an inch taller, and wore a severe black dress. Mourning? Brandt wondered. The collar reached her chin and the pleated skirt dropped around her ankles, but there was abundant evidence of a lithe, active body beneath. Perhaps, Brandt thought, he had miscalculated in not checking the servants' quarters last night. Sport had been afoot.

Brandt rose without a sound from the sofa and casually announced, "You can cook breakfast, I suppose."

The woman's head whipped around, but without the gasp of surprise that Brandt had expected. Her sharp green eyes appraised him coolly.

"You do cook?" Brandt asked, stretching ostentatiously. "I've had a long ride and only an hour's sleep. Some breakfast would be nice before I suffer a meeting with some tedious government agent."

"My responsibilities do not include cooking," the woman responded in a cold, mocking tone—a voice accustomed only to giving orders, not taking them. "I'm afraid, Mr. Karrelian, that there will be no breakfast before tedium sets in today."

Brandt's brow creased in pain as he realized his miscalculation. This woman was no maid.

"You're Imbress?"

The woman casually crossed the room and, as she passed a window, Brandt noted that her short hair was not black, as he'd thought, but a remarkably deep red that flashed with sudden brilliance only, it seemed, when it chose.

"Elena Imbress," she stated simply. "I see our security has been less than rigorous. No one was supposed to be admitted last night—certainly not you."

"I didn't ask permission," Brandt replied, gratified by Imbress's concerned frown. At last, he'd found an opportunity to shift the momentum of this dismaying conversation. "But, if you're going to starve me until you've had your say, say it quickly. What happened here, and what does Taylor Ash expect me to do about it?"

Imbress took a seat across from Brandt, the frown still twitching across her face as she studied him.

"The murderer made an attempt on Duke Calador early last morning," she explained. "It would seem that the duke and his wife resisted successfully, although they didn't leave behind the body of our assassin. It was a stalemate, apparently, and both sides fled."

The murderer? So they were maintaining the fiction that one killer was responsible for the mayhem that Intelligence had carefully erased. Judging by what he'd found last night, Brandt guessed that several killers were involved. It was infuriating that Intelligence would insist on his riding a hundred miles only to be misinformed. But Taylor Ash had no real interest in giving Brandt information. What he wanted was to orchestrate Brandt's involvement as carefully as possible, and the best way to do that was to saddle him with a "control agent" who would dole out whatever fake stories were most convenient. If they could control what he knew, then they could control what he'd do. And that was Elena Imbress's job—to spin Brandt around like a child's toy.

For a moment, he considered confronting the woman, but she seemed too well trained to blurt out anything useful because of momentary surprise. Better that he keep his secrets and that she keep hers. In time, the better operative would ferret out what the other was hiding. For now, Brandt decided, he would do best to appear utterly ignorant.

"Frankly," Brandt said in a nonchalant tone, "I don't see why I'm here. You people seem to have things under control."

"For the first time," Imbress replied sharply, "I agree with you. I protested your involvement in this thing with Ash, but he seemed set on including you." She frowned bitterly at the memory of a past encounter with the Minister of Intelligence. "But you're here. I suppose I should show you around."

"Why not?" Brandt responded lightly, struggling to keep the edge out of his voice. "Seems like a nice place. If it turns out the duke was murdered, maybe the heirs will sell. How much do you think it'll go for?"

Imbress shot him a dark look, turned on her heel and left the room. She wondered whether she could have simply shot Brandt that night from the rooftop and convinced Taylor Ash that her hand had slipped . . .

"The intruder appears to have come in the early morning," Elena said, launching into the story she had prepared, "hoping to surprise the Caladors while they slept. Apparently, the duke and duchess were earlier risers, or we'd have found their bodies rather than a simple mess."

Brandt permitted himself the luxury of a smile as he followed the agent upstairs. "So where did it happen? The attack, I mean."

"The master bedroom," Imbress replied as she threw open the heavy oak door to that chamber. "As you can see, there was something of a struggle." She pointed out the unmade bed, an overturned chair, the shards of a broken pitcher lying next to a scratched end table.

The chamber had been neat as a pin last night.

Apparently, the government had rethought its strategy. They had cleaned up the house too well—they had to convince Brandt that an attack had happened, after all. So Imbress had wreaked some quiet havoc up here earlier in the morning.

Brandt walked up to a landscape hung crookedly over a dressing table—a pleasing pastoral scene suffused with light—and straightened it. "Is this a Cozotte?" he asked in as vacuous a voice as he could muster. "Looks like his work, but it's not signed." He turned to Imbress and smiled engagingly. "Normally, I wouldn't know, but my broker advises me to invest in Cozottes. The old man's about to die, apparently, and there's sure to be an appreciation on the work. You should consider buying one. . . . But how much does the government pay you?"

"*Wouldn't you like to inspect the room?*" Imbress snapped. "Seeing that you rode all this way—"

"Oh, I'm sure your people found everything here worth finding. You know, on second thought, I don't think this is a Cozotte," added Brandt, who had never seen a Cozotte in his life, although his broker had recommended the artist two weeks earlier. "Cozotte's palette is usually much redder."

Frustrated, Imbress tried to draw Brandt's attention to her reconstruction of the "attack." She was describing how the duke must have repulsed the assassin, who promptly fled, when Brandt again interrupted: "How'd he get in?"

"In? We think through the main entrance."

"Really?" Brandt said, feigning interest.

"I'll show you," Imbress replied as she led the way out of the room. After a last adjustment to the displaced picture frame, Brandt followed her. They walked along the central hallway, down the circular stairs into the main atrium, and up to the imposing pair of brass-handled doors. Imbress walked outside and crouched near the lock, motioning Brandt to do the same.

"Do you see those scratches?" the agent asked, tapping her finger near the keyhole. "We believe that he picked the lock to gain entry."

"Oh, *these* scratches," Brandt said between clenched teeth. "I see. You must be right."

It took monumental discipline for Brandt not simply to walk away from the insult. Having picked his share of locks—thousands of them, in fact—he knew very well that a skilled thief was the last person to leave scratches. When you're concentrating on picking a lock, the chances of missing the hole, provided you aren't a hopeless buffoon, are vanishingly slim. Invariably, it was owners who would carelessly jab keys at their locks and scratch them. If Imbress thought he would be hood-winked *that* easily, then she must have decided he was a total idiot. Of course, that had been the intent of Brandt's posturing all morning—but the entirety of his success nevertheless rankled.

"Well," Brandt concluded, "you seem to have every-thing figured out. I'll be going back to Chaldus, then."

"Not so fast," Imbress snapped as she rose to her feet. She had been hoping that Karrelian would finally con-front her about this lame business of the lock. If the man possessed skill equal to even a fraction of his reputation, he would have to know better. That he said nothing told her a lot: it said that he would not cooperate willingly. It said, Elena decided sourly, that thanks to Taylor Ash, her life was about to become an unparalleled pain in the ass. "I'm to take you back to the city and supervise your involvement hereafter. Didn't you read the memoran-dum? I'm—"

"My control agent. Yes, I read the bloody thing," Brandt replied impatiently. His tolerance had finally worn out, and he abandoned his facade of amiable gul-libility. "Tell Ash or whoever's *your* control agent that I'm no payrolled government employee. You don't sim-ply assign me to one chore or another, you see, because I don't work for Intelligence, and I certainly don't work for a woman."

Imbress's eyes narrowed in fury, and Brandt got the distinct impression that he'd finally figured out how to get under Imbress's skin as successfully as she was get-ting under his.

"With Calador's disappearance," the agent said qui-etly, "everyone has become a lot more nervous. People want to know what's happening to all the ex-ministers, and you, Mr. Karrelian, remain the most likely explanation. Disobey me, and I will gladly throw you to the wolves."

Brandt studied the hard lines of the young agent's face and realized that she wasn't kidding. Elena Imbress looked more than ready to use Brandt as a scapegoat . . . and ruin his life in so doing.

"I guess that *we're* going back to Prandis, then," Brandt announced with ill humor. "You'd better keep up."

CHAPTER 8

Carn sat in misery, staring at the sea of paper before him. The ease with which he had acquired a list of the Ministry of Intelligence's safe houses had made that term seem sadly inappropriate. On the other hand, what the ministry lacked in secrecy, it made up for in sheer numbers. Taylor Ash's sprawling organization owned hundreds of properties across the country, and dozens in Prandis alone. Searching them all could take weeks, and there was no guarantee that Barr Aston was holed up in any of them.

Carn laid a massive hand on his brow and tried to massage away the beginnings of a headache. During the twelve years that he and Brandt had worked the underside of Prandis, Carn had watched his curly brown hair recede and these habitual migraines increase—and he had no doubt that there had been a connection among all three phenomena. The more recent years since Brandt had abandoned his old trade had been good ones—Carn's hairline had stabilized, even if the brown was losing ground to gray, and his migraines had disappeared. Now, though, the incipient throbbing of his brow was an evil omen for the days to come. He thought of Masya, of her knack of rubbing his temples in a way that banished any headache. But she was busy working, satisying her need to feel self-sufficient. Working, as he should be.

During the last three hours, Carn had eliminated from his list every safe house purchased in the last three years, assuming that Aston would not know of anything established after his retirement. He had also ruled out any location farther than one hundred miles from the city. Aston's advanced age made such a sustained journey unlikely. Even so, more than eighty addresses remained on the list before him. In his prime, Carn had become a master thief because he possessed the methodical patience for tedious tasks like this, but some jobs even Carn dreaded. There had to be a better way.

Aston would not simply choose a refuge at random, Carn reasoned. There would be some reason—prior use of it, a strategic advantage to the location. The choice would depend on Barr Aston's past, on the man's character. Carn knew little about Aston, and Brandt's files contained nothing helpful.

It was time, then, to visit Barr Aston's house.

The funeral had been simple: an oak box from a nearby mortuary, a spade and shovel from the gardening shed. Taylor dug the hole himself while the morning sun shrank from view and a fitful rain began. Jolah stood quietly by his side, heedless of the ruin of her new dress, and watched him struggle with the wet, uncooperative earth. She had offered to dig beside him, but he had waved her away. Taylor sought help only when it came time to lower the coffin into the ground.

Kermane Ash had been a tall man, and he had put on substantial weight in his last years. Even with Jolah's help, the coffin fought their efforts as if it were possessed by some mute, perverse intelligence. Finally, Taylor slid down into the open grave, feeling his feet sink into the mud that awaited his father. From below, he gripped one end of the coffin, and with Jolah pushing from above, managed to lower the wooden casket diagonally into the hole. As Taylor's end of the coffin swung downward, he could feel the burden within it shift, feel his father's mass slide toward the bottom of the box, disarranging limbs that had been carefully composed in the stately posture of death.

Kermane Ash would have raged at the indignity, but the only sound that rose from the grave was his son's labored breathing. Exhausted from digging, Taylor collapsed against the leaning coffin, his limbs trembling from stress, his cheek pressed against the rough grain of the wood.

There seemed to be no way of sliding the coffin down to a horizontal position without sending it crashing into Taylor's legs, so after he caught his breath, he climbed from the grave. The wet earth came crumbling down from the side every time Taylor tried to gain purchase with his foot. It was like running up a mudslide, and by the time Taylor finally struggled to the sod above, he was unrecognizable—caked with mud like some elemental creature of the earth that had clawed a savage birth from her womb.

Ignoring Jolah's strange stare, Taylor walked to the head of the grave. There, the top of his father's coffin leaned only a few inches below the ground. With one sharp kick, he drove the casket down farther into the slick mud, where its momentum grew. It slid downward and out, finally falling to the bottom of the grave with a huge crash, accompanied by a small eruption of mud. Slowly, it settled into the wet, brown earth.

Taylor turned back toward the shovel.

"Shouldn't we say something?" Jolah asked.

She was surprised by his harsh laugh. "Say what you

want. He won't hear you any better now than he heard before."

She watched mutely as Taylor dug into the mound of dirt and sent the first shovelful tumbling onto the coffin. Wet, the dirt stuck to the wood where it hit. Savagely, Taylor plunged his shovel again into the earth, and again. Burying proved to be faster work than excavating, and after twenty minutes, Taylor was able to toss aside the shovel. It was only then that he noticed Jolah had left.

Turning back to his work, he stared at the small mound of broken sod that was the only trace of his father's remains. Undoubtedly, the elder Ash would have been furious. No regal marble mausoleum to mark his final rest, not even a tombstone. It was not Kermane Ash's style. The old man's will, Taylor reflected, probably contained some provisions for burial. Most likely some elaborate state-built crypt, open to the public for a modest admission fee. Finally, after his death, his father might have become a man of the people. Kermane's lawyers would probably have Taylor tied up for years about this burial. Stall the inheritance.

Fine, Taylor thought. He had long ago received all the inheritance he would need: a sense of self-reliance crafted by years of studied neglect. It was only the job that mattered, Kermane had taught him, if only by example and, Taylor thought ruefully, if only there was a hereafter, Kermane would be enjoying his first laugh of the afterlife over the way his son had failed both his father and his job at once.

As soon as he could wash and change clothes, Taylor rode Scry back to Council Tower, ignoring the rain that soaked him for the second time that day. He found Jolah behind her desk, wearing a dry dress and a calm look, as if nothing had happened that morning.

If only nothing had.

"Any news on Aston?" Taylor asked quietly.

"No."

"Has Imbress's report come in from Calador?"

"No."

The tone of Jolah's replies hinted at some petulance, but Taylor was in no mood to soothe her irritation. He was more than irritated himself. He had returned to the office praying for news, for some piece of information that he could focus on, for anything that might erase the last twelve hours of his life.

Instead, there was only the waiting game, and he would have to force himself to concentrate on the more mundane aspects of his job. There were hours of work to catch up on, piles of dispatches and reports that threatened to crack his desk under their weight. The fingers of Chaldean intelligence stretched throughout the civilized world. Every day, thousands of operatives and informants groped to find the news that shaped the continent, and they would transmit it to one of the three hundred regional offices that the ministry operated clandestinely worldwide. From there, the news was relayed to Council Tower, where twelve district chiefs and their staffs condensed the regional gleanings into coherent reports that daily found their way onto Taylor's desk.

For the past few weeks, these reports had been growing ominously thicker.

Taylor sighed as he pushed away the Gathon report and lifted one from Yndor. The principal news was bad: the king's longtime adviser, Holoakhan, was steadily losing favor with the court. A new adviser, Sardos, had grown in power. Intelligence had no background on Sardos—an oversight that he would soon see corrected, Taylor noted—but any waning of the moderate Holoakhan's power was sure to be a change for the worse. A conservative shift in Yndrian politics, combined with Amet Pale's intemperate troop movements near the border, might be all both countries needed to embroil themselves in another unnecessary war.

But if this was news to groan about, a small item deeper in the report made Taylor gasp. Parth Naidjur had been found dead, having seemingly been killed in a duel. Such affairs of honor were not uncommon in Yndor, but that a Parth should die—here was cause for alarm. Each of the five provinces of Yndor was ruled by one Parth, and they, along with the emperor, formed the hereditary leadership of the nation.

Six Chaldean ministers, the emperor of Yndor, and five Parths: twelve men in whose hands the fate of the world rested. Twelve men, twelve Phrases.

And now, for all that Taylor could tell, half of them were dead—perhaps more, depending on the fate of Barr Aston.

A timid knock on the door roused Taylor from his gloomy reverie. Jolah was supposed to handle all his visitors, but when the knock came again, he rose to find a courier in the deserted outer office.

"Where's Jolah?" the minister asked sharply.

The young man quailed and stuttered an explanation. "I don't know. I need a signature, or I wouldn't have bothered you, sir—"

But Taylor had already looked at the clock above Jolah's vacant desk. In his absorption, he'd lost track of time. It was well past noon, and understandable that Jolah had left for lunch. Lately, her lunches had grown increasingly long, but given her martyr's hours, Taylor didn't begrudge her the midday break. He ought to see about finding a lunchtime replacement, though.

He smiled at the young man, trying to make amends for the harsh impression he'd given, and signed for the proffered envelope. Taylor's name was written on its back in a graceful, precisely drawn script that he recognized as Imbress's hand. Taylor thanked the messenger quickly and, shutting his door, retreated to his desk.

He'd awaited her full report on the Calador incident for some time, but now that he had it, Taylor dreaded to see what it would contain.

Delay, however, was not one of the prerogatives of his office. A quick stroke of a paperknife slit open the envelope and, with a grimace of foreboding, Taylor extracted the report.

To his surprise, Taylor was greeted with the first good news of the day. Imbress confirmed that the Caladors had escaped. Servants of the family had seen them ride off after the attack, although everyone denied knowledge of their destination. Taylor now had the logistical problem of finding them—but a minister in the bush, Taylor reasoned, was preferable to a corpse in hand.

Taylor flipped the page over and received with rather less pleasure the news on the opposite side. Imbress had identified the attackers positively: they belonged to the Sixth Division of the Chaldean National Army. A paralyzing chill crept along Taylor's spine as he fit this news into place.

Amet Pale, not the mysterious assassin, had tried to kill Duke Calador. Now, beyond a shadow of a doubt, Taylor knew whom he had chased from his home last night: more of Pale's men. They had not been in time to kill his father, it was true—but they gladly would have murdered the old man had they been given the opportunity.

Taylor crumpled the dispatch and slammed it against his desk as he pondered the implications. The day of the vote, Amet Pale had been the most bloodthirsty minister on the Council, and Taylor had suspected that the paper warrior would clamor for proof of the executions later that week. Even so, Taylor had assumed Pale would allow him at least three days to demonstrate Intelligence's completion of the unpleasant task. To have immediately dispatched the army's own death squads, though . . . if discovered, that would risk an open breach in the Council. Finally, Taylor thought with grim satisfaction, Pale had acted too rashly. At the very least, he would be censured for such action. Perhaps even removed from office. Taylor determined to call an emergency Council session immediately. Let the general try to justify himself to the assembled ministers. It would only hasten his downfall.

Unless Pale had somehow acquired hard evidence that Taylor was disobeying the Council vote. A moist chill broke across his brow as he realized that this was the solution. Pale was too patently a reptile to act in this matter without a face-saving recourse.

Taylor called for Jolah before he remembered that his assistant was gone. He wanted a list of all the operatives privy to his orders to apprehend the ministers. There were only a few, and he proceeded to draw up the list himself. Nine names.

Nine men and women, each of whom he would have thought, up until that very moment, incapable of betraying him. Jin Annard, Taylor's deputy minister, had been a close friend since the Academy. Elena Imbress, despite her fiery temper, treated him like a brother—often, to Taylor's chagrin, a little brother. The others seemed equally inconceivable suspects. . . . He studied the list again, trying to remember any irregularities of behavior. Could any of these agents have sold themselves to Amet Pale without even a hint of treachery? It seemed impossible.

Taylor decided to begin from the start, this time more methodically. He numbered the operatives according to the chain of command and, as an afterthought, wrote his name at the top of the chain. Somewhere there was a weak link.

No, he realized with horror, not a weak link. A missing one. Almost all of his orders passed through Jolah's hands.

Yes, Jolah's hands—they had acquired a new and

expensive-looking ring, Taylor remembered. Her wardrobe had been taking a turn for the better. Taylor was too well acquainted with her wages to believe she'd bought all these things herself. And given the hours that Jolah worked at the ministry, it was doubtful she had time to find a generous lover. Unless it was someone very convenient.

And Taylor suspected that he knew just who to look for.

The staff on the eighth floor of Council Tower was accustomed to two manners of visitors. There were the haughty, stiff-kneed officers who marched proudly to Amet Pale's office, dreaming of the extra stripe or star that successful duty might earn them. And then there were the failures who, commanded to Pale's presence, slipped quietly through the halls in a cloud of disgrace. All in all, upward of forty visitors might come to the minister's offices each day, but not even the oldest staffers could remember anyone storming through the mahogany-paneled corridor, shouldering aside the guards, and bursting into Pale's outer chamber.

Taylor Ash would be the first.

The robust captain who served as Pale's assistant rose immediately as Taylor strode into the office, and perceiving that the irate minister had no intention of asking for an appointment, placed himself before the door to Pale's closed inner sanctum.

"Out of my way," Taylor warned.

"Beg your pardon, Minister," the captain began deferentially, "but General Pale is occupied at the moment—"

Ash's fist shot out at the man's larynx, and the unfortunate soldier fell choking to the floor.

Instantly, a cry went up, and an armed guard charged down the hallway toward Pale's office. Along with the guard came Agon Celwan, Pale's Underminister of War. A curious expression rose to Celwan's face as he saw the Minister of Intelligence at the threshold of Pale's office. Quietly, he placed a restraining hand on the guard's shoulder. The curtain of a very rare show, Celwan suspected, was about to rise.

Taylor Ash kicked open Pale's door and burst into the dim, elegantly appointed office. He found the Minister of War where he expected him, behind the spacious oak desk that had once belonged to Roland, Duke Calador.

Taylor had not, however, expected to find the general with his trousers collapsed around his boots.

Nor had he expected to find Jolah perched hands and knees on the desk, her dress pushed up over her hips as she stoically received the military thrusts of the Minister of War.

"I was going to fire you, Jolah," Ash observed with distaste, "but I see you've already found a new position."

"Damn you, Ash!" Pale cried as the blood rose to his cheeks. "What right have you—"

"Don't talk to me of rights," Taylor growled, advancing.

Jolah pulled herself away from the general, adjusted her dress, and rushed toward Taylor. He pushed her away roughly, and she flew into a scaled display of Chaldus, scattering the general's tiny ivory forces of foot and horse, archers and engineers. Agon Celwan slipped into the room and took hold of the woman, dragging her out to the custody of the guard.

"I swear to you, Ash, I'll have your head for this!" The general was fumbling for the sword that he had dropped, minutes earlier, along with his pants.

Taylor could hardly hear for the hot rush of blood in his ears, but he responded in the cool, mocking tone that had marked his father's career.

"I suggest you concentrate on your own breeches first, General."

Later, he would not be able to determine why the next sentence tumbled from his tongue, if not for the Yndrian report he'd just finished reading, but in a moment it was done:

"But if it's my head you want, you'll find it at Hawken Heights come dawn tomorrow."

CHAPTER 9

Among the residents of Yndor, Prandls was known as Kihal a'Tyr, the City of One Tower, which was at once a joke and an age-old curse, for among the clustered spires of Thyrsus, the idea of a city without towers was a city not at all. Slender and delicate, the multicolored Thyrsian monoliths strained in frozen competition toward the sky, reaching for the one moisture-laden cloud that had hung motionless over the city all day like a solitary and enigmatic emissary from heaven.

But below that unchanging sky, within and among the unmoving towers of Thyrsus, the city was in turmoil. The commotion had begun, as commotions do, with whispering, and the subject of the whispering was the death of Parth Naidjur. Not that the Yndrians were a people who whispered about death. During centuries of internecine strife between provinces before the Empire was established, and during the course of countless bloody wars with neighboring Chaldus thereafter, the Yndrians had become accustomed to death. Even in these increasingly peaceful times, the citizens of Thyrsus were far from shy of blood. No, it was not the fact of bloodshed that set the people whispering. It was how that blood was shed.

Or, rather, who had shed it.

Each of the five provinces of Yndor was divided into innumerable smaller fiefdoms, each ruled by a thane. And in the province of Aginath, one of the most notorious thanes was Crassus. He was not famous for his wealth or the size of his holdings, for although these were great, many possessed far greater. Rather, Crassus was known throughout the Empire by an epithet usually preceded by a curse: *sympathizer.* When an Yndrian used the term, no one needed to ask what the person so named sympathized with. It was understood: a sympathizer advocated closer relations with Chaldus, an easing of the centuries-old hostility that, despite the new era of peace, still defined for many citizens exactly what it meant to be an Yndrian.

Thus, when Parth Naidjur, as proud an Yndrian as ever walked the land, surveyed his domain, he was disturbed. His was a large province, stretching from the southwestern spur of the Grimpikes down to Tyr Odom, and then northward along the Cirran River where it ran through the heart of the Ulthorn Forest. Much of this land was uninhabited, for few men chose to live in the harsh mountains or in the dark and dangerous interior of the forest. But his people were hardy, and he prided himself on the stout warriors with whom he garrisoned Tyr Odom, one of the twin fortress-cities that defended Yndor's Chaldean border. Among all his vast lands and all his doughty people, the parth was pleased.

Except when he thought of Crassus. The thane was a living affront to Naidjur's nature, and so the two had coexisted uneasily, maintaining a continual trade of slights and covert insults. Naidjur drew more heavily on the radical thane's fiefdom to stock the province's troops, and Crassus in turn made his lands as independent of the parth's power as was possible. Indeed, over the years, the two began to relish their hatred with an odd sort of cordial enthusiasm.

But five days ago, the people whispered, an insult had been delivered that Crassus would not brook. The outraged thane took recourse in the age-old remedy for insults among the nobility: a duel. Challenged by a fellow nobleman, Parth Naidjur could not simply decline, and he would not retract whatever he had said. So, like generations of thanes and parths before them, the two met on the field of honor and hacked at each other with a pair of pedigreed blades, until one of them had the decency to end the contest by dying.

Duels took place so frequently in Yndor that they seldom were accorded any attention. The stature of these specific duelists, however, ensured that the public would take notice. But what really set the people of Yndor abuzz, what sent them running barefoot into the street to consult with their neighbors, what got passed over counters between clerk and customer more often than merchandise, what set a generation of Yndrian men to honing their swords, was the rumor of Naidjur's insult itself: Thane Crassus was a Chaldean agent.

Where this rumor began, no one could say for certain. It had been heard whispered in corners by men who had heard it whispered in other corners, and the only thing about the affair that remained perfectly sure was that after four days, the whisper had grown to a murmur, the murmur to a clamor, and ultimately, the clamor to a national uproar.

So it was that on this windless day the shops remained darkened and goods sat rotting on the Thyrsian docks. The people gathered in the streets, avidly discussing the possibility that one of the most powerful men in their country had been assassinated by a Chaldean agent. Most of all, they wondered why the emperor had said nothing, had sent no word to the people to explain what had happened. And so the crowds eventually drifted to the Thyrsian Way—the wide, tree-lined boulevard that wound from the Imperial Port of Thyrsus through the lower regions of the city, into the aristocratic neighborhoods of the foothills, up to the huge cobbled square that surrounded the Imperial Palace. By noon, so many people had packed into the square that not one red cobblestone could be seen. The milling throng filled the area, pressing up against the walls of Martyr's Square—the vast courtyard that occupied the space between the palace and the Jurin Crypts—and spilling back down the Thyrsian Way for nearly half a mile.

From a window high in one of his towers, Emperor Mallioch could see the gathering, and he brooded.

"You must speak to them, my lord."

The emperor turned from the window to consider the speaker. Holoakhan, the Imperial Wizard, had served the emperor since Mallioch was an irresponsible prince. That was more than four decades past, and the years had left their mark on Holoakhan's visage. The hair that Mallioch remembered as black had turned a silvery white, and it had receded until only a fringe was left around the wizard's ears, growing long in the Yndrian fashion and formed into a foot-long braid. The old man's face had shrunken into a series of bony angles and deep creases—a birdlike face. Holoakhan's body seemed almost lost within his voluminous gray robes, except where a frail hand peeked forth from beneath a sleeve, clutching the polished cherry staff of office for support.

The wizard's policies, Mallioch reflected sadly, were as old and tired as the man himself. The roads of conciliation led only so far. Yndor had prospered for years, but now progress seemed to have lurched to a stop. Commerce with Chaldus had been surprisingly profitable since Mallioch had opened trade with them early in his reign, but the enterprising Chaldeans, bolstered by their clever technology, had begun to surpass Yndor. Yndrian goods were beginning to falter even in their home market. Why, the commerce Chaldus enjoyed in the export of generators alone was staggering. Worse yet, the last three harvests had been awful—blasted by freak weather. In the past weeks, Mallioch had begun to consider protective tariffs. . . .

The emperor looked again through the window and saw a crowd enraged less by the death of a parth than by mounting hunger and joblessness. It would take more, he knew, than a tariff to please them.

Suddenly, all the light in the small tower room vanished, as if the sun had been eclipsed. And, indeed, it had. Mallioch's other close adviser had taken a step forward, and his huge frame completely blocked the window. This man, too, wore robes, but beneath the thick black fabric one could note the play of tremendous muscles, of unthinkable force. He must be seven feet tall, Mallioch mused for at least the hundredth time. Perhaps that was why his words were uncannily prescient, because he could see over the heads of other men.

"And what say you, Sardos?" the emperor asked wearily.

"I say what I have said before," the man answered in a voice so deep that Mallioch could feel the vibrations in his chest.

The emperor almost smiled. That was the way with Sardos, never wasting a word. Earlier he had offered to interrogate Crassus, to determine whether the man was indeed a Chaldean agent. Sardos's interrogation would no doubt have been magical but, Mallioch reflected upon studying the tremendous silhouette of his adviser, the magic would surely have proven unnecessary. The king could imagine no man so daring as to tell Sardos a lie.

Indeed, Mallioch did not himself know what to tell Sardos. Holoakhan, on the other hand, did.

"It is not our way," the old wizard replied. "Crassus is a thane, and no less a thane for having killed Naidjur in a duel. Whatever we think of his politics, his blood is owed respect."

"As Naidjur's blood was respected?" Sardos rumbled.

"The field of honor is another matter entirely," Holoakhan said irritably. "You should know that. Were we to apprehend a thane and interrogate him without cause, the entire aristocracy would cry out against imperial tyranny."

"The other thanes hate him," Mallioch said softly. "They would be glad to see him dead."

"Yes, but not by our hands," Holoakhan replied. "They will not allow a precedent of their own rights being trampled." The old man turned to Mallioch. "But it is not the thanes you need now consider, my liege; you can hear your audience below you."

And, indeed, as had happened on a few occasions earlier that afternoon, the crowd's chaotic roar had resolved itself into a purposeful chant: "Mallioch! Mallioch! Mallioch!" The entire city had gathered in the streets below, and it would not be denied.

Wearily, the emperor rose from his chair.

Alone in his ability to ignore the chanting crowds gathered in Martyr's Square, Prince Clannoch, Mallioch's only son, sat hunched over a large, leatherbound tome in his study, high within one of the palace's innumerable spires. His dark eyes traced each line of the scribe's hand, then flickered back to the margin of the page to begin again, never straying from the ancient vellum. If the prince noticed when the broad door opened, admitting his sister to the room, he showed no sign of it. Cyrintha observed her younger brother for a moment, then turned toward the nearest row of bookshelves, browsing through the titles. She envied Clannoch's implacable concentration and wished she, too, could find a book to throw herself into. But she knew that nothing there possessed the power to distract her.

"It scares me," Cyrintha said, pondering the vast crowd that chanted a hundred feet below the tower window.

Prince Clannoch looked up from his book. "I didn't hear you knock," he said, scowling. He swept his arm in an arc, indicating the long desk and the formidable rows of bookshelves that cluttered the room. "I come to the study," he announced irritably, "to study."

Cyrintha walked along a row of shelves to the curved tower wall and peered down at the chanting masses. From here, the people were indistinguishable—a heaving mass of color and noise. After a moment, she turned back toward her brother and appraised him critically. That deep crease in his brow, she thought, rather ruined his fine features. She wondered whether she should warn him against letting that frown become permanent, but said instead, "I never used to knock when we were children."

"Which we are no longer," Clannoch replied. "Unlike you, I shall one day have an empire to govern. *My* studies are no idle plaything."

It was Cyrintha's turn to frown. For the past three years, she had been studying magic with Holoakhan—not that she had learned much yet, but it was a challenging field to master. She was disturbed that her brother—her younger brother, whom she had always chided for his caprices—should think of her efforts as idle.

She wondered whether they were.

"And what, pray, should I be doing?"

Clannoch's handsome mouth twisted into a rakish smile. "One might consider finding a suitable husband. Why waste such a promising youth on the barren paths of coquetry?"

The princess laughed and batted her eyes experimentally. "After twenty-three years, I'm afraid my feminine charms have all but expired. Nothing is left for me but my studies."

"Tell that to Rogaska," Clannoch replied mischievously.

"Rogaska? Ah, my Thorn. . . ."

"Is that what you call him?" Clannoch asked, an eyebrow rising in curiosity. "Thorn?"

Cyrintha smiled ironically. "The thorn in my side. But, ultimately, even he abandoned me."

Clannoch chuckled. "Abandoned you? Ah, yes, for the dubious charms of Tyr Senil's barracks. That's quite an infidelity."

Rogaska had been neither the first nor the last in Cyrintha's long line of disappointed suitors, but he had certainly been the most melodramatic. The youngest son of the Parth of Todar, he had been sent to the imperial court as a functionary for his father, and there he had met Cyrintha. Rather quickly, they had become good friends, but Rogaska made the mistake of confusing her easy affection with love of a different sort. For the better part of a year, he had applied himself unstintingly to the pursuit of the princess's heart. Cyrintha had shown not the least reciprocation, and finally, almost a year ago, Rogaska had enlisted at the imperial garrison of Tyr Senil, drowning his despair in the strict discipline of military duty and, upon occasion, the dubiously romantic indulgence of an afternoon's stroll through the Bismet Fens.

She had not thought of the young lord for months, Cyrintha realized. Oddly, she felt a small pang of regret—not that she missed his attentions, but she supposed that she had treated him cruelly in the end. Nevertheless, Rogaska was the last thing on Cyrintha's mind today. The crowd below had begun again to chant her father's name.

"Are you scared?" she asked.

"Of that rabble?" Clannoch replied, laughing in disbelief. "It would take ten times that number to breach our walls, and if they did, I'd skewer the first hundred like rats."

The princess blinked in disbelief. Of late, she seemed less and less able to comprehend the peculiar turnings of her brother's mind. There were enormous pressures on the heir to an empire, she knew, but she could not begin to fathom how they had actually operated on the young man with whom she had played for years of carefree childhood.

"I didn't mean that you were afraid of them," Cyrintha said softly. "They protest because they want to hear the emperor. They gather not in hostility to the Jurin dynasty, but in loyalty. The people seek to learn whether the country is threatened, and if so, what our father intends to do."

Clannoch turned back to the text he had been reading. "I've more than sufficient civics lessons to study here," he replied with an edge to his voice, "if that's what you've come to deliver."

Cyrintha sighed. This was not working out at all as she had expected. She had come to her brother for comfort, not further vexation. She looked down into the square again, amazed at the size of the roiling mass. She hadn't imagined that so many people lived in the entire province. Many of them were thrusting their fists into the air in time to the chant of the emperor's name. Cyrintha wondered what it must feel like in the midst of that great throng, tossed about on the tide of bodies, no one quite an individual but rather a cell of the crowd, swept by its will, breathing air made damp by the breath and sweat and fear of thousands.

The thought terrified her, yet it also lured her with a strange appeal, so different than the charm of her well-decorated towers.

"I fear what we shall do with them," she said finally.

Clannoch looked up again from his book, his broad brow furrowed. "And that is . . . ?"

"They believe Crassus is a Chaldean tool. If that is true, the peace cannot last. Even if it is false, and they persist in thinking it true—"

The princess lapsed into silence.

Clannoch gazed at his older sister with a gleam in his eye that she could not recall seeing before. "And would war be that bad?"

CHAPTER 10

"**I**f I'm slowing you down too much, let me know."

Brandt grumbled a curse and kicked his heels sharply into the flanks of his sorrel, but the horse had decided that after last night's ill usage, she would never gallop again. Not for Brandt, at any rate. Meanwhile, Elena Imbress rode a fine black-and-white dappled gelding whose enthusiasm for the road could hardly be contained. The first hour of the ride had consisted of Imbress pulling steadily away from Brandt until finally she reined in and let him catch up, only to pull away quickly again. This would have been fine with Brandt—he had no desire to ride with her at all—except that every time he drew close, she would offer a sardonic apology for *her* slowing *him* down. Apparently, she had no intention of forgetting Brandt's dour warning that she'd better keep up, and she intended to punish him for it all day long.

When Brandt drew close to the Four Marks Inn, he slowed his horse even more, letting Imbress disappear around a bend in the road. Still muttering curses to himself, he tethered his nag to the inn's hitching post and stormed inside in search of the innkeeper. Orvin, it turned out, was more than happy to trade back Brandt's bay for the sorrel . . . for an extra consideration of two hundred capitals. The sum was outrageous, of course. In two transactions at the Four Marks, Brandt had accomplished nothing more than renting a broken-down sorrel for one night at the cost of five hundred capitals—enough money to buy three fine horses outright. But if a faster horse could make Imbress shut up, he would account the money a splendid investment.

The investment soured quickly. There was a brief moment of satisfaction as Brandt overtook and passed the Intelligence agent, rushing by her at a spirited gallop, but all she did was laugh and spur her gelding in chase. It took her only a moment to draw even, and to Brandt's dismay, there was a look of sheer delight on her face. Elena Imbress was a natural rider for whom no pace was too brisk. Her body dipped down and drove forward with the rhythm of her horse as if their flesh were joined. He should have known from her riding gear, he realized: a jacket and trousers, both crafted of soft leather, that looked as if they had seen thousands of miles of road. Brandt, on the other hand, had begun to regret his gallop almost immediately. He rode only infrequently, and yesterday's long journey had created a soreness that the jarring speed of the bay soon aggravated into agony.

"I see you stopped for a little business transaction," Imbress observed merrily as she eyed his new horse.

Brandt said nothing in reply, but Imbress was not to be discouraged. Now that she'd begun talking, she seemed determined upon a conversation.

"How is the electrical generator business these days? Have you sold many of them lately?"

Brandt glared at the woman. The question was innocuous enough, but her tone remained amused, as if some enormous joke hovered just beyond Brandt's grasp.

"I don't sell generators," he snapped. "I just finance

their production. There are retail firms that handle sales
and installation."

"Oh," Imbress said, drawing out the syllable as if
Brandt had revealed some transcendent truth. "I see. Of
course you don't sell them yourself. I suppose you
haven't done any door-to-door work since you gave up
. . . your old vocation."

Brandt shook his head, cursing himself for having
been stupid enough to answer her. If this mockery kept
up, he swore to himself, Taylor Ash would find the head
of his "control agent" delivered in lieu of Brandt's first
report.

"Although, I must say," Imbress continued, the
amused twist of her lips growing, "I hear you were a
good enough thief in your day."

"I managed," Brandt grumbled.

"What I don't understand is the bit about the coins.
Why did you leave a gold capital in the mouth of each
man you murdered?"

"Killed," Brandt corrected. "I'm no murderer."

"Oh, I'm sorry," the young agent said, the amused
undertone growing in her voice. "I didn't mean to offend
you. I suppose it must be vexing to be called a murderer
when you're merely a killer."

Brandt ground his teeth together and kicked his horse
into an even faster gallop. Effortlessly, Imbress's gelding
kept pace. She slipped her hand into her pocket and
fished out a cigarette that she had rolled in anticipation
of the long ride. She began to lift it to her lips, then
shrugged and held it out toward Brandt.

Brandt shook his head, not bothering to explain that
he didn't smoke. Then he glanced again at the cigarette
in her hand, a connection forming in his mind. If Elena
Imbress was his "control agent," it certainly made sense
that she had shot at him from the roof. And if she shot
with anything approaching her skill at riding . . . Brandt
glanced down at the crossbow that hung from her pom-

mel and ground his teeth together. He supposed that Imbress had enjoyed a hearty laugh at his expense that night. A cold fury began to creep through him.

"You still haven't explained the coins," she called over the clatter of their horses' hooves. Her hair flashed red in the dappled sunlight.

Brandt considered ignoring her, but Elena Imbress did not seem the type of woman to be ignored. She would probably pester him for the next ninety miles, if that's what it took to get an answer.

"I never wanted to kill anyone," Brandt growled. "The coins were a promise of compensation."

"Ah, compensation. Yes, I suppose that ten or fifteen years ago a gold capital might just about cover the costs of a pine box. Very considerate of you."

Brandt yanked back on the reins, jerking the bit sharply into the bay's gums. The horse whinnied in pain and reared, threatening to topple onto its back. After one terrifying, teetering moment, it caught its balance and returned to the ground, kicking petulantly at the road and trying to grab the bit in its teeth. Imbress reined in her mount more gently and brought it about to face a glowering Brandt Karrelian.

"Is it something I said?" she asked with disingenuous innocence.

"I've killed eight men in my life," Brandt said, his voice low and menacing. "Eight—and that's eight more than I ever wanted to kill. The coins were *symbols*, not that it's any business of yours. Not compensation, but symbols that I would take care of the families. And I have. Each one of those families has seen more money from me than those men would earn in a century. I've bought them houses, arranged guild entry for their children—"

"Quite humane of you," Imbress interrupted coolly. "Generous, as well. Almost like winning the lottery, I suppose. It's a good thing you never advertised your

policy, Mr. Karrelian, or everyone in Prandis would
have started volunteering family members for the edge
of your sword."

Brandt drew in his breath sharply as he glared at Imbress. He spurred his horse into a mild canter, forcing
himself not to look at her as he passed.

"You know, I said that I've never enjoyed killing anyone. You may just prove the exception."

Elena Imbress laughed at the threat. "Good thing for
me, old man, that you're retired."

The hooves of the two horses clattered noisily
in the gathering darkness as they passed over the rough
wooden planks of a covered bridge. This and the horses'
occasional snuffling were about as much noise as the
travelers had made since leaving the vicinity of Calador.
After their argument, Brandt and Imbress had proceeded
at a moderate pace for the remainder of the day, pausing
only long enough to eat and to rest their horses. For
Brandt, however, the ride was becoming too painful too
bear, in more than one respect. Although they were only
twenty miles north of Prandis, Brandt stopped at a small
roadside inn that lay just beyond the bridge. Imbress shot
him a curious look, but said nothing. When they went
inside, the innkeeper attended first to the pretty young
woman from Intelligence, ushering her politely to a
room and turning down her bed. For Brandt, he simply
grunted and pointed down the hallway.

Despite his exhaustion, Brandt found himself unable
to sleep. He lay on the beaten-down straw mattress for
two hours, silently cursing Taylor Ash and his own awful luck. He wondered whether Ash was really vindictive
enough to have him killed if he failed to cooperate.
Somehow, he doubted it, and in the middle of the night
he determined to find out. This entire business—and
Elena Imbress in particular—had become altogether too

infuriating, and he would have nothing more to do with it. To hell with Intelligence and retired ministers. Let the old men drop like flies. If anyone thought he was responsible, they would discover otherwise . . . to their eternal regret.

Brandt slipped out of bed and got dressed. He walked quietly down the hall, smiling as he passed the closed door of Imbress's room. She would have a little surprise awaiting her tomorrow morning when she found his bed empty. It was all he could do to avoid laughing at the thought.

As he approached the ramshackle old stable, he saw light spilling from beneath the doorway. It was odd that the innkeeper would waste oil on the stables in the middle of the night, but Brandt didn't think much about it. If he was lucky, one of the stable hands was working late and Brandt wouldn't have to saddle his own horse. When he opened the door, though, he found only Imbress inside, busily grooming her gelding. His look of dismay brought a slight smile to her lips.

"I thought you might like to get an early start," Imbress explained. "There's nothing like a man who shows initiative."

Brandt saddled his horse in silence and they set off into the darkness at a brisk pace. Twenty miles, he promised himself. Only twenty miles more.

After those miles had passed, Brandt pulled himself erect in the saddle and surveyed the road before him with pleasure. They were in the northwestern outskirts of Prandis, in an affluent area that Brandt knew well. A familiar fork lay only a few hundred yards away in the hazy twilight, and he spurred his mount toward it. Without a word in response, Elena did the same, keeping her gelding within a few paces of Brandt's tired bay.

At the fork, the wide trade road ran into the heart of

Prandis; the other, smaller route wound into the expensive suburbs where Brandt resided. Without a word of farewell, he turned onto this road and urged his horse into a brisk trot.

But Elena Imbress followed.

Brandt hauled abruptly on the reins, again bringing the bay up short.

"Somehow," he began with a smile that quivered on the edge of a sneer, "I don't imagine you live in this neighborhood."

Elena reined in alongside Brandt and fixed him with a weary stare. It was true enough that she lived nowhere near that region of sprawling estates. Her own lodgings were more modest: a three-room flat on the second floor of a widow's house, not far from the center of the city. Of course, she could as easily have written for money and bought a house of her own; her father had never disinherited her, despite his repeated threats. Elena simply had never asked the executor of her father's will to forward her funds. But her family was not a subject she was about to discuss with Brandt Karrelian—and Elena knew that any contest of fortunes was sure to prove a losing game.

"I'm your control agent," she said patiently, as if it explained everything. "Until this entire crisis is resolved, you don't move a step without me, unless under my express directions. Little as either of us may relish the arrangement, I'll nevertheless be staying with you today, tonight, and indefinitely thereafter."

Just until Taylor Ash comes to his senses, Elena silently amended, *and dispenses with small-time crooks, no matter how rich they've become.*

"Well, then," Brandt responded, the smile twisting like an unwelcome visitor on his features, "I suppose I'll do my best to be hospitable."

Turning back to the road, he let his horse have its head and canter patiently into the well-groomed estates that lay north of the city. Every mile or so, Brandt would choose a side road, leading them into a hilly, well-wooded region that contained the most luxurious mansions of Prandis. Finally, they arrived at a little path that led to a massive wrought-iron gate set into a high stone wall. Two large men dressed in crisp black suits attended the gate, and they nodded gravely at Brandt's approach.

"Master Karrelian," the first said pleasantly as he swung open the iron portal for Brandt to pass through. They said nothing, but watched with curiosity as Brandt's stern companion followed him. It might have been a smile that flickered briefly on one guard's features as he closed the gate behind them.

Inside, Elena found herself following a broad flag-stone path through a garden. Although the vibrant hues of the flowers were muted in the overcast dawn light, she was nevertheless impressed by the garden's meticulous and intricate arrangement. Such floral delicacy, she thought, did not seem in Karrelian's character. If she envied him anything, Elena decided as they passed the vibrant flower beds, it was his gardener.

In the center of the garden, the path divided along either side of a large marble fountain that was dominated by the festive figures of a satyr struggling with a nymph. Here, she noted, was a feature more in keeping with her estimate of Karrelian's character.

They passed the fountain and began the climb up a mild slope to the crest of the hill upon which the mansion stood. Elena had heard some rumors about Galatine Hazard in earlier years, and in the scanty time allotted to her before she began this current assignment, she had learned a little more. She expected that his house would be one of the finest in Prandis. But even so, she was impressed by the massive, graceful brownstone building that sprawled upon the hilltop. In the classic, open Prandis style, the facade was dominated by a number of spacious windows. Through their sheer curtains a veritable blaze of steady electric light poured onto the grounds, as if the old brown building caressed the grass with slender white fingers.

Another pair of soberly clad men attended the mansion's red double doors. One descended the steps as Brandt approached and took the reins as he dismounted. A moment later, he performed the same service for Elena, who had approached more slowly as she examined the grounds.

"Well," Brandt prompted, "do you intend to remain outdoors all day?"

Elena looked up. Brandt stood at the top of the short flight of steps. Quickly, she ascended to his side and the other attendant opened one of the gleaming red doors. Brandt strolled casually inside, stamping his dust-covered boots on an exotic hand-stitched rug from Gathony. Elena followed a step behind him, looking up at the ceiling of the entry hall, thirty feet above her head. A huge, crystal chandelier shed the refracted radiance of a hundred electric bulbs, dispelling any shadows from the elegant chamber. The walls were hung with a variety of paintings and tapestries, except where a stairway swept along the curved hall up to an open, balustraded walkway on the second floor. Several doors faced this airy corridor, none of them open.

On their own level, there were only the doors they had just entered and a twin pair across the way, this time painted a sedate white. Brandt had walked to these doors and was on the point of throwing them open when he remarked, a bit too cheerfully, "As long as you're here, I want you to enjoy *all* the diversions we can offer."

But Elena was busy gazing at the design that a Gathon artisan had labored so long to weave, and at the large oil paintings that adorned the walls to either side. There was a certain disturbing motif in the art of this chamber—

"Brandt, dear!"

Elena turned around. The inner doors stood open, revealing a large, dimly lit room shrouded with heavily perfumed, perhaps narcotic, mists. The speaker, leaning in the doorway, was an impeccably groomed woman of perhaps fifty years, sheathed in a clinging, low-cut, indigo dress that, to Elena's taste, would not have suited a woman half her age. But this was apparently the mode of the premises. Inside the room, Elena could see perhaps a dozen more women—a few of them hardly more than girls—each dressed more provocatively than their mistress. Many appeared tired after what had obviously been a long night. They lounged on deeply cushioned divans, some hidden half-coyly behind sheer silken curtains as they sipped drinks or smoked slender pipes. Indeed, a nearby pair lifted their pipes in silent greeting when they saw Brandt. Their smiles grew arch as they observed the dusty, bulky leather riding gear that Elena wore and the dark red hair that tumbled in disarray after a day of hard travel.

Without a word, Elena turned on her heel and walked out. The doorman snapped the red portal smartly closed behind her.

"Silene," Brandt laughed, for the first time that day, "you've saved me again."

"Anything," the madam replied, the words floating lazily from her painted lips, "to keep you, dear Brandt, from the dreaded embrace of matrimony."

Brandt's brow knitted for a moment, then relaxed as he laughed again. "That is definitely *not* what you saved me from—and you've slighted my taste in the bargain. But all's forgotten between friends."

Especially now that he was rid of Elena Imbress.

"Speaking of taste," Silene continued smoothly, "what might be yours tonight?"

"I'm afraid it's already morning, Silene. Unfortunately, I rode through most of the night."

The madam smiled and traced a manicured fingernail along the edge of Brandt's jaw.

"Dear Brandt, of all people, you should know that night is a state of mind . . . and in this house, that state is perpetual. Forget the sun, and choose."

Brandt turned his attention to the dim interior of the room and the somewhat familiar buffet of delight that it offered. He was about to nod toward a small, energetic blond who had become a favorite, when he spied a new countenance toward the back of the room: a shy young woman, lithe and long-legged, from whose head fell an abundance of perfumed red locks.

"Her," Brandt said simply, gesturing in the girl's direction, and he turned and ascended the circular staircase before Silene could regale him with her customary approval of a choice well made.

Silene frowned at Brandt's more than usual moodiness and merely delayed her young employee long enough to exhort her to perform admirably for the kind and generous man who had, years ago, given to Silene the house's massive electrical generator.

When Loriale reached the darkened bedroom upstairs, she found Brandt brooding by the window. He was staring through a tiny space between the curtains, at what she couldn't say.

Elena Imbress stood on the lawn outside, as still as the statues in the fountain, looking upward resolutely at the line of windows that she knew must be the bedrooms.

"My name is Loriale," the young woman said softly.

Brandt said nothing. Usually, Loriale's clients introduced themselves, even if they lied about their names. But some men preferred silence, and she proceeded, unruffled, to lay a small hand on Brandt's shoulder. He continued to stare out the window while she ran her fingers through his hair, tracing delicate lines on his scalp with her nails, smoothing out the tangles of a day's ride.

Imbress refused to turn away, staring directly at his window—though Brandt knew she could not possibly see him.

Wordlessly, Loriale eased off Brandt's riding jacket and lifted the worn shirt over his head. Then, starting at the nape of his neck, she pressed a trail of kisses down his spine. Finally, Brandt turned around and, looking at the woman on her knees before him, caught a strand of her flame-colored hair between his fingers.

"What did you say your name was?"

CHAPTER 11

The commotion in the adjoining room roused Emina Pale well before dawn. Unable to imagine what might be the matter at such an early hour, the aging matron pulled a thick green robe over her shoulders and opened the door to her husband's chamber. Amet Pale sat at the edge of his bed, his ample belly spilling over his boxer shorts as he pulled on a new black sock. The electric light was jarring, and Emina realized, not for the first time, that Amet in the morning was no longer an inspiring sight.

"Go back to bed, Amet. Surely, the country cannot demand your devotion twenty-four hours a day."

"I've matters to attend to," Pale growled, "and, yes, when Chaldus calls, I shall answer—day or night."

The truth was, on this particular day, Chaldus could hardly have called early enough to suit the Minister of War. Indeed, he was grateful that Ash had set such an early meeting—he could not imagine having to wait any longer to get on with it. Unfortunately, much as he wished to think so, Pale's emotions were not wholly due to anticipation. Although he relished the idea of squashing that young upstart from Intelligence, the fact was that the minister had been up all night, wrestling with an acute attack of gastric distress. For all his decorations, the general had graduated from the military academy as an officer during peacetime; he had won his promotions by sending men to the field rather than by leading them there. Truth to tell, Amet Pale was a poor swordsman, and few knew it better than he.

Although by morning's end, Taylor Ash would certainly discover that fact.

Not that he would live long enough to divulge it.

"Yes, Chaldus calls," Pale grumbled again, as if trying to convince himself. And with that explanation, Emina retired to her chamber. She was not, however, comforted in the least by Amet's old patriotic saw. After twenty-two years, she knew full well that Chaldus called. Indeed, Chaldus called Amet daily—to troop reviews, to government banquets, to matériel contractors' estates, and, Emina suspected, to sweaty, clandestine wrestling matches in more than a few Chaldean bedrooms. Nevertheless, she expected Chaldus to call; all she asked, as she slid back into bed, was that Amet begin to answer less noisily.

A knock at Pale's outer door boosted his spirits considerably. He called for the visitor to enter, and saluted curtly as Captain Harzon stepped inside. Harzon was Pale's personal assistant, the man whom Ash had assaulted the afternoon before. *Assistants*, Pale mused, surveying Harzon's rigid form in the doorway. Assistants would prove to be Taylor Ash's downfall. *Never hire anyone you might possibly want to screw,* was Pale's motto. Because after you did, you'd surely want to get rid of them—and that could prove inconvenient. How cheap, by comparison, the few dresses and baubles that had been Jolah's price. That and, of course, the minister's requited passion, which had proved cheapest of all. An infantryman might live and die by the sword, but a general's subject was human passions. And these, Pale noted smugly, he had studied well.

For instance, the general considered it almost a foregone conclusion that Taylor Ash would come alone to Hawken Heights that morning.

Hawken Heights was, properly speaking, a range of gentle, wooded hills that skirted the River Mirth. When spoken of as a meeting place, however, everyone understood the reference to mean a long, secluded meadow that lay nestled between the southernmost group of hills. Taylor Ash sat cross-legged in the middle of that meadow, his sheathed sword resting across his knees. He had arrived early, hoping to find time for contemplation, but found instead that he'd done rather enough thinking lately. His next thought, Taylor worried, might be his last—the one that drove him over sanity's precipice. Instead, Taylor abandoned his preoccupations with dead ex-ministers and contemptible living ones, with Phrases and geopolitics, assassins and Jolah. He concentrated instead on the way the long grass, blown by a fickle breeze, tickled his knee; on how the dew had soaked through the seat of his pants; and on the cold weight of the blade across his knees.

The sun had just peered over the crest of the Heights when, with typical military punctuality, Amet Pale arrived. Taylor realized that the general had donned his full dress uniform, and he supposed that he should feel flattered. The thought that weighed on Taylor's mind, though, as he watched the general swagger across the meadow, was that his father would not have done things this way. Kermane Ash would have destroyed Amet Pale, but not on the field of battle—the elder Ash had fought with memoranda and innuendo. If you roused his ire, he would merely smile at you . . . but the next week you would discover that you had resigned your position, that your bank accounts were frozen for an audit, that there were irregularities in the deed to your land. Kermane Ash would never seek revenge in a mode so thoroughly antiquated, so absurdly . . . Taylor searched for the proper word—

Sentimental.

Perhaps the only sentimental thing Kermane Ash had done in the last half-century was to visit his son on the way to the Council Tower. And that had cost him his life.

"Minister Ash."

Taylor lifted his eyes to Pale's face, but did not stand. "Minister Pale."

"I presume you feel fit for this morning's exercise."

"Perfectly," Taylor responded. "Have you anything more you wish to say before we engage?"

"Nothing," Pale said with blank finality.

Taylor shrugged and rose to his feet. He slid his blade free into the damp morning air and discarded the scabbard to the side.

"Ah," Pale observed as he drew his own sword, "your father was fond of that blade." As he spoke, he took a first, tentative cut at Taylor. The younger man parried the blow easily, as it was meant to be parried. More of a greeting than an attack. Pale smiled as he resumed a position en garde. "Have you inscribed your own name on it?"

The elder Ash had spent years seeking an ancient, unadorned sword. Once he succeeded, with a typical dynastic flourish, he had inscribed the blade with the names of six generations of paternal Ashes. Nevertheless, Kermane's ironic nature had demanded its due; the last name on the sword read, "Kermane, Prime Minister of Chaldus," the first read "Fleon, Cobbler of Belfar." The gentle curve of the blade belied a century of sharply fluctuating Ash fortunes.

Taylor had not inscribed his name in the ancient steel,

but his only reply to the general took the form of a cut at the man's head. The blades met with a spark, then sprang apart.

"You see," Pale continued, apparently heedless of the blow, "I realized from the first that you would betray us—"

"Betray you?" Taylor repeated incredulously as he parried a thrust by Pale.

"You deliberately disobeyed a Council vote," the older man grunted as he swung again. "What name would you grace that with, save betrayal?"

"I knew what I was doing—"

Smiling, Pale feinted left, then snapped his blade quickly back toward Taylor's sword arm. The blow was easily countered.

"Three centuries of experience sit in that room," Pale went on, "and you think you know better? What induced Aston to elevate you to such a position, I'll never understand."

Furious, Taylor launched himself forward with a vicious downward stroke. It would have cleaved the general's head in two, but Pale seemed ready for it. He slid out of the way with more dexterity than his bulk would suggest, and his sword swung about in a neat riposte. Taylor, off balance, could neither bring his own blade up nor evade the blow entirely. He pulled himself back but felt his arm burn as the tip of Pale's sword sliced through the flesh of his left biceps.

"Just a prick," Pale laughed, savoring Ash's reaction. "Are all the men in Intelligence scared of blood?"

"We see our share," Taylor responded as he stepped back. For the next few moments, he fought purely defensively, trying to settle down and analyze what was going wrong. He had never seen the general so garrulous before, and he doubted that this new volubility was a coincidence. The running patter was intended to upset

Taylor, and it was working well. A disturbed duelist most often wound up a dead one, Taylor knew.

"You see," the general continued, "you should all serve an apprenticeship with the army, in the field. Get used to blood. Watch a few of your friends die. In fact, I highly recommend it. Sacrifices are natural in the service of a noble cause."

Sacrifices like Calador or Kermane Ash, no doubt. But Taylor refused to answer. He concentrated only on the bladework—no more wild thrusts, only a series of sharp, measured blows. Pale was able to fend them off, but with each parry Taylor drew him farther and farther out of position. A sweat had broken across the general's brow and in the fat creases of his neck. As Pale realized that he had failed to unnerve the younger man, he began to yield ground before the steady hail of blows, retreating slowly toward the wooded hills behind them. Each of his parries grew weaker, and Ash realized that, in a moment, he would beat down Pale's guard completely. Despite the canny way he'd drawn first blood, the general had never posed a real threat, and the misgiving struck Taylor that, truly, he was about to commit a cold-blooded murder.

This thought so disturbed him that he failed at first to note the high-pitched whine that rose from the trees before him. He swung a sharp, two-handed blow that made Pale stumble backward in desperation, his own sword jerking upward, leaving a fatal opening. The whine rose in pitch as Taylor prepared himself for the final thrust. An odd sound, he thought. And then something struck him explosively in his temple, and he dropped senseless to the ground.

"A lovely shot. Captain Harzon." the general cried, "although a little late. You were beginning to make me nervous. The young upstart isn't half bad with a blade."

Despite the bravado of his talk, Pale felt himself trembling as he stared at his unconscious enemy. It had been so very close . . . But it was paramount that he compose himself before Harzon came out of the woods and glimpsed the fading terror in Pale's eyes. No, that wouldn't do at all. The general used his sleeve to wipe the sweat from his face while he awaited Harzon's approach. There was a rustling as a figure pushed through some tall shrubs at the meadow's edge.

"I do believe," Pale continued, "that we can dispose of this garbage—" he kicked Ash's shoulder to indicate what he meant—"and still make it back to Prandis in time for a celebratory breakfast. How does that sound, *Major?*"

But Pale's forced glee diminished as he realized that the man who emerged from the woods was not Captain Harzon. Indeed, he was no soldier at all.

"Harzon sleeps," the bald man replied in rasping tones, "as you shall shortly."

"Who are you?" Pale demanded warily, raising his sword. "Was it you who shot the sling?"

Hain's teeth glittered as his smile caught the morning sun. "Indeed it was, my dear general. I've so much wanted to meet you, you see. And we wouldn't want you to get hurt . . . prematurely."

Hain's stone had just darkened to an angry green when he heard the hoofbeats in the distance. At least six, perhaps eight, horses, the assassin guessed, and they would arrive within a minute. The woods had muffled the sound until they were close by.

"And the fun was just beginning," Hain apologized, patting the general's cheek almost tenderly. "You'll forgive me for cutting things short."

"You, there!"

The assassin glanced upward, quickly counting seven horsemen on the far side of the clearing. Hunters, by their dress: men used to traveling quietly through the woods and, more than likely, not carrying those long-bows for show. Mere seconds away at a full gallop, Hain reckoned. It was almost worth disposing of them, just to be allowed the leisure of finishing the masterpiece he had begun making of Amet Pale. But Madh, damn his eyes, kept stressing circumspection.

With a sigh of regret, Hain applied one last, departing stroke of his razor and slipped something between Pale's teeth. Then he rose and sprinted toward the forest.

It was the hunters' uncertainty as to who Hain was and what he was doing that prevented a volley of arrows being loosed at his back. But, by the time Hain's flight signaled that he was up to no good, the assassin had already disappeared into the trees. Four of the riders spurred their horses in pursuit while the remaining trio headed for the two figures that lay unmoving in the tall grass.

A man riding a large roan was the first to arrive, dropping his bow to the ground as he swung out of the saddle.

"No normal duel this," he muttered in horror as he approached the first of the bodies, a middle-aged man in uniform. From a distance, the hunter had supposed that a red net had been laid over the soldier's head, but as he stepped closer, he realized that there was no net at all. Rather, a fine grid of cuts entirely riddled the man's face. A deeper cut ran across his throat.

Appalled, the hunter knelt by the soldier's side and examined the bloody wound. Then he pulled a handkerchief from his pocket and pressed it to the man's neck.

"Well, my friend, you can thank your cook today, for it's your fat that saved your life. Your jugular's been spared." He looked away from Pale's gruesome visage to his two remaining companions, who were still mounted. "Quickly, boys! Don't you see there's another man to be tended here?"

One of the men dismounted and, bringing a waterskin with him, began to wash Taylor's face. After a moment, Taylor groaned and lifted his hand to his head, frankly surprised to find himself alive.

"Thank you," he groaned, pushing away the hunter's hand. "I'll be fine."

Fine was perhaps an overestimate, he realized. He was acutely nauseous and, for some reason, his eyes refused to focus.

"Just what happened here?" his nurse demanded curtly. A hunter, by the looks of him, Taylor thought.

"Happened . . . ? I'd like to know. Where's Pale?"

Taylor turned his head to find a double image of the general's ample frame spread out on the grass. With an effort that sent an acute stab of pain through his head, he struggled to his feet and, supported by one of the hunters, stumbled toward Pale. The twin image of the general's face was doubly horrible.

"Will he live?" Taylor asked weakly.

The hunter at Pale's side looked up, and the worry in his eyes gave Taylor his answer.

"I may have stopped the bleeding, but the issue is in doubt. Our only consolation today may be punishing the scoundrel who did this."

"You saw him?" Taylor asked, his dizziness suddenly receding. Finally, a real lead—

The hunter shrugged. "Not well enough to describe him, save to say he was middling height, middling weight. But four of my party are tracking him on horseback. No doubt, they're dragging him back as we speak."

Taylor sighed. The four men would find themselves in a different type of hunt than they had bargained for. . . .

At that moment, a great retching sound issued from Pale's throat, and the general's body spasmed in pain. The hunter shook his head.

"The bleeding's under control," he began. "There's little else—"

"He's choking!" Taylor cried. "Open his mouth!"

The hunter pried the general's jaws open and slid two fingers into his throat. A moment later, he pulled back his hand and Pale's convulsion subsided. The general's body slackened, and his breathing eased as he lay in the bright sun of the meadow.

The hunter opened his hand for all to see.

A newly minted capital.

"So much for your plans." Hain laughed. flushed with success and veridine. He propped his boots up on the cheap hotel bed and locked his hands behind his neck. "The old pig was already up and in his carriage by the time I reached his estate."

Madh frowned. "I don't like this. Pale seldom varies his morning schedule."

"Relax," Hain sneered. "As I told you, I got the Phrase and left the old fart belly up in the woods."

"What *exactly* happened?" Madh asked, not for the first time. Getting information from Hain, rather than mere self-congratulations, was always a trying experience. He pushed his chair farther into the shadows and closed his eyes.

"A duel," Hain laughed. "An affair of honor. Except our conniving general isn't much on honor, it seems. He had left one of his men in the woods with a sling, just in case the duel took a turn for the worse. Good thing for that sling. Pale's an awful swordsman. He would have been killed before I could get to him."

"Who would Pale be fighting?" Madh mused, concerned. "Describe his opponent."

Hain sighed. He'd had his fill of Madh's tiresome questions. But he knew the smaller man well enough by now to know that Madh would not leave him alone until he had the answers he wanted.

"About my height, I suppose. Jet black hair, athletic build. Good looker—one of those aristocratic old Prandis families, I guess. Interesting sword, too—lots of names written on it. I should have taken it," the assassin added after a moment, with a twinge of regret.

As Hain completed the description, Madh rose to his feet in horror. "You fool!" he hissed as he grabbed Hain by the collar and jerked the assassin from his chair. Hain responded instantly, swinging his right fist inward to Madh's abdomen, but the older man caught the assassin's wrist in midblow. Hain hadn't suspected such strength.

"Do you know who Pale was fighting?" Madh asked quietly, each syllable short, clipped with disgust. Madh's furious face was but a hair's breadth away from Hain's own, and the assassin was overwhelmed by the sour smell of the seeds which Madh habitually chewed. "You've just described Taylor Ash, the current Minister of Intelligence. Idiot! Our only remaining Phrase is the one carried by Intelligence—you had Ash under your very nose and you let him get away. We could be well on the road to Thyrsus right now."

Hain allowed himself to relax, and a grin spread slowly across his face. Madh was not the first employer of his to become presumptuous. The best reply, Hain had found, was always the blunt one.

"I'll remind you, foreigner, that I'm but paid to kill them. It's your job to find the victims. Or am I to murder all of Chaldus and leave you to sort through the bodies for the few you seek?"

Madh released Hain's wrist and pushed him back into his seat. Much as Madh hated to admit it, the assassin was right.

"Where is Aston, anyway?" Hain continued, pressing what he saw was a winning point. "You had vowed to find him days ago."

Madh's dark features twisted with frustration. "By all appearances, the man has vanished from the face of the earth."

"No one simply vanishes. Where have you looked for him?"

"Looked?" Madh laughed bitterly. "I look where few can see."

Hain shifted uncomfortably in his seat. He hated his employer's habit of ominous and cryptic pronouncements.

"Speak in a language I understand, damn you."

Madh swept his long black hair away from his brow and looked deep into Hain's eyes. They were glassy with veridine.

"Would you like to see where I've looked?" Madh asked. "Perhaps it is well that I try again."

Madh pulled his pack out from its place beneath the inn's old bed and reached deep inside it. Momentarily, he withdrew a shallow bowl and a small box, both fashioned of a reddish-brown wood.

"Fetch the ewer," he rasped.

Reluctantly, Hain brought the pitcher of water that rested on the nightstand. Madh half-filled the bowl and put the pitcher aside. Then, with great care, he opened the box's brass latch and lifted the top. The interior was lined with black velvet, against which it was difficult to discern the dark object inside. Hain leaned closer and made out a wooden sphere about the size of a walnut, from which sprouted an innumerable cluster of needle-sharp, woody spikes.

"What is it?" Hain asked, almost against his will. The less he knew about Madh's arcane dealings, the happier he was.

Madh looked up for a moment, his dark eyes suffused with a deadly fire. "It is called kahanes root, though it is a root like no other. The kahanes is a black and twisted tree found only in the fens north of Bismet Bay. The kahanes is shorter than the other trees of the swamp, so the light of the sun does not touch it. Instead, it must draw its sustenance from the ground. These nodules form on the roots, just beneath the surface of the mud. The spines contain a poison of extreme potency. Paralysis comes instantly, but death follows slowly and quite painfully. The corpses provide the trees with their nutrition."

"Charming," Hain replied in an attempted jaunty manner, trying to regain his composure. "What do you want with such a thing?"

Madh pressed his thin lips together in a mirthless smile. Without a word, he upended the box and let the kahanes root fall onto his outstretched palm.

"What—" Hain cried, jumping backward. In the better light, he could see the sticky, poisoned tips of the spines resting lightly against the callused skin of Madh's palm. The needles' weight formed tiny depressions where they met his hand, but they did not break the skin. "Don't jest," Hain continued. "You can kill yourself for all I care, but not until I've been paid for my services."

"Kill myself?" Madh repeated, amused. "No, surely not that."

And his hand snapped closed around the deadly root. Hain stepped forward, but it was too late to intervene. Instead, the awful deed done, the assassin relaxed and began to study his employer with clinical interest. Death was a field in which Hain often strode, but there was always something new to learn. He watched with curiosity as Madh's body convulsed and, just as suddenly, turned rigid. The muscles of the older man's jaws bunched together and a long, tortured breath escaped him.

Slowly, blood crept along the contours of Madh's hand, gathering at the bottom of his fist and dripping into the bowl.

Hain looked around, wondering how to proceed. Madh's death did not in itself bother him—he had never liked the small, mysterious foreigner—but there was a substantial portion of his fee which remained to be paid, and Madh had long ago assured him that a trip to Thyrsus was the condition of payment. If Madh died now, Hain would lose a small fortune.

The assassin knew a few doctors in Prandis, but none who could treat a poison found only halfway across the continent. Perhaps a wizard. . . .

A strange, choked sound tore its way through Madh's throat. A death rattle. Neither doctor nor mage could save him now.

But the sound persisted far longer than any death rattle Hain had heard before, and the bald assassin had conducted a veritable symphony of them. With time, the throaty rasp became more intelligible, and Hain realized that this was no death rattle at all.

Madh was speaking.

If it was speech, though, it resembled no language that Hain had ever heard. Held rapt by the impossible sight, he watched the knotted muscles of Madh's jaw slowly relax. The small man's eyes fluttered and opened, but they focused on nothing. Each word was now distinct and loud, but no more familiar than ever. Madh's head slowly bent forward, facing the bowl on the floor.

Only a few drops of blood had fallen, but they spread quickly across the surface, seeming to infect the pure water around them. In moments, the contents of the bowl had turned a deep crimson. As Madh continued his tortured chant, bubbles began forming deep in the bowl, agitating the liquid as they rose. Soon, the entire surface was roiling and the fluid threatened to splash over the edge.

Finally, Madh pronounced two words that Hain recognized: Barr Aston. The tumultuous liquid instantly subsided into a dark, placid sheet. "Barr Aston!" Madh repeated vehemently, but nothing happened. The man's shoulders slumped, and his eyes returned to their normal, piercing glance.

"You see," he said, sounding entirely natural again, "the old man is protected. Somehow, he has shielded himself from my inquiries."

Hain found himself suppressing a shudder. First there had been Tarem Selod, now Madh. . . . When Hain watched a man die, he was accustomed to his remaining that way. Madh's casual ease was entirely unnerving, and Hain concluded that it would be best to avoid making himself the target of Madh's "inquiries."

On the other hand, Barr Aston had somehow frustrated Madh's mysterious efforts.

"I thought Aston was the Minister of Intelligence," Hain said, "not a mage."

"He is no mage," Madh agreed, as his hand slowly unclenched and he let the kahanes root fall back into its box, "but he must have an ally who is powerful indeed. This scrying spell is a costly one and not easily frustrated. But Aston is a wily old fiend and not to be found without labor. It would have been far simpler to have taken Ash this morning, while no one suspected."

"Perhaps it's easier still. Ash—where is he now?"

"It little matters," Madh responded. "Assuming you did not kill him with the sling, he woke up beside his dead colleague. Until today, we have hunted only the retired ministers. Now that we have taken an active one, the full resources of Chaldus will be mustered in the Council's defense. I will be surprised if the entire National Arcane Authority is not marshaled to protect them." Madh paused, frowning. "I fear I have miscalculated. Having tipped our hand to the Council, they will put themselves safely out of reach. No matter how difficult, we must now find Aston."

"And how do you propose to do that?"

"Tomorrow morning," Madh replied, "I shall make inquiries of a more direct nature."

Had Madh bothered to focus his mystical ener•gies on Taylor Ash, he would not have found the minister holed up in some Council stronghold, surrounded by soldiers and mages, but hunched low over the neck of Scry. Taylor had waited at Hawken Heights only long enough to discover that Amet Pale would regain consciousness no time soon. He would live, it seemed, but the extent of his recovery was uncertain. Taylor rather doubted that a man could survive such torture with his mind intact.

In an odd sense, Taylor felt cheated. He had been on the verge of exacting his own vengeance from Amet Pale, but the assassin had beaten him to it. Now more than ever, Taylor felt that he and the killer were rivals of a sort, racing against one another toward the same goal. It was a race that Taylor desperately needed to win, but his conviction was growing that he'd given his opponent a dangerous head start.

On the other hand, the attack on Pale told Taylor a lot. First, it meant that Duke Calador had escaped not only Pale's men but the mysterious assassin as well. Second, it indicated that, rather than follow Calador, the assassin had opted to switch his strategy and attack a sitting minister. That in itself entailed several conclusions. Interestingly, it hinted that the enemy's resources were limited, too concentrated in Prandis to track the duke into the countryside—or that a pressing time schedule forbade a lengthy chase. Moreover, and more ominously, it suggested to Taylor that the assassin's mis-

sion was complete, or almost so. Attacking Pale was sure
to rouse the entire force of the Council; that was something the enemy would probably avoid until the last moment.

As Scry pounded over a small wooden bridge into a
quiet Prandis suburb, Taylor tried to ignore the pounding
in his head as he worked the arithmetic for the hundredth
time. Ell, Loft, and his father were dead, and they represented half the total. Pale, though a possible survivor,
had certainly surrendered his Phrase. The assassin would
hardly have crammed a coin down his throat if he had
been waiting for Pale to speak. That made four. Tarem
Selod, at least, remained a mystery. Taylor's agents outside the house had been attacked, and that indicated an
attempt on the old mage. On the other hand, no bodies
had been found—either Selod's or an assassin's. It was
possible that Selod had simply not been home, although
Taylor's agents swore to the contrary. Yet, if the old
wizard had been there, why the broken pattern? Why no
bodies? Lacking an obvious solution, Taylor had little
choice but to assume the worst.

The final element in Taylor's calculus was Barr Aston, his old, dear mentor. Aston, wise in the ways only
an old spy could be, had evaded Intelligence's best efforts to find him. And if he could disappear that thoroughly, perhaps he would be able to frustrate the
assassin as well. Throughout these nervous weeks, Taylor had cherished the hope that Aston would remain their
final safeguard, that no matter how many other ministers
were killed, Aston would remain free.

Now, however, Taylor's heart sank under the possibility that Barr Aston was dead. How else to explain that
the assassin had tortured Amet Pale for his Phrase without so much as touching Taylor? After all, if Aston
couldn't be found, Taylor knew very well that he was
the next target. And there he'd been, lying on the grass

next to Pale, a convenient double feature for the killer's bloody work . . . yet he was unharmed.

No, Barr Aston must be dead.

Taylor harbored a single possibility, no matter how unlikely it might prove. Perhaps that group of hunters had disturbed the assassin just as he had finished with Pale, before he could begin to torture Taylor. Only that explanation would leave both Taylor and Aston alive, but Taylor was wary of indulging such unwarranted optimism. Barr Aston would have railed at him, he thought dourly. How many times had the old man lectured him about the dangers of optimism and overconfidence? To indulge either was to become sloppy, to assume facts where it was the job of Intelligence simply to procure them. Hope for the best, Aston had taught, but always calculate the odds honestly.

And so Taylor calculated. At best, two ministers remained beyond the enemy's grasp—and as long as even one Phrase was missing, all the rest were worthless.

On the other hand, even as Taylor drew Scry off onto an ill-marked dirt path and thundered through the densely clustered trees, he considered that the assassin might be riding off as well, secure in the possession of all the Phrases. And if that were true, the entire world would be shattered by the consequences.

Which left Taylor only one option.

The narrow path opened into a small clearing, toward the rear of which was an old cottage. An idyllic, isolated location—the perfect antidote to the intricacy of its owner's job.

Taylor pulled Scry up short before the front door and vaulted to the ground. Before he could seize the brightly polished knocker, however, the door was opened. Clad in a robe and slippers but holding a wicked sword, a small, blond-haired man stepped out of the cottage. A pair of sparkling green eyes settled instantly on the welt on Taylor's forehead.

"What happened to you?" Jin Annard asked quietly.

Taylor chose to ignore the question.

"Sorry to bother you in the morning, Jin, but shouldn't you be dressed by now, anyway?"

The Underminister of Intelligence shrugged. "Elena Imbress showed up more than an hour ago and all but dragged me out of bed. She was too anxious to start complaining to let me get dressed. I had just about calmed her down, and I was hoping to get some clothes on and eat breakfast, but now you show up. I suppose that will only get her started again."

"Damned right it will."

Taylor looked up to find a furious Elena Imbress standing in the shadows behind the doorway. The anger in her eyes wavered, though, as she saw the purple bruise on Taylor's temple.

"What happened to you?" she asked.

"He's avoiding that question," Annard explained.

"Ah," Imbress replied, nodding as if that were a sufficient answer.

"So I suppose," Annard went on, "that we'll never find out whether he killed our rust-for-brains Minister of War."

Annard regretted his tone as he watched a troubled cloud pass over Taylor's face.

"I would have killed him," Taylor sighed, leaning his head back against the doorpost. "That in itself was probably a poor idea—"

"A greater favor to the nation could hardly be done," Jin said in a softer tone.

"Perhaps." Taylor was in no mood to argue the point. "But how on earth do you know that I met Pale for a duel?"

"I *am* the underminister of the finest Intelligence network on this continent," Jin replied, mock-offended. "Although, considering the way you stormed into Pale's office yesterday, secrecy couldn't have been uppermost in your mind."

That almost brought a grin to Taylor's lips. "Well, in case you didn't get the full report of those events, you should know that Jolah is on Pale's payroll—not to mention his desk. Don't let her back into the office under any circumstances. If she wants to collect her personal belongings, *you* do it and send her the stuff."

At this news, Imbress slipped past Annard onto the lawn. There was a dangerous look in her eyes. "If you think she's a security risk . . . well, departmental policy on that is clear from the day we sign up. She should know what to expect."

Taylor sighed and shook his head. "Whatever damage she could do is done already. Leave her alone—we have more pressing problems. You see, I didn't get to Pale."

For the first time that morning, Annard's brow creased with confusion.

"The assassin did," Taylor concluded.

"Oh my lord . . . ," Annard muttered slowly as his mind ran through the list. "Pale could be the last one."

"Precisely. So we all have a lot of work to do, and quickly. Here's your part. First, get everyone in the area looking for Aston. If he's still alive, it's essential that we find him before the assassin does—or find his corpse if not. We have to know what they've got and what they need."

"And if we find him . . . ?" Annard asked slowly.

"The policy is the same," Taylor ordered firmly. "We're not murdering old men, not under any circumstances. No, if you find Aston, put him under the care of Orbis Thale. Let Thale hide him in the deepest dungeon of the NAA, just so long as he keeps him safe."

Imbress snorted and shot Taylor a sour look. "In Aston's place, I'd rather be killed, I think."

"Look, Elena, Thale may not be the most congenial host in Chaldus, but he's the best insurance I know. It's important that we secure his cooperation. The NAA is the only independent source of power that can rival the army—and we know what the army will do if they find any of the ex-ministers."

"If they fumble the way they did with Calador," Imbress muttered, "we needn't worry a whit. The only thing Amet Pale accomplished up north was the early payment of widow's benefits."

Taylor frowned. "There have been a lot of fumblers in this business, ourselves included. That's got to stop. For instance, Elena, unless you've got Brandt Karrelian inside there . . . ?"

Imbress's mouth twisted with distaste. "I lay the blame at your feet. What in the world were you thinking when you got Karrelian involved in this? The man is a chauvinistic, irresponsible, uncooperative, egocentric mess." Elena's voice had risen to a bellow, and the look in her eyes was turning murderous. "And I can tell you right now that he won't help a bit in locating the assassin. I doubt he could locate his boots if his butler didn't lay them out for him—"

Even for Imbress, such a fit of pique was uncharacteristic. While Elena continued her tirade, Taylor shot Annard a questioning glance.

"He led her to a brothel this morning," Annard volunteered in a very low voice. It had not been low enough, however, to avoid drawing a glare from Imbress. This was fortunate for Taylor, because it gave him time to erase his smile.

"Elena," Taylor said, "given these current developments, you can forget about Karrelian. Even had he been willing to help, it's too late now. The assassin may already have finished his mission. I want you personally to supervise the hunt for Aston. I've got a couple of new ideas about where he might be, assuming he's alive, and I'd like you to start checking on them immediately. Stick with that unless you get some information on the assassin himself. If you do, you're the field agent I want out there. Track the bastard down, wherever he goes, whatever it takes."

Imbress nodded, and she flicked a quick smile of gratitude at her director. Annard, however, took no comfort from Taylor's instructions. He was beginning to suspect where all this was headed.

"Sounds to me," he said suspiciously, "like you're preparing us for an awful lot of contingencies. Now why would that be?"

Taylor turned toward the small blond man and shrugged. "I still can't sneak anything by you, can I, Jin?"

"If you could, I wouldn't deserve my job."

"Speaking of which," Taylor continued, "I have some instructions for you, too. I want more of our resources concentrated on Yndor. Parth Naidjur has been killed in a duel . . . so Chaldean Phrase-keepers aren't the only ones meeting misfortune these days. Perhaps that's coincidence, but I'm not willing to bet on it. Keep heavy surveillance on the other parths and on the palace. Blow the budget on it if you have to, but we need to know what's happening to our counterparts."

"And where will you be," Annard asked as he glanced anxiously at the full saddlebags balanced on Scry's haunches, "while we're busy carrying out these directives?"

"I'll be where I can do the most good," Taylor told them softly. "I'm going back to the field."

CHAPTER 12

Loriale lay awake, watching the morning sun creep silently through the curtains and suffuse the room with a gentle, misty light. She felt Brandt stir next to her, but she lay quietly a moment longer, not wanting to disturb him. He had slept only two hours. Let him awaken just a little more.

Morning was a propitious time to embark upon the tender endeavors at which she excelled. Most men took their time in awakening, and Loriale could use those blurry moments of half-consciousness to her advantage. But Brandt did not awaken like most men. Instead of returning slowly to consciousness, his eyes snapped open and he swiveled out of bed, neatly disengaging himself from Loriale's embrace. She fluttered her eyelids and yawned delicately, moistening her lips, but the artifice was lost on Brandt, who strode immediately to the window. He was about to push aside the curtain when, abruptly, he paused. His fingers hovered over the sheer white fabric, twitching indecisively.

"We can try again, you know," Loriale suggested

mildly, although she realized that she had lost his attention already.

"I have to go," Brandt replied hoarsely. He paused for a moment more at the window, then snatched his hand away as if he were afraid of what he might see. Or as if he already knew.

Loriale arched her back provocatively and forced herself to smile.

"You were tired last night, but a few hours' sleep can do wonders." She reached out a finger and lightly stroked his stomach. "I'd really like to," she added, a bit too urgently.

But Brandt merely began pulling on his clothes as if he were the only one in the room. Loriale feared the consequences when a report of the night's futile efforts reached Silene. Brandt had not exactly been pleasant after his failure, and Loriale had no doubt that he would complain to the madam. It was always, Loriale reflected wryly, the woman's fault.

Just so long as the customer was a man.

With one hand on the doorknob, Brandt suddenly turned around, his gray eyes locking onto Loriale's across the dim room. Reflexively, she pulled the sheet over her bosom, somehow frightened by his expression.

"Do you like what you do?" he asked abruptly, and then added, as if specificity were crucial, "Being a whore?"

Loriale blinked, surprised by the question. Could he possibly mean *last night* . . . ? But that would be the height of arrogance, if he expected compliments now.

"Everyone assumes that whoring is . . . an act of necessity," Brandt went on. "That you only do it until you earn enough to start over, find a husband, become respectable. . . ."

Respectable. How oddly he pronounced that word. Loriale pulled the sheet up to her neck, amazed at how this man could pile cruelties one upon the next.

"Do you like whoring?" he repeated, his voice insistent.

To hell with him, Loriale thought. And to hell with Silene, if he went complaining to the old hag. Silene could make her life only so miserable. There were other madams, other cathouses in Prandis than this one. And give or take the size of their purse, the men were all the same.

"No," she said softly, but firmly, her voice rasping through the chill morning air. "No, I don't like it at all."

Brandt's eyebrows rose a fraction of an inch, but Loriale could not guess what the expression meant.

"You may find you miss it some day," he said, "impossible as that seems. Not because you like it now, or will like it one day, or will like even the memory of what you've done. But because we miss things after we've done them so long that nothing else seems possible."

With that, he left.

Loriale watched the door slam, felt her red hair flutter in the breeze of its closing. And then she lay back down, burying her head beneath a pillow, and speculated bitterly about the money that Brandt must possess, despite his plain clothes and brusque manner, that allowed him to breeze from the room while she was left to spend a few more sleepless hours alone between the sheets.

Brandt left the familiar hallway of the front bedrooms and threaded his way through a series of narrow corridors that led to the back of the building. People in Brandt's profession quickly developed an architectural sense that allowed them to visualize the relations of interior rooms to the walls outside. For a thief, this skill was often the difference between riches and prison bars.

Back so easily, he thought, to the wagon ruts in the old road. And it felt better, somehow, than wasting his days in a mansion, fussing over reports. Better, yet still not right.

He opened a door to a small storeroom that held linens, soaps, and sundry items indispensable to the pursuit of Silene's particular commerce, and walked to the small window in back. No one was in sight. The window slid open almost noiselessly, and Brandt lowered himself out. It had been years since the last time he had been forced to sneak out of a woman's house, and even longer since he'd had to escape the scene of a crime, so Brandt negotiated the rough, brownstone wall with care. Even so, his fingertips remembered how to seek cracks in the stone, his limbs remembered the intricacies of leverage, and it took only a few seconds for Brandt to descend to the garden below. He paused amidst the azaleas and rhododendrons, pondering his choices.

Somehow, he suspected that Elena Imbress remained waiting for him on the front lawn, as rigid as a statue. Imbress, he knew, lay in some indefinable way at the root of his growing ill temper. She was so openly contemptuous of him, either as a thief or as an industrialist. And the problem, Brandt suspected, was that he somehow shared her opinion. However this assassination business concluded, he felt he could not simply go back to a cloistered life in his mansion. Nor could he return to his days of espionage. The act of uncovering secrets remained engaging, but the secrets themselves. . . . There were enough files, enough iniquities, entombed in his basement.

Brandt sighed and cast a mournful glance at the stables. It would be impossible to retrieve his horse without alerting Imbress that he'd risen, if indeed she was still there, so he left the animal as a present for Silene and silently slipped into the arbor behind the mansion. It was at least ten miles to his estate, and that might take the better part of three hours by foot. But Brandt was in no hurry, just so long as he walked alone.

Bent over the large. tin laundry tub. Masya hummed a tune her mother had taught her while she scrubbed people's clothes. Through the thin cotton of her dress, Carn could watch the play of her muscles as she worked, admire the tense column of her neck beneath her pinned-up mass of brown hair. Let Aston's house wait, he thought, at least for a while. Quietly, he eased across the room until he stood only inches behind her, the scent of detergent and the henna in her hair mingling pleasantly. Suddenly, he shot his arms around her, catching her in a tremendous hug.

Masya cried out and thrashed for a moment, water sloshing over the rim of the tub onto the countertop and across her dress. Then she recognized the large hairy hands that were clasped around her middle, and twisted about in Carn's embrace.

He leaned over to kiss her, but received only a perfunctory peck for his efforts. Instead, Masya placed both hands on his chest and pushed him firmly backward.

"I told you not to bother me while I'm working," she chided, frowning at the sudsy trail that climbed from her fingers to her elbows. "Look at me."

With a sharp glance at Carn, she snatched a towel and patted the wet spot that stretched across her belly.

"No hope," she muttered, tossing the towel onto the countertop. "I'll have to change."

Carn smiled and shrugged. "Sorry, but I couldn't help myself. You looked irresistible."

She snatched up the towel again, this time to throw it at him.

"Liar! And what are you doing here at dawn's first light, anyway?"

Carn caught the towel, folded it neatly, and put it aside. "I have some chores in the city today, and they brought me near your house."

"And what kind of chores are they, that they have you looking like a cat with a belly full of sparrows?"

Carn laughed. He supposed he did look odd, excited as he was about the venture at hand. But he couldn't very well tell Masya that the morning's "chore" was breaking into another man's house. .

Instead, he told Masya that some of Brandt's old foes in the government were making trouble for him again. He had never told Masya exactly what he and Brandt had once done for a living, but she had a general sense that their history was less than reputable.

"And why," she asked, a suspicious edge to her voice, "would trouble put a grin on your face?"

"It's a healthy kick in the ass," he replied, wincing at the look she gave him for his language. "It's got Brandt looking like I haven't seen him for years—like he's got something to do besides watch his bank accounts grow. This is when you should meet him, Masya, when he's his old self. Why not come to the house tonight—"

"Not unless you've got laundry to do," she snapped.

Carn shook his head and grabbed the woman by the shoulders, locking their eyes together. If only his words, he thought, possessed the strength of his hands. . . .

"Just for a few minutes," he pleaded. "I'll introduce you to Brandt, and then we can leave, go to the theater. There's a chorus from Belfar in town."

"Cheat," she accused, slapping him playfully on the arm. She had a fondness for choral music that Carn was just now learning to exploit. But the newspapers said this Belfarian group was excellent.

"It would mean the world to me," Carn said, his voice

a low, seductive rumble, "to have the two people I love under the same roof . . . even for five minutes."

And how was she supposed to resist a request like that . . . or the silent appeal of his eyes? Masya craned her neck around and glanced wistfully at the laundry tub, thinking that she had nothing to wear.

"I'll never have my work done in time," she complained.

Carn's face lit up. "Then you'll come? Wonderful!"

He snatched her up in another of his enormous hugs, feeling a cool spot grow across his belly where her wet dress was pressed against him.

He put her down and grinned. "And now we should get you out of that dress before you catch cold."

But, before he knew where she'd found it, there was a wooden spoon in Masya's hand—and it was moving with speed toward his rump.

"Out!" she cried, gratified by his yelp when she made contact. "I have work to do."

"But you'll be there tonight?"

"Out!" she repeated, striking again with the spoon, laughing now as she chased him toward the door.

"I'll send a carriage for you," Carn called, fending off the spoon as he ducked outside into the dawnlit morning. "Until tonight!"

Barr Aston's residence was an unpretentious townhouse not far from Council Tower. It was the sort of house, Carn decided, that you could walk past every day for years without looking at it twice. Across the street, the onetime thief paused at a smoke shop that had not yet opened. He walked back and forth by the window, feigning interest in the wares. Pipes and tobacco, however, were less on his mind than the more elusive smoke that the old minister had used to obscure his trail.

In the darkened plate glass of the tobacconist, Carn

was able to survey the entire reflected street behind him. A few people hurried by, on their way to unlock their offices and begin another routine day's search for profit. No one seemed interested in the quiet, brown brick facade that was the home of Barr Aston. Carn wheeled leisurely away from the tobacconist and crossed the street toward a bookseller, looking up as if to ascertain the mood of the feathery clouds above. When he looked down again, he was satisfied that it would not rain, and satisfied as well that there were no unwelcome observers lurking behind the windows of the apartments nearby. Apparently, when Aston disappeared, the government had decided it would be too costly to maintain surveillance on the house. Carn smiled, falling back with leisurely comfort into long-abandoned habits as he considered the government's folly. False economy had always been the chief ally of a thief.

With two quick bounds, Carn sprang up the small flight of steps that led to Aston's door. His broad frame and loose overcoat blocked any possible view from the street as he slid two slender metal probes into the lock and began to maneuver them against the pins. It had been some time since Carn had last practiced such tricks, and as he expected, the retired intelligence chief had bought a lock of exceptional quality. For several long moments, Carn continued to manipulate his tiny calipers, beginning to flush at the cheeks and neck. Before long, he realized, his atrophied skills would grow from a simple embarrassment to a certain danger.

Suddenly, he felt the well-oiled cylinder rotate and, rapidly twisting the handle, Carn let himself inside. Working with Brandt over the course of so many years, Carn had seen the interiors of dozens of politicians' houses, and if this one surprised him, it was by its simplicity. The rooms abounded in the niceties one would expect from a man of high rank—the polished parquet floors, crystal chandeliers, rich brocade curtains, mahogany wainscoting—but Aston's furnishings manifested a simplicity that bespoke more spartan habits. Nothing called attention to itself. Indeed, everything seemed as old as Aston: simple, serviceable, faithful. Carn glided smoothly through the first floor, quietly absorbing the details.

Small framed portraits of friends and relatives, geological oddities that the minister's voracious curiosity had latched upon in foreign climes, souvenirs of state, candlesticks (Aston, it seemed, eschewed electricity), vases holding long-dead flowers: Carn examined everything for some clue to Aston's character, for something that would lead to the man. But for all that the minister's personal effects spoke of an old age that had not forgotten the better days of youth, Carn learned nothing crucial.

After thoroughly canvassing the first floor, he began to grow discouraged. Brandt would probably return from Calador early that morning, and Carn was anxious to greet his friend with good news. It was a simple task Brandt had given him: find me an old man. If Carn could no longer accomplish even that much. . . .

After a few moments more, Carn ascended the stairs, hoping to discover something useful in the rooms that never failed to reveal character: the bedroom and study. If Aston's bedroom spoke of the old man's character, though, it said nothing that Carn had not learned before. A small, exceptionally firm bed occupied the center of the room, flanked on one side by a nightstand and on the other by a wardrobe. Carn opened the latter and found it filled with clothes, most of them the unassuming gray and brown suits that formed the uniform of a typical civil servant. It had been years since Aston had worn some of those suits, and the wardrobe exhaled a smell of disuse that reminded Carn of his grandparents, long dead. He should return to Belfar, he thought, chiding himself. Visit their graves . . .

Carn sighed and looked again at the wardrobe.

Wherever Aston had gone, he certainly hadn't seen the need for a change of clothing. By the looks of the wardrobe, very little had been taken. On the bottom shelf, Carn found a shoe rack, filled with pair after pair of respectable office shoes—brown, black, oxblood. Strangely, each slot in the rack was occupied. Either the minister had fled barefoot or he had shod himself from a different supply. Either way, the bedroom told Carn nothing about Aston's present whereabouts, and that was the only question that mattered.

Aston's study was found through a door that communicated with the bedroom. The large desk was unnaturally empty, and a quick glance at the fireplace told Carn why: the minister, before leaving, had reduced years of personal correspondence to ash. A thorough man, Carn decided, and perhaps too skilled for a simple thief to find, after all. But, Carn reminded himself, he was no simple thief. He and Brandt had pried secrets out of hiding places so dark and remote that even their possessors had forgotten them. He had never failed Brandt, and this was no time to begin. So he turned toward the two walls that contained Aston's books. In the course of his long lifetime, Aston had read hundreds of volumes. Carn prayed that, in the books, he could read the man.

One column of shelves held poetry and drama. Whether Aston preferred comedy to tragedy, or the epic to the ode, Carn considered beside the point. Instead, he focused his attention on the surrounding shelves that contained histories, both political and cultural. These were to be expected from a man in Aston's position. The books were categorized according to geographical location and, within those locations, by chronology. The whole history of the world stood before the old thief, and truly, he seemed to have all the world in which to search.

Dispirited, Carn studied the remaining rows of shelves

and found treatises on natural science, magic, and an exhaustive collection of all the research that had recently been done on electricity. Odd, Carn thought, that a man who read so thoroughly about it should eschew its use.

As he turned to leave, his eye alit on a series of histories that comprised the annals of Prandis itself. This was not mere chance, Carn realized; rather, three full shelves had been devoted to the city's record. The subject seemed to be of particular interest to Aston. One group of these books appeared older, more worn than the rest, and Carn gave them closer scrutiny.

The Excavations of the Atahr Vin, Carn read. *A Record of the Khrine in Eastern Chaldus. The Revised Khrine-Chaldean Dictionary.*

It had been years since Carn had given any real thought to the Khrine, a race long-disappeared from the face of the world. They had withered in the days after the Binding, when their magic and that of the whole world had been diminished to its present state. The old days of high sorcery had witnessed the destruction of much that civilization held dear, but in fashioning a Binding, much else had been destroyed as well. All the creatures that had depended on the liberal flow of Chaldus's arcane energies had degenerated, fled from the sight of man, died away.

The Khrine were such a race. Always they had held themselves aloof from man, whom they so much resembled. While man lived in cities above ground, the rare and long-lived Khrine built intricate underground dwellings, well suited to their isolated habits. Such a place was the Atahr Vin, not fifteen miles from the outskirts of Prandis. It had been discovered by archaeologists from the university seventy years ago, quite by accident. The discovery, however, proved to be only the first of many accidents. Two of the scholars had been killed by clever traps during their first day of exploration, but this had not discouraged the others. Instead, the traps seemed to convince everyone that fabulous treasures waited to be found. Huge crowds gathered outside the entrance to the ruins, awaiting the discovery of mountains of gold and jewels. After another day, however, the crowds went home disappointed. Rather than wonders of intricate workmanship, what the scholars found was a series of cold, forbidding chambers, empty both of treasure and life.

Curiosity blossoming, Carn began to remove all the books related to the Khrine. Opening the dictionary, he found a name elaborately inked on the flyleaf: Wegman Aston.

The minister's father?

A slight rustling reached Carn's ears, and not one that he attributed to the pages in his hand. Softly, he laid the book on a nearby table and, loosening in its sheath a long dirk that nestled inside his overcoat, the old thief slipped from the library. He had never checked the rest of the second floor, he realized—a mistake compounded by spending too long in one room.

Aside from a bathroom, all the remaining chambers were spare bedrooms, three in all. Each was simply furnished and, by all appearances, long unused. Certainly, each was now empty and quiet.

Carn sighed. Good thing they had retired, he thought, if he had become so skittish by the age of fifty. Between good sense and an obscene amount of ready cash, there had been no obvious reason to keep working. Carn smiled almost nostalgically. No sum had been enough to convince Marwick to abandon the trade, he remembered. He wondered if that mercurial joker was still in business—

Business, indeed. That was the order of the day, and the big thief chided himself for such useless reminiscence. Returning to the library, he began to examine the two dozen books on the Khrine, one at a time. Each bore the name of Aston's father on the flyleaf.

Except that one bore it on the cover. With a thrill of discovery, Carn realized that Wegman Aston had been one of the three authors of *The Excavations of the Atahr Vin.* The elder Aston, it seemed, had been a member of the archaeological team that had found the place. Carn made a quick calculation: Barr Aston had been a boy during the weeks his father had worked in the empty Khrine caverns. Perhaps the boy had come to know them well.

With a grim smile of satisfaction, Carn grew certain that he had discovered Aston's secret. If the old man had sought refuge in the Atahr Vin, it was no wonder that he had spurned his office shoes.

Carn slipped *The Excavations of the Atahr Vin* beneath his coat and replaced the others on the shelves. The book he'd taken was slim, and its absence left no conspicuous gap between its old neighbors. A moment's scrutiny assured Carn that, with the exception of the stolen volume, he was leaving Aston's home exactly as he had entered it. Barr Aston, Brandt, and Masya all under one roof tonight: this day promised to exceed all his expectations. Whistling like a schoolboy, he skipped lightly down the steps into the brisk April morning.

Riding back toward the mansion, Carn found it difficult to suppress what he guessed was a very undignified-looking grin. The grin arose not merely from his sense of having located Aston, although that was part of it. Nor was it the feeling that, once again, he and Brandt were about to become players in a game of national scope. He had abandoned that years ago, when Brandt and he had made the decision to leave the business of espionage and, truth to tell, Carn did not miss it. What he did miss was the shared sense of purpose that used to suffuse Brandt and himself when they were working. For a decade now, life had been too easy and, in some perverse way that Carn could not fathom, the ease of Brandt's life and his enjoyment of it existed in an inverse proportion.

Carn could remember his first encounter with Brandt, more than two decades ago. Brandt and his irreverent partner Marwick, neither more than fifteen years old, had burglarized a home that Carn had been casing for a week. Carn had thought to teach the two youths a lesson, but had found himself liking them instead. Liking Marwick had never been hard—that red-haired joker lived for fun. And, back then, Brandt had been full of a certain intense exuberance, the high spirits of a young man who felt that no challenge was too great for his skills.

Carn sighed. In one way, it was too bad that no challenge ever had proven too great. Brandt always had seemed happiest when struggling, when pushed to the edge of his abilities. That had not happened for more than a decade and, in that time, Brandt had slipped into a quiet, impenetrable depression.

But a challenge had risen anew, Carn reminded himself as he patted the book in his jacket and ran up the front steps of the mansion two at a time. There was a mystery afoot, and it led to the Atahr Vin. Carn could not have planned a more promising development.

"Brandt!" he called as he burst through the mansion's double doors.

But the only answer was a maid looking up and shaking her head. Brandt had not yet come home. Carn frowned. Apparently, the business with the Caladors was more complicated than they had feared. He was tempted to wait—nothing seemed more appealing than embarking together with Brandt on a task fraught with enigmas and urgency—but he had no idea how long Brandt would be delayed. And Carn forced himself to consider that he and Brandt were not the only ones seeking Barr Aston. There was also an unnamed assassin . . . and finding Aston first might prove to be the difference between the old minister's life and death. Carn would have to go alone.

The old thief changed into warm woolen riding clothes and gathered some gear that he expected to be useful in the long-vacant passages of the Atahr Vin. When he had finished, Brandt still hadn't returned. Disappointed, Carn wrote a succinct note for his friend before he went to the stables. There he chose a horse for himself and an extra mount as well—intended, optimistically, for Barr Aston. Satisfied with his preparations, Carn spurred his mare east toward the Atahr Vin. The ride would not be too long, and he wondered whether he would beat Brandt home. The idea brought a grin to his face: Barr Aston would make a nice present to welcome Brandt back.

The countryside around Prandis was generally composed of soft, rolling fields and light woods. Toward the northeast, however, one gradually entered a sparser land of rocky gullies through which a vanished waterway had once cut a tortuous path to the coastal bluffs and the sea. It was not far into this area of gullies that the entrance to the Atahr Vin lay, nor was it hard to find. The capital's commerce had thrived so greatly over the centuries that what had once been uninhabited land was now dotted with small villages and hamlets, each sustaining itself by trade with the nearby metropolis. One of these growing communities, thriving on the profits of a nearby granite quarry, had staked its place almost upon the old Khrine doorstep itself. It was but a small matter for Carn, when he reached the quarry an hour before noon, to obtain precise directions from a stonecutter. The worker eyed Carn's fine riding clothes with some distrust, and the traveler's destination proved more surprising still. But if some citified gentleman was fool enough to go looking for the Atahr Vin, and more fool still to pay a good gold capital for the directions, what was an honest laborer to do except oblige?

•   •   •

As Carn's horse bore him slowly toward the interior of the bleak region, the rocky inclines grew taller
and steeper on each side, until the midday sun could
barely penetrate to the dried riverbed below. Carn rode
on cautiously into the deepening gloom, fearful that the
horses would break a leg on this sharp and treacherous
ground. He wondered what had possessed the Khrine to
make their ancient home in such a forbidding locale
when the rich, fertile fields around Prandis had lain open
for settlement.

Soon the path plunged precipitously downward into
an abyssal gully, hardly more than a narrow cleft between the towering, craggy walls of black rock on either
side. Carn dismounted and carefully led the horses down
the defile into the murky twilight beyond. Slowly, his
thoughts reverted from the Khrine to Barr Aston. Could
the aged minister have truly negotiated this arduous journey? At first, the forgotten Khrine abode had sounded
like a perfect hiding place, but now Carn began to suspect he had set himself upon a fool's errand. If *he* found
the trip strenuous, how could an octogenarian have negotiated the path?

Once the ground became level again, Carn swung
himself back into the saddle and urged his horse along
the twisting rockbed. The echo and re-echo of the clat-
tering hooves began to tell on his imagination, and he
fancied that he heard other sounds following him
through the ravine. Often, he cast worried glances over
his shoulder into the gloom, but apprehended only the
broken trail behind him. Perhaps, he decided, his nerves
were no longer up to this sort of thing. He tried to push
the thought from his mind. Barr Aston *would* be found
in the Atahr Vin, Carn told himself, and if the eighty-
year-old could make it, so could he.

At length, Carn arrived before a tall stone door set

into the face of the gray rock. It seemed as incongruous now as it had appeared upon its discovery decades ago—like a window set imperturbably in the side of a tree—but after a few moments of staring at it, the door's strangeness began to subside. Despite the sheer improbability of finding a cliff side with a front door, the door itself possessed such a calm and ancient air of *belonging* that one could almost imagine the Khrine having fashioned the gullies to accommodate their portal, rather than the reverse.

Carn slid out of the saddle and tethered the horses to a nearby outcropping of rock. Pulling a black velvet pouch from his breast pocket, he approached the Khrine doorway. Now his anxiety wholly disappeared. Not suited for rides through gullies or the strange sounds of the wilderness, Carn was a child of cities—a thief, perfectly at home in his native habitat and confident in his natural calling, which was entering doors no matter how secure, no matter where they happened to be placed. With a quiet satisfaction, Carn set himself to the task of breaking in.

The Khrine were a race whose reputed genius ran not only to the magical arts, but the mechanical as well. In the small, intricate lock that protected their rocky abode, Carn found a piece of craftsmanship well matched to his years of experience, far outpacing in complexity the lock on Aston's door that had defied him only momentarily that morning. Luckily, Carn thought, the Khrine had not settled on one of the busiest streets of Prandis, so he would have all the leisure in the world for his work. Time and again, he drew a slender tool from his little pouch and, slipping it delicately into the mysterious recesses of the Khrine keyhole, probed the lock's interior. After a moment, a low grunt issued from his throat as he became satisfied that the tool was insufficient for the job. Eyes glittering with a determined satisfaction, Carn drew a yet more subtle instrument from his collection and proceeded apace, until few of his tools remained untested.

Finally, he took hold of a slim pick of his own invention, a glittering lattice of interwoven wires. After long moments of adjusting his temperamental instrument, he slipped it into the lock. The cunning springs slid upward against the alien Khrine pins and settled snugly against them. Carn carefully rotated the pick, and with a smoothness that even a new Prandis lock could not match, the ancient cylinder turned. Gratified by his victory, Carn returned his tools to his pocket and fetched the supplies from his saddlebags. A moment later, he had lit a small hooded lantern. With one push, the Khrine door sighed slowly inward and Carn stared into hallways that no man had entered for years.

Except, perhaps, Barr Aston.

Carn had hoped to ascertain evidence of the minister's presence immediately, but Khrine workmanship stymied his plans. Although the ancient stone passageways had been abandoned for ages, a ventilation system provided a steady breeze in every corner of the forsaken place. No dust had found a peaceful abode on the floor and, consequently, if Aston had passed this way, he had left no tracks.

As he took his first step inside, Carn's senses sprang to the alert. At Brandt's side, Carn had broken into some of the most elaborate fortresses in the country, eluded the most sophisticated traps that man's bloodthirsty genius could devise. But the Khrine had a genius all their own, and Carn was careful not to underestimate their ancient work. He reminded himself of the archaeologists who had died here in the age of Wegman Aston. The last thing Carn wanted was to lose his life by falling through a trapdoor designed to protect a people who centuries ago had yielded to extinction.

The dark corridor was narrow—Carn's broad shoulders nearly brushed the wall on either side—but its ceiling towered twenty feet above him. In this way, the passage resembled the narrow defile which had brought Carn to the Atahr Vin. The Khrine appeared fond of such constricted spaces. But, in marked contrast to the broken rock outside, the passages of the Atahr Vin were carved seamlessly from the bowels of the stone. How such corridors had been crafted baffled Carn's imagination. Whether in magic or mechanics, the Khrine had been mighty indeed.

Thankfully, he thought, they had been equally orderly. No labyrinthine warrens greeted the dim but steady beam of his lantern. Instead, the corridor ran straight as an arrow as far as he could see. Every twenty feet, alternating on the left and right, Carn found a doorway into a side chamber, each one forty feet on a side and an equal measure in height. Each of these cavernous spaces was entirely empty, devoid of furniture, other exits, or markings of any sort. Whether the Khrine had emptied the stronghold themselves, or robbers and archaeologists had done the job for them, Carn did not know. Perhaps he would have been well served to have read more of Aston's book than the first two pages, which did no more than describe the Atahr Vin's location.

Carn had passed countless identical, bare chambers and had long since lost sight of the exit when the corridor terminated in a tall arched doorway. Above this door, at least, there was something different than the endless monotony of straight, seamless stone. A series of the Khrine's strange, spiky letters were inscribed above the opening, but they surpassed Carn's powers of interpretation. Curious, he slipped through the doorway into a huge, circular hall. The place was at least a hundred feet in diameter, and a tremendous domed ceiling stretched sixty feet above the polished stone floor. Again, not a seam or crack was to be found in the entire chamber. By all appearances, the stone had been hollowed out as easily as one would scoop the flesh from a melon.

Most striking of all, this room bore evidence of the Khrine who had fashioned it. Standing in the exact center of the chamber was a large, circular dais, intricately inscribed with a variety of figures. Almost forgetting his purpose, Carn walked, rapt, to the abandoned monument and gazed in wonder at the carvings. The dais bore the likenesses of dozens of Khrine, each tall and remarkably slender. The artist had captured with astonishing fluidity their lithe, athletic forms and long, sensuous limbs. The figures, Carn noted, were depicted in a variety of poses. Some Khrine, arrayed for war, held long javelins and small, spiked shields. Others sat cross-legged in apparent contemplation. More surprising still were outdoor scenes in which rural Khrine hunted game with long bows or tilled fields that groaned under heavy harvests. All the stories spoke of the Khrine's magical prowess; Carn could hardly imagine them as common farmers or hunters.

But one thing remained common to each figure. Instead of a head, there was simply an inch-round hole that appeared to be drilled deep into the dais. Carn's finger idly traced the lip of one of these head-holes, and he almost thrust his digit into it before thinking better of the idea. Strange that such minutely detailed renderings of Khrine life would omit what Carn supposed to be the most interesting item: their faces.

Such musings, Carn realized, might well have held importance to a scholar like Barr Aston's father. But whatever Carn learned about the Khrine that day, his mission, practically speaking, was an utter failure: Barr Aston was nowhere to be found. The only way out of this great hall was the doorway Carn had already used, and he had neglected no chambers before this one. Carn had reached the innermost depth of the Atahr Vin, only to find that he was alone.

But to concede failure meant nothing but a return trip through the gully—and frankly, Carn preferred the eerie stillness of the Atahr Vin to the troublesome trek home. Perhaps he had missed something, he thought halfheartedly. Unconvinced, but unwilling to give up just yet, he walked along the perimeter of the chamber, running his hand lightly over the smooth gray wall. If the Khrine had fashioned a secret passage, it surpassed his skill to detect it. As he completed this futile revolution, his glance alit once more on the dais— the only curious object in the entire keep—and he returned to it. It was odd, Carn noted, that the relief carvings on the rock formed a continuous line just below the top of the cylinder. He held his lantern close to the stone and conducted a more intense inspection.

Sure enough, a hairline fissure ran from one carving to the next—from one figure's arm to a nearby tree branch, from a menacing javelin to a man reclined in sleep—completely around the top of the stone. The dais was some sort of well, he realized, capped by a heavy lid of rock. Carn pressed his hands to the cool stone and, bracing himself against the floor, applied all his strength to lifting the cap. His effort was entirely fruitless: the stone refused to budge, and three further attempts proved no more successful.

Again Carn turned his attention to the holes that had replaced the figures' heads. He almost thrust a finger inside but again decided against it. Despite the fearsome legends of its deadly traps, the Atahr Vin seemed entirely innocuous—as safe as a vacant warehouse. Indeed, Carn had begun to wonder whether the legends had been created by the archaeologists themselves as a means of scaring people away from the place, the better to preserve it for scientific scrutiny. But he wasn't willing to bet parts of his body on that hunch.

Instead, he pulled a pencil from his pocket and slipped it inside the nearest hole. When the tip had traveled a few inches, Carn heard a low, sharp click and felt the pencil twitch in his fingers. Withdrawing the instrument, he noted with grim satisfaction that the tip had been sheared off by a hidden blade. Far easier, Carn mused, to sharpen a pencil than to grow a new finger.

With growing excitement, Carn plumbed the depths of hole after hole with his ever-shrinking pencil. Each test brought only another click and another bit of wood sliced off. Finally, though, in a hole where the head of a young warrior should have been, Carn pushed the remaining few inches of his pencil inside and encountered no resistance, no obstacles. He removed the useless writing implement and, for the first time, tested the cavity with his finger. There had to be some sort of hidden catch that would open the dais for his inspection. Yet, probe as he might, the old thief found nothing but the smooth cylinder that had been drilled into the rock.

Disappointed, he glowered at the carved figures of the dais as if they'd betrayed him. It was then that a thought struck him. Judging by the lanky proportions of the carvings, even if a Khrine were only as tall as a man, each of his slender fingers would be a good deal longer than human. It was possible that the secret catch did indeed exist, but that it lay, by Khrine standards, beyond the reach of Carn's stubby forefinger.

Carn reached again for his tools and extracted a stiff piece of wire. In a few seconds, he twisted the end into a loop and inserted it into the cavity. A moment's probing yielded the results he had sought: the little loop caught around the edge of a small trigger in the rock. Carn pulled gently and, with a sigh like that of the front door opening, the dais's circular lid swiveled to the side, revealing a cylindrical shaft that plunged down into the ancient and profound darkness below.

Slowly, a smile of deep satisfaction spread across Carn's features as he aimed his lantern's beam down the shaft. A series of stone rungs protruded from the circular wall, but the beam could not penetrate to the bottom. Undaunted, Carn clamped the lantern's wooden handle in his teeth and, lowering himself silently into the shaft, cautiously began to descend. His shoulders scraped against the rock on either side of the slender passage, and the hot metal of the lamp, pressed against his chest, burned his skin. But Carn hardly noticed the discomfort. Opening the secret door had also roused an old emotion, one that Carn had supposed dead from disuse: the thrill of discovery, of being where no one should be, on the verge of laying eyes upon things he had not been meant to see. More alluring than the secreted treasures of any wealthy merchant, the unknown lair of the Khrine drew Carn on, and in his mounting fascination, he almost forgot it was Barr Aston whom he sought.

The shaft seemed to descend forever. He had been counting rungs as a way of concentrating on the task of climbing down, and by the time he reached sixty his jaw had begun to ache from gripping the handle of the lantern. But he was not yet halfway down. He paused for a few moments, taking the lantern in one hand and clinging to a rung with the other while he caught his breath. Then he began to lower himself again, counting another eighty rungs to the bottom. It was a total dead end—no passageways, no doors, and not a clue about what to do next. Carn stamped his feet against a floor that seemed disappointingly solid, and he cast the lantern's beam about him, studying the inscrutable face of the rock. The well seemed to have led nowhere, but it defied logic that the Khrine would have so meticulously hidden a useless shaft. Nevertheless, Carn realized, logic did not define the Khrine's eerie dwelling—or if it did, it was logic beyond a man's ability to grasp. He thought of all those symmetrical, cubical chambers, lacking any convenience adopted by the human race. It seemed impossible to Carn that living creatures might choose such a place to live, devoid of comfort, devoid of light.

While Carn silently debated these finer points of Khrine lore, he continued to study the circular wall of the well, unwilling to believe that the shaft had been carved to no purpose. After a few moments, he found the hairline fissure that characterized the Khrine's subtle engineering: a faint outline of a door. This door, Carn supposed, would be at least as challenging to open as the front door and the dais, but one firm push sent the portal sliding silently outward, revealing a long, narrow corridor beyond.

Carn expected the same spartan workmanship, the same utterly smooth stone walls, interrupted only at uniform intervals by the opening to a room. He was instead surprised to find that the walls of this corridor, like the dais above, had been elaborately carved. The scenes were various and fantastic. They all depicted the Khrine, but not in their subterranean abodes. Instead, they were pictured among the hills and valleys of Chaldus in a variety of attitudes. Carn gazed in fascination at the graceful bas-reliefs. He saw long caravans of Khrine trekking across the plains, festivals in the woods where the fluid Khrine danced in concentric circles, and even scenes of storm-tossed ships at sea. But the carvings which most interested him were the hunt scenes in which the Khrine, their long javelins and slender swords in hand, were pictured fighting a collection of beasts that Carn had once considered as mythical as their long-extinct hunters. The thief ran his fingers lightly over the stone, feeling the precisely articulated scales of huge reptiles that flew through the air, breathing fire onto Khrine hunters. Elsewhere, there were two-headed giants, naked but bearing huge clubs, pierced in several places by the sharp Khrine javelins but fighting on. There were beasts that looked like winged lions, others like snakes with several heads. Carn, like everyone else, had heard stories of such magical creatures as a child. Some people believed that these creatures had actually lived in an elder age, when magic blew through the world as freely as the wind. Others put the stories down as the products of overly fanciful imaginations. Carn had once included himself in those ranks.

But someone had built these passages. The Khrine had lived. And why would they bother to carve images of imaginary beasts? Carn stared in awe as he realized he had been allowed a privileged discovery. He had been permitted to glimpse a world that had long ago died off—a world vastly more colorful and wondrous than the one he inhabited today. What must it have been like, he wondered, to live in the age of the Khrine? How lucky they had been.

Carn felt an acute twinge of regret that even on these walls, the Khrine faces were missing. The ancient artist who had so painstakingly carved these images had neglected to etch in the faces of his people, leaving only strange blanks within the graceful ovals of their skulls. Carn wondered what sort of untold beauty they might have possessed, what tales their faces might have told. When the present trouble faded, Carn resolved, he would take a deeper look into the Khrine. And into the world before the Binding.

Today, however, Carn was hunting neither imaginary dragons nor vanished Khrine, but a very real—if elusive—old man. As the memory of his task returned to him, he sped his steps along the passage, paying less attention to the baroque images graven in the walls. The corridor stretched on nearly two hundred feet and finally terminated in a small, arched doorway. The wall above the opening was more elaborately carved than elsewhere, Carn realized, and a moment's inspection revealed to him the subject of the carvings: death. Long rows of faceless Khrine figures were depicted, arranged head to foot in stiff, withered postures. The bodies showed no visible wounds, merely a terrible emaciation, as if these people had simply wasted away. The carving filled Carn with horror. What bloody sort of inner sanctum lay beyond the arch, he could not guess. But he had come this far and, wrenching his eyes from the dismal scene above, the old thief stepped through the archway into the large, high-ceilinged room beyond.

The chamber was square like the many rooms that had preceded it, but this one measured almost eighty feet on a side. The ceiling was low, however—perhaps only seven feet high—and supported by carved columns spaced at ten-foot intervals. No, not columns, Carn realized as he looked closer. Only a few of the pillars quite reached the top; most of them terminated in an oblong bulb a few inches shy of the ceiling. Carn cast his lantern's beam on the pillar closest to him and realized that the slender mast of stone was not architectural at all. Rather, it was a sculpture of a tall, slender Khrine. Again, the face had been left a smooth, cryptic blank, but this only emphasized the statue's otherworldly delicacy. Even rendered in stone, the Khrine was a beautiful creature. The figure possessed a certain elongation, a tapering of the limbs that was seldom observed in the Khrine's clumsier human cousins. Carn cast his beam at other nearby statues. The postures and proportions varied, but a certain dignity inhered in each statue. And their missing faces seemed to be lifted toward the ceiling above.

Again, Carn had to recall himself forcefully to the task at hand. There were at least fifty statues in the room and, consequently, the far walls were completely obscured from his view. Almost anything could be hidden in the interior of the chamber. Quietly, Carn proceeded inside, searching through the darkness with his lantern as he navigated between the statues. A sweep of the beam cast an odd shadow on the floor to his right and, returning his light to the spot, the thief detected a figure stretched out along the far wall. His heart leaped in excitement:

the man had to be Barr Aston! But was he sleeping or dead?

Quickening his pace, Carn drew nearer still, but his triumph subsided as the increasing light revealed the true nature of what he had found. One of the statues had tumbled over in the remote past and he beheld only its cracked form on the floor. He had not found Barr Aston after all.

"Hello."

Carn whirled about, shocked at the sound of a voice, and beheld a wizened old man behind him, dressed entirely in black and leaning lightly against one of the statues.

Barr Aston, it seemed, had found *him*.

"And goodbye," the old man continued, pushing sharply against the statue's hip. With the fluidity of all Khrine workmanship, the pillar of stone toppled straight at Carn The thief dropped his lantern and dived to the left, but his old legs were no match for the far more ancient statue. The cold stone hit him on his back as he tried to spring away and, with a terrific crash, bore him to the floor and into darkness.

A light was bothering him. That was the only sensation that seemed to matter, and Carn lifted his head to avoid it. With a painful flutter, he forced open an eye and recognized his own lantern set down on the floor only a few feet away. The lantern's flame was making the flesh of his face uncomfortably hot, but the rest of his body felt utterly cold, almost frozen.

Sitting cross-legged behind the lantern was the shadowy figure of Barr Aston.

"Ah, you're back," Aston said in a voice smooth and hollow from years of use. "I was afraid for a moment that I'd missed my aim and had actually killed you, which would be a shame. Old men, you see, tend toward the garrulous and, as I'm the oldest man I know, I'm also the most talkative. As I'm sure you can imagine, my friend, spending days down here in the dark hasn't helped my disposition one bit. A lonely situation until you came along."

Carn opened his mouth and tasted blood. It came from his lower lip, which was split and swollen to twice its usual size. He ran a shaky hand along his skull but found no more blood, not even a bump.

"Oh, nothing's wrong with your head," the old man said, chuckling quietly at Carn's distress. "You weren't unconscious half a minute. No, you'll live—just as long as I let you, which is the same deal I suppose you had meant to offer me."

Carn put his palms against the floor, tried to turn himself over. This produced only another chuckle from Aston. The old man ran a knobby hand through his thin white hair, bemused.

"You're not going anywhere, my friend, with a half-ton of fine Khrine art resting on your buttocks. It's a shame to see another ruined, you know. My poor departed father would have been distraught to know that I was the agent of such negligence. The Khrine, those graceful creatures, were too dexterous ever to bump into things—they thought nothing of perching these tall statues on such tiny feet. As soon as my father found this place, though, and knocked over the first one, he knew it would never do to let the rest of the world in. He never even told his colleagues what lay beyond the dais, though he took me down here once. Frankly, I had my doubts that you would find me, although anyone bent on purposes such as yours would clearly possess resources—"

"Aston!" Carn rasped. He began to fear that the man was not merely talkative, but thoroughly mad, perhaps driven so by sitting in the dark of the Atahr Vin too long. "You don't understand who I am."

"Of course I don't," the ex-minister replied testily, slapping the cold stone with impatience. "I've never understood any of the lunatics who believe it's in their best interest to destroy the world. I have devoted an entire career, however, to *trying*. And I'm sure that this little interview will go a long way toward enlightening me. So, why don't you tell me exactly who you are."

Perhaps he was not mad after all. Carn could form no clear opinion of this odd, old man, but one thing remained clear: he was entirely at Aston's mercy, and if he did not convince the former minister of his good intentions, he might well wind up as dead as the Khrine themselves.

"I work with Brandt Karrelian," Carn began.

"Galatine Hazard," Aston said softly to himself. "An interesting man, but not someone I'd associate with designs such as yours. I'm afraid that your attempt to frame Hazard for the murders was as useless as it was transparent. Hazard is as harmless as I am . . . except, of course," Aston added with a smile, "when provoked."

Carn shook his head, regretting the wave of nausea that incited. He took a moment to clear his head before throwing himself again at the rampart of Aston's skepticism.

"I *am* Hazard's partner," Carn insisted. "I've worked with him for years, since he was a boy in Belfar. These days, I help oversee his investments. Let me prove it, let me explain."

His urgency was having an effect, Carn realized. As the old man listened, the smile melted from his deeply lined visage and a growing look of horror took its place.

"Whoever *has* been killing retired ministers," Carn continued, "has been trying to frame Brandt—you're right about that. Taylor Ash used Brandt's apparent guilt in this mess to extort our help. So we've both been working with Intelligence for the last week. I was supposed to find you in order to *protect you*."

"A noble but useless gesture." Carn's and Aston's heads snapped to the side in search of the owner of this new, hissing voice. "You led me to him instead."

Something moved in the darkness. Carn could barely make out the gleam of very white teeth, the smooth curve of a hairless skull.

Aston recovered from the surprise more quickly than Carn. The old man sprang to his feet with remarkable fluidity.

"So you're the man I was waiting for," Aston said thoughtfully. "I suppose you have me at something of a disadvantage."

But at the very moment he said this, the old minister leaped away into the darkness and Carn beheld a nearby statue topple toward the newcomer. By the time it crashed to the floor, however, Hain had vanished into the gloom. Carn strained his eyes, but the weak beam of light remained pointed at his face, not at the interior of the room, and he could see nothing.

A long moment of silence followed during which Carn tried to pull himself from beneath the statue, but the tremendous weight of the stone made the attempt as futile as if the entire weight of a mountain rested upon his legs. Then he tried to wriggle just one leg free at a time, and realized that it seemed unable to respond. In fact, beneath the crushing weight of the statue, he should have been in excruciating pain. Instead, he felt nothing, simply an inability to move. Not even a toe wiggled upon his command.

With a growing sense of horror, Carn realized that the statue's fall had broken his back.

Another crash suddenly rocked the room, and then two more in quick succession. Each was followed by a short, cold chuckle as Hain evaded the ponderous missiles. There was another silence, followed by the sound of more statues falling.

"Come now, minister," Hain said amiably in the darkness, "you're running out of ammunition."

This taunt prompted another explosion of stone, and then a loud curse as the sound of a scuffle reached Carn's ears. Carn could almost feel the desperation of Aston's struggle; he pounded in frustration at the cold floor, but there was nothing he could do. There was nothing, Carn thought, that he would ever be able to do again. His arms began to tremble at the thought, and he felt his heart beating like a hurricane within his chest. He wanted to scream, but even that was beyond him. His throat had constricted into a burning knot. He was a cripple, forever useless—useless to Aston, to Brandt, to Masya, to Chaldus. Useless to himself.

A moment later, Hain's athletic figure entered the dim halo of the lantern. The assassin was carrying Aston like a child in his arms. The old man's hands and feet had been bound with wire. Hain dropped the minister roughly to the floor and approached Carn. A chill ran through the old thief as he met the other's merciless red eyes. The killer was grinning, his upper lip pulled taut over his teeth in an expression that was more feral than human. Here was the animal that would kill them all, yet Carn could not so much as move. A great, soundless sob wracked his body.

Hain lifted the lantern and placed it directly before Carn's eyes.

"Mind if I borrow this?"

Carn clenched his eyes closed and whipped his head away. Hot tears streaked along his cheeks.

"Don't cry," Hain said with a chuckle. "I promise I'll give it back."

The assassin moved away and set the lantern down near Aston. Now Carn had a clear view of the old minister, who, though bound, was sitting up and facing Hain with a dignity that Carn desperately wished he could equal. Best that he follow the old man's example and die well. But a vast sense of failure overwhelmed him and he could not stop trembling.

"I would ask you a question," Aston told the assassin quietly.

Hain merely smiled as he reached into a pouch tied to his belt.

"Why do this?" Aston continued. "Is the world not to your liking?"

"The world is perfectly to my liking," Hain replied with a gravity that was unusual for him. He met the minister's eye calmly and continued. "My job suits me well, as do its rewards."

Aston frowned, his suspicion confirmed. "So you are simply a lackey. Has your employer told you exactly what he means to do with the information that he has set you gathering?"

Hain smiled. "I'm not to be made a pawn of, old man. Yes, I've been told and, frankly, I don't care a turd about the consequences. Let all Chaldus weep, so long as I am paid." He drew a dark, pear-shaped gem, no larger than a robin's egg, from the pouch. "And, speaking of suffering, you'll soon be singing a different tune."

Hain held the gem before Aston's face, rolling it between his forefinger and thumb.

"Do you know who I was?" Aston asked. It took Carn a moment to realize that the man did not mean the question rhetorically.

"Some politician, like the others," Hain shrugged.

Aston's eyes narrowed as he shook his head. "Not quite a politician. I was the head of the Ministry of Intelligence. Every method of torture known to man, I know. Every method of resisting it, I've mastered. So I wouldn't count on getting paid quite yet. You may kill me, but you won't have the satisfaction of hearing one word pass my lips."

"I was warned about that," Hain replied evenly, "so I consulted my pharmacist."

Saying that, he held up the hypodermic in his left hand.

"And, regrettably," the assassin added as he moved across the room and kicked Carn sharply in the head, "I'm not allowed the luxury of an audience."

The halls of the Atahr Vin had not seen so much traffic for the better part of a millennium, nor had it offered so surprising a sight as it did to Brandt Karrelian. Toward the rear of a room littered with the cracked remains of Khrine burial statuary, in the soft lambency of a half-hooded lantern, Brandt beheld a bald man holding a gem over the body of a very old man. And, half-shrouded in the darkness beyond, he saw Carn's lifeless figure, head framed within a black halo of blood. The sight struck Brandt visibly, like a blow in the gut, and he felt momentarily sick. There followed no thought, only a blur of action that best resembled the Brandt Karrelian of twenty years ago—an ambitious but impetuous adolescent who had just been adopted by a bemused thief twice his age. In the sepulchral silence of the Khrine keep, Galatine Hazard slipped into the shadows, his blood pounding like war drums in his temples.

"And now, old man," Hain chuckled, "let's finish this so I can finally get paid."

Just then, Hain caught a sound behind him and whirled around to see a smallish, dark-haired man spring furiously from behind a statue, his sword cutting through the air. Hain rolled away in time to see sparks burst forth as the blade hit the floor where he had been perched a moment ago. The assassin was amazed at the stealth of the man's approach. Had his veridine-sharpened hearing not warned him at the last moment, his bald head would have been split in two.

Hain prolonged his dive into a somersault, coming up neatly on his feet. Quickly, he slipped the gem into his

pocket and ducked behind a nearby statue. Karrelian was
already charging forward, blade whistling through the
chill air. Karrelian's sword put Hain at a distinct disadvantage, for the assassin carried none himself. Still,
with one foot of steel in his right hand and a small
throwing dagger secreted in his left, Hain felt more than
capable of handling any intruder. In fact, he almost relished the opportunity. Madh had forbidden wanton violence and, save Hain's encounter with Kermane Ash's
chauffeur, the assassin had been denied the joy of an
old-fashioned killing for some time.

Brandt approached warily from the left, and Hain
found it impossible to maneuver the statue directly between them. Instead, he feinted, as if to flee, and then
hurled the little dagger from his left hand. In the gloom
of the Khrine chamber, the blade appeared as little more
than an obscure blur. Brandt had no time to duck. Instead, he whipped his blade up and around, striking the
dagger from the air in midflight.

It had been a very lucky swing. By all rights, both
Brandt and Hain should now have been dead men.

Capitalizing on the surprise that momentarily clouded
the assassin's face, Brandt leaped forward, screaming at
the top of his lungs. But Hain was not to be taken off
guard so easily. He dodged backward and began to de-
fend himself against a flurry of cuts, either deflecting
them with his dirk or leaping aside with a panther's agil-
ity. He was amazed not only by the sheer savagery of
Brandt's attack but by the bloodcurdling cries that accompanied each thrust. Hain had no idea who the
swordsman was, but he seemed to have gone utterly in-
sane.

Slowly, the thrusting, parrying course of the two men
led them back to the supine body of Aston and the
greater illumination of the lantern. Brandt threw all of
his weight into a downward cut that Hain met with his
knife, checking the momentum of Brandt's blade bare

inches from his face. There they stood for a moment, locked together, Brandt trying to drive his sword forward, Hain holding it back. Brandt glared past the cross of steel at Hain's twisted features and, in the better light, was taken aback.

"You're not the man who tried to hire me," he rasped between long, tired breaths.

The remark struck home, forged a connection, and Hain smiled. "So you're Hazard," he replied almost cheerfully as he continued to struggle against the other's blade. "They say you were something . . . in your day."

But Hain's jab at Brandt's age rang hollow, and despite his glib patter, Hain knew it. For whatever reason, the elder thief was fighting like a man possessed, and his skill with a sword was formidable. His best chance, Hain knew, was to remove Hazard's advantage—his sword— and the temporary clench offered a perfect opportunity. Hain had wrapped both hands around his knife, seeking sufficient leverage to hold off Hazard's blade. Now, he removed his left hand, ducking his head as Hazard's momentum drove the sword forward, and grabbed Hazard's wrist.

In response, Brandt's left hand moved from the hilt of his sword to Hain's throat, his fingers digging into the flesh around the assassin's larynx, threatening to crush it. Hain twisted violently aside, retreating between the rows of silent Khrine statues. Brandt spun after him, forcing Hain backward with a series of short, controlled thrusts that the assassin parried only with difficulty.

Despite Hazard's inspired fury, Hain would still wager that he could beat him—but it was a fool's bet. The length of Hazard's blade kept Hain on the defensive, and even one missed parry would spell disaster. No, there would be another day for Hazard, a day of Hain's choosing. On the chance that Hazard could beat him, on the chance that these unfamiliar Khrine passages held other unpleasant surprises, the most rational choice was to cut short a combat that, in other circumstances, he would have relished.

Hain allowed himself to be borne backward a few steps by Brandt's force. Seizing his apparent advantage, Brandt committed all his strength into a broad cut of his sword, intending to use the memorial to the Khrine dead as the chopping block for a decapitating blow. But Brandt did not expect, as Hain did, that the statue would topple over as soon as Hain hit it. While the ancient stone shattered into piercing shards against the floor, Hain slipped adeptly to the side, rolled to his feet, and dashed toward the door. Deceived by his momentum, Brandt flew off his feet. He landed lightly on the floor only a few yards from Carn and saw now what he had not discerned from afar: despite the growing puddle of blood in which his friend's head lay, Carn's eyes twitched beneath their lids in an uneasy sleep, his nostrils dilated as he inhaled.

He was alive.

Brandt turned momentarily to watch Hain vanish into the Khrine gloom. In his fury, he was tempted to follow, bent on claiming blood. But there was blood enough in the Atahr Vin already, and it belonged entirely to Carn. Any time Brandt wasted on the assassin was time better spent helping his friend. Forgetting Hain, Brandt rushed to Carn's side, stripping off his shirt in midstride. He stooped to examine the wound on Carn's brow and, heaving a sigh of relief, found that it was far from crippling. Hain's boot had caught Carn near the right temple and, opening the delicate flesh above the eye, caused far more bleeding than real damage. Brandt blotted the cut with his shirt and held it steadily against the wound until, after a few minutes, the bleeding stopped. Then he tore off a clean sleeve and carefully bandaged Carn's skull.

What to do about the statue that crossed the man's lower back, pinning him to the ground, was not so easily solved. But Carn was beginning to show some signs of stirring, and that alone lifted Brandt's spirits.

A low groan from behind him caught his ear, and Brandt turned to see Barr Aston's eyelids flutter open, his pupils dilated in a drugged haze. The old man shook his head and blinked, trying to dispel the fog from his brain.

"Must . . . stop. . . ."

Aston shook his head and took a few long, deep breaths. When he looked up again, some of the old light had returned to his eyes—eyes that narrowed as they settled on Brandt's face.

"Karrelian?" the old man croaked, his voice slurred by drugs. Brandt was surprised by this recognition, but he should not have been. If someone bore even the slightest relation to matters of Chaldean security, chances were that the former Minister of Intelligence knew him by sight. But Aston did not stare long at Brandt; rather, his old eyes cast about in a hopeful search for Hain's corpse. Disappointed, they turned to the door and immediately back to Brandt.

"After him, you fool!" Aston snapped, his lips still fumbling over the words.

Brandt glared at the old man. He had always looked with favor on government officials, considering how very useful they had been to the cherished cause of his enrichment. Now, however, the sight of a Chaldean minister had become distinctly distasteful. Brandt almost regretted having interrupted Hain's handiwork.

"After him yourself," he growled, turning back to Carn.

The minister cursed and thrashed about weakly, struggling with the wire that still bound his hands and feet. In a moment, it became obvious that he would not be able to free himself, much less chase the assassin.

"Your friend will live," Aston argued, "but your generator business is in jeopardy."

The old man's words were crisper now as the effects of the drug continued to subside, but they didn't seem to make sense. Brandt ignored the apparent non sequitur.

"Prattle on, you old bastard, and you just may convince me to continue where your attacker left off."

Brandt rose again and studied the slab of rock that was pinning Carn down. The statue's feet rested upon the ground. Just beneath its shoulders, the statue crossed the small of Carn's back, leaving the stone head a foot above the floor. Brandt wrapped his hands around the smooth, featureless face and strained against the weight, but the Khrine rock was too much for him. He tried again, groaning at the effort, and managed to shift the statue, but not to lift it.

Aston cast a last, doleful look at the doorway and shook his head. The assassin couldn't have gone far . . . but Karrelian seemed determined to ignore that fact. Aston sighed. It seemed that nothing further would happen until Karrelian helped his friend.

"Untie me, and I'll give you a hand," the retired spymaster suggested.

Brandt looked up, frowning, but decided that the old man might be right. It took only a few moments to twist free the wires that had held Aston in place. The old man sat up and began rubbing his wrists, then his forearms.

"It will take a moment or two for my circulation to come back," Aston explained.

Brandt quickly grew tired of watching the old man massage his muscles back to life. Instead, he returned to Carn and tried his luck once more with the Khrine statue. It moved no more than a half-inch.

"Wake him up first," Aston advised sourly. The retired spymaster had come around quicker than Brandt had thought. Quickly enough to quietly pocket the gem that Hain had left behind "You'll need his cooperation to get him out."

Without a word, Brandt let go of the statue and began

gently prodding Carn's side—an old signal they had used to wake each other up in former, rougher days. Slowly, the older thief came around, and Brandt felt a surge of relief at even this moderately hopeful sign.

Carn said nothing, but fixed his watery eyes on his smaller friend.

"Brandt . . . I thought I'd never see you again, unless we were granted adjoining rooms by the devil."

But Carn's cavalier tone was forced, and it was all that Brandt could manage to reply in kind.

"It hasn't come to that. Although I do see you've taken up strange bedmates lately," he concluded, patting the statue.

"These Khrine are forward fellows," Carn joked back softly, but his voice cracked as he said it.

"Enough banter," Aston ordered. "Let's get you out of there."

But the minister had a difficult time raising himself to his feet, and Brandt doubted that the old man could offer substantial help. Nevertheless, Aston bent over alongside Brandt and took a firm grip of the statue's head.

"We won't be able to lift this for long," the old minister told Carn, "so as soon as we get it off your back, you scramble out quick as can be, you hear?"

Carn's face convulsed nervously, and he turned to Brandt. "I don't think I can scramble anywhere. I—" He took a long, shuddering breath before he continued. "I can't move my legs. Brandt, I can't *feel* my legs."

Brandt turned away, his face twisting with emotion that he would not have Carn see. His teeth ground together furiously. "I should have killed him. I should have— "

But then Brandt realized there had been three people in the room when he had arrived. Carn, the assassin, and Barr Aston. Another possibility began to grow in his mind.

"Who did this?" he asked in a strained, low tone. "Did that bald bastard cripple you—" Brandt turned back menacingly toward Aston, and his voice rose in one single word—"*or . . .*"

"The assassin," Carn replied sharply, not entirely understanding the lie even as he said it. But it seemed important, somehow, that Brandt not know.

"This is getting us nowhere," Aston interrupted quietly, "and the longer we wait, the more damage may be done to your friend's back." He looked curiously at Carn. "If you can't use your legs, simply pull yourself forward with your arms. Will that work?"

Carn nodded as Brandt and Aston bent low over the statue, taking hold of the head and neck. In concert, they strained at the stubborn stone. As before, Brandt felt his muscles protest, burning at the limits of their power. But Aston's wiry old strength added just what was needed, and the statue rose reluctantly a few inches above Carn's back. Immediately, the old thief pressed his fingers against the smooth stone floor and pulled himself a few inches forward.

"Hurry!" Brandt hissed through clenched teeth, cords of muscle straining at the skin of his neck.

Carn reached out and pulled himself along the floor again, and again. He could hear the men's labored breathing and tried to work faster, but the smooth floor yielded little traction. A long, nervous minute passed before his toes cleared the statue. Instantly, both Brandt and Aston released the Khrine relic and sprang backward. Without the accommodating cushion of a human body, the ancient stone cracked against the floor, spitting out jagged chips in all directions.

"Are you all right?" Brandt asked, still breathing heavily from his exertion.

Carn merely nodded, but he was very far from all right. He had hoped, foolish as such hope might be, that only the weight of the rock had cut off the sensation of his legs. Now he was free, yet they remained dead to him. And for all his money and for all his influence, Carn knew there was not a healer on earth whose power could mend his legs.

"Let's get you off your stomach," Brandt suggested.

Without waiting for help, Carn rolled himself over heavily, his legs twisting with the motion of his torso like some great unwieldy tail. He watched as his feet lolled to either side at the ankles, forever severed from his will.

"Is that better?" Brandt asked.

Carn propped himself up on his elbows. "I'll be fine," he said quietly.

"Good," Aston snapped. "Then let's be off after the villain. The information that man has stolen in one month, Mr. Karrelian, is worth a thousand times more than all the petty secrets you managed to collect in your lifetime. It's high time that we catch him."

But what Brandt caught instead was the arm of Barr Aston as the old minister turned toward the doorway.

"What it's time for," Brandt replied, a steel edge in his voice, "is an explanation."

CHAPTER 13

The northwest tower of the imperial palace was reserved for the exclusive use of the princess. It rose seventy feet above the main body of the palace, a tapering cylinder of lazy arabesques of tan and rose stones. On the highest floor of that tower, Cyrintha had chosen a chamber for a sitting room. It was furnished with a few armchairs and a small round table. Cyrintha loved this place because it offered a stunning vista of the bay without showing much of the city. Today, as on many days, she was in no mood to look upon Thyrsus—or, for that matter, to concentrate on her daily lesson, which was her ostensible reason for coming to the chamber in the first place.

"They still clamor for war," the young princess observed somewhat testily. "What gives them the idea that Chaldus was behind Naidjur's death, I still don't understand. Crassus and Naidjur hated each other for ages, yet no one accused Crassus of treason until now."

Of course, Crassus hadn't killed anyone until recently, either.

Cyrintha thought back to the speech that her father

had delivered to the crowd a day earlier. The old man had stood on the northern balcony of the palace, a tiny dot of a monarch before the throng gathered in the plaza below. If not for the magical assistance of Holoakhan, the Thyrsians would not have heard a word he had said. Which, as it turned out, might well have been for the best.

The citizens had come that day not necessarily for a declaration of war, or for the exoneration of Crassus—but certainly for one or the other. What they wanted was certainty—an imperial mandate of what to think. Emperor Mallioch had instead reminded them that while everyone shared alike the great loss of Parth Naidjur, and no one need acknowledge love for Thane Crassus, a thane was still a thane, and Yndor remained Yndor. As long as these facts held true, the sacred ritual of the duel could not be violated

And then Mallioch had simply walked away.

The crowd had milled about for a few moments more, trying to digest Mallioch's unexpected speech. Had Crassus sold himself to the Chaldeans or not? If he was no traitor, why hadn't the emperor simply said so? But if Crassus had betrayed them, were they supposed to continue nourishing this serpent in their bosom, without any retribution . . . ? Slowly, with sinking spirits, the citizens of Thyrsus dispersed. Rather than putting a stop to their grumblings, the emperor's speech had only spurred them on anew.

But the princess could fathom neither the reasons nor the depths of their discontent.

"Why should they think it was anything more than the duel it was?"

Sitting across from Cyrintha, in the cool shade which soothed his aged skin, Holoakhan stirred within his voluminous robes. He peered quizzically at the princess, his eyes half-hidden by drooping white eyebrows. "It is uncharacteristic that one in your family consider why and what the citizens think. More than likely, dear Princess, this is an unwholesome occupation. Certainly, neither your father nor your brother cares a whit for public opinion. Such apathy is, after all, the primary benefit of a hereditary monarchy, so long as you are numbered among the hereditary monarchs."

The corners of Cyrintha's mouth curled downward as she contemplated her elderly tutor. Holoakhan had fallen into his cryptic, worldly-wise demeanor today. Indeed, he was falling into it far more often of late, and this in itself was enough to concern the princess. She knew from experience that the old mage relied most on his cynical epigrams when matters were afoot that he thought best to keep from her. But the young Yndrian princess was fast becoming tired of life as an ornament of the reigning Jurin family. It was a job that admitted no excitement and promised no improvement. Indeed, this was the very reason she had first sought instruction from Holoakhan in the magical arts.

At least, it was one of the reasons.

Cyrintha leaned back in her chair and wound a strand of rich brown hair around her finger. Her hair was a prized possession. The Yndrian style for noble women was to grow one's hair long, and Cyrintha's cascaded well below the small of her back. It was a habit of hers to play with it when disturbed—a habit almost as frequent, Holoakhan thought, as asking questions about politics, although playing with hair was not nearly so dangerous.

"Loa," the princess began sweetly. The old mage roused his mental defenses. Loa was a pet name that none but Cyrintha called him, and the way she used it at the moment was ample warning for the wizard to guard himself. Cyrintha was often most calculating when she sought to be pleasant. "Loa, has all mirth fled Thyrsus?"

"I have lived so long in my books, Princess," the wizened man replied, "that I fear I've forgotten what mirth is. How, then, may I say whether it has departed?"

Cyrintha rose abruptly and crossed the half-lit tower room. She bent over the mage and kissed the brown skin of his head, right at the very crown, before the edge of his receded hairline. With her finger she traced the course of his white hair as it twisted into a braid fifteen inches long, down to the small jade ring that held the braid together. Cyrintha tugged on the braid playfully and bade him farewell.

"No lesson today, I think, Loa. Magic will have to wait until I discover whether I, like the rest of the city, should be angry and demonstrating in the streets."

Cyrintha turned lightly on her toes and strode through the doorway. Silently, a shadow detached itself from the deeper shadows of the room's corner—a tall, dark man who followed Cyrintha quietly into the interior of the palace. This was Akmar, her trothblade. Every member of the imperial family had a trothblade, an elite soldier sworn by his life to protect the imperial line. As Akmar departed, the tip of his long, curved sword tapped against a metal urn, leaving Holoakhan to contemplate the fading, musical ring of steel on brass.

And, of course, to contemplate Cyrintha herself. Akmar lived to protect the princess from the physical threats of life in the palace, but these, Holoakhan reflected grimly, were as nothing. Although Holoakhan could think of no place in Yndor more dangerous, the menaces of the imperial palace were not the type to be stopped by a sword. No, for the most part, they were much worse. In truth, the aged wizard was Cyrintha's real trothblade, and he feared his task would prove more difficult than Akmar's. Akmar need only protect Cyrintha from others, but it fell to Holoakhan to save the young princess from the excesses of her own folly.

The receding footsteps dissolved into silence at the very moment that the urn ceased to ring, and Holoakhan

sat unmoving in the quiet and gathering darkness, his
thoughts turned to a man named Sardos.

As a woman not yet two dozen years of age and
possessing all the fiery blood of the Jurin family, quiet
contemplation was not Cyrintha's ordinary way of dealing with troubles. The most sensible thing, of course,
would be to ask her father or her brother what was going
on. Was Crassus a traitor? Would they be going to war?
But the doings of the empire were seldom sensible, Cyrintha feared, and direct inquiries were out of the question—especially because Emperor Mallioch considered
politics to lie beyond the grasp of the female brain. Her
father's obstinacy on this point infuriated her, but Mallioch was too old to change his ways. She would learn
nothing from him.

There had once been a time when she could go to
Clannoch for news or consolation. Years ago, he had
happily shared with her anything that he knew, but even
this was changing. Cyrintha thought back ruefully to
yesterday's encounter in Clannoch's study. Her younger
brother seemed to be growing ever more distant as the
days passed . . . and about as likely to discuss politics as
Mallioch himself.

That left few direct options. And so, as Cyrintha approached the tower stairs, she considered the indirect
ones. Since she had been a little girl, she had known
that the easiest way of examining the true disposition of
the rulers of Yndor was simply to create mischief—
something that little children were incomparably well
equipped to do. It saddened Cyrintha that, at the age of
twenty-three, she was forced to resort to such old tricks,
but if they were the only means that worked. . . .

Ask, she thought, *and you shall receive nothing. An-
noy, and there are all manner of interesting secrets to
be pried loose.*

She descended a long flight of circular stairs, not noticing the echoing steps of Akmar on the red-veined marble behind her. Akmar had been her trothblade for the entire span of her conscious life, and she paid him no more heed than she would her own shadow. The two were equally quiet and, in her opinion, equally superfluous.

The staircase terminated at a large arched doorway, through which Cyrintha strode into the main corridor of the palace. This hallway was thirty feet wide and equally high, the whole of it clothed in an elaborate geometrical design of brilliantly polished marble. With the fluidity of painters, the stonecutters of Yndor fashioned marble into interlocking patterns of color as striking and intricate as any tapestry. Down the hall stood the pair of plain but massive double doors that led to her father's audience chamber, and it was there that the princess intended to go. But, as she drew near, she heard her brother's voice issue from an adjoining chamber. The door was slightly ajar, so she peeked inside.

Clannoch stood with his back to her, his entire body animated with the force of his speech. As he leaped from one word to the next, the tip of his sword bobbed up and down, keeping time as well as a conductor's baton. The sword was a recent affectation, Cyrintha mused. No member of the Jurin family needed to carry arms—indeed, even through the limited view afforded by the narrowly cracked door, Cyrintha could make out the shadow of Clannoch's trothblade, Senz. It seemed to Cyrintha an affront to Senz's competence that Clannoch now bore weapons, and she could not even begin to understand his motives. It was this keen annoyance at her brother's newfound inscrutability that suggested him as a more appropriate target for mischief than her father.

Clannoch took a step forward—carried, it seemed, by the momentum of his speech—and Cyrintha gained a glimpse of her brother's audience. Seated motionlessly before the prince, as still and cold as the marble that clad the palace walls, sat a giant of a man. More than seven feet tall, even seated he was almost eye level with young Clannoch. He wore thick robes of such absolute blackness that they threatened to soak up all the light in the chamber, even as they absorbed Clannoch's words, even as the man's own body seemed lost. Nothing—not a foot or a finger—was visible beyond those robes; nothing save the pale unmoving head that sat atop them, the face lined with creases as deep as gorges, the eyes as black as underground lakes and just as likely to drown you. The man's face was framed by a wild tangle of raven locks, so black that they blended imperceptibly into his robes.

This was the way with Sardos, Cyrintha reflected. You could never tell where the man began or where he ended. Two years ago, he had come from nowhere, becoming in a matter of months a trusted adviser to the prince and emperor both, and Cyrintha would be just as glad to see him return to nowhere.

But there was nothing that she could do about Sardos—the man seemed as implacable as a mountain and about as likely to be gotten rid of. Instead, her annoyance increased at her brother, and redoubled again when she realized the topic of his spirited monologue: he was inveighing against the Chaldeans.

"It is high time," Clannoch declared, his short brown ponytail dancing along with his words, "that the sovereign empire of Yndor reassert its natural rights. To abide by a dishonorable peace is little better than to live as a slave!"

Sardos did not reply to the prince's inflammatory conclusion. Indeed, part of the man's unnatural air derived from his utter lack of movement. Even when consciously striving to remain still, an ordinary man moves, his body swaying slightly, his chest expanding and collapsing with his breath, his eyes flickering. Not so Sardos. He sat as still as if he had been carved from the same stone as the palace. Yet his eyes seemed to devour Clannoch's words, as if, Cyrintha thought, they were calling them forth.

Still, it was Clannoch she was annoyed with, not Sardos. Cyrintha disliked Clannoch's new and increasingly solemn moods. Two years younger than she, Clannoch had always been the baby—and such a pretty baby. As a little girl, Cyrintha had devoted herself to playing with him, running through the palace in games of tag or hide-and-seek, deceiving him with petty tricks and practical jokes. For almost twelve years, it had been an idyllic childhood for both of them, but childhood must inevitably end, and that end came far more quickly for the offspring of the imperial line. As Cyrintha had grown into adolescence, she quickly realized that, as the imperial princess, she was destined to cement one or another of her father's more tenuous political alliances through marriage—a role which she resisted by studying magic with Holoakhan, for the rulers of Yndor dreaded nothing so much as the thought of marriage to a witch. Meanwhile, her brother began the arduous process of grooming and education necessary to prepare him to assume the leadership of the nation. As the years passed, the two children found ever fewer hours for games as the official business of the Jurin family began to claim their time. Cyrintha could not recall the day exactly, but there had been one day, she realized, when they had become less Cyrintha and Clannoch than the Imperial Princess and Prince. That was the day they had truly begun to grow apart.

And, Cyrintha realized, perhaps her annoyance at her brother and her instinctive dislike of Sardos stemmed from a motive as simple as petty jealousy. Her brother, by a fluke of heredity, would receive the job that she coveted.

But Clannoch's gender was not, of course, his fault,

and Cyrintha knew that she had little reason to be angry with him.

Very well. On that particular day, Cyrintha was in no mood to restrain herself in the name of so pale a motive as logic.

The young princess's brow furrowed as she turned her mind toward the task at hand. Imposing one's will on the brute objects of the material world was a strenuous chore for any wizard, even when the object in question was as simple as the leather drawstring that held up Prince Clannoch's breeches. Small beads of sweat began to form on Cyrintha's forehead and palms as she muttered inaudibly the words that imposed the domain of her will. She bent all her concentration to the simple act of tugging.

Then, suddenly, the tension in her body evaporated as the stubborn leather slid free. Clannoch's pants, already weighed down by the uncustomary burden of a sword, crumpled to the floor.

The flustered prince let out an unintelligible cry of surprise and, deflected from the course of his harangue, began to apologize to Sardos for the inexplicable event. Flushing deeply, he reached for his pants and tied the drawstring with particular emphasis.

Sardos said nothing, but he finally moved. His eyes shifted in one deliberate motion from Clannoch's face to the half-closed door. Clannoch followed the gesture and, comprehending, turned around. Cyrintha did not bother to flee. The corridor was too long and altogether too bare for any hope of escape. Besides, Sardos had somehow known that she was there. Indeed, Cyrintha realized that she had no desire to run away. She was in a combative mood, and this confrontation was what she had come for.

So, as Clannoch swung open the door, she smiled sweetly into his flushed face. As she expected, this mild gesture enraged him further. Scowling, he stepped forward and shook her by the shoulders.

"The most beautiful woman in the nation," he hissed, "and good for nothing save playing pranks. Why our fool father consented to your study of magic, I'll never understand—but when the old man dies, I promise you, I'll see you married within a week."

His words were punctuated by increasingly violent shakes. This was going too far. No one was suffered to lay hands on the imperial family, much less assault them. Akmar stepped forward silently and, from inside the room, Senz also slid into motion. Each man's hand moved lightly to his sword.

"Enough!"

The word resounded through the hallway like an avalanche, and was equally resistless. For the first time that day, Sardos had spoken, and his voice froze the blood of both young Jurins and their trothblades. All eyes turned toward the inscrutable adviser, but he sat as impassive as before. One would hardly believe that he had spoken.

It was Cyrintha who finally moved. She shot an angry, betrayed look at her brother, turned on her heel, and strode off. Akmar's hand left his sword's hilt and, with one curious glance at Senz, the trothblade followed his ward. Never before in the long history of the Jurin family had a trothblade been forced to lift his hand against a member of the imperial family. For Akmar, this seemed a dark omen of the days to come.

Cyrintha was still flushed with outrage when she reached her suite of rooms in the northwest tower. Akmar took up his position in the outermost antechamber, but Cyrintha hastened through sitting room, dressing room, and bedroom, slamming each door behind her as she passed. Finally, she drew closed the thick damask drapes and collapsed into the cool softness of her bed, her face buried in her arms.

She had long ago accepted the fact that Clannoch was no more the little brother she had played with around the palace. At the age of ten his imperial education had begun in earnest, and Clannoch spent most of his days studying the history of Yndor and the business of running it. Yet, for all that their childhood love had died away, they had maintained a common respect for it and treated one another with an easy geniality. Never, after even the most humiliating practical jokes, had Clannoch responded with such vitriol.

Cyrintha rolled over and sat up, pulling her knees up to her chin and wrapping her arms around her legs. She tried to dismiss the bitter pang of Clannoch's words and concentrate on what she had learned from them . . . for, despite the outburst—in fact, because of it—she had learned all she wanted, and perhaps more. Never before had Cyrintha heard her brother speak of the day that their father would follow their mother to the earth. Of course, Clannoch was the sole male heir to the imperial throne of Yndor and, as such, was obliged to consider his future as a monarch. Yet, that he comforted himself with thoughts of future power, that such ideas lay so close to the surface of his mind—this was a shocking discovery.

And, worse yet, Cyrintha had learned more than her brother's eagerness to assume the throne. She had also learned of his plans for her. If Cyrintha was able to put off many of her suitors by her eccentric behavior and magical apprenticeship, and was further able to convince a still-indulgent father that the remaining suitors were inadequate, she would suffer no such indulgence from Clannoch. Somehow, Cyrintha had always imagined that, on the strength of their childhood bond, her brother would have respected her wishes about matrimony. Instead, young Clannoch seemed eager to be the only Jurin left in the imperial palace, and this struck Cyrintha as suspicious.

She was suddenly seized with a desire to know more, to see what her brother was doing at that very moment. She had not learned very many practical spells from Holoakhan—the ways of magic were tortuously difficult to master—but she did possess the means for this particular task. Atop the nightstand next to her bed lay a small, silver-handled mirror. She snatched this up and laid it on the bed before her, then retrieved from a drawer in the nightstand a long pearl-tipped hairpin. She jabbed the end of the pin into the flesh of her pinkie and squeezed her finger until a single bright drop of blood fell like a bead onto the face of the mirror. As she wrapped her finger in a handkerchief, Cyrintha began to sing a low, melodious tune.

Once again, the exercise of magic made her body go rigid with exertion. Simple as the clairvoyance spell was, it demanded the utmost investment by the caster. And, even then, if Clannoch had left the immediate vicinity, the spell would fail. Indeed, even the more remote reaches of the palace lay beyond the limits of Cyrintha's fledgling power. Ignoring the possibility of failure, however, she focused her entire imagination on the figure of her brother. The princess continued singing, and her body began to tremble. The blue silk of her dress started to spot darkly with perspiration.

Suddenly, the drop of blood moved on the mirror. It rolled an inch, stopped, and rolled back randomly in a different direction. Wherever the drop had moved, a streak of color appeared, as if with every movement the drop was ripping free the covering from a painting that lay beneath the glass.

A low hissing sound reached her ears and, as a slender wisp of smoke arose from the mirror, it became obvious that the blood was heating up. Its motions became more frantic and it rolled quickly now, sliding across the mirror's slick surface until it hit the silver frame, then bouncing away in a different direction. The reflection of Cyrintha's face was soon streaked with unintelligible lines of color. In only a few moments more, there was little reflection left at all. As the drop continued its crazy flight across the glass, the random blotches joined together, turning disjointed patches of color into unified forms. A scene was taking shape and, finally, Cyrintha could begin to make out her brother's figure. Once again, his back was toward her.

After a few more seconds, the entire surface of the mirror became a coherent oval picture and the drop of blood evaporated completely. Now, faintly, Cyrintha could make out a voice—but it was not Prince Clannoch's.

"Naidjur is dead and the new parth must be anointed. It is tradition."

The low, cracked voice was that of her father. Cyrintha focused her will, and slowly the figure of her brother dwindled. Her mind's eye drew back, took in more of the scene, and soon she realized that her brother stood in her father's audience chamber—not the ornate throne room, which was used only for formal ceremonies, but the smaller hall in which Mallioch conducted the daily business of empire. He sat in a huge oaken chair, cushioned by elaborately embroidered pillows. His sturdy old frame was swathed in velvet robes and a simple gold circlet sat on his brow. The emperor was thoughtfully stroking his close-cropped white beard as he regarded his son.

Clannoch stood at the far end of a long wooden table that was strewn with maps, papers, and reports. A host of counselors and servants bustled about on errands, but many of them were watching the exchange with barely concealed interest. Cyrintha realized that the audience was public; she could just as well have walked downstairs, saving herself both the effort of the spell and a tender finger. But she held onto the image, reluctant to abandon the spell now that she had completed it.

"You should not leave Thyrsus," Clannoch warned. "Naidjur was killed by Chaldean treachery—"

"He was killed in an affair of *honor*, a challenge honorably tendered and honorably accepted. It is a shame that Naidjur did not prevail, and that it is not Crassus being buried on this day—"

"The earth is too noble to accept a burden so horrible!" Clannoch shot back. "Crassus, that Chaldean lapdog, should be executed and his body hung from a tree for the vultures."

The old monarch's eyes narrowed. "I do not expect you to sympathize with Crassus's politics," Mallioch rumbled, "but the role of a ruler is to enforce the law. Without the law, we have nothing."

"You *are* the law," Clannoch replied hotly.

"Yes," Mallioch agreed, smiling craftily, "yes, I am. And so long as I am, I will see myself obeyed. Had Crassus foully murdered Naidjur, he would be executed in the name of justice. But a duel fairly fought and widely witnessed shall not be punished, lest we mock our most hallowed traditions. And one such tradition, my dear son, is the emperor's anointing of new parths. Now, I will go to Aginath to anoint Garadjur parth in his father's place, and all shall be as it has been for generations."

"I still say it is dangerous for you to leave Thyrsus at this time. There is nothing the Chaldeans would relish more than an opportunity on your life."

Cyrintha drew in her breath sharply. Just a few minutes earlier, Clannoch had seemed to welcome nothing more than their father's early demise. Why this sudden solicitude? Had he repented his hot words? Or, Cyrintha wondered, was he maneuvering toward some mysterious aim?

But Mallioch waved a hand negligently at his son's remark.

"If I cannot leave my capital, then I am no monarch at all, and the Chaldeans have already conquered us." Then the old man smiled coyly and leaned back in his chair. "But what would you have me do, my son?"

"I would have you stay here in safety."

"And Garadjur would not be anointed parth?"

"I would go in your place and anoint him by your leave. And while there, I would speak to the people of Aginath."

"Speak to them of . . . ?"

Clannoch put his fists on the stout wooden table and leaned forward. "I would speak to them of Chaldus and the insidious subversion that led to Parth Naidjur's death. I would speak to them of *war*."

The entire image in the mirror swam wildly as Cyrintha heard her brother's words. It took the entire force of her will to calm down and stabilize the vision.

Mallioch had drawn himself up in his seat, and she could now see the outlines of the still-robust body that was often obscured beneath the emperor's velvet robes. He replied to his son with vigor. "There is no cause for war—"

Clannoch threw his arms wide, as if one had only to look to see cause aplenty. "They mobilize their troops on the banks of the Cirran—"

"As we mobilize our own," Mallioch finished sharply. "I know more of the doings in Chaldus than you, my son, and there shall be no war. Not yet." Then the monarch settled back into his seat and resumed his benign smile. "And what of you, Sardos? What say you of these evil times?"

Cyrintha realized with a shock that she had not yet drawn back her magical eye to a full view of the room. The images of Clannoch and Mallioch shrank somewhat as the far walls of the chamber slid into view along the edges of the mirror. There, in a corner by the fire, towering over the other men in the room, stood Sardos. He inclined his head slightly in recognition of the monarch's favor to speak.

"You are wise, as always, my liege. There need be no war yet, though it is well that your troops are prepared. Go to Aginath and anoint Garadjur, but take care. Clannoch speaks well. Trouble is afoot in Yndor, and our emperor is too precious to be risked."

Although his words were as deferential as any of Mallioch's courtiers', there was a strange impassive quality to Sardos's deep voice, as if nothing that he said in any way touched him.

In response, Mallioch merely nodded and smiled his unfathomable smile.

Slowly, Sardos turned his head until, it seemed, his eyes met Cyrintha's own. That was impossible, of course, but the very illusion chilled her. She could not bear the dead gulfs of Sardos' eyes.

Then, without her wishing it, the scene of the audience chamber vanished abruptly, leaving Cyrintha seated on her bed, staring into the image of her own ashen face.

CHAPTER 14

"**S**ome explanations are best left unknown," Barr Aston said, peering intently into Brandt's hazel eyes. The ex-minister's voice was suffused with weariness—a weariness beyond the years even he could boast of. "I have lived within Chaldus's secretive underside for the better part of a century, Mr. Karrelian, so I understand a man like you well—your compulsion to *know*, to ferret out the answer to any puzzle, no matter how insignificant or how obscure. You're young yet, and the secrets you've learned haven't begun to bow those fine shoulders of yours. But live another decade or two, and you'll begin to feel the weight of those secrets."

Aston paused and studied Brandt's face, his gaze searching past skin and bone for some sympathetic kernel of the man that could understand his plea. But Brandt sneered at the old minister. These pious government types with their precious responsibilities and cherished self-righteousness. . . . Aston was right, of course: secrets did weigh upon the soul. Brandt only had to consider the sewer of forbidden knowledge that rotted in his basement for confirmation of that theory. But that hardly meant that ignorance was preferable. If there was one thing Brandt *had* learned over the years, it was simply this: there was no piece of information that he trusted more in the government's hands than his own. What you knew hurt you, Bradt reflected, but what you didn't know might kill you—and he merely had to look at his oldest friend, lying crippled on the floor, for proof of that sad maxim. Carn seemed oblivious to the conversation. Propped against the wall, he sat staring at his legs, his brow creased and sweaty despite the sharp air of the Atahr Vin. Slowly, feeling a boiling rush rise through his veins, Brandt turned back toward the old man.

"We'll have that explanation now."

But Aston was not cowed by Brandt's glowering stare.

"Are you sure you've thought this through, Karrelian? When this business is over, you'll want to return to your mansion still able to enjoy it. But every word you learn from me will become a weary load to carry for the rest of your days."

Indeed, Aston reflected, only he understood just how heavy a load. No one had shouldered the truth longer than he.

"Spare me the melodramatic garbage," Brandt replied, fuming at the old man's sanctimony. "Carn and I have no innocence left to protect, thank you. Government corruption, clandestine wars, backstabbings, scandals—we know them all, and we sleep fine at night. But I won't move another finger unless I understand who you're so eager for me to find . . . and why."

Aston cleared his throat and spat on the ground. "Don't think you're so immune to the events around you, Karrelian. Every moment you waste here, your precious empire of generators comes closer to collapse. That should be information enough for you. Catch that assassin, or your fortune will crumble."

Brandt shrugged and turned his back to the old man. "You won't be able to climb out of here, will you, Carn?"

The older thief hadn't been paying attention to Brandt and Aston's conversation, and Brandt had to repeat his question. Finally, Carn looked up and shook his head. His heart was racing and his stomach felt strangely hollowed by disaster. If he tried to move, he knew, he would fall into a fit of trembling—perhaps even weep. Hysteria crouched at his shoulder, whispering the comforts of oblivion. But Carn knew that, having failed once today, he must not fail again. Brandt, as ever, was depending on him in ways that he could feel, yet not begin to fathom.

"I'm sorry, Brandt." At first, Carn's words came only with great effort, but his voice began to steady itself as he went on. "It's too long a climb for me to manage with my arms alone."

Brandt knelt by his friend's side and squeezed his shoulder. "I'll get a rope," he said quietly. "That means returning to the quarries. You'll be all right?"

The question was, of course, ludicrous. With greater desire than Carn had ever felt for anything, he burned simply to move his legs—just a twitch of his toes to tell him he would get better, that he would walk again. He would sacrifice everything he owned simply to be able to climb by himself out of the Khrine ruins and back into the sunlight of Prandis.

No, Carn thought, he wouldn't be all right, not ever again—but he bit back the thought and the bitter replies he could have made. Instead, he simply nodded and smiled at his old friend.

Brandt shot a last, dark look at Aston and turned to leave. At the doorway, he paused for a parting comment, without looking back. "Try to flee, and I'll track *you* down. It won't improve my temper."

But Aston was in no mood to be told what to do. He

advanced a step, wagging an index finger at Brandt.

"Someone's got to alert Intelligence. Karrelian, even if you won't help, it's crucial that we—What are you doing?"

Midway through Aston's speech, Brandt had turned around, an ugly look in his eyes, and headed back toward the old minister. Bending over, he retrieved one of the wires Hain had used to bind Aston's hands.

"Karrelian!"

Brandt caught Aston by the wrist and spun him around toward the nearest of the Khrine statues. He forced the old man's arms around the stone, hugging the statue around the waist, and quickly lashed his wrists together.

"Damn you, Karrelian, these statues aren't very stable. If I lose my balance—"

"Don't," Brandt suggested.

Then he disappeared into the Khrine tunnel and, within a moment, his soft footsteps faded away.

Barr Aston carefully turned his head toward Carn and surveyed the wreck of the man's legs with something like regret. Regret was not an emotion the old spymaster had experienced often in life, but he seemed to suffer it more and more these days. It was the true curse, he thought, of growing old.

"You know," Aston said softly, "you needn't have done that."

"Done what?" Carn replied, distracted.

"Lied. Told him that the assassin pushed that statue."

Carn considered this a moment, and a somber light kindled in his eyes. "When Brandt gets back, you'll tell him what he wants to know."

Then the two men lapsed into silence, Carn contemplating his crippled legs, and Aston his crippled world.

•   •   •

"He killed all our horses." Brandt announced with distaste when he returned. "I hired three from the quarry, as well as two men who weren't afraid of entering the tunnels—for enough money. They're waiting at the top of the shaft with the rope. We should have no trouble getting out of here—" Brandt said to Carn, casting a sidelong glance at Aston—"and taking a long vacation to Gathony."

Aston let a long breath escape his lungs. He did not in the least care about Brandt's implied threat. By almost any standards, Aston's eighty-two years made him an old, old man. He had been prepared to die throughout most of them—in his line of work, he had even expected to. Although he didn't relish the idea, he was no less prepared to die now.

No, Brandt's threat hadn't mattered a whit. Rather, what started Aston thinking was the room he had been hiding in for the last eight days. He still did not know, and would never know, what the large, dark chamber was for. Why had the Khrine wrought these fine, precarious statues of themselves, so many of which now lay in shards on the floor? Why did they never depict their own faces? Only the Khrine could say, but they were long extinct. And why had they died? Questions on questions that none could answer; one could only stare at the ruined fragments of a dead race and wonder.

And Barr Aston wondered how long it would take, if his bald attacker were allowed to escape, before some man walked the ruined streets of Prandis in the future and wondered what sort of people had lived there—and how and why they had died.

That last question Aston was only too capable of answering. He stood in the gloom, embracing a monument to the dead, pondering the ruin of all he had ever known, and reflecting bitterly on his circumstances. As ill luck would have it, the only man in all of Chaldus with the power to avert catastrophe was a thief and a scoundrel. Brandt Karrelian could not care less whether his country lived or died. Perhaps Aston could make him care, but to do so would mean to utter a thing that no one had uttered for centuries, to tell a tale that had been carefully scoured from the minds of men. But, Aston calculated, it was better to do this than to see his country scoured from the globe.

"I will tell you what you wish to know," Aston quietly announced, "if you swear two things: never to repeat what I say to a living soul, and to chase the assassin to the ends of the earth, if that's what it takes to kill him."

Brandt turned to the old man with some surprise. He had resigned himself to the idea that Aston would not speak. His curiosity surged at the prospect of discovering what, ultimately, had been behind all this tumult. But he shrugged as if he were no more interested in Aston's secrets than in discussing the weather. Brandt did, however, take a moment to twist free the wire that was holding Aston in place.

"I break my oaths all the time," Brandt replied, "so there's little point making them. Tell me what you want or be still. The choice is yours."

Aston's mouth twisted bitterly. This Hazard made nothing easy . . . except insofar as he was an easy man to dislike.

"Take your time thinking things over," Brandt added. "I'm not interested in anything you have to say until I've taken Carn to his doctor. Now, let's get out of here before the stonecutters I hired lose their nerve and flee this godforsaken place."

Taylor Ash's "new ideas" about Aston's where-abouts, Elena Imbress reflected, were beginning to drive her to distraction. Ash had wracked his brains trying to remember every anecdote Aston had every shared over lemonade in his office. Mostly, they had been childhood anecdotes, childhood places ... and, if populated by Barr Aston, only by his ghost.

A campground by a lake north of Prandis that Ashton had once frequented: Empty.

An old summer cabin once owned by an aunt: Now it was an animist church in the middle of the woods.

Finally, this red herring of ancient ruins called the Atahr Vin. From what Taylor remembered, Aston had never set foot in the place himself, but Aston's father had supposedly known it well. The scrapings at the bottom of the pot, Elena thought. She'd spent two hours that afternoon procuring maps and a key from the university that Wegman Aston had once worked for—two hours wasted on red tape, which meant that she'd never make it back to Prandis before dark. With her luck, she'd wind up having to spend the night at the limestone quarry she had passed before entering the ravine. Worse yet, as the sun's afternoon decline plunged the ravine into twilight, she began to wonder whether she'd even find the entrance to the caverns. From what she'd discovered at the university, the Atahr Vin was not exactly built to attract visitors.

Ten minutes later, she saw that finding the entrance would not be a problem. Not when two dead horses had been left there, no more than three hours earlier, as a signpost.

Damn it to hell, she thought. *Late again. And no surprise if there's a bloody gold capital in each of the horse's mouths. ...*

She struck the first match so hard that it broke. Cursing, she tried again and lit her lantern. There was nothing to do now but collect Aston's body. And, if she was lucky, find some locals who were more perceptive than they looked.

• • •

Upon returning to his estate, the first thing Brandt did was carry Carn upstairs, shooing aside the servants who rushed to help. Instead, he ordered the maid to turn down his bed so Carn could be put under the covers.

"You mean my bed," Carn suggested, all the while hoping that Brandt didn't trip underneath his weight. The way his luck was running, he'd fall on top of Brandt and break *his* back. . . .

"No," Brandt corrected. "I mean my own. It's bigger, and you may need the extra room."

Carn's brow creased with confusion. "Extra room? For what? I'd rather—"

"Too late," Brandt replied, cutting off further protest. He rushed through the sitting room that began his bedroom suite, headed for the larger room beyond. The center of that chamber was dominated by a huge bed of black wood, overhung by a canopy of ivory cloth. Brandt deposited Carn in the center of the pressed sheets and arranged the blankets neatly over his legs.

"Just give me a moment to get our other guest settled," Brandt said, glancing pointedly at Aston, "and I'll be back."

It was the work of a moment for Brandt to lock Aston in an adjacent bedroom, leaving one of his stablemen standing guard. He did not bother lying to Aston that the currier was there for the old man's protection; they both knew the guard's purpose was to prevent Aston from running away. Brandt paused in the hallway, alone for the first time in hours, and leaned his head back against the mahogany paneling. The day had been a damned disaster, he reflected. If only he had come straight home, bypassing Silene's and ignoring Elena Imbress. If only his pride hadn't pushed him to leave Silene's on foot that morning, he might have caught

Carn before his friend left for the Atahr Vin. If only he had been a fraction faster with his sword or a mite stronger. . . .

Instead, disaster. Carn crippled, and nothing more than a doddering old bureaucrat to show for it. Brandt closed his eyes, seeking a brief respite, but an image loomed over his imagination, bald and leering. Better to keep moving, to do something.

During his trip to the quarry, Brandt had written two quick notes and paid handsomely for an errand boy to deliver them to Prandis. The notes, he had noticed a few minutes ago, had borne their intended fruit. Two men sat nervously in a large, north-facing sitting room, awaiting Brandt's return. Time to turn his attention to them, he decided as he headed downstairs.

"Thank you for coming on such short notice, Dr. Pardi," Brandt said to a stout fellow of middle age, dressed in an embroidered blue robe. Pardi avoided the snug pants that were the style that year because of the substantial size of his paunch. Whatever the reason, there was something about a healer in robes that Brandt found comforting. "Your patient is upstairs in my bedroom."

Brandt turned to his other visitor, a slim, goateed man a few years Dr. Pardi's elder. He was settled in a huge armchair, poring over a number of very thick documents.

"Your job, Solan, depends on what the good doctor can tell us. It may be a while longer."

"I'm in no rush, Mr. Karrelian," the other said, his voice thin and high as a boy's.

Brandt nodded in reply before leading the doctor out into the hall and up a wide stairway to the second floor. Pardi was huffing by the time he reached the entrance to Brandt's suite, but he ignored his discomfort upon his first glimpse of the patient. The doctor's trained eyes fell immediately upon Carn's legs. They lay straight together, the feet hanging to either side. It was a posture

no man would ordinarily take, and Pardi could see that
Carn's legs had been arranged that way.

"How are you, my friend?" the doctor asked with
buoyant good cheer. Such a bedside manner, he had discovered after long years of practice, was less for his
patients' benefit than his own. Invariably, the exuberance of Pardi's spirits forced at least a grudging levity
. . . even upon the dying. There was no use, Pardi
thought, enduring the daily complaints of cripples.

And, indeed, Carn found himself swallowing back a
bitter reply to what seemed such a senseless question.
He spread his arms and attempted to grin. "Who could
be happier, doctor? I went forth today a working man
and, it seems, I return a man of leisure."

Pardi smiled briefly and began his examination, stripping Carn and rolling him onto his stomach. He probed
Carn's spine from the base of his skull down to his buttocks, paying special attention to the lumbar area. Here,
Carn's flesh was swollen and discolored. Without a
word, Pardi probed the purple and black bruises. He
shook his head and paused to rummage through his medical bag.

"Feel anything?" Pardi asked after a moment.

"Not at all," Carn replied.

"Now?" the doctor asked, a moment later.

"Nothing."

Pardi looked up at Brandt, who grimaced in return.
The doctor had inserted a straight pin slowly into Carn's
hamstring. By the time Pardi was done, the better part
of an inch had penetrated Carn's flesh, but the man
hadn't even twitched.

Pardi sighed and removed the pin, swabbing with a
ball of cotton the bead of blood that rose to Carn's skin.
The doctor then closed his eyes for a moment, collecting
himself. He laid his hands again upon Carn's spine and
began to chant an odd, lulling tune. After a moment, he
stopped and removed his hands. Where he had touched

Carn, the bruised flesh had become pale and was turning paler still. Brandt took a step closer, curious. Carn's skin had become as colorless as a jellyfish, and just as translucent. Beneath, Brandt could see the twined red bunches of muscles and the blood vessels that ran along and between them. Soon these, too, began to look bleached, and Brandt found himself staring, as if through a window in his friend's back, at Carn's very skeleton.

Pardi was clucking his tongue softly to himself, shaking his head as he did so. He began to trace lines with his finger along his patient's vertebrae. "Here . . . and here: fractures. Perhaps there would be some hope. . . ." Then the doctor placed a thick finger below a dark, jagged line that ran through the base of Carn's spine. Without a word, he looked at Brandt and shook his head.

Brandt returned the doctor's stare, glassy-eyed.

Pardi shrugged and rolled Carn over again, but the man's legs didn't move with the rest of the body. They remained crossed, the feet lolling lazily from the motion of his torso. Grimly, Brandt reached down and arranged his friend's legs. Then he drew up a thin woolen blanket that was folded at the foot of the bed, covering Carn to the waist.

"I'm not cold," Carn replied. Indeed, there was a sheen of perspiration gathered beneath his gray-brown, curly hair. Brandt paused a moment, then nodded and removed the blanket.

"I'd like to see my legs," Carn continued, "if I'm denied the privilege of using them." He turned to the doctor. "What can be done?"

Pardi opened his arms expansively. "Everything can be done. There's little reason why you shouldn't live a full and productive life—"

"That's not what I meant," Carn interrupted as he began to sense the direction of the doctor's reply. His eyes roved about wildly in his skull, as if seeking escape.

"What can be done about your injury itself?" the doc-

tor asked softly, understanding. "Nothing. The damage
is extensive."

"Is there no magic . . . ?" Carn began, but he choked
on the question.

"Magic is a blunt instrument," Pardi explained. "It has
its uses, of course, but this. . . . There is no cure subtle
enough to repair the extent of nerve damage that you've
suffered."

He had known, of course. From the first moment in
the Atahr Vin that he realized he couldn't move his legs,
Carn had known that he would never walk again. But
there had been more to think of: the danger of violence
between Brandt and Aston, the escaping assassin. . . .
Now, removed to the familiar domesticity of their house,
the house where Carn had gone about his daily routine
for years, the utter *change* of his situation struck him
with the force of a killing blow. Each of the doctor's
words pierced him, seemed to scoop out a portion of his
spirit, until, done speaking, the doctor had left him hollow. More gourd than man, Carn thought grimly. He
would echo inside when he spoke.

"Leave me." The command was not directed simply
at the doctor. He turned toward Brandt, and their eyes
locked. No words would suffice.

"Leave me," he repeated, almost a sob.

Brandt wanted to reply softly, to say that everything
would be all right, but that was a mockery. He had never
lied to Carn, and would not begin now. Taking Pardi by
the arm, Brandt left.

It was not a house. she thought. It was a city.
A small city within its very own walls, with room
enough for artisans, workmen, sailors, and soldiers—
room enough to warrant a mayor of its own. The entire
homeless population of Prandis could be sheltered
within those walls, spend their days from birth till death.

"Stop!" she called, as the carriage passed through the gates onto the broad cobbled avenue that led to the front doors. She feared she could not be heard over the clatter of the hooves. "Stop!"

The driver reined in his team, then turned back to look through the front window of the carriage. Tomas was a young man, but already four years in Master Karrelian's employ. Of all the passengers he had served during this tenure, Masya was one of the few who had cared to ask his name. She looked very small in the coach, he thought, nestled into a corner of the broad leather seat. Her flesh seemed paler than the moonlight.

"Can we wait here? Just for a moment?"

Tomas nodded crisply, fighting off the urge to smile. He was used to passengers telling him what to do, not asking his permission.

"As long as you wish, ma'am. Just tap on the glass when you'd like to ride on."

Masya nodded, and turned back toward the mansion. Impossible, she thought, that Carn spent his days and nights in this place, sharing it only with his employer and a few other servants. No, it was possible—possible, but wrong. How many rooms, just for a few men? Dozens? Hundreds?

Too much room, she knew, for her.

She leaned forward, wondering what she would say to Brandt Karrelian when she met him. Some pleasant-sounding lies that would burn her tongue for the rest of the evening. Not worth a dozen choirs from Belfar. But there was no escaping now. Tomas's straight back seemed to admit no possibilities other than proceeding to the mansion. And if she did turn away now, Carn would be upset. And he would not understand.

Sighing, Masya leaned forward and tapped on the glass.

•   •   •

When Aston's door opened, the force of the deed echoed through the room. A small shower of plaster fell from where the door handle had made a crater in the plaster.

Aston looked up to find a seething Brandt Karrelian.

"Time for you to talk."

By the tone of Brandt's voice, Aston could not tell whether that had been a statement or a threat. For a moment, he reconsidered his decision. Rather than spending time with Karrelian, if he could only get to Taylor Ash, tell him what he had learned about the assassin. . . .

"Well?" Brandt prompted. "I haven't all day."

"The first correct thing I've heard you say," Aston muttered to himself. "You and your business have less time than you think. . . ." But he abandoned his reverie and turned to the task at hand Without winning at least Karrelian's temporary allegiance, he could accomplish nothing.

"Have a seat," Aston proposed. "This may be some time in the telling."

Instead, Brandt grabbed the old man by the wrist and pulled him out of his chair.

"It isn't me who needs telling," he replied, dragging Aston out of the room and down the hallway. Brandt paused by the door to the master suite and leaned close to the minister, their noses almost touching. The muscles in his jaw bunched as he ground his teeth together.

"Now," Brandt growled, his fist growing tighter around Aston's wrist, "you're going to walk in there and talk to my friend. You're going to tell him what's so damned important that it's worth killing old men for. You're going to tell him why he walked into those ruins today to save your worthless neck. And you're going to tell him why that was the last bloody time he'll ever walk again."

Before Aston could respond, Brandt opened the door

and pushed the old man through. Aston stumbled a few steps forward, then regained his balance and continued under his own power, pausing at the threshold of Brandt's bedroom. Carn was sitting up in the large canopy bed, his broad torso propped up against the pillows. His head leaned back against the engraved headboard, eyes fixed on the white billows of cloth above him.

In his years at Intelligence, Aston had seen men broken. Ultimately, there was a place they retreated to, beyond the world's grasp. Carn, Aston supposed, had caught his first glimpse of that place upon the white muslin of the bed's canopy.

Before Brandt could prod him again, Aston proceeded into the room and seated himself in one of a pair of upholstered armchairs beside the bed. Brandt walked past the other chair and sat down lightly on the edge of the mattress. Carn's eyes did not move.

Gently, Brandt leaned forward and patted his friend's leg. The gesture provoked no reaction and, when Brandt realized why, he pulled his hand back and grimaced.

"Aston has something he wants to say."

Carn didn't seem to hear.

"Perhaps another time?" the old man suggested, half-rising from his chair.

"Now," Brandt growled, his voice barely audible. It was late enough already . . . and there was another man downstairs whom he had to see.

"As you wish," Aston replied. Then he leaned forward and, with an infusion of new energy, asked, "What year is this?"

Brandt blinked at the non sequitur. "What does that have to do—" But he saw that Aston was serious. "One hundred and seventy-eight," he answered.

"One hundred and seventy-eight *what*?"

This was absurd. Brandt began to wonder whether the assassin's drug had permanently addled the minister's senses. But the old man was peering at him with dis-

concertingly lucid eyes and an expression that spoke of
annoyance at Brandt's stupidity.

"This is the one hundred and seventy-eighth year of
the Republic," Brandt replied, feeling like a schoolchild
as he recited the formal answer.

"Ah, yes," Aston said, his eyes attaining a dreamlike
look. "That's what we say in Chaldus. The year of the
Republic. But what did we say before the Republic was
formed, when Chaldus was a hereditary kingdom like
Yndor?"

Brandt cast his mind back through the scattered bits
of Chaldean history that he had cobbled together during
his irregular education. One hundred and ninety years
ago, he knew, Chaldus had undertaken the Great Reformation. The country had been too large, too populated,
and too complicated to be run by a handful of hereditary
aristocrats whose abilities were subject to the wildest
flukes of genetic chance. More often than not, not one
in the bunch was competent to rule the kingdom.

Ultimately, the nobility had set about arranging a co-
operative system in which a general bureaucracy was set
up in Prandis, staffed by competent officials rather than
hereditary rulers. The idea was to remove the burden of
governance from the shoulders of the nobility while re-
taining all the privileges that nobility brought. The aristocracy's one mistake was authorizing the bureaucracy
to levy taxes—a prerogative it immediately began to exercise. Before long, a national army was in existence,
and it owed no allegiance to anyone but the ministers
who sat in the lower floors of a tower whose construction had just commenced in the heart of the city. Of
course, many of the nobles protested, some by force of
arms. But each one proved little more than a nuisance
to the national government they had created. After the
ineffectual nature of resistance became apparent, things
settled down into a political routine that had not much
changed until this day. Slowly, the aristocracy had run

out of money or simply died out, so only a few remnants like the Caladors could claim noble Chaldean blood.

When the Great Reformation was completed, almost nine score years ago, the calendars of Chaldus were altered to commemorate the event. From that moment onward, all days were numbered from the inception of the civil government. But before that . . . ?

"We counted from the Binding," Brandt said slowly.

"We counted from the Binding," Aston repeated with relish, "even as the Yndrians do today."

"So?" Brandt prompted, but now his voice lacked any hint of irritation. Despite himself, his curiosity was irresistibly roused by the bizarre preface to Aston's explanation. "What do calendars have to do with murdered civil servants?"

"Everything in the world," Aston replied inscrutably, nudging a corner of the rug with his toe. "What year would this be numbered in Yndor?"

Brandt shrugged. "I haven't the slightest—"

"Four hundred and thirteen," Carn answered, his voice gravelly.

Brandt shot his friend a curious look.

"The magnets we use in the generators are mined in the mountains north of Aginath," Carn explained, still staring up at the bed's canopy. "Naturally, their invoices are dated in the Yndrian manner."

"Four hundred and thirteen years," Aston repeated. "That's a long time, wouldn't you say? Too long for you to recall what the Binding was, Mr. Karrelian?"

"Centuries ago," Brandt replied, annoyed at Aston's superior tune, "Yndor and Chaldus fought the father of all wars. It was wizards, mostly, that did the killing— tens of thousands dead. Supposedly, the carnage sickened everyone so thoroughly that after the war was over, the most powerful of the surviving mages decided that the kind of magic they had used was too dangerous. They banded together and swore some oath about not practicing destructive magic—the Binding."

"That's the history we teach in schools," Aston acknowledged, "but the real details are somewhat different. In the first place, Yndor and Chaldus were warring, as usual, but they were not the only ones. Indeed, our ancestors were little better than heathens back then. The only thing that made them dangerous—and they *were* dangerous; millions, not thousands, died in the Devastation—was magic. Far beyond the limits of their wisdom, they had acquired immense arcane powers, taught to them by the Khrine. The Khrine themselves were largely a pacific race, and at first they did nothing but watch as their human pupils slaughtered each other wholesale. This caused strife within the ranks of the Khrine, and soon everyone was at war: Chaldeans, Yndrians, Khrine, and more. Great beasts lived in those days: dragons that destroyed houses with the mere beating of their wings and ogres whose footsteps shook the ground."

"Are you telling me my friend has been crippled because of fairy tales?" Brandt asked, his anger beginning to return.

"Let him speak," Carn said sternly, his eyes now closed, the lids twitching.

Aston paused a moment to peer at Carn before continuing. He would have to revise his estimates of at least some thieves, he thought.

"These are no fairy tales," the old minister said, returning to his explanation. "Would that they were. The general destruction was inconceivable, and it was worse nowhere than in Kirilei, the land in which Khrine civilization was centered. We now call Kirilei the Gonwyr."

Brandt drew in his breath. He had never been to the Gonwyr—indeed, as far as he knew, no man had been there and survived. It was a huge, blasted island that lay east of Gathony. Nothing lived, nothing grew in those barren wastes. It was said that the man who touched his foot to that blighted shore killed himself as surely as by slitting his own throat.

"The Gonwyr," Aston repeated. "It is a Khrine word, and in their language it means 'Our Sorrow.' For so it was. The devastation of the mages was vast and terrible. A land of gardens and graceful cities was swallowed up. Mountains vomited out of the earth itself and, in a short time, Kirilei was no more."

"What does any of this have to do with murdered ministers or my generator business?" Brandt asked, becoming more and more uncomfortable with the mythic proportions of Aston's tale. The old man, however, seemed to relish Brandt's discomfort. The thief had insisted on hearing, and hear he would. Aston would tell it his way.

"When the survivors looked upon what they had wrought, they swore that never more would magical war be waged upon the land. But they knew that such vows were futile. Men hate, and men war; and when they do, no one forsakes a potent weapon because of ethical concerns. No, our forebears were wise enough to see that, one day, mystic war would once again visit destruction upon us . . . provided there was magic to use. The only true solution was to prevent men from using this sort of magic again. There were two ways to do this. The first was to stop teaching the arcane lore—which is what most people think the Binding means—but, in truth, this solution could never work. Too many were adept, and not everyone would agree to take such knowledge to the grave. Indeed, even if every mage in the land had died instantaneously, the race would have started again from scratch—experimented, tested, improvised, until wizards once again walked the earth. The only real answer, then, was not to do away with magicians, but to eradicate the magic itself."

"The Binding stopped magic?" Carn whispered.

"Yes. It was an experiment of unthinkable proportions. The greatest of the surviving mages, Tarem Hamir, toiled for years in pursuit of a way to rid the land of magic. Ultimately, he concluded that magic was everywhere and that energy could not be destroyed. Nor could it be exhausted, as it was infinite. Since it could be neither eradicated nor depleted, the only solution left was somehow to control it. Thus, he devised a spell that would channel all of the world's magical energy into a set of rigid, predictable pathways. No longer would man be able to warp the natural fabric of existence so easily. His access to power would be cut off. And it was only after the Binding that electricity—including your generator business—became a possible alternative."

"This Hamir of yours didn't do such a great job," Brandt observed wryly, "or I wouldn't have so much trouble insulating generators from magical fields. If the idea was to eliminate magic from the world, I'd say the Binding was a flop."

Aston's eyes narrowed. "Truly? Then where are the dragons, the ogres, the great trolls that dwelt in the Grimpikes? What has become of all the fabled creatures of old, and even of the Khrine themselves? All these creatures existed by dint of magic. Their lives were sustained by the energy that they were so easily able to draw from the very air around them. Once the Binding cut off that energy, they withered and died."

"It seems that someone—the Khrine, if they were so powerful—would have objected," Brandt replied.

"Oh," Aston chuckled, considering the scope of Brandt's understatement, "there were countless 'objections.' Very bloody objections. But the Khrine were ever a sparse race, and few survived the Devastation. Those who did could not agree on what to do, and they fought among themselves. It is said that one Khrine in particular was fast friends with Hamir and, without him, the Binding never would have succeeded."

"Insofar as it did succeed," Brandt muttered.

Aston considered this thought as he stretched his back. "Sadly, you are correct, young man. The spell was not a complete success. Indeed, Hamir feared it might be too complete—that he would cut off the world from energy it desperately needed. All of civilization depended on the potency of magic, after all, and Hamir sought only to prevent its destructive excesses. It was a tricky business, arranging such a result. And remember, as soon as Hamir completed the spell, he would have to live with the results, for at the moment he spoke the last word, his own magic would diminish along with everyone else's. Neither he nor any other man would ever have the power to override the Binding."

Aston paused and sighed. It was here that the story should end, the great wizard having done his job. But, instead, it was here that the true story began.

"No, the wizard could not be sure . . . so Hamir, to our everlasting regret, built in a safety valve. When you have the chance to do something only once, and the result is uncertain, you hedge your bets. Hamir contrived within the spell a reversal, a way to undo the Binding and make the world again as it was before."

Brandt's eyes narrowed. "I'm finally learning something, old man—but not about murders."

Aston smiled at the thief's impatience. Brandt Karrelian was not so jaded as he liked people to believe. "It was of paramount importance to Hamir that the formula for reversal be carefully guarded—otherwise, all his work would be in vain. Thus, he split the spell for reversal into twelve Phrases. One Phrase he entrusted to the Emperor of Yndor, and five more to each of the Yndrian parths. The other six he bestowed upon the most powerful dukes of Chaldus."

"I'm beginning to like this Hamir," Brandt commented. "A neat scheme: splitting the reversal spell between two enemies ensures that it's never used, except in circumstances so pressing that even Yndor and Chaldus finally agree."

Aston nodded. "Exactly. Moreover, even the twelve Phrases will not themselves suffice to unmake the Binding. It is rumored that there is a key that Hamir and the Khrine wrought, and then hid away beyond the sight of men. What and where this key is, no one has ever discovered."

"As far as you know," Brandt added.

"As far as I know," Aston agreed. "But what Hamir hid would not easily be found. Men of his genius do not often walk the land—one of our few safeguards." The old man sighed. "In any case, there is little more to tell. Each Phrase automatically passes down from its possessor to his or her designated heir at the moment of death—or, in the case of Chaldean ministers, retirement. The Chaldean phrases were transferred from the nobility to the ministry during the Great Reformation. For more than four centuries, each Phrase has passed quietly from one guardian to the next—until now."

Until, Aston added silently, *some maniac decided to ruin the delicate balance that Tarem Hamir had so delicately crafted—and, in so doing, to push the entire continent toward the bloody embrace of war.*

"What do you mean?" Brandt asked. For days he had tortured himself, trying to imagine what might move someone to murder doddering old men. Finally, he had caught a glimmer of what could motivate such crimes. "Are you saying the Yndrians are stealing our Phrases?"

"Stealing?" Aston's face twisted in anguish. "Stolen, you should say. The assassin told me I was the last one. I have no choice but to assume that, while I was drugged, the bastard got what he had come for."

Brandt absorbed this information in silence, considering the implications of Aston's tale.

"And why," he asked finally, "would the Yndrians

want to undo the Binding? If the world before was as horrid as you describe . . . ?"

Aston chuckled grimly at the comment. "Of all people, Hazard, you should understand the answer to that question. Only a madman would seek to unravel the Binding. Perhaps a madman is behind the murders . . . but, more likely, the Yndrians intend to use the knowledge as leverage—perhaps to counter the economic edge we've gained of late. Blackmail, Hazard: surely you understand that."

Brandt responded with a sour smile.

"Not that we can be sure the Yndrians are responsible," Aston continued, more thoughtfully than a moment before. "There are other players to contend with as well: Brindis, Gathony, the northern tribes. None of these peoples was developed enough in Hamir's day to entrust a Phrase to them. Perhaps they seek a share of the legacy, little good that it will do them."

Again, Brandt paused to ponder what he had learned. Before, Aston's talk of dragons and Khrine and magical wars had only irritated him, hinting at a problem with dimensions so broad that it defied comprehension. But this idea of stealing Phrases to gain political leverage . . . Brandt was able to calculate the contingencies with ruthless efficiency.

"You're right, Aston. Blackmail is something I understand, and blackmail's first rule is that no information has value unless it can be *used*. It seems to me that only a fool would ever use these Phrases. From what you say, the Yndrians would have as much to lose as we would if the Binding were undone. Why not simply laugh in their faces if they try their blackmail?"

Aston stepped close to the thief and gripped his arm with a surprising, wiry strength. The old man's weathered face leaned within an inch of Brandt's.

"Because, Hazard, unlikely as it is that they will ever be used, these twelve Phrases should never be possessed by any one man or government. Because, indeed, if any madman should chance to use them one day, we would cease to recognize the very world we stand on."

The corners of Brandt's mouth twitched with amusement. "You sound like a lunatic preacher, Aston, foretelling the apocalypse. It's a pity I'm not the churchgoing type."

The old minister trembled with fury. "Is there nothing, Hazard, that does not fill you with amusement? With ignorant contempt? This is no joke, and I ask you again, what will you do?"

Brandt stood there for a moment, his arms hanging loosely at his sides, then turned back towards Carn. *It all depends on you*, he thought. But Carn seemed to have drifted away from the conversation again, his eyes fixed upon a vacant spot on the wall.

Aston followed Brandt's glance to Carn and frowned. He had done worse things to men before in his life, but never as mistakenly. He began to say something, then paused as he realized that he had forgotten the crippled man's name. Quietly, he cursed his spotty memory. Perhaps it had been the adrenaline of the moment . . . or perhaps he was simply growing too old.

"What is his name?" Aston whispered, leaning forward.

Brandt paused, hoping Carn would answer the question himself, but his friend showed no sign of having heard. Frowning, Brandt turned to Aston to answer.

But before the words reached his lips, they were echoing up from the entrance hall, framed by a voice he didn't recognize.

"Carn! Carn Eliando!"

Tomas helped Masya down from the carriage and accompanied her up the broad flight of steps that led to the mansion's double doors. Impossible, she thought, that such doors would open for the likes of her.

And they didn't.

After half a moment, it became apparent that the twin doormen were not just slow to react. They did not mean to let her in. Tomas took a step forward, looking one in the eyes, then the other.

"We are expected," he said quietly, embarrassed to be arguing in front of his passenger, as if the doormen's intransigence were somehow his fault. Despite the size of the estate, Brandt Karrelian kept a small staff, so Tomas knew these men well: Dannel, always quiet, and Baley, who strained the seams of his uniform.

"Master Karrelian instructed us that the house would not be taking visitors tonight," Baley replied.

Tomas glanced backward, absorbing in an instant the look of confusion on his passenger's face. It seemed unfair that she be penalized for one of Master Karrelian's moods, especially when it was Master Eliando who expected her company.

Tomas was tempted to push past Baley and open the door himself, but he knew those handles too well. His first day on the job, Master Eliando had asked Tomas to open those doors—the same doors that Carn himself had just opened by way of demonstration. Upon touching the handle, Tomas had snatched his hand back, having received a shock—not painful, but certainly unpleasant. Every door in the mansion, Carn had explained, was magically keyed to open only to specified personnel— one of the mansion's numerous security measures.

Tomas turned back to his passenger, trying to keep his face placid.

"Begging pardon, ma'am, but I'll have to ask you to return to the carriage now."

Masya's fingers fluttered nervously upon the clasp of her purse.

"But—"

"They won't let us in, ma'am. I'm sorry, but there's nothing to be done."

With that, Tomas took her gently by the elbow and helped her back into the carriage, closing the door gingerly after she climbed inside.

"I'll thrash that man soundly," Masya muttered as she settled into the cushions.

But, no, she decided—*she* was the one who deserved the thrashing. It was no one's fault but her own that she had felt as uncertain as a schoolgirl on Brandt Karrelian's front steps. Slowly, humiliation began to turn to anger. She had not wanted to come here at all, not wanted to glimpse the place she feared would keep Carn apart from her. Masya had always known, in a vague way, that her lover's life at the Karrelian estate was opulent . . . but knowing was different from seeing it. And far different from having it rubbed in her face that she did not belong, was not even welcome within the front door. She should have known better than to have come, to have been bribed by the promise of choral tickets.

The carriage had come to a halt again. Masya looked up, puzzled to find that Tomas had not taken them back to the road. Instead, they had circled to the rear of the mansion. Through the slim windows set in the gray stone, Masya could glimpse a kitchen larger than her entire home.

The carriage door opened. A nervous-looking Tomas proffered his hand.

"Some doors of this house," he explained, "I can open for you. I can't explain the doormen's actions, ma'am, but I know Master Eliando was firm that I bring you here on time."

Tomas helped her down from the carriage and led her to the kitchen door, one of three servants' entrances that he was authorized to unlock. As he opened the door, he noted that the room was vacant, sparing him the difficulty of explaining why he was bringing a guest through the kitchen.

Copper pots, Masya thought as Tomas led her by hand past rows of burnished cookware. *No tin for this cook.*

They walked quickly through a series of narrow servants' hallways, then passed through a paneled door into a broad entrance hall. The hardwood floors gleamed beneath the light of a hundred electric bulbs. And, standing before the first step of a long, curved stairway, his face flushed, was the doorman Baley.

"What's got into you, Tomas?" the large man huffed. "Trying to get us all into trouble, are you?"

Tomas stepped forward, interposing himself between Baley and Masya.

"Whatever Master Karrelian told you, my instructions from Master Eliando were clear. He wanted to see this woman here, tonight. Now."

Baley frowned and tugged at his collar. "Things have changed. Master Carn won't be seeing anyone tonight."

It was the tone of his voice as much as what Baley said that struck her. Something was terribly wrong—and, suddenly, Masya didn't care whose house she was in. Before either Tomas or Baley could react, she had slipped past both of them, springing up the stairs two at a time while she called her lover's name.

When the door at the top of the stairs swung open, it wasn't Carn who greeted her. Instead, it was a smaller, younger man with a sword in his hand. His momentum carried him to the very edge of the stairs, bringing the tip of his blade only inches from Masya's nose. Startled, Masya came to a sudden stop, grabbing the banister to keep from falling backward. The man paused, glancing at her and then at the sword in his hand. Warily, he lowered the weapon.

"Who the hell are you?" he demanded.

It was, Masya thought, the tone of voice she would expect from a man who owned a house the size of a small city.

"You must be Brandt Karrelian," she said, half to herself.

So this was her rival for Carn's loyalty. Not quite what she had expected, Masya thought as she assessed the man. He looked bone-tired and was wearing three-day-worn clothes—not satin robes and gold chains. His hazel eyes were guarded, inscrutable. Whatever Carn saw in the man, Masya decided, lay far beneath the surface.

Brandt frowned, weighing the sword in his hand and wishing it felt more useful.

"I know my own bloody name," he replied. "I asked for yours."

At that moment, Tomas reached the top of the stairs, his posture all fear and apologies.

"This is Lady Masya, sir," Tomas began. "I'm terribly sorry to have disturbed your evening, but Master Carn was quite explicit that the lady here be brought on time for the chorale."

Chorale? Everyone was talking nonsense tonight. But Masya . . . ? That name rang a bell. This was the woman that Carn visited in the city so often. Brandt looked again at the sword in his hand and grimaced ruefully before sheathing it.

"No, I'm the one who's sorry," he replied wearily. How was he to explain any of this to Masya, this confused-looking woman in her simple floral dress? "I'm afraid there's been an accident," he said, glancing over his shoulder at the door to the bedroom suite.

Before he could go on, Masya had shot past him, up the last few stairs, and across the hallway, into the bedroom.

"I'm so sorry, Master Karrelian," Tomas continued,

his face ashen. "I'll take her home just as soon as—"

"Forget it," Brandt answered. "Just leave us be."

And then he turned back toward his rooms, wondering what else this night might bring.

When Brandt entered the bedroom, he found Masya seated at the edge of the bed, her arms wrapped around Carn, her face buried in the hollow of his neck, as his was buried in hers. She was murmuring something to him, though Brandt could not make out the words. And Carn . . . Carn was sobbing. Brandt had never seen him shed a single tear over the course of two decades, much less this—this almost-howl that wracked him. Masya continued to cling to him, like a small ship tossed upon the waves, whispering incessantly. Carn's arms were wrapped around her waist, and Brandt could see the play of his muscles beneath the fabric of his shirt. He was hugging her so hard he must be hurting her, but the woman didn't complain.

Aston was the first to move, rising from his chair and retreating toward the door, touching Brandt lightly on the arm as he walked by. The look on Aston's face said what Brandt knew all too well—that this was a private moment, with neither of them invited. But Brandt lingered a moment longer, watching Carn's sobs slowly subside and his tortured breathing calm. And he realized that what he was feeling was jealousy, the envy of something he had never known.

Standing there, jealous of his only friend, a man he'd seen crippled that day, Brandt had never felt smaller. Cursing himself, he finally left the room.

Aston was waiting in the hallway, staring at Baley, who had resumed his position downstairs by the front doors.

"May I leave now?" he asked quietly as Brandt emerged.

"Go anywhere you like," Brandt snapped back. "Go to hell for all I care."

Then he stopped and paused, looking up at the old man. Aston said nothing, but Brandt could see the judgment lurking behind his blue eyes.

"Go anywhere," Brandt added, "but you may not want to go home."

Briefly, Brandt sketched out what he had learned at Calador's estate: that the assassin they had met in the Atahr Vin was not the only killer on the loose. Aston nodded as he absorbed the information. Neither had to voice the unspoken conclusion—that there would be elements of the government willing to kill him to keep the Phrases out of the enemy's hands.

"If you want," Brandt concluded, "I'll have Tomas drive you back to the Atahr Vin. But if I were your age, I'd avoid the chill air. Stay here, if you like. The house is well protected and I doubt anyone would think to look for you here."

Aston's lips slowly curled into a smile. "You surprise me, Karrelian."

Brandt shrugged and headed downstairs, to the sitting room where Solan was waiting.

When Tomas saw Masya emerge from Master Karrelian's rooms, she looked like a different woman. Tear-streaked, yes, but stiff-backed, with determination in her eyes. She seemed, somehow, bigger than the hallway.

"Tomas, just the man I need."

"Shall I be taking you home, ma'am?"

Masya nodded. "Yes, but only long enough to pack my things. Carn will need looking after . . . and it's clear that no one in this house is up to the job."

Tomas's eyes widened in surprise. He doubted that Master Karrelian would agree with the woman—or simply allow her to move in—but it seemed that Masya was not interested in asking anyone's permission. The edges of Tomas's lips twitched upward in a barely suppressed smile. It was high time a woman took up residence in the mansion.

He held out his arm and escorted her down the stairs.

Half an hour later, when Brandt and Solan entered the room, they found Carn asleep. Brandt walked straight to the bedside, but hesitated to wake his friend. Carn could use a little peace, a brief respite from a situation that seemed unreal, impossible. This morning, a man wakes up, swings out of bed under his own power. Now, a few hours later . . . hours? The difference had been minutes. A few ticks of the clock, Brandt reflected, and he could have been there early enough to stop the assassin. Ride straight home, instead of stopping at Silene's, and he would have been by Carn's side in the Atahr Vin—not a few damned minutes late.

Squint my eyes, Brandt thought, *and time rolls backward.*

In the dim light, the gray in Carn's hair vanished, the wrinkles disappeared—he seemed whole again, snoring gently, no different from the first time Brandt had seen Carn sleep, years ago in Belfar. Barely sixteen years old, Brandt and another street thief, Marwick, had broken into an industrialist's house, looking for jewels. Hell, looking for anything valuable, portable, and easy to fence. Little did they know that Carn had already broken into the house, searching for papers that the industrialist's rival needed. And little did they intend to trip an alarm that Carn had skillfully avoided, almost getting all three of them caught by the city guard in the process.

A mad sprint through the streets of Belfar had ensued,

terminating in the safety of Carn's one-room flat where, somehow, Marwick had convinced Carn not to thrash them for ruining his job. Typical Marwick, Brandt thought, talking fast as a carnival barker—and making little more sense—until Carn had no choice but to laugh at them both. Cooked them dinner and, when he found out they were living on the street, offered them a place to stay—provided they bathe off their alleyway stench. By the time Brandt emerged from the tub, Carn had retired to bed, his chest rising and falling steadily, as if he were asleep.

Waiting to catch us rummage through his things, Brandt had thought. *Playing possum to see whether he can trust us.*

Young Brandt had sat in the corner of the room, studying Carn intently for the next two hours. The only change he'd observed was a sporadic snore. Long after midnight, Brandt had realized that Carn *had* been asleep the entire time—he already did trust them. The first time anyone had trusted street rats like them.

"Perhaps," the lawyer suggested in his strangely whistling, high-pitched tones, "we should come back later."

Solan's voice recalled Brandt to the present—to a time that could not be rolled backward, where Carn was not just sleeping, but crippled.

Fine way to repay that trust, Brandt thought. *Carn would've been better off beating us and kicking us out, where we belonged.*

Brandt motioned for Solan to join him at the bedside. The lawyer hesitated, uncomfortable at the intrusion. Despite his age, he looked somewhat childlike, Brandt realized—always half-swallowed by the large black suits he wore.

"There is no later," Brandt said. "This has to happen now."

The lawyer came forward and deposited the documents he was carrying on the side of the large bed. Carefully, he separated the papers into three piles, fidgeting with the edges to make the piles neat.

"I suppose I'll be signing these for the better part of an hour," Brandt sighed.

"No, your part is simple," Solan countered. This was a standard refrain of his, but what was simple for the lawyer invariably left Brandt with a colossal headache.

Solan produced a pen and handed it to Brandt, who began to sign in a variety of spaces that the lawyer dutifully pointed out. All told, it took a mercifully short time.

"Now it's his turn," the attorney said, turning toward Carn, who was softly snoring.

For the second time that day, Brandt woke Carn with their old sign, a gentle prod just above the hip. Carn rubbed his eyes and looked about, surprised to see Solan in the room. Then he saw the stacks of papers laid out beside him.

"What's this all this about?"

Solan stroked his goatee, as if preening himself in preparation for a formal dissertation on the law.

"Briefly," Carn added, and his eye found Brandt's. A glint of humor almost caught there, but neither man's mood could nourish that weak spark into laughter.

"Briefly," Solan began, oblivious, "this is a power of attorney."

Brief, for Solan, unfortunately meant cryptic.

"Power of attorney?" Carn repeated. "You're the attorney. What do you mean?"

Solan sighed, appalled as usual by his clients' ignorance of the law that regulated their lives.

"I mean that once you sign these papers, you assume sole control of all Karrelian business enterprises. You oversee and direct all corporate activities and ventures, you authorize budgets, you determine production. You even assume the management of Mr. Karrelian's private assets, for the purposes of investment, estate maintenance, and the like. The salary terms are the most generous I've ever seen, so I assume you won't balk—but any emendations in that area can be made simply."

Carn turned to Brandt, still puzzled. "You're giving me . . ."

"Giving nothing," Solan interrupted with pedantic precision. "This is a matter of control, not ownership. You merely run all of Mr. Karrelian's concerns until his return."

"His return," Carn echoed. He drew in a breath, cool and damp. In the gathering darkness, he could almost believe himself back in the Atahr Vin. "The Binding. You're going after him."

"To hell with the Binding," Brandt growled in return. "To hell with Aston and to hell with Imbress and to hell with the entire Ministry of Intelligence." As he spoke, he could feel the boiling surge of rage, just as he had in the Atahr Vin, but his voice remained low and cold. "Damn them all, and damn all of Chaldus and Yndor besides. I'm going after *him*."

And the image hung in Brandt's mind, as clear as Carn's own: the bald skull beaded with sweat, the pupils dilated so the irises seemed only thin, dark bands. That leering smile.

Galatine Hazard was going to find an assassin named Hain.

And, when he did, he was going to cut his legs off.

CHAPTER 15

"**O**ur ranks are somewhat slim today," Andus Ravenwood commented as he entered the room.

"I can make up amply for those who are missing," Jame Kordor replied, patting the rich curve of his paunch. And then, characteristically, Kordor killed the already weak joke by calling further attention to it. "Never accuse a party of slimness," he announced broadly, "while I'm in attendance."

Landa Wells, the Minister of the Interior, rolled her eyes.

Chaldean Ministers of Finance, Ravenwood reflected glumly, had never been famous for their wit. It was strange, though, to see Kordor in such a good mood when, only yesterday, he had seemed greatly disturbed. Now he acted like a man from whose shoulders a great weight had been lifted. Like a man who had made a decision. Andus wondered what sort of decision it could be.

"Our attendance is lagging," Orbis Thale said soberly, ignoring Kordor's joke. In the wizard's presence, humor fared as well as a drop of water on a hot skillet. "During such a crisis, I would expect more diligence."

Ravenwood took his seat in the deeply cushioned leather chair at the head of the table and looked around. Neither the Minister of Intelligence nor his counterpart from War was to be seen. Rather than six ministers gathered around the large, dark table, there were only four, as well as Kevin Arnod, Ravenwood's Underminister from Foreign Affairs. Arnod functioned as acting minister of that department while Ravenwood held the Prime Minister's chair. The representation of four ministries constituted a quorum, but given the tidings lately blown their way from the west, it was the Ministers of War and Intelligence who were most needed.

Ravenwood grimaced as a pain shot through his side. If only he had time to consult his doctor, perhaps discover he was dying of a tumor—now *that* would be a blessing. Instead, he had, as always, only his work to look forward to.

"I'm afraid I can't explain our colleagues' lateness," Ravenwood sighed. "I sent both their offices notice of this special meeting. I assumed they would be here—"

Just as Ravenwood finished these words, the large oak door swung open and a young, soberly dressed man entered. Beneath his blond hair was a drawn, grave face that all the ministers recognized.

"Mr. Annard," Kordor said in greeting, "I assume you are here to explain your superior's absence?"

Jin Annard unbuttoned the jacket of his dark blue suit and took a seat next to Orbis Thale. It was Taylor Ash's chair, the traditional seat of the Minister of Intelligence. More than a few ministerial eyebrows were raised.

"My explanation," Annard began, "will be brief. There are far more pressing matters than Minister Ash's whereabouts."

"But as for those whereabouts . . . ?" Landa Wells had leaned forward, placing her elbows on the table.

"Yndor."

"Yndor?" It was a chorus of surprised cries. Everyone seemed shocked except Orbis Thale, who had neither moved nor spoken, and remained as hidden beneath his cowl as ever. Ravenwood, however, had risen from his seat.

"You had better explain yourself, Mr. Annard," Ravenwood said, regaining his composure and slowly sinking back into his chair. "And never mind how long it takes. Explain yourself well."

Annard seemed unruffled by the commotion he'd caused. Indeed, he'd expected worse.

"The minister felt that, considering the enormity of the current situation, he was obliged to enter the field."

"That's absurd," Ravenwood countered. "That's why he has a network of thousands of operatives—so he can stay here and coordinate them."

Annard smiled slightly—a reaction that Ravenwood interpreted as Annard's subtle way of demonstrating frustration with minds less dexterous than his own.

"The minister is still coordinating," Annard explained. "We do have a network of thousands of operatives, and that means we can funnel our reports wherever we like. We center our administrative operations in the Tower out of convenience, not necessity. Wherever he goes, Minister Ash contacts local agencies to gather current intelligence and redirect our activities. And, this way, he also gets to see what's happening himself."

"It's an unnecessary risk," Kordor commented, aghast, his jowls trembling with outrage. "He's too important!"

Privately, Jin Annard agreed only too acutely with Kordor's conclusion. Although Taylor had been as fine a field operative as the ministry could produce, there were dozens of other fine operatives, each one of them perfectly expendable. Imbress, for instance . . . or even himself. Everyone was expendable, Jin thought grimly, except Taylor Ash—the one man who had chosen to voyage directly to Thyrsus, the most dangerous city of all. What mad compulsion had driven Taylor to Yndor, Jin could not begin to guess, but he knew one thing: it was irresistible. Taylor had refused even to listen to Jin's and Imbress's arguments before he'd thundered off on that great chestnut stallion of his. Fleeing like a madman, Jin thought. And that left Jin here, in Council Tower, feeling a little resentful and very, very alone.

But Jin would admit none of these qualms to the High Council, and especially not to Jame Kordor.

"At the moment," Annard replied, "no one is too important." He reflected that Kordor would never have made a career for himself if the man's job had required fieldwork of any sort. "Moreover, most of the minister's prior fieldwork was Yndrian. He's acquainted with the territory, the language, and the people."

"He can't be in Yndor yet," Ravenwood observed. "He attended our last meeting only a few days ago."

"I overstated," Annard conceded. "He is currently en route."

"Then we could order him to return," Kordor suggested. "He must have just embarked."

Ravenwood considered this for a moment. "No. Ash has always known what he's doing. This is utterly unprecedented, but I'm inclined to trust him."

"These times," Orbis Thale rumbled, "are unprecedented. It is only natural that our actions correspond."

"It's settled, then," Ravenwood decided. "In Ash's absence, Mr. Annard will represent the Ministry of Intelligence in all Council affairs. Now, if only Pale would show up—"

"I believe I can explain that as well," Annard said quietly. All eyes turned to him, more curious than ever. "This morning, Minister Pale and Minister Ash dueled on Hawken Heights."

"What?"

For the second time that day, the ministers had reacted

with a gasp of astonishment, and this time Ravenwood was not the only one to jump from his seat. Even Jame Kordor had half risen, leaning heavily on the mahogany table before him. Only Orbis Thale remained in his seat, but even his dark eyes were glowering from beneath his cowl at Jin. Jin could not remember such unrelenting scrutiny since his confirmation day as underminister.

"The reasons are extraneous," Annard continued, keeping his voice calm, "although it should suffice to say that both men were justified in their actions, and that the reason for the duel was personal."

"This will bear looking into," Ravenwood murmured. "Much looking into."

Kordor's eye wandered to the empty seat nearby where Amet Pale was wont to sit. His usually ruddy face had turned a sickly pale.

"Then . . . Ash . . . ?"

Inwardly, Jin sighed. This would be the truly difficult part.

"No, Minister Ash did not kill Minister Pale. Before the duel ended, Minister Ash was rendered unconscious by a sling bullet."

"But Pale didn't kill Ash?" Ravenwood asked. It was a tactless comment, he knew as soon as he'd uttered it. It implied that Pale would take unfair advantage during an affair of honor. But, frankly, Pale had never impressed Ravenwood as the type to stand on ceremony when he wanted something done. Indeed, how else was the sling bullet to be explained?

"He had no chance," Annard explained, "because he was rather more occupied with the man who began torturing him for his Phrase."

This time, the uproar lasted much longer as the ministers drowned out each other's questions with the sheer volume of their cries.

Orbis Thale arose, spreading his arms wide enough for his black robes to blot out the light from the window behind him. "Quiet!" he said, his voice low and urgent. "Quiet!"

Slowly, the ministers settled down, but none of them seemed calm. One of their own had been attacked, a sitting minister. Kordor glanced about nervously, trying to reassure himself with the thought that Kermane Ash was dead. His own Phrase, Kordor told himself, had already been taken by the enemy. He should be safe.

"Why weren't we told of this immediately?" Ravenwood demanded.

Annard's slim shoulders rose in a noncommittal shrug.

"All our efforts have been bent toward finding the culprit," he replied.

"And?"

Annard sighed. "And it has been a very busy day Just one hour ago, we found the dead body of Barr Aston. We believe that our assassin now possesses all the Chaldean Phrases."

This time, there was no commotion. Everyone around the table absorbed the information in silence, looking about nervously, hesitantly.

"Since Pale is dead," Ravenwood finally said, "General Celwan should be here in his place. We need to consult with the Ministry of War immediately about this."

"Pale is not dead," Annard announced.

This raised more eyebrows. To the best of their knowledge, no one had ever survived an attack by the mysterious assassin.

"Apparently, the killer was interrupted by a group of riders and, having what he wanted, fled. The minister is convalescing, and I am unsure why Celwan has not come in his place."

"Because I intended to be here."

The voice issued from behind the door which had very quietly opened, how long ago no one could say. It was a hollow voice, without resonance, and everyone recognized it immediately. They turned to watch the entrance of Amet Pale.

The minister was arrayed in full battle garb: steel plate armor, the breastplate of which had been enameled in black and decorated with the seal of Chaldus. A velvet cape was fastened at each shoulder and billowed behind him. Ravenwood could not remember a day that Pale had arrived at the Council Chamber in armor, but this was only a momentary thought. Ravenwood, like each of his colleagues, could not draw his eyes away from Amet Pale's face.

A grid had been snapped upon it, a horrible network of lines that crossed and recrossed what had once been smooth, rounded flesh. Two horizontal lines ran across his brow, another across the middle of his nose, the next just above his lips, and the last across the chin. These were intersected by a vertical set: one barely forward of each ear, another bisecting the eyelids and cheeks, and a last along his nose, dividing the general's face exactly in half. The lines ran from his hairline down to his collar, leaving not a patch of skin unmarred.

Pale took a step closer, his scarred mouth twitching into a smile. With horror, Ravenwood could perceive the *depth* of those black lines, as if a network of wires ran across Pale's face and had been pulled tight behind his head, creating deep channels in the man's flesh.

Ravenwood considered his long acquaintance with Pale, especially the frequent, insufferable military banquets. The man had always preened himself, womanized, loved his features. How could he stand such horror?

"I see you found a competent healer," Orbis Thale said, the first to greet the Minister of War.

Pale ran a gloved finger down his central, vertical scar

and his smile twitched more deeply in private appreciation.

"Yes, indeed. These would have been pink for months yet, but a wizard I know accelerated the process."

Pale walked around the table and took his chair, leaning closer to Jame Kordor than strictly necessary as he bent to sit down. He relished the look of terror that flew across the Minister of Finance's soft features.

So this, Pale thought to himself, is what it is to be feared. He savored the feeling, and decided that it would provide a rare and fine sustenance.

"Now, gentlemen," Pale suggested in his odd half-whisper, "shall we discuss war?"

Twenty feet beneath him, Madh could feel the thrum of the River Mirth against the pilings that supported this sorry excuse for a sailor's inn. The peeling paint, the thin straw mattresses upon the cots—none of the inn's squalor mattered to him. What he liked was the distant feel of the river, inexorable and passionless upon its course to the sea. There lay a purity that fascinated him: neither agent nor instrument, but a thing unto itself.

Rising against the syncopated beat of the river came the steadier rhythm of Hain ascending the stairs. Briefly, Madh pondered the image of Hain immersed in the river, blue-tinged body borne to sea. A peaceful thought. And so it was that Madh was smiling when the assassin threw open the door to their room.

"Congratulate me," Hain announced, jauntily tapping his temple. "I've got the last of your gibberish."

"Excellent," Madh replied, his smile fading, "but why are you late?"

Hain ignored the question, glancing through the grimy window at a sky that was now only half-lit by the dying rays of a setting sun. He did not suppose Madh was truly curious about an afternoon of celebration upon the docks.

"What business is it of yours, as long as my job is done?"

"Your job isn't done until you deliver what you've learned to my master." Madh leaned closer, noticing that the assassin smelled of brandy and women. "Now tell me what happened at the crypt."

Hain shrugged. Madh always insisted on the details, although it was only the results that counted. The assassin pulled off his boots and tossed himself on the musty-smelling cot in the corner.

"I followed that gray-haired man into the Atahr Vin, as you ordered."

"His name is Carn, I believe," Madh said softly. Yes, that's what Karrelian had shouted in his study so many weeks ago: *Carn, fetch my sword!*

"I couldn't care less about his name," Hain said, "but how did you know he'd be going to Aston?"

Madh said nothing in reply, thinking back to his for-tuitous trip to Aston's house that morning. If Carn had not searched Aston's library so thoroughly, Madh might still have been looking for the old minister. In a way, Madh supposed, Galatine Hazard had wound up working for him after all. This was just the sort of irony that Madh relished; he feared it would serve as his sole en-tertainment as long as he was saddled with Hain.

When it became apparent that he would receive no answer, Hain went on. "I followed at something of a distance, waiting for this Carn of yours to find Aston." The assassin laughed. "He shouldn't have been so eager to succeed. When he did find Aston, the old man at-tacked him. Carn is either dead now or a cripple. I don't suppose he was a friend of yours?"

Madh looked with distaste at the assassin. The man was leering, enjoying a private joke.

"What then?" Madh asked simply.

"I overpowered the old man and took his Phrase."

"No complications?"

Hain laughed. "Complications, no. Entertainment, yes. That Hazard character showed his face and we fought."

Madh stepped forward, unable to mask his curiosity. "And . . . ?"

The assassin's smile grew broader. "You were wise to hire me for the job, rather than that washed-up fool."

"Then you killed Karrelian?" Madh asked with some surprise.

"I certainly could have," Hain replied a little too quickly. "But I didn't want to risk your precious Phrases . . . or the fortune you owe me for them. I escaped and went to the docks for a little celebration."

Madh stepped backward, surveying the assassin with distaste. "Do you realize the trail you've now left behind? Barr Aston, Amet Pale, Hazard, and his partner. Perhaps even Tarem Selod and Taylor Ash have seen you and lived."

Hain grinned. "I'll stop shaving my skull today."

"Moreover, you've wasted an entire afternoon we could have used to put distance between us and our pursuers."

Hain laughed. "What pursuers?"

Seething, Madh restrained himself from killing the fool assassin upon the spot—he needed Hain alive, at least for the moment.

"Would you like to see the pursuers I mean?" Madh asked, as if speaking to a child.

Without waiting for a reply, he dug into his pack and brought out the box that contained the kahanes root. He turned to the nightstand, and the pitcher and bowl it held. Hain watched with increasing fascination as Madh once more went through the odd ritual of the scrying spell. Again, he was amazed that any man could willingly pierce himself with such deadly poison and survive, much less cast a spell as he suffered agony that, from

Hain's point of view, seemed positively exquisite.

"Now we will know whether anyone pursues us," Madh announced, his voice hoarse from the effort of the spell.

Hain swung himself off the bed and took his place at Madh's side. The red waters of the bowl were roiling. Only slowly did they resolve into a face.

A face that Hain recognized from that very morning. A face bent on killing him.

Madh turned to his hireling. "It seems you've made an enemy."

"I can dispose of Hazard easily," Hain boasted. "No doubt, they've holed up in his mansion, thinking it's safe. I can finish them all tonight."

Madh, who had been in Karrelian's house, *knew* it was safe. Karrelian had paid for safeguards that Hain's eyes could not see. Easier, Madh thought, to break into Council Tower.

"We won't risk putting you to the test. But we certainly do not want Hazard following us across the continent."

Madh turned toward the corner of the dimly lit room and muttered a word in a language that Hain did not recognize. No, he did recognize it, although he could not put a name to it. He had heard Madh use it once before.

There was a rustling beneath the cot that Hain had been lying upon, and the assassin turned about to see what was responsible, a hand automatically going to his knife. An old gray blanket was draped over the edge of the cot and fell into a woolen puddle on the floorboards. Now the blanket stirred—a rat, no doubt—and Hain reversed his grip on the dagger, holding it by the tip of the blade, ready to throw it. Rat-skewering had always been a favorite amusement.

But the creature that pulled away the blanket was by no stretch of the imagination a rat. It was bigger than

the largest wharf rats Hain had ever seen—a full foot in
height—and resembled more than anything a naked,
gnarled old man with deep green, leathery skin and bat's
wings. It was another of Madh's homunculi. Hain had
never before seen one up close.

A shudder ran through his body and, suddenly, the
smile he'd worn all afternoon melted.

The homunculus seemed to sense his unease, for it
launched into the air and flew just past Hain's face on
its way to Madh's shoulder. Inches away, Hain could
see its pointed black beard and a preternaturally stiff
member.

What, exactly, did they do with that?

Again, Hain shuddered.

Meanwhile, a second homunculus, looking much like
the first except for a small pair of curved horns, emerged
from beneath the cot and took its place on Madh's other
shoulder. Madh spoke to them in that odd language he
used, spending a few minutes with each. When Madh
had finished speaking, the two creatures descended upon
the nightstand, lowering their faces toward the bowl of
bloody water that still held Brandt's fading image. As
they began to lap noisily at the liquid, the image shuddered, diffracting into a fun-house nightmare. Within
moments, every drop had been consumed.

Madh lifted the sash of the window and watched as
his familiars launched themselves into the darkening
sky.

"One for my master," Madh announced, "and one for
Galatine Hazard."

He left the window open and resumed his place in the
corner.

"Aston is a wily man, an intelligence operative with
decades of experience. You're sure the words he gave
you were authentic?"

Hain reached into his pocket and produced the pouch
that contained Madh's odd gem. He held the stone up

to the light. As the afternoon had worn on, it had faded to its original blue color.

"As long as this did its job," Hain answered, "it was the real Phrase. The stone turned green as grass."

"Good," Madh replied, smiling. Then he gestured toward the gem. "I'll have it back now."

Hain turned over the pear-shaped stone in his palm. It might be useful, a talisman that showed the truth. Useful or, at least, salable.

"Perhaps I'll claim it," Hain mused, "as the first installment of my payment."

"The stone is mine," Madh replied, "not my master's. If you desire, he can fashion you another like it, but that one is my own."

Hain shrugged. "Very well."

He tossed the stone in a steep arc toward the open window. Madh's hand shot out and swallowed the gem in a motion so smooth that Hain found himself envious. Why, he wondered, hadn't Madh simply done the dirty work himself? And that, of course, was answer enough: the work was *dirty*. Hain had made a fabulous career simply because his employers found such work distasteful. Very well. He would take a fortune built on squeamishness as well as anything else.

"So when do we start for Thyrsus?" Hain asked. "I'm eager to collect what's owed me."

"Leaving after dusk would draw attention," Madh replied, "so we'll have to wait for morning."

"Fine with me," Hain answered, leaning back onto his cot. "I hate riding through the night." He looked about the room, at the two cots, the two dingy chairs, the closet with its broken rod. "Perhaps you should rent me my own room from now on."

"If you insist," Madh replied. The money was no object and, after all, there was little he relished less than spending the night with Hain. Until just a moment ago, however, the assassin had needed a certain amount of supervision.

"You want to keep me happy, after all," Hain continued. "What would happen if I simply decided not to go to Thyrsus? Or not to tell your master what I know?" His grin deepened maliciously. "Or to double my price? It would be rather difficult to go through all this again, considering that I've killed all the men who possessed the information you want."

"Very difficult indeed," Madh replied, smiling slightly as he rolled the blue gem between his fingers.

Jin Annard stepped from the twilight into the well-lit vestibule and nodded his thanks to the doorman. His entire house, he realized, was dwarfed by this entrance chamber. He laughed and was surprised by the responding echo.

His laugh startled a knot of men who were waiting in the vestibule—tired-looking businessmen whose rumpled shirts spoke of having been roused from comfortable beds. They carried satchels bulging at the seams, and folders full of papers lay at their feet.

"This way, please," the doorman said, leading Annard across the antechamber and up the wide, sweeping staircase to the second floor.

For this time of night, there was a surprising amount of activity in Brandt Karrelian's house. A door near the staircase opened and two more businessmen emerged, ushered out, Annard thought, by Karrelian himself. Farther down the long corridor, an older, handsome woman was carrying a stack of clothes toward Karrelian's room. They passed her without a word and, two doors to the right, the servant admitted Annard into a dimly lit study. Annard slipped inside, waiting not only for the door to close but to hear the sound of the doorman's retreating footsteps. There were few things he liked less than conducting sensitive conversations in places he could not trust to be secure.

"Oh, stop fussing and have a seat," said the old man who waited behind the leather-inlaid desk at the far end of the room. Barr Aston was having an iced tea. It was what he had missed most during his week in the Atahr Vin.

"How did it go?" Aston asked, taking another sip through the paper straw as he awaited Annard's reply.

"They accepted me as Taylor's representative. They have no idea that you're still alive."

Aston sighed with relief. "Well, you've got my help, then."

"I still don't see the need for secrecy—"

"Not secrecy, my boy," Aston grinned. "Dread of paperwork. I hated it then, I hate it now. No retired minister has ever returned to the service before. Imagine the pile of forms they'd have me fill out for that."

Annard said nothing. He had never precisely understood the odd humor of his former superior in the ministry. But when Annard had received the old man's coded note earlier that day, he understood that such a resource was not to be wasted during the current crisis— even if Aston refused to rejoin the ministry formally. Annard's trips to Karrelian's mansion would be a small price to pay for the ex-minister's experience.

Just so long, Annard amended, as Elena Imbress didn't discover where he was sneaking off to. The woman was still in a mood to murder Brandt Karrelian upon sight. It had been all Annard could do, after his first meeting with Aston, to sidetrack Imbress with a description of the assassin and a firm injunction that her only task now was to find him. Brandt Karrelian, he had informed her, would trouble her no longer.

"So tell me," the old man said. "In detail."

Annard complied, recounting almost verbatim the council meeting that had only recently adjourned.

Aston sucked the last ounce of his iced tea noisily through the straw when Annard finished.

"Theatrics."

"Excuse me?" Annard replied.

"Theatrics, I said. Pale's entrance into the chamber was too well-timed. Somehow, he'd been eavesdropping and waiting for the proper moment to make his appearance." Aston chuckled. "I always suspected that friend Amet had a frustrated thespian lurking somewhere within that very unmartial body of his. Very well. He'll bear watching."

Annard nodded. Aston's confidence was beginning to alleviate Jin's anxiety. He no longer felt quite so alone—that awful weight of responsibility that had oppressed him since Taylor's departure that morning.

"Otherwise," Aston continued, "we sit back and wait."

"For what?"

"For Pale to make a move. For the Council to vote on Pale's motion for war. For Elena Imbress to find the assassin and his masters. For the next gust of ill tidings to blow along the foul westerly winds from Thyrsus." Aston gestured toward his half-filled pitcher. "Care for a glass of iced tea while we wait?"

CHAPTER 16

"**M**ay the beast rot in hell!" Gorman swore as he snatched his bloodied hand away from the stallion's teeth.

"Seaman Gorman," a deep voice bellowed, "we'll have no profanity aboard the *Grampus*, nor about the docks. Like all God's creatures, the horse is to be treated with respect."

Gorman sighed and bowed deeply before Captain Torm, who had just appeared above the cutter's railing. The sailor felt triply cursed: first, there was still this contrary horse to coax into the winch's harness; worse, he felt keenly the guilt of having profaned; and, finally, there was the misfortune of having profaned before Torm, who, like every Gathon captain, was not only the temporal but also spiritual authority of the ship. Such a transgression would not pass unpunished.

And, indeed, Captain Torm waited only long enough for Gorman to straighten his back before announcing sternly, "I will expect your confession this evening, once we are safely offshore."

The captain's peppery beard was so thick that Gorman

could not perceive a mouth behind it. Torm seemed almost a living incarnation of the Gathon God, whose voice rang clear from a mouth sewn shut.

"Moreover," Torm added, "you may holystone the deck with both fore and aft watches until we reach sight of New Hope. Now get that beast on board."

With that, the captain disappeared and Gorman turned back toward his hoofed adversary. The horse was far taller at the shoulder than he, and Gorman was among the largest members of the *Grampus*'s crew. The creature's coat was a rich, lustrous brown, entirely devoid of markings, and its fathomless black eyes revealed an intelligence and independence that augured no good for the already injured seaman. With his good hand, Gorman reached toward the horse's bridle, but the beast reared back, kicking at Gorman with its front hooves

"Scry!"

In the way it was said, the name was a command, as clear and sharp as any that Captain Torm might aspire to. Gorman risked a glance down the docks to find the horse's owner, a young Gathon merchant named Pass, striding swiftly along the wooden pier. At the call of its name, the horse snorted in recognition and awaited its master as calmly as if nothing had happened.

"My apologies about the horse," Pass said as he approached Gorman, looking pointedly at the sailor's hand. "Scry dislikes strangers, and he has never been aboard ship before. He must be a bit jittery."

As he concluded his explanation, the merchant patted Gorman on the shoulder and dropped something into the sailor's good hand. But his words rang hollow to Gorman, who was sure Pass suspected him of mishandling the horse. Gorman had always hated merchants. Although clumsy and useless aboard ship, they strutted around as if they owned the works. Worse still, usually they did.

Gorman could only watch ruefully as Pass swung the

wide leather cradle in Scry's direction and, running it
beneath the steed's stomach and up along its other side,
strapped the harness securely into place. The horse
hadn't stirred an inch, accepting its master's touch plac-
idly. Disgusted, Gorman whistled shrilly, signaling the
men above to start working at the winch. In a few
minutes, they managed to haul the heavy beast high into
the air, then pivot the winch arm around to deposit Scry
on deck. There, Pass had paid for the construction of a
special pen, so that the horse might be spared the indignity of the hold. The horse, Gorman observed bitterly,
would be better quartered during the voyage than he.

At that thought, he turned again toward the handsome,
black-haired merchant who could afford so much so
young, but the man had already clambered up the gang-
plank onto the deck of the ship. Gorman frowned and
looked down at his two hands, one stained with blood,
the other with the merchant's gold, and wondered how
those hands would fare scrubbing the deck every day
that week.

Taylor Ash locked his cabin door behind him and
collapsed into the small chamber's bunk. The bed was
little more than a thin mattress tied to the top of three
wooden cabinets, each two feet high, that served as the
cabin's only storage. He could feel the wooden planks
distinctly through the padding, but Taylor always preferred a firm bed. It wouldn't be a luxurious voyage, he
thought, but it would serve its purpose. And, all things
considered, the passage to Thyrsus would prove far more
comfortable aboard the *Grampus* than aboard Scry's
back for weeks on end. Much as Taylor loved his horse,
a transcontinental gallop seemed less than an appealing
prospect. And, in any case, such a trip would take far
too long.

Indeed, Taylor had abandoned his overland plans almost as soon as he had begun to consider them. Despite the spring storms, it would be far swifter, and probably safer, to sail to Thyrsus. A Gathon ship made the most sense on two counts. First, because Gathony was a neutral nation, its ships were received cordially at Yndrian ports. Posing as a Gathon merchant, Taylor hoped to benefit from the reduced scrutiny the *Grampus* would receive when it docked at Thyrsus. Better still, Gathon ships were the only vessels in the world that dared sail the Sawtooth Straits in spring, when the sudden infusion of warm currents made the long, narrow straits unpredictable and, for less nimble ships, often fatal. But Captain Torm's vessel was narrow in the beam, sharp in the prow—a long, agile, three-masted cutter with a skilled crew. The danger would be slight and, Taylor calculated, the savings in time would be invaluable. In this season, the larger, clumsier Yndrian and Chaldean galleons steered southwest around both Gonwyr and Brindis. The deep, safer waters of the southern sea offered a passage that most competent captains could navigate, but the detour added ten full days to the journey.

And despite Taylor's careful pose as a Gathon merchant of spices, he knew that the most precious commodity of all was time.

Taylor was surprised by a knock at his door. He rolled from the bed to his feet, almost hitting his head on the low ceiling beams, and cautiously drew back the bolt of the door. Captain Torm stood in the passageway beyond.

"Captain," Taylor said in a careful Gathon accent, "I am honored." He swung the door wide and ushered the captain inside. "To what do I owe the pleasure of your visit?"

Taylor did not anticipate any real pleasure from the captain's call. The lines of Torm's face seemed even stiffer than the starched white expanse of his uniform.

"Brother Pass," the captain began, using the Gathon term for a man of the same social caste, "you will be pleased to know that a few moments hence we shall lift anchor and set sail."

Taylor bowed slightly in acknowledgment of this fact. "If we are to be soon under way," he said, "I will waste no more of your valuable time than what is necessary to thank you for the notice."

"Yours is a gracious tongue," Torm replied from behind his impenetrable beard. He was looking at Taylor oddly. "But surely you know that the harbor captain will guide us safely beyond Chaldean waters. Only when we are received into the deep bosom of the sea shall he take to his pinnace and I to my bridge."

Taylor smiled amiably—a difficult feat, considering his chagrin. He had hoped to maintain as little contact with the Gathon captain as possible, lest his pose as a fellow countryman be penetrated. It was becoming obvious, though, that the captain saw him as one of his few social equals on the ship. Torm would probably make a point of seeking the company of "Brother Pass."

Now, however, Taylor's immediate problem was excusing his very genuine lack of nautical expertise.

"As I said when I hired your ship, Brother Torm, this is my family's first foray into the seaborne trade. Our very modest success has constrained us to the caravan routes of the north."

Torm nodded gravely, apparently accepting Taylor's explanation.

"I should warn you, then," the old seaman said, "that we sail southerly through a strong equatorial current. Those new at sea often find the roughness of the passage disconcerting. Be warned."

"I thank you again. I hope my stomach proves a match for the journey."

"God willing," Torm intoned.

"God willing," Taylor agreed.

The captain appeared pleased with the gravity of his reply. "I came down here," he explained, "to petition your presence in my cabin. It is customary that we begin each voyage with prayer."

"I would be honored to join with you in our sacred duty," Taylor said, "after a proper interval."

He indicated his old, worn clothes, and Torm nodded with understanding.

"In a few moments then," he said as he left the room.

Taylor sighed as the door closed, cursing quietly as he began to hunt through his bags for the robes he had packed in case of such an eventuality. It was the last thing he craved, but it seemed there would be little choice but to bend knees with Captain Torm in tribute to Gathony's mutilated god.

Taylor would never have tried passing for a Gath had he not known that Gathon prayer was always unspoken. The Gaths conducted silent, kneeling vigils with an occasional bow that brought one's brow to the floor. He had read the Gathon Gospels, and so was conversant in a general way with the country's religious tenets—enough so, in any case, that he could pass as a northern merchant on his first sea voyage, making up in enthusiasm for his cargo of spice what he lacked in piety.

After prayer, Captain Torm asked Brother Pass to dine with him, and Taylor used this opportunity to flesh out his carefully crafted mercantile persona. Ignoring the captain's obvious desire to haggle over esoteric theological paradoxes, Taylor instead waxed eloquent on turmeric and coriander until the grave captain entirely lost interest in Brother Pass. From then on, Taylor managed to circumvent many of the twice-daily prayer sessions by keeping to his room, seasick. This last excuse required no subterfuge on his part. For the first three days, the incessant pitching and rolling of the ship set his stomach twisting with proportional intensity, and more than once Taylor had to dash from his cabin to the rail.

Progress was slow because the *Grampus* had both the current and the prevailing winds to fight. As Taylor tossed in his bunk hour after hour, the dark wooden walls of his cabin seemed to creep ever inward, threatening to suffocate him. He would drift from a nauseous stupor into fitful sleep and back, and his dreams were often as troubled as the *Grampus*' passage. During the third night out, he dreamed of Captain Torm's cabin, reliving the ceremony they had enacted before the ship set sail. It was an ancient ceremony in which the ship's captain took a handful of black Gathon earth from a small box and scattered it about the floor of the cabin, thus asking that God keep the ship as safe as their precious motherland. In his dream, Taylor watched the earth fall with unnatural fluidity from Torm's sunbrowned hand and tumble slowly downward until it hit not the floor of the cabin but the dead, maimed face of Kermane Ash. Where the dirt fell, it clung to Ash's cold skin. And then, through his sealed lips, Torm began to read the Chaldean rites of the dead.

It was the next day that Taylor determined to go up on deck. He was feeling somewhat less seasick and he wanted to tend to Scry, but he also suspected that further confinement in his cabin would drive him mad. He had been sleeping so irregularly that he had no idea of the time and, upon emerging into the sunlight, was surprised to discover it was almost noon. As he turned toward Scry's pen, a hoarse cry fell from the mastheads.

"Teeth ho!"

The deck grew hushed at these words, although there was no visible change of activity, no new orders bellowed by the mates. Yet, as the sailors heaved at their lines, their songs became muted, a bit more grave, and a few of them gazed across the sparkling blue waters to the southwest. Taylor craned his neck in that direction but could see nothing more than the ever-receding crests of the waves. Shrugging, he made his way fore, where a small covered pen had been set up in the shadow of the mizzenmast. There, Scry stood regally, his mane whipping about in the wind, his nostrils dilating to consume the salt air. At Taylor's approach, the stallion stamped the deck in greeting. Taylor smiled, climbed over the stall's top post, and reached into his pocket for a carrot that he had saved from yesterday's uneaten dinner. For a moment, as he fed his horse, Taylor forgot entirely why he was aboard ship, sailing toward Thyrsus. With an utter, thoughtless contentment that knew nothing of murders or intrigue or war, Taylor spent the next hour brushing down Scry's coat.

When he finished, Taylor patted the horse's neck affectionately and climbed out of the stall. He was feeling as well as he had since Torm had set sail. The day was bright and warm, and although he knew the least risk of discovery lay in staying as far from the crew as possible, he loathed the idea of returning to his cabin, so dark and stagnant. Instead, he wandered toward the ship's prow, marveling at the sailors who hung suspended like leaves from the yards high above, where they daubed lines with tar and adjusted the rigging.

Taylor rounded the mainmast on the starboard side and stumbled upon a group of men hunched over the deck, scraping at the planks with large, flat pieces of sandstone. The stones made a peculiar grinding noise against the wood, and Taylor recognized it as one of the many unfamiliar sounds that had troubled his ill sleep the last three days. Apparently, Captain Torm kept the men working at the decks on a frequent basis, although Taylor could hardly fathom such an obsession for neatness. Perhaps it was yet another quirk of Gathon religious doctrine.

"Good day, Brothers," Taylor said as he made his way among the men, feeling a momentary burst of pity for their labor. One of the men looked up from his work and glared at Taylor from eyes sunken behind deep, dark circles—it was sailor Gorman, whom Taylor had helped with Scry. Immediately, Taylor understood his mistake. Within the rigid caste system of Gathony, a prosperous merchant would seldom stoop to greet common sailors, much less call them "Brothers," a term reserved for equals. He strode away, not looking back until he reached the *Grampus's* prow. The men had fallen back to work without saying a word. The incident had passed quickly and, doubtless, would be just as quickly forgotten.

As he gazed over the prow, Taylor saw what had been apparent an hour earlier only to the men high up in the rigging: there was land to the south, and more than land. Indeed, jagged peaks were rising like stalagmites from the sea, still miles away, but looming ominously like a behemoth's teeth.

The Sawtooth Strait.

The sight brought back Taylor's sense of mission with immediate urgency. The strait was a narrow channel of water that wound for a hundred miles between the eastern coast of Gathony and the western edge of the isle of Gonwyr. Gonwyr, the histories said, had once been part of the mainland, attached to Gathony by the daunting range of mountains that still defined Gathony's border with Chaldus. But the same cataclysm that destroyed Gonwyr had caused an entire chain of the mountains to sink beneath the sea, separating the homeland of the Khrine from the rest of the continent.

Unbidden, the origin of the name sprang to Taylor's mind. The land had not been called Gonwyr until after the cataclysm, after the Binding. Gonwyr, in the language of the Khrine, meant Our Sorrow.

And the *Grampus* would pass beneath its very shadow.

This was another reason why the ships of Yndor and

Chaldus seldom sailed the strait, superstitious as sailors were. Taylor doubted that the Gaths were any more enlightened, but their nation's age-old proximity to Gonwyr had perhaps tempered their fear, and their superior ships allowed them to navigate the difficult channel more easily. Curious now, Taylor remained on deck, settling himself on a large coil of rope that gave him a comfortable view over the prow. He wanted to see this Gonwyr for himself, the ancestral seat of the extinct Khrine, the scene of the most devastating conflict the world had ever witnessed and, in an indirect way, the cause of Taylor's current woes.

Perhaps, too, the cause of a new war the likes of which the land had not seen for decades. Taylor's mind retraced the miles to Prandis and alit on the image of Amet Pale, maimed but alive, sprawled on the earth of Hawken Heights. He wondered how long Pale's convalescence would take and whether, by the end of it, the man would learn anything—or would he remain the same stiff-necked jingoist as before? If so, Taylor brooded, how long could Andus Ravenwood hold out?

As the ship sailed on, driven by a rising tailwind, the Sawtooth Mountains loomed larger, as if they were growing from the sea. They seemed an unbroken chain, and the crazy thought flitted through Taylor's head that Captain Torm intended to drive the *Grampus* directly into the jaw of the black rocks, impaling everyone on those stony knives as final sacrifices to the Gathon God.

"Truly, such sights humble us properly before the omnipotence of God."

Startled by the interruption, Taylor nearly fell from his perch atop the hawser.

"It is good to see you on deck, Brother Pass," Captain Torm continued in his customary rumble. "I had begun to fear you would never find your sea legs, little as I could believe that possible of the lowliest Gath."

Taylor cleared his throat and tried to smile. "My illness seems to have passed, Brother Torm." And through clenched teeth he added, "Praise be to God."

"Praise be to God," Torm replied. "Now that you have recovered, I expect the pleasure of your company at prayer. Five bells, in my cabin."

The captain turned to leave.

"One moment more, Brother Torm?" Taylor called out. "I see that we approach land, but where is the Sawtooth Strait?"

Torm paused for a moment, then broke into a laugh so broad that, for the first time, it became apparent he did indeed possess a mouth.

"If ever a man tries to persuade you to take up the sailing life, Brother Pass, be sure to stick to your spices, for a more unsailorly man than yourself I've yet to find."

Then, resuming his typically stoic composure, the captain advanced to the very tip of the prow and, nestled in the merging crotch of the gunwales, stretched his arm due south.

"There, Brother Pass, there," the captain said as he pointed, "see you how one mountain trails into the sea, obscuring the peak behind it? From this distance, those two rocks seem almost to merge, the front of one into the other's back. The furthest reach of Gathony's Sawtooth range extends so far east that it appears to overlap the westernmost peaks of Gonwyr. In truth, as you shall soon see, a spacious bay lies nestled between those mountains, but you should never spy it unless you approach from the east. The Sawtooth itself is as fearsome a strait as God has chosen to fashion, but it does not yet gnash those teeth at will. Have no fear, Brother Pass," the captain said as he turned to leave, "and think only of the profit on your spice."

But as the captain disappeared aft and Taylor turned back toward the ever-growing peaks, his thoughts were not of spice. Instead, he pondered the way the captain continually referred to the Strait as the proof of God's

hand on earth. *God indeed*, Taylor thought, scowling.
Whatever Torm might think, Taylor knew that what was
now a watery channel had once been filled with mountains as perilously high as any in the Sawtooth chain.
There had been mountains . . . and they had been lev-
eled.

Not by God, but by men who had thought they were
He.

Taylor remained on deck often during the next
three days, strangely compelled by the massive stone
walls of the strait that hemmed in the *Grampus* on either
side.

Torm had been quite right. Once the ship had swung
east and then tacked southwest, Taylor could make out
a distinct opening between the mountains of Gathony
and Gonwyr. Torm had stayed on deck for this passage,
bellowing orders that couldn't be misheard at the uppermost reaches of the rigging. All the sails were furled
save the mainsail, and under the power of this single,
broad sheet of canvas, the *Grampus* slipped between the
looming rocks that marked the opening of the Sawtooth
Strait. The gap was little more than a hundred yards
wide, bringing the ship within a stone's throw of the
ancient rocks. Little grew upon those sheer slopes: some
lichen near the waterline and some occasional scrub
higher up, where life had found an improbable way to
take root among the age-blackened stones.

Beyond this towering portal, the ship slid into a broad
bay, almost three miles in diameter and entirely encir-
cled by the towering mountains, save for the slim opening behind them and a slender channel that split the
rocks to the south. It was a chilling feeling, Taylor
thought, to be sailing along those calm waters, cradled
in the shadow of mountains ten thousand feet high. As
if the world had swallowed them.

God's Handbasin, the captain called the bay.

As they approached the far opening between the rocks, Taylor realized it was even narrower than the first. The sheer faces of the mountains rose abruptly from the water, stretching upward to a dizzying distance where they blocked out the sun. The men, usually so vocal, had ceased singing entirely and now, in the shadow of the rocks, they heaved at their lines in an intense silence. As the bow penetrated the tiny neck of the channel, Taylor realized he was holding his breath; he did not release it until the stern had slipped past the rocks as well. At the worst moment, jagged blades of black stone had stood only fifty feet away on either side. And Taylor shuddered to think how close they might lie beneath the hull.

He was grateful that Torm did not mention until after that evening's prayer how lucky their timing had been. Ships could pass through the inner portal of the strait only near high tide, for the channel there was extremely shallow. Long ago, a ship had been wrecked through ignorance of this fact, and clearing the debris from the rocky bottleneck had taken months. Had the *Grampus* been any later, she would have had to drop anchor for hours before the water rose high enough for the next passage.

Beyond this spot, however, the walls of the strait fell away on either side, revealing a channel that reached as much as two miles in breadth, though more often it was less than half that wide. Taylor stared in wonder at the watery corridor with its mountainous walls, twisting tortuously to the south. When the mountains grew closer on either side, Gathony to the right and Gonwyr to the left, Taylor craned his neck upward, growing dizzy from the rocky heights above him. The *Grampus*, even with its towering masts, seemed a mere speck by comparison.

For a few miles, the strait dwindled to a passage only a few hundred yards wide. The men's songs echoed eerily off the barren rocks, and when the breeze picked up, it sounded like a ghostly wail. Taylor was unnerved at times by how close the ship came to the mountains on either side, but the strait offered more than enough room for Captain Torm, who had ordered the mizzen, maintopsail, and foresail unfurled long ago. At a pace that seemed brisk, judging by the way the mountains raced by on either side, the *Grampus* cut south toward the Sea of Ashes.

"How long will the passage take?" Taylor asked when he and Captain Torm rose stiffly from their knees after the evening prayer.

"It varies," the Gath explained. "We sailed well this afternoon, but the winds in the Sawtooth are capricious. Once I saw the Sea of Ashes only two days after passing through God's Handbasin. On another passage, I spent a week in these waters, most of those days becalmed. A captain of my acquaintance was once trapped in the strait fifteen days. He swore the wind had died as surely as if God had ceased breathing. Even so, the passage took him no longer than it might have to circumnavigate Gonwyr."

Taylor took his leave of the captain, wondering what might happen in the space of fifteen days should they become becalmed in the Sawtooth Strait. Already, after only a week, he felt woefully severed from the world, from the shifting web of information that he had spun across the continent. Taylor never took vacations, and it had been years since he had gone even half this long without daily poring over the various intelligence reports that rushed to Prandis. Everything, he thought, was going on *out there*, and here he was trapped on a ship full of religious fanatics.

Even so, that was preferable to sealing himself up in his coffin-like cabin. There were still three hours of daylight, and Taylor brought a couple of pillows up to the deck. These he arranged in the sloping hollow of the hawser, making a comfortable nest for himself, and he lay within the coiled lines, wondering how Imbress and Annard were faring in far-off Prandis, wondering whether Barr Aston was still alive.

He was woken gently by a sailor soon after the sun had set. The looming mountains obscured much of the heavens, leaving only a blue-black swath of starry sky above the path of the channel. A pleasant breeze played over Taylor's skin and, contented, he thought of spending the night on deck. No doubt, it would not fit well with Gathon custom, but more particularly, it did not conform to sailorly custom.

"We must drop anchor for the night, Revered Father," the sailor apologized, "because it is impossible to navigate the Strait in darkness."

The large coil of rope Taylor had appropriated for a couch, it turned out, ran through the hawser hole to the starboard anchor. Had Taylor remained atop the line while the men dropped anchor, it would have proved a rude awakening indeed. Bestowing his thanks on the seaman, he took a last look at the starry ribbon above and retreated regretfully to his cabin.

Despite Taylor's fears, Captain Torm made exⵙcellent time through the strait. The wind held steady, pushing the *Grampus* quickly along the channel. Sail was shortened only when the ship approached particularly narrow openings. A few times, rocks cut through the waters of the strait itself—stony bergs that had been, before the cataclysm, the snowy peaks of mountains thousands of feet high. Torm was familiar with each of these obstacles, and he steered the ship slowly and prudently around them, raising sail again as soon as they slid by.

Two full days passed and, on the morning of the third, the mountains fell back swiftly to either side, never to

approach each other again. The *Grampus* had reached
the black and bitter waters of the Sea of Ashes. This sea
had once been as blue as its neighbors but, it was rumored, on the day of the cataclysm, a vast volcano had
risen from the depths to belch lava and ash for months
to come. The volcano still stood above the waters near
the center of the sea, and from time to time sailors would
see a dark cloud hover over the spot. Other times, there
would be a strange glow after sunset. No ship sailed
close enough to see more than that.

The coast of Gonwyr receded quickly to the east and
Taylor, who had never seen any of the island except for
the inscrutable face of the Sawtooth Mountains, gazed
at it curiously. At the southern mouth of the strait, the
mountains dwindled rapidly into a range of short and
jagged rock formations, nothing like their towering
brethren to the north. Soon, these outcroppings disappeared before a distant line of dense, dark woods. At a
half mile's distance, Taylor could barely discern the
stunted, twisted forms of the trees, and yet he was
shocked, for he had never imagined anything growing
on the cursed soil of Gonwyr. Still, he noted that
whereas birds wheeled above the Gathon coast a few
hundred yards to the west, not one could be seen over
Gonwyr and the Sea of Ashes. Taylor pondered the
power that could destroy a land so utterly, and he pondered as well what sort of man might wish to loose it
once again upon the world. If it was indeed Mallioch
who was stealing the Chaldean Phrases, Taylor had to
wonder why. Before this voyage, he had simply assumed
that the Yndrian emperor sought the political leverage
over Chaldus that possession of all the Phrases might
bring. But now, gazing on a blasted land, Taylor began
to turn over in his mind the extent of human ambition.

And the extent of human folly.

•   •   •

Four days of swift sailing brought them into the harbor of New Hope on a chilly, overcast morning. They would dock at the Gathon capital only until the next morning's tide while the crew unloaded a priceless shipment of Deshi steel and replaced it with a consignment of Gathon goods headed for Thyrsus. Taylor felt bad for Scry, and ordered the stallion to be hoisted down to the docks for a day of liberty. Taylor had been to New Hope before, although never by sea, and he knew that most of the city was built to the north and east. Westward, beyond a scattering of the bleached adobe homes that the Gaths built low to the ground, lest they affront their god, Taylor knew there was only farmland and wild fields. It was in this direction that he spurred Scry, who, after so much enforced inactivity, galloped from the docks like a brown bolt from heaven.

And behind his wiry beard, Captain Neveh Torm scowled as he watched Brother Pass gallop away in a direction that held no temples, when the morning prayer was less than half an hour away.

After two hours of brisk riding, Scry had loos-ened his knotted muscles and worked up a satisfactory lather. Turning the horse back toward the city, Taylor realized that not only Scry had needed to purge nervous energy. He, too, had felt good—really, thoroughly good—for the first time since leaving Prandis as he had wheeled aimlessly about the Gathon countryside, enjoying the play of Scry's powerful muscles beneath him and the whip of a breeze that smelled of grass instead of salt. Ultimately, however, Taylor's thoughts had returned to the city where, in the basement of an import-export dealer, Chaldus kept the office of its New Hope division of the Ministry of Intelligence. Although the *Grampus* had made quick work of the journey, Taylor still expected news to be awaiting him there—in fact, he hungered for it like a starving man. This branch office, which oversaw all Intelligence activities in Gathony, was large enough to pay a wizard for on-the-spot communications. If anything important had happened since his departure—even that very morning—the New Hope office would have word of it.

It was well before noon when Taylor rode back into the vast sprawl of New Hope's outlying bedroom communities. In New Hope, it was sometimes difficult to tell one neighborhood from another; almost all the buildings were squat, white or cream-colored adobe structures. Little distinguished a business from a home except the modest wooden signs that hung above the doors or the somewhat larger front windows through which the shopkeepers displayed their goods. As Taylor rode toward the center of the city, the buildings tended to become somewhat larger, but remained just as plain on the outside. He had been in southern Gathony often enough to know that pride of place had not been stamped out of the race—indeed, far from it. Within some of those unassuming adobe façades lay sumptuous interiors, filled with fine brocades and plush, upholstered furniture. For Taylor, this paradox always remained uppermost in his mind when dealing with the Gaths: a placid, humble exterior that often disguised powerful depths of ambition.

The import-export shop that served as a front for Chaldus's intelligence office was located in a once-prosperous area near the wharves that now bore only moderate commercial traffic. It was the sort of modest business, exporting china in exchange for a plethora of foreign-made goods, that generated enough revenue to make it seem legitimate. But what truly was imported and exported from that shop, via the wharves and the caravan routes, was an unceasing freight of information—and Taylor was greedy for it as he hitched Scry to a nearby post and dashed past a half-dozen clerks' desks to the dimly lit office in back.

New Hope's chief intelligence officer was a fat, balding man named Hinks who squirmed in his chair when he noted the minister's arrival. His thick mouth twitched as he offered Taylor a seat in one of the worn armchairs that flanked his desk. Hinks's fingers twitched at the edge of one manila file, then another, as if he were unsure where to begin. The reason for his discomfort soon became apparent. The news Taylor received in New Hope was mixed: bad and worse.

"Where would you like to start, Minister Ash?" Hinks asked with a distinct lack of enthusiasm.

"How about the High Council. Any news?"

From the look on Hinks's face, the answer was yes.

"Something about Pale?" Taylor guessed.

"Yes . . . ," Hinks replied slowly. Obviously, Amet Pale was not on Hinks's mind, but because Taylor had addressed the issue, Hinks briefed him on Pale's latest activities. The very afternoon of the duel, the general had been reported walking the streets of Prandis, hideously disfigured. What's more, Pale had initiated a shake-up in the army's chain of command. Many older officers were being relegated to merely decorative posts, and younger officers—many of whom owed their entire careers to Pale—had taken their places.

"That's bad," Taylor muttered, chewing on a thumbnail. "The last thing we need is Pale playing power games within the chain of command. I want you to send a message to Annard. Tell him to pay particular attention to the Ministry of War, and especially to Pale's assistant, Agon Celwan. General Celwan has shown some independence in the past. He may prove to be useful."

Hinks merely nodded at these instructions. Nothing, if it could be avoided, would be written down.

"Anything else from the Council?"

Hinks cleared his throat. "There is the matter of Jame Kordor. . . ."

The matter of Jame Kordor? Taylor's eyebrows rose in surprise. It was very seldom indeed that the portly Minister of Finance figured into calculations of Intelligence.

"What about Kordor?"

Again, Hinks paused uncomfortably. "He's dead."

"Dead?" Taylor repeated, stupefied. Obviously, this was no natural death, or Hinks would not have mentioned it. Some sort of foul play—foul play touching upon the security of Chaldus— had to be involved. But Jame Kordor seemed as unlikely a target as a matronly aunt.

"What on earth happened? Our assassin . . . ?"

"It would appear not," Hinks answered. "Early on the morning that your ship departed, a young boy appeared at Minister Kordor's house. He delivered a note . . . and a single gold capital."

"Hazard," Taylor whispered.

"Kordor's servants remembered the minister seeming very agitated after reading the note, which he proceeded to burn. He refused to go to the office that day, citing illness. But around noon, Kordor's chef reports that the minister's mood seemed to be improving. For lunch, he ordered a feast—dish after dish of his favorite foods. And while the chef worked at the main dishes, the minister himself prepared a tart for dessert. Apparently, this was something he did upon occasion when his spirits were high. Kordor's butler reported that the minister seemed to enjoy lunch immensely, finishing every dish completely, except for that dessert."

"Dessert?" Taylor prompted, growing impatient. He failed to see why Hinks stressed this particular detail, especially when time was so short. He had only a few more minutes to spend with the man before returning to the ship, yet the most pressing topics remained untouched.

Hinks's mouth twitched nervously, shaking his

rounded cheeks. "It seems that Kordor mixed lyc into the dough. He managed to eat only half the tart before he began vomiting blood."

Taylor shuddered. He could hardly imagine the jovial minister preparing such a dish, much less possessing the courage to sit down and eat it.

"He didn't die until later that evening, but he refused to answer any questions that were put to him. Of course, his voice was gone, but he might have written. . . ."

"Did we discover the reason for this, then?" Taylor asked.

Hinks paused. This was the part he dreaded to discuss.

"The next morning," Hinks said quietly, "the news-paper's headline story claimed that for years Jame Kordor had been in the pay of the theocracy here in New Hope. The story was exhaustively detailed and, from everything we can tell, each of those details checks out."

Taylor's face drained of color as he weighed Hinks's explanation. All this time, Kordor had been a Gathon agent, and though Galatine Hazard had known it, Intelligence had possessed no idea! It was scandalous . . . and the fault, Taylor realized, lay in the very room in which he was sitting. It was New Hope's business to keep a rein on Gathon activities. He was about to reprimand Hinks when he realized that Kordor must have been re-cruited more than two decades ago. At that time, Hinks had been some inconsequential junior officer. It wasn't his fault.

Taylor sighed. It wasn't anyone's fault, and even if it was, it really didn't matter. Given what else was going on, Kordor's death was insignificant by comparison. He was almost relieved, though, to be in the field; he didn't envy the questions that Ravenwood would be putting to Jin Annard right now.

"And Kordor is only the tip of it," Hinks proceeded, wringing his hands as he spoke. "The capital seems to have gone half crazy. The financial markets—"

"Damn the financial markets!" Taylor snapped. "Hinks, what about Agent Imbress? Has she forwarded any reports?"

"There was one," the man answered, but he seemed no more enthusiastic about this change of topic. Wordlessly, he handed Taylor a sealed envelope. Taylor ripped it open and withdrew a single sheet of paper, unfolding it to find a sketch. It was a man's face—the head a smooth curve devoid of hair, the jawline sharp and strong, the lips thin and pressed together in a sneer. Below a broad brow, two eyes stared at Taylor malevolently.

On the bottom of the page, Elena had printed two words: Your Assassin.

Taylor's teeth ground together as he stared at the portrait, engraving those features in his mind. Then he flipped the paper over to find a brief note from Elena:

"Explanation forthcoming from Annard. No time here. On the hunt."

On the hunt. Then she had seen the killer, perhaps, but she had not caught him. He fumed at the lack of details. Had she found Aston? Had the assassin? What had happened?

"No other reports from her?" Taylor asked.

Hinks sighed and squirmed again in his chair. "Apparently, Agent Imbress was headed toward Belfar."

"On the trail of the assassin?"

"We assume so. All we know is that a few days ago, a fire broke out in one of Belfar's poorer neighborhoods. It proceeded to ravage more than fifty city blocks."

"And what has this to do with Imbress?" Taylor asked, a chill settling over him.

"It's impossible to say. But ever since, we haven't heard a word from her."

Taylor frowned and pressed a hand to his temple, which had suddenly started to throb.

"Annard, then?" he asked curtly.

Hinks produced a message that the local wizard had transcribed and sealed for Taylor's eyes only. Although Imbress had promised that Annard would send details, the senior intelligence officer was curt and cryptic, the better to ensure security. Security be damned, Taylor thought as he opened the message to find two scant sentences. How much will this tell me?

The first line read, *All Six Snatched*, and Taylor's heart sank as he read it. If all of the Phrases were taken, it meant Aston's death. Having lost one father, losing another was more than Taylor could bear. But even as a black wave of grief swept over him, he read Annard's second and last line: *Old Crow Rules from Hazard's Roost*. Old Crow was a name Taylor used to call Aston in jest.

Annard was telling him that the old minister had survived somehow, just as Amet Pale had survived—there seemed to be some balance left in the world yet. Moreover, the wily veteran had taken covert charge of Intelligence. Despite the gravity of the loss of the Phrases, Taylor reflected that New Hope had perhaps been correctly named. If Barr Aston was alive and well, Taylor could cease worrying about affairs in Chaldus.

All that remained for him to do was intercept six Phrases before they were delivered into the eager hands of Yndor's emperor. And now he knew whom to look for.

Taylor rode back to the docks with buoyed spir‐its. Despite the grim news about Kordor and Pale, the disaster of having lost the sixth Phrase, Hinks's ominous allusions to disarray in Prandis, and the unwelcome disappearance of Elena Imbress, Taylor had truly reached bottom in that split second when he had thought Aston dead. Whatever else might go awry, the knowledge of Aston's survival gave Taylor the first glimmer of victory that he'd seen in weeks. And so he thundered along the pier, anxious for the *Grampus* to get under way, to bring him to Thyrsus where this drama would end. Cheerfully, Taylor helped the ever-scowling chief of lading, seaman Gorman, strap Scry into the harness that would hoist him back into his pen. The Gaths seemed rather dour as they toiled upon the docks, but Taylor supposed they were no different than before. Glum as his own mood had been the past week, a ship full of fatalistic Gaths had been ideal company. Even if they did spend half of each day on their knees, at least they prayed silently, and Taylor had been able to use the time to study the clouds on his own horizons. Now, infused with a renewed sense of purpose, Taylor suspected the voyage to Thyrsus would prove an unendurable exercise in tedium and feigned piety. The *Grampus* rode low, its hold filled to capacity. That would slow its progress, but because all the goods were destined for Thyrsus, at least there would be no other landfalls to delay them.

"I hope the passage to Thyrsus proves swift," he said cheerfully to Captain Torm as he passed the old officer on deck.

"You would have to petition God for an answer," the old man said before he turned away.

The *Grampus* bore westward from New Hope under full sail, flying over the waves like a zephyr, as if nothing had been loaded into her spacious holds but the very pith of speed. It was not until midmorning of their first day out that Taylor realized the captain had not invited him to prayer. He thought little of it. After all, the ship had taken on more than a dozen passengers for Thyrsus and Torm seemed to know a few of them quite well. Undoubtedly, his interest in Brother Pass had passed, and few things could suit Taylor better. To maintain appearances, he was sure to retire to his cabin during the devotional hours, but at least he could spend this enforced captivity sprawled on his bunk, reading one of the volumes of pre-Binding history he had brought with him, rather than wearing out his knees. The rest of the day he usually spent tending to Scry or reclining in his habitual nest in the bow.

Four days and nights of steady sailing brought them within sight of Cape Haven, the westernmost city of Gathony. From there they would cross the expanse of Bismet Bay—a misnomer, Taylor thought, for a body of water large enough to be a sea, but one could little expect better from the Yndrians who had named it. At the far end of the bay, Yndrian land would come into sight near the peninsula of Khartoum. Rounding Khartoum and bearing north, if the weather held, it would be little more than a week before they reached Thyrsus.

But the weather did not hold. Taylor was on deck late that afternoon, admiring the crystalline waters of the southern seas, when he saw a sailor descend from the rigging and hurry over to the second mate. The mate had been checking some lines that ran from the foresail to the deck, leaving Taylor in his hawser close enough to overhear the one word the sailor said to his superior:

"Sou'wester."

The mate's brow creased, and he turned to peer over the port gunwale. There, Taylor could see, against the southwestern horizon, gathered a hunched line of black clouds. Indeed, it was becoming colder, and Taylor realized that for the last five minutes he had been pulling his shirt tight around his neck, fending off the licking breeze.

The mate did not hesitate to act on the sailor's information. In a stentorian tone hardly outmatched by Torm himself, the man issued a rapid set of orders. Taylor went belowdecks to fetch a jacket, then returned to watch the flurry of activity above. Save the mainsail and foresail, all the other canvas had been furled and lashed

securely to the yards. A small group of men with fresh
pots of tar had begun waterproofing the seals on the
large hatches that led to the hold.

They must be expecting one hell of a storm, Taylor
thought, looking again at the massed clouds that had
begun to obscure the setting sun.

The first mate walked by, pointing at a loose line on
the foreyard, and Taylor stopped him.

"What of my horse?" he asked, realizing that he now
had to raise his voice over a growing wind.

"It is too late for that, Revered Father," the mate answered quickly, with very little semblance of sympathy.
"You asked for a stall on deck, that the beast might
enjoy the air and sun. Now he may enjoy the storm as
well."

The man paused and seemed to repent a bit. "God
protects the innocent," he added quietly before turning
back to his work.

Troubled, Taylor made his way carefully aft toward
Scry's stall. The waves were growing into large swells,
throwing Taylor off balance as the deck pitched to and
fro. He noticed a group of sailors stringing lines between
the masts and along the gunwales—to secure themselves
when the weather grew worse, no doubt.

Scry seemed placid despite the coming storm, shifting
his weight stoically to adjust to the bucking deck, but
that hardly made Taylor feel better. He realized for the
first time how needless it had been to bring the horse.
He was *sailing* to Thyrsus, after all, and although it
would depend on circumstances how he would return, it
would have been simple enough to purchase a mount in
Yndor had he needed one. Instead, he had risked the
animal's life gratuitously.

He hadn't wanted to leave Prandis alone, he realized.
And of all the people he knew in the vast city, there had
been no one as comforting to bring as the large chestnut,
with his steady black eyes. In fact, Taylor realized with

a wry frown, he hadn't spent more time with any one person than he had with Scry—not since the day his father had died. He laughed harshly as the rain began to fall. While the crew accelerated the near-frenzied pace of their preparations, Taylor Ash was left alone to comfort his horse against the brewing storm and to contemplate the odd infirmities of human nature.

The drops were large at first, but soon gave way to a dense downpour of small, stinging beads. The waves had grown to the height of a house; they had begun to breach the gunwales, washing the decks in brine. Glowering at the weather, Captain Torm supervised the furling of the last sail and the deployment of the sea anchor. With any luck, this large canvas cone would catch the waves well enough to keep the *Grampus*'s bow headed into the wind. It would be a rough ride, but given a bit of luck, they would suffer nothing worse than a wet and miserable night.

Torm did not care to consider the alternatives. Should the vessel swing athwart the storm's force, she would be at risk of capsizing. Indeed, the intensity of the waves was frightening already, and Torm could feel in his bones that there was worse to come. Should the sea anchor fail. . . . Torm hated even to voice it in his thoughts, but he knew there would be no choice but to run the ship before the wind. And running before such a wind as was coming made even the grizzled Gathon captain shake to his God-fearing bones.

It was then that Torm pulled himself fore along the starboard gunwale line and saw that crazy spice merchant clinging to a post in his horse's stall. Tempted sorely to swear, Torm fought his way along the steeply pitched deck and grabbed hold of the stall before another wave threw the entire ship backward.

"Get to your cabin, Brother Pass!" the old captain

bellowed into the wind. "This is no place for a landsman!"

Apparently, Taylor heard him. He swung around to face the captain, his eyes obscured by a ragged black curtain of wet hair. "But—"

Torm cut him off with an angry gesture. "I'll not be responsible for your death. Below deck, I say!"

There was no use trying to answer. Taylor felt that his life was his own to risk, but it was folly to distract the captain from the paramount task of preserving the ship. Taylor paused to pat Scry on the neck once more before he slipped between the rails of the stall. Then, carefully, he made his way back to his cabin.

The captain's steward, whose duties never brought him on deck, even during the needs of a storm, had lit Taylor's cabin lantern, as he did every night. The old iron lamp swung crazily from its hook in the ceiling, its hood clanging wildly open and shut as it pitched this way and that. The effect was maddening, as if a creature of light had been trapped in the small space of the cabin and was crashing from wall to wall in a desperate attempt to escape. In what little he could make out in the aimless light, Taylor realized the steward had removed the glass and pitcher of water that usually sat upon his table, thereby saving them from certain destruction. He had not, however, stowed the books and clothes that Taylor had left about the cabin, and these things flew wildly around the room, even as the furniture, all bolted into place, seemed strangely indifferent to the tempest.

The cabin door was banging repeatedly behind him. Taylor pulled it firmly shut and latched it. Then he collected his things, lest he be brained by a flying book, and tossed them into one of the cabinets below his bunk, latching that as well. He was tempted to blow out the lantern, but he knew that if he did, he would never succeed in lighting it again. Instead, he crawled carefully into his bunk and, wrapping his fingers around the cords that held the mattress in place, tried to relax.

It was impossible. The groaning of the ship's timbers seemed deafening as, with each wave, the bow was lifted high out of the water, only to come crashing down again with an impact that threatened to burst the vessel into splinters. And, try as he might, Taylor was thrown from his bunk repeatedly, once bruising his ribs against the nearby table leg. Swearing under his breath, he struggled to his feet and snatched his blanket from the cabin floor. For the first time, he realized that the series of little cords that ran along the edge of the blanket might be something more than another inscrutable Gathon embellishment. As the ship continued to buck, he haltingly ran these cords through the same metal eyelets by which the mattress was tied down, creating a snug pocket between blanket and mattress from which he could not be thrown. Taylor crawled inside this improvised haven and wished for an interval of peace, but although he was not thrown to the floor again, peace would not come. He could not stop thinking of Scry above.

And he could not stop thinking of a bald man who was even now, no doubt, making his comfortable way toward Thyrsus, in untroubled possession of words that no one man should own.

Whether it was only minutes or hours or an entire tortured day later, Taylor could not say. Time dilated by a means that misery alone knew, and Taylor could cling only to the certain knowledge that his back felt broken from the bucking of the ship, and that each unsurpassable crescendo of the wind proved, beyond all philosophy, only the overture to a still greater wail of pain, like some grieving chorus of infinite membership. Finally, he could endure no more. Scry was still on deck, as were the Gaths, and why should he hide beneath his bedclothes while they faced the elemental fury of the tempest? He struggled out of his bunk, almost sprawling headlong as he put his foot to the floorboards, and staggered toward the door across what seemed like an impossible uphill slope. Abruptly, the *Grampus* plummeted downward, throwing Taylor headfirst at the door. He bore the impact silently, content to get a firm grasp on the handle, and wrenched the door open as the deck began to rise again. He caromed wildly off the walls of the passage as the ship pitched about, but it took only a few more steps to bring him to the end of the corridor. There, a half-flight of steps led upward to the door that opened upon the deck. Bracing himself, he threw this door open.

Nothing he had imagined had prepared Taylor for the shock that greeted him. A sheet of water struck him full in the face as the door swung open. Between the stinging rain and the utter darkness, he couldn't see a thing. The wind tore through his clothes as if they meant nothing. The gale rattled his teeth in his skull, drove his eyes back into their sockets. Above him, from the quarterdeck, Taylor could make out Torm's distant cries. The captain's voice sounded raw, bloodied. There seemed not to be an intelligible word in it, only a primeval howl to meet the greater howl of the wind.

It was then that a stroke of lightning struck nearby, illuminating the deck with painful intensity and filling Taylor's nostrils with ozone. Before him, he could see groups of sailors tied to the guy ropes, frozen in that instant of light in the postures of boneless corpses. And half-obscured by the mainmast, he glimpsed Scry in the paddock, reared high upon his back hooves at a crazy angle from the deck, mouth open and eyes wide with fear.

Driven by an impulse far beyond thought, he sprang onto the deck and was thrown promptly forward, sliding on his belly through the salt water that covered the planks. He hit something hard and rolled over. It was the mainmast. There should be a line tied about it at waist level, Taylor remembered, if it had not already been torn loose. He flailed desperately with his right hand, and his palm found the tarred rope. He clung to it as the next wave hit, spinning him around and slamming him back into the mast.

Another stroke of lightning split the sky. He saw Torm towering over the quarterdeck railing, as steady as a fourth mast. And Torm saw him.

"Get below!" the captain cried. "Back to your cabin, you fool, or I swear I'll keelhaul you myself before I let this storm claim you!"

Taylor had little choice but to obey. Another great convulsion of the sea ripped him free of his mooring and sent him spinning aft, sliding on his belly across the planks as if they'd been greased. The only safe haven was the nearby door to the halfdeck cabins, held yawning open by the wild pitch of the deck. In the moment of equilibrium before the ship came crashing down again, Taylor kicked himself toward the doorway and slid straight through, bouncing harshly down the steps. His head hit the floor and he took a mouthful of water before rolling over onto his back. Coughing convulsively, he crawled along the passageway to his cabin and edged inside. The door slammed shut after him as the ship tilted perilously to starboard. When it swung open again, it revealed Captain Torm standing behind it. Torm wore only his white shirt now and, as he braced himself against the doorjambs, Taylor could see every cord of the captain's lean, old muscles through the wet linen. Water streamed down his cabled beard and fell in runnels to the floor.

"This is a hurricane," he growled. "A hurricane from the southwest."

The old Gath seemed to put a peculiar emphasis on that last fact, but Taylor could not in the least fathom why the man had left his post to brief a passenger on the weather.

"This is spring," the captain added with dangerous

intensity. "No storms like this come from the southwest, not during spring."

Taylor tried to speak, only managed to cough, and tried again. "Apparently, this storm did."

"No storm does," Torm repeated.

Taylor let his head drop to the wet deck. Nothing, it seemed, would ever make sense again.

"I don't understand. I'm no sailor. . . ."

"No, that you are not," the captain agreed. He paused a moment before continuing in a lower tone. "The sea anchor is all but shredded. As we swing athwart of the waves, we risk capsizing. Should we stay thus more than a moment, nothing else could be our fate."

In the face of doom so mildly announced, Taylor could think of nothing to say.

"The sea anchor matters little, however," Torm went on. "By God's grace, we have taken little water thus far, but surely the timbers can stand such a buffeting no longer. We have no choice but to come about and run before the wind. If the storm does not shred every inch of canvas we carry, or does not simply tear out our masts by the root, we may perhaps run out the storm."

Torm paused, apparently waiting for a response, but Taylor remained mute. Finally, Torm shook his head with a slow, fateful stroke.

"Can you imagine, Brother Landsman, what it is to ask a man to climb the rigging and set a double-reefed foresail on a morning such as this?"

And then he slammed Taylor's door shut.

The young man lay exhausted in the water for a long time before he fully understood what the captain had said. The utter darkness outside was a new day's morning.

It was not long after Taylor pulled himself miserably into his bunk, wet clothes and all, that he was slammed violently into the cabin wall. The ship felt as if it had been lifted clear out of the sea and smashed down on its starboard side. And yet, at the same time that the cabin wall came perilously close to becoming the floor, the ship rotated violently on its axis like a wildly spinning bottle. Suddenly, as the vessel came about, a huge force grabbed hold of it, as if Torm's God had perched the *Grampus* on his forefinger and shot it forward like a marble. The acceleration pressed at the base of Taylor's skull, a sickening weight.

On a lone, double-reefed sail, Captain Torm was running the *Grampus* before the wind. And never, through a long seaborne life, had a vessel of his run half so fast.

But the speed, in its way, proved far better than fighting the storm. Driven by the implacable gale, the sharp-prowed *Grampus* drove through the sea like a fury, settling into a pounding rhythm that was nevertheless less punishing than the tossing it had endured before. The timbers screamed under the strain like nothing Taylor had ever heard or imagined, but the banshee wail seemed somehow welcome. After a time, he could no longer tell whether it was the beams screaming or himself, and he fell not into sleep, but into some unthinking state, a compound of wind and wave and pain.

Strong arms pulled him from his bunk and, before he quite realized what was happening, he was dragged along the passageway to the deck. It took a moment before he could rouse himself from the stupor he had lain in, for how long he could not tell. He glanced wildly at the two burly sailors who were dragging him by the arms.

"What on earth is going on?" he shouted above the roar of the storm and the creaking of the beams.

"The captain wishes to speak with you, Reverend Father," one of the sailors replied, pronouncing the epithet with a dark undertone.

He would say no more, and because Taylor had no choice in the matter, he allowed himself to be carried onto the deck, into the stinging rain. It was still dark outside, but not impenetrably so. Taylor could make out the dusky silhouettes of sailors moving about and the churning masses of black clouds above. The ship seemed more still than it had since the first breeze had crept deceptively upon them from the southwest, but Taylor realized this stillness was yet another deception. The wind was fierce and, beneath his feet, Taylor could feel the timbers vibrating under the strain of terrific speed. The *Grampus* would be safe as long as it continued to run before the storm, a helpless instrument of the wind. The only question was, how long could the ship continue its devil's run?

It was a question that Torm was disposed to answer immediately.

"The tempest has carried us for almost a full day," the captain said as Taylor was led before him. The man's dark eyes were fixed on his passenger, but he spoke in tones loud enough to be heard by all. It was not a conversation that Torm intended, Taylor realized, but some sort of formal announcement. And as the captain spoke, the crew drew closer, ringing the two men. Only then was Taylor released.

"Half our sheets are ragged," the old man continued, "and this ship is weary from her mastheads to her keel. But, one way or another, rest cannot be far off. If we abandon sail, we shall capsize. If we continue to run this wind, we shall soon break ourselves upon the shore. For, as I reckon it, in this one day, we have made three days of normal sailing, and not far off, there—" the captain flung his arm toward the bow, his finger pointing over the gunwales into the waiting darkness—"there, lie the deadly bogs of Bismet, whether leagues away yet or only yards, I cannot say. This I can say: Should we founder there, we shall die as surely as by drowning, though far less wholesomely."

The old Gath paused here, seeming to expect an answer, as he had a day earlier in Taylor's cabin. Only when he saw that no words were forthcoming did he continue.

"The men whisper that this is no ordinary storm."

A murmur arose from the crew at this, and Torm looked about him, embracing his men with his gaze.

"They are right," the captain said, as if pronouncing sentence. "A tempest such as this is the handiwork of God. Such wave and wind speak divine protest, protest against human sin."

Torm paused again here, and a chill swept through Taylor that was not entirely due to the cold, vicious gale. When you were dragged from your bed to hear a Gath rave about his God, it boded very little good indeed.

"Such sin breathes aboard this ship that our divine Father has seen fit to erase it from the sight of man, to sink it below the waves or suck it beneath the mud of the bogs, that the sun may shine upon it nevermore. But must thirty men die for one man's sin?" the captain implored, his strong voice cracking. Then he continued more quietly. "I have examined the souls of my crew this everlasting night, and though I have found some men weak, there is not one whose soul is stained with deadly crime."

The captain took one long step forward, casting his dark eyes upon Taylor, and from behind his broad beard he asked, "Have you anything to tell us, Brother Pass?"

Taylor ground his teeth together and glared at the old, addled captain before him. He had had more than his fill of preposterous Gathon piety.

"I'll tell you this," Taylor growled, loud enough for everyone to hear. "Odd as it may be, this is a storm. No more, no less. God doesn't send storms to show his displeasure with one man."

A few of the sailors gasped, and Torm's eyes crinkled

in such a way that, if Taylor had been able to see the man's lips, he knew that he would have witnessed a smile. Too late, he realized that whatever he'd said had only answered Torm's wishes, convinced the old Gath of his suspicions.

"Long have I watched you, Brother Pass, and you are no Gathon man. You speak as we speak, but your thoughts are not our own. Who are you, in truth?"

In a fleeting moment, Taylor considered his options— an easy task, because there were few. Torm was already convinced of his suspicions, and there was nothing Taylor could say to the contrary. There seemed little point in prolonging the masquerade.

"My name is Taylor Ash," he replied wearily. "I am the Minister of Intelligence for the Republic of Chaldus."

"Thank you, Minister Ash," Torm said with genuine gratitude. Then he lifted his voice again in clarion tones for all the crew to hear. "Centuries ago, God laid upon Gathony the duty to withdraw from the bloody affairs of the nations to the north. We might walk among them and trade with them, but never were we to assist one nation more than the other in the eternal strife that sets them apart. When Minister Ash came among us, he pitched us at odds with our duty, although we knew it not. Having found the truth, we may step back from the precipice of disaster and atone for this sacrilege.

"Seize him."

Immediately, two sturdy sailors took hold of Taylor's arms. He struggled for a moment, but it was clear that he would never shake loose hands inured to years of hauling lines and climbing rigging.

The captain looked for the last time at Taylor, almost sadly. "Throw him over the side, to port, whence he first climbed aboard ship and whence as well this plague of a tempest came upon us."

The tight knot of sailors drew apart as Taylor's two captors dragged him toward the port gunwale. Desper-

ately, he tried to brace himself, but the deck was still
wet, and his frantically slipping feet could find no purchase against the planks. In a moment more, they thrust
him against the gunwale. The sailor on his right grabbed
hold of his head and pushed Taylor's torso over the railing, slamming his ribs against the wood. The wind
whipped wildly at his hair and Taylor could make out
the writhing waves lapping greedily at the hull of the
ship, awaiting him.

"Captain, may I speak?"

Taylor could hardly hear the voice over the wind, but it
sounded like Gorman. He could hardly believe that, of the
entire crew, this particular sailor would risk speaking on
his behalf. But Gorman had indeed spoken, and the interruption gave Taylor's captors pause. They held him firmly
against the rail as they awaited the captain's response.

"Speak freely, my son."

And then, as Gorman spoke, Taylor's last, desperate
hope died stillborn: "Should we not offer to the sea the
blasphemer's horse as well, demon that it is? And his
spices from the hold?"

Another voice rose up now, the second mate's, Taylor
thought. "The horse is a fine beast. It will fetch a high
price at market. And shall not this man's spices pay for
the repair of our ship and for new canvas?"

"Are we then to profit," Gorman countered, "from the
wages of sin? And ought not we, then, to drown as
surely as the Chaldean, provoking God's displeasure?"

The argument began to absorb the crew's attention,
including the sailors who held Taylor. On Gathon ships,
crew members were not paid wages, but instead received
a specified fraction of the voyage's profits. Were the
Gaths to dump Taylor's spices overboard, they would
see no profit at all. As Gorman continued his inspired,
devout harangue on the evil of Taylor's goods, the two
sailors who held Taylor against the railing began to see
their payment slipping away, and their grip on him be-

gan slipping as well, although they hardly realized it.
Taylor quietly shifted his feet until they were braced
firmly against the gunwale. Then he drew his upper lip
tightly across his teeth and blew a long, shrill whistle.

Scry's trumpeting call answered immediately and, at
its sound, Taylor pushed against the gunwale with all his
strength, tearing himself free from the Gaths' grasp. As he
fell backward onto the deck and began sliding to starboard, he saw a huge, dark figure split the air. The planks
shivered as Scry landed beyond his stall and, charging
across the deck, split the ranks of the astonished sailors. It
took only a moment for the horse to reach Taylor's side,
knocking away one of the crewmen who had been chasing him. Taylor pulled himself clumsily upon Scry's wet,
bare back and struggled to keep his balance as the horse
wheeled around to face the massed crew.

The stallion's initial charge had caught them unaware,
but now they were ready. Bearing knives, or drawing
belaying pins from the rail, the men swiftly began to
advance. The momentary surge of elation that had accompanied Taylor's escape now ebbed quickly from his
body. The entire notion of escape was foolish—escape
to where? And if not escape, what then? Conquest? Even
if, by some absurd miracle, he could manage to defeat
the entire crew, who then would sail the Grampus? No,
although temporarily at liberty, Taylor still possessed no
options.

Only a choice of dooms.

The choice was quickly made. Wrapping his arms
around Scry's great neck, Taylor kicked sharply at the
horse's ribs. Scry reared like a giant upon his back legs,
kicking out with his forehooves at the nearest of the sailors. Then, returning to the planks with a clatter, the horse
exploded like a shot across the deck, charging past the
crew until, with a fluid leap, he cleared the port gunwale.

There was a huge concussion, a stinging spray of salt
water, and then the black waves closed hungrily above
them.

The night that Taylor Ash set sail from Prandis, Cyrintha determined to dine with Holoakhan. She issued no invitation. She simply arrived at his rooms, Akmar trailing silently behind her, and informed the old mage that dinner would be served shortly. Such were the prerogatives of a princess.

Nevertheless, Cyrintha was not normally one to impose her presence on others, despite her imperial blood. The old wizard knew this, and wondered what was wrong.

Cyrintha stood there, her fists perched delicately upon her hips, and stared impatiently at her aged mentor.

"You know, Loa, to dine standing upright is very bad for your digestion."

Holoakhan smiled and bowed in apology. Then he ushered the princess and her trothblade into his study. The room was small and the high walls were entirely lined with books; Holoakhan had even bricked up the windows in order to install more shelves. The place was lit only dimly by two candles on a cluttered desk. Holoakhan carefully moved his books and papers from the desk to the already overburdened shelves behind it.

"A poor enough dinner table for a princess of the Jurin family," he observed, motioning toward the old desk, "but it will have to serve. What brings the princess to so beggarly a banquet hall as this?"

Cyrintha smiled in spite of herself. She had determined not to let Khan's amusements distract her tonight.

"There was an important audience this afternoon," she replied, resuming her grave demeanor. "Why did you not attend?"

Khan's eyes twinkled with dark humor. "And how do you know I did not, when you were not there yourself?"

"How—?" Cyrintha stifled the question, once more surprised by her old mentor's resources. "Answer my question," she responded in a tone she reserved for her most imperial moods.

"Gladly," Khan replied as he positioned three chairs around the desk. "I did not attend because I knew what your brother was going to say—and what your father would respond. It seemed too thoroughly a waste of my afternoon."

"There was a time," Cyrintha observed, "when my father would not hold an audience without you by his side."

"Ah, yes," Holoakhan assented softly, as if lost in nostalgic reminiscence. "But that was before he so generously allowed me to devote my fuller attentions to your education. I fear I have stumbled so badly in this capacity that he trusts me no longer in any other."

Again, Cyrintha had to suppress a smile. "Don't jest."

"I'm not, entirely," the old man replied gravely, his olive brow creasing with concern.

He settled wearily into a seat and invited Cyrintha and the trothblade to do likewise. This was something of a running joke between Khan and Akmar, for the dour trothblade consented to sit on very few occasions indeed. His duties forbade it.

"Your father no longer knows whom to trust," Holoakhan continued. "Since Sardos arrived at the palace two years ago, his advice to the emperor has been unerring. Every course of action Sardos suggests, succeeds. Everything he undertakes, he accomplishes. The man has been an invaluable asset to the empire."

"*You* have been an invaluable asset to the empire!" Cyrintha replied hotly.

Holoakhan shifted uncomfortably in his seat before responding. "Your father sees that as the past . . . and a rather remote past, I'm afraid. This is not to say that I have completely lost my standing. My suggestions succeed as well as Sardos's, upon occasion. My advice, too, is not wholly without worth. Yet, of late, my counsel and Sardos's seem to agree less and less, and so the emperor is confused more and more. He listens to Sardos, he listens to me, but in truth he hearkens to neither of us. Emperor Mallioch sits upon his throne and considers which of his advisers to trust. In the meantime, he will trust no one, and he is a better man for it."

A knock interrupted Khan's speech, and he called for the visitor to enter. It was a palace servant wheeling a cart laden with food. Imperturbable, the waiter steered his burden around the columns of books that littered Holoakhan's floor at random intervals, and he glanced fearlessly at the stained old desk which was to be the princess's dining table. From a lower shelf of the cart, the servant brought forth a rich burgundy-colored tablecloth and hid the desk beneath it. He proceeded to set the table with china, crystal, and silver, and then brought forth dish after dish of steaming food. Cyrintha inhaled the rich aromas and smiled; a feast was one of the few things, perhaps, that could improve her spirits today. She waited impatiently while the servant poured wine into the three goblets, left the bottle on the table, bowed, and disappeared.

Cyrintha reached toward a platter of roasted herbed

venison. It was then that Akmar cleared his throat. It was more noise than he had made all day.

. Part of the trothblade's duty was to sample anything that the imperial family would eat. An old and useless ritual, for in Cyrintha's entire lifetime she could not remember a single case of poisoning in the palace. But she enjoyed the routine nonetheless. There was something reassuring about it, something redolent of her childhood, a reminder of a time when everything seemed secure and protected. So, as usual, Cyrintha withdrew her hand and waited with a slight smile while Akmar stepped forward and helped himself to a small portion from each platter on the table. He would not sit, but stood as he efficiently consumed a few bites of each dish and concluded his abbreviated meal with a swig of wine. It was the heroic expediency of Akmar's dinner that entertained Cyrintha—the way the stoic soldier chewed like a rabbit so that he would delay the princess's meal as little as possible. She felt a sudden urge to hug her stern protector, and wondered whether such a thing could succeed in producing a blush on Akmar's impassive cheeks. Now that would be rare entertainment indeed.

Satisfied with the food, Akmar stepped backward, allowing Cyrintha and the wizard to proceed. With a smile, Cyrintha reached toward the venison.

She was stopped by the sound of gagging.

Both she and Khan whipped around in their chairs to confront a horrible sight. Akmar was clutching his neck, desperately ripping at the collar of his thick black shirt, as if to make room to breathe. In the scant seconds that had passed, his flesh had turned purple—not only his face, but his hands as well. His fingernails shone black.

"He's choking!" Cyrintha cried. "Help him!"

Holoakhan had already jumped from his seat with a spryness surprising in a man of his years. He raced around the desk toward the gagging trothblade, but before he reached him, Akmar fell to his knees with a tremendous crash. His massive body began trembling violently, and his hands now shook too much to clutch his neck. Somehow, though, the warrior fought the pain long enough to look one last time upon Cyrintha, his blue eyes wide with an unspoken apology. And then he toppled onto his side, dead before he hit the floor.

Cyrintha screamed, but only once. Then she stood up, feeling herself waver on her feet, and took a tentative step forward. Tears had begun to gather along the margins of her eyes and spill down her pale cheeks. She felt faint, as if the world had been wrenched inside out.

Akmar, her shadow—Akmar, who never spoke or smiled or winced or blushed—Akmar, her eternal companion, was dead. She fell to her knees and took his swollen face between her hands. His flesh was still hot but utterly lax. Cyrintha realized she had never touched his face before, and with a start, drew her hands back.

Holoakhan, kneeling at the trothblade's side, shook his head as he examined the man. Then, gently, he closed Akmar's eyes and straightened the fingers that had convulsed into fists. Wearily, the mage rose to his feet and turned to Cyrintha with a terrible sadness in his eyes.

"He suffocated," the wizard said softly, drawing Cyrintha away from the corpse.

Suffocated. It made no sense. Nothing that Akmar had eaten should have been able to choke him so quickly, so thoroughly.

"Was it a bone?" Cyrintha asked hoarsely.

"No bone," Holoakhan answered. "Poison."

The princess recoiled. The room seemed to reel into motion with a sickening lurch. "Poison? Are you saying that someone wanted to kill me?"

"Not at all," Holoakhan replied.

Cyrintha stumbled backward and fell into a chair. The

sound of her breathing seemed very loud and her heart felt ready to burst.

"Don't jest with me," she said weakly, "not now, Loa."

"Oh, I'm not jesting," the old wizard replied grimly. "The trothblades are trained to recognize virtually every poison known to man and, if the means are available, they're trained to resist them as well. Unless I miss my guess, Akmar is a victim of amarilis. It's one of the few really effective poisons that is impossible to detect—colorless, odorless, tasteless."

Cyrintha shuddered at the thought of such an insidious, unsuspected death. "Then why didn't he develop a resistance to that, too?"

"Quite simply, because there was never the need. Amarilis is so potent that no assassin would be foolish enough to use it on the imperial family. The trothblade would die far too swiftly, alerting the real target that the food had been poisoned. And that is exactly what happened here. Even in death," Khan concluded sadly, "Akmar did his job."

"What are you saying?" Cyrintha asked, confused. She rested her elbow upon the desk for support, but touched a platter accidentally and jerked her arm away.

"I am saying," Khan explained, capturing her eyes in the comforting gaze of his own soft brown irises, "that this was not an attempt on your life. Someone is sending you a message. And that message is, stay away from your brother. Stay away from Sardos."

CHAPTER 18

In the end, of the two doctors Brandt provided for Carn, it was the doctor of law who proved more curative. The ultimate result of Pardi's work was to remind Carn more acutely than before that he was forever a cripple. After his examination, all Pardi had been able to do was instruct a servant in special massages for Carn's legs and order the construction of a fine wheelchair—specially designed to cradle Carn's figure, made of sturdy oak, and cushioned in all the right places. (Days later, when Carn first beheld the upholstered seat, he thought: *They could have saved the trouble; I'll never feel anything there again.*) Nor did the massages possess any curative value. They would merely fend off atrophy of the muscles, an entirely cosmetic matter. It was a different kind of atrophy Brandt feared—one that lay beyond the scope of Pardi's healing arts.

Solan was a different matter. Innocuous as the lawyer's stacks of papers seemed, they had a profound and immediate effect on the signatories. With a sort of ruthless efficiency, Solan had already informed every company and organization even remotely related to Karrelian

Industries that Carn Eliando had become the ultimate authority in all financial matters. Indeed, Solan had barely left the door before employees began to arrive, bearing contracts to be pored over, bids to be considered. And they all addressed themselves to Carn, ignoring Brandt as if he were not there. They brushed aside his protestations of fatigue with explanations of why each document was more urgent than the one that preceded it. Just as Brandt had planned, there was no respite from the press of business.

At first, Carn's response had been annoyance. But when it became apparent that Brandt would do no more than stand in the corner and watch, Carn sighed and began to examine the paperwork they brought him. He knew, of course, that all of this was simply Brandt's crude psychology—an amateurish attempt to distract him from what had now become the central fact of his existence: half a body.

But it was the crudest psychology that sometimes worked the best. And, before long, despite himself, Carn was absorbed in the consuming details of Brandt's sprawling enterprises. When Masya returned to the mansion with her things (packed in pillowcases, for she had never had need of a suitcase in her life), she was pleased to see Carn absorbed in his work. She lingered only long enough to kiss him on the forehead before settling into her new room.

After watching Carn work for two hours, Brandt was satisfied—and he feared he could afford to wait no longer. He dismissed the servants clustered about the bed and, moving aside a pile of the papers that now covered the entire mattress, he took a seat beside his old partner.

"I need to leave," he said quietly. The sun was already going down. "They've got enough of a head start already."

Carn looked up and his eyes darkened. For a moment, lost in the tangles of paperwork, he'd forgotten that

Brandt intended to go after Hain. Carn considered trying to dissuade him, but then, in a flash, he was flooded again by the feeling that had overwhelmed him in the Atahr Vin. He could not explain it—this premonition that had compelled him to lie to Brandt about Aston, this dread that had seized him while he had listened to the old minister's story. Carn had the inexplicable sensation that, for what he had suffered physically, he had been given a vision in return. But what a dismal vision it was. . . . The whole world, which had once seemed so solid, was merely a stage propped up on a foundation called the Binding. And that foundation was in dire danger of collapse. Carn didn't trust the government to save it—his years of work with Brandt had taught him too well the Republic's folly, ineptitude, and apathy.

Apathy. It had infected more than just the government, Carn thought. Over the last decade, he had watched his friend devolve from an ambitious spy into a jaded magnate—a man who had become little more than a spectator to the parade of his own wealth. But now Carn saw a smoldering purpose in Brandt's eyes, and the years of apathy seemed to have burned away in that heat. He looked like the Brandt of old—a man whose mind was always half on some distant, all-consuming purpose. He looked, Carn thought, like Galatine Hazard.

Carn shook his head, emotions torn. It was good to see Brandt infused again with a sense of mission. But that sense itself. . . .

"Please, Brandt," Carn said softly, "if you go, go for the right reasons."

Brandt sighed. "What's that supposed to mean?"

"It means—" Carn almost choked on the words. "It means, don't do anything for me."

A cloud passed over Brandt's features. When Brandt's reply came, it was barely audible.

"You're the only reason I have."

The words hung in the air between them, and they said nothing more for a few moments. It was, Carn realized, the closest Brandt had ever come to sentiment. And it was the gesture of a friend who knew he might not return.

"Be careful," Carn warned.

Brandt merely nodded.

"One invalid is enough."

At that, Brandt smiled. "At least we'd have wheelchair races to look forward to."

Carn laughed. "I'll beat you."

"I'm lighter."

"I'm stronger."

Brandt shrugged. "We'll see. For now, my problem isn't killing the killer; it's simply finding him."

Carn pulled himself upright against the headboard. He tended to slide down along the mattress, and getting back up was difficult without his legs to brace himself.

"How do you intend to go about it?" he asked.

Brandt frowned. "I was hoping you'd help me there. Let's assume that he's an Yndrian agent—"

"Why not Gathony or Brindis?" Carn asked. "Gathony has tried in the past to play Chaldus and Yndor against each other, hoping to emerge as the preeminent continental power after a war. They've got that bizarre religious sense of destiny. And they look like atheists compared to Brindis. I wouldn't put anything past the Brindisians: a bunch of idol-worshipping fanatics running around the forest in loincloths. . . ."

"We'll assume Yndor," Brandt explained, "simply because it seems most likely. If he heads for Gathony, it won't make much difference. The route would start out the same. If he's bound for Brindis, we've gambled and lost—but there are only so many contingencies I can cover. So, assuming that his destination is Yndor, the important question is, how does he get there?"

"Fastest way?" Carn asked. "That would be by ship,

beyond doubt. A sea passage would save a month or more of cross-country riding."

"That's what I thought," Brandt said, "but put yourself in the situation of a fugitive."

Carn did, and he saw Brandt's point. The Ministry of Intelligence would surely be keeping a tight watch on the docks, probably blockading the port and searching every ship. Now that the government had a description of the assassin, the chance of escape by sea was unlikely.

"So he leaves by the roads," Carn said, after outlining his thinking, "and heads for the most convenient port. More likely still, he'll have a ship of his own waiting in some deserted inlet. There are dozens of navigable bays and rivers along this stretch of coast."

This last fact Carn knew well, having occasionally worked as a smuggler when thievery and espionage grew boring decades ago.

Brandt, too, had thought back to Carn's smuggling days.

"How many ships would you lose each month between Chaldus and Yndor?" he asked.

Carn shrugged. "Depends on the time of year. In the best circumstances, the Sawtooth Strait can be a death trap. If you wanted to play it safe, you'd have to sail south around Gonwyr and Brindis. That would take time, and the seas in that area aren't exactly what you'd call tame, either."

Brandt nodded. "Playing it safe: I've been thinking a lot about that. Let's assume Aston wasn't lying. Let's assume that Yndor really has stolen the key to a spell so powerful that it would change the world as we know it, or at least bring Chaldus to its knees. The circumstances of these thefts are incredible—the kind of thing you can pull off only once, by moving very quickly while your opponent's guard is down. Do you think they'd risk such treasure on the high seas? Lose it once and, now that the Council is vigilant, generations might pass before the next chance."

Carn nodded. "By road, then. Slowly, but safely, by road."

"My thoughts exactly. It's spring. The trade routes are lousy with merchants, travelers, pilgrims, you name it. Draw no attention to yourself—all the right papers, no traveling at night—and you can easily get lost in that traffic. Right now, I bet he's riding slowly at the head of a little caravan, carrying a legitimate load of cloth or pickles."

"You should be able to catch up easily."

"Catch up," Brandt said, grinning, "or even get there with a day to spare."

"There?" Carn asked.

"Belfar. Everything hinges on my finding them in Belfar."

Carn nodded as he weighed Brandt's logic. There was only one major trade route that traveled west of Prandis, and it led to Belfar, the mercantile hub of the nation. After Belfar, however, roads radiated out like spokes. There were at least three well-traveled routes to Yndor.

Belfar, Carn remembered, was where they had first met, with two guttersnipe thieves interrupting a careful bit of commercial espionage he had been conducting.

The chase had been merry and long.

And it would have ended in the most solid drubbing of Brandt's life, if not for another snotty sixteen-year-old guttersnipe. Carn could see him clearly—it was not a face you were liable to forget: curly carrot hair, constellations of freckles splayed across ruddy cheeks, and a crooked smile. A boy who could talk his way out of any trouble.

"What about Marwick?" Carn asked.

"What about him?" Brandt replied darkly.

"Will you see him?"

"I doubt he's still alive. Not clever enough to avoid the authorities without me there."

Carn laughed, amused as always at Brandt's selective memory of his youth in Belfar.

"Don't flatter yourself. I was the one who saved both your necks from the patrols."

Brandt shrugged. "Have it your way."

"Will you see him?" Carn asked again, suddenly grave.

"Not if I can help it."

Carn sighed. It was a bad habit Brandt had, burning bridges for no good reason, casting off the best parts of his youth along with the worst. Carn wondered whether Brandt would ever learn to embrace his past, to mine the gold in those buried veins. But he did not want to get in an argument about Marwick; for the moment, there were more important issues at hand.

"Go, then. But be careful," Carn reminded. "The bald one is dangerous."

"So am I," Brandt replied, ending the conversation by leaving the room and the house, and lifting himself into the saddle of a fast horse he'd prepared two hours earlier.

It was late at night when the messenger arrived. Carn had almost cleared the mattress of papers. He took that to be a reasonable goal: uncover the bed, and you get to sleep in it. Masya had tried staying awake with him, but had fallen asleep in a chair in the corner. The announcement of a messenger therefore vexed him. He had been through enough already.

But when Baley ushered in the boy, keeping a firm hold on his collar, Carn's interest awakened. The lad looked no older than twelve and was utterly filthy, his clothes little more than a cleverly arranged collection of rags. At the moment, he had a firm, two-fisted grip

around a small ebony statuette that habitually spent the
night on a pedestal in the vestibule.

"This is a messenger?" Carn asked, amused.

"He says so," Baley replied. "He's also taken that
statue and refuses to give it back."

"He said it was mine!" the boy replied, demonstrating
the unfortunate childhood belief that, the louder you
spoke, the more credible you'd sound. Carn winced at
the racket.

"Softly, boy, softly." But it was too late. Masya had
already awakened, rubbing her eyes as she stared curiously at the guttersnipe.

"But he *did*—"

"Softly, I said. Now, who said it was yours?"

"The man who sent the message. Brandt."

As the boy said the name, he looked up smugly at the
doorman who continued to hold his collar, as if invoking
the name was an irrefutable token of authority.

"Well, you've proved that you know who lives here,"
Carn said, "but not much else. What did this Brandt look
like?"

The child lifted his hand high above his head, perhaps
five feet in the air.

"He was a midget, then, this Brandt?" Carn asked,
laughing.

"Hey, watch the cracks about midgets," the boy replied with a threatening undertone that amused Carn. On
a second look, Carn decided that the boy was older than
he had first thought, perhaps in his early teens. Rather
short for his age.

"I can't reach his head," the boy went on. "But that's
about where his shoulder was."

Carn shrugged. It was about right.

"Black hair—"

"What color eyes?"

"I don't know what color eyes," the child replied,

peeved. "He's not my girlfriend, y'know. But his clothes were all black—"

So far, accurate, Carn thought.

"—except for the blood on 'em."

Carn leaned forward, his patience suddenly at an end. *Blood?*

"You'd better get to the point of this message faster," Carn snapped.

"Not till I know I'm getting paid," the kid replied. "He said if I came here I could have the Yojo."

That was it. That was the sign Brandt had contrived to convince Carn that the boy was genuine. Eighteen years ago, Brandt and Carn had stolen the little statuette from a double-crossing Brindisian merchant in Gathony who worshiped it as an idol. The merchant had called his diminutive black god the Yojo. No one but Brandt would know such a detail.

"And what did Brandt say?" Carn asked intently.

"Do I get to keep it?"

"That and more," he replied impatiently, "if you ever tell me the message."

The boy closed his eyes, as if better to remember, and pressed the Yojo to his chest.

"Time to slaughter our pig," he recited, "and serve him on our best china. Fires burn red and yellow, leaving black ashes for all to see."

"For all to see . . . ," Carn repeated, incredulous. The magnitude of the instructions were enormous. What could possibly have transpired in two short hours? "You're *sure* that's what he said?"

The boy rolled his eyes. "He made me repeat it twice. Sure, I'm sure."

Carn glanced down at the few files that lay scattered along the edge of the bed. Trivial, he realized now, compared to what would come on the morrow.

"Prepare a room for our friend," he ordered Baley. "He'll be spending the night."

"But what does that message mean?" Masya asked.

"We're about to find out." And then Carn turned back to the boy. "Now, you're going to tell me from the beginning, and with every detail you can remember, exactly what happened."

What had happened had begun as a stomach ache. That was easy enough to attribute to a traumatic day, and a traumatic night before it. What a catalog of misery, Brandt thought. There had been the frightened, big-eyed whore at Silene's, and Imbress at the window below; the rapid ride to the Atahr Vin and the nervous trip within those ancient tunnels; Carn's crippling; the duel with Hain; Aston's disturbing story, which Brandt still distrusted; and even the loaf of bread that Brandt had eaten on horseback as he'd started his journey through Prandis. Indeed, Brandt realized, that loaf was the first thing he'd eaten for more than a day, and the jarring rhythm of the horse was not the best digestive aid.

All in all, after such a day, a mere stomach ache was merciful.

But the world did not obey the laws of mercy anymore. Soon, although the night was chill, a sweat began to break across Brandt's brow. He loosened his cloak to the wind, but the fever began to spread nonetheless. The sweat covered him now, gummed his clothes to his limbs. He momentarily considered returning to the mansion, but he could be sick indefinitely, and it was certain that the assassin wouldn't delay departing for Yndor just to give Brandt a sporting chance. Nor was Brandt willing to sacrifice vengeance in order to sweat out a stomach flu in a comfortable bed. Hell, he'd rip out his belly himself if that would help him find Hain.

So, bowed in the saddle, he let his horse walk on through the streets of downtown Prandis. Above the row of two-story offices that lined the avenue, he could see

Council Tower looming not far off. *More lights than usual burning tonight*, he thought. *Their precious secrets are galloping west and the keepers of the Chaldean flame are frightened.* Despite his pain, Brandt grinned at the idea. At least he had partners in misery. Before killing Hain, he would have to thank the man for keeping the government apes out of their beds.

And beyond Hain . . . ? Brandt thought back to the night of his annual ball—almost a month ago—and the swarthy man who had intruded. Features like a bird of prey, all angles. And who was he? Secrets and secrets: they were all in that business, and his mysterious visitor wasn't far out of line, after all, in coming to Brandt. The visitor stole secrets, Brandt stole secrets. As Aston pointed out, it was a game he should understand well.

Except that Brandt never used any of the secrets he stole, or at least he hadn't used them recently. A couple of his earliest "clients" had responded to his modest requests for annuities by trying to have him killed. Three total, Brandt recalled. But his clients' assassins had proved to be less dangerous than information, the only secrets he'd ever published. In a flash, three careers had been ruined, and since then, none of Brandt's clients had attempted to strike back. They just sent him the cash, in satchels or vases or sewed in stuffed animals, to dozens of always changing pickup points. And they rested in comfort that their hidden lives remained tucked away safely in Galatine Hazard's files.

A provocative question, Brandt thought: Was the hidden life of Chaldus safe? Would the spy *use* the secret Phrases? In a hypothetical sense, Brandt was curious to find out, almost curious enough to let the swarthy man escape. It might be interesting to see things shaken up a bit. . . . But the reason that Brandt was out on horseback again—despite the cold night, despite his sore backside and aching gut and rising fever—was anything but hypothetical. There was a certain bald assassin out there whose anatomy Brandt yearned to rearrange, and alongside that purpose, speculation about the Phrases meant nothing.

A sharp pang ripped through his belly. He exhaled slowly and shook his head, hoping to clear it. It was no help.

And he knew it would be a long, miserable night.

His teeth had begun to chatter by the time he was stopped by the guard. There were four of them, and all on horseback, which was odd. The city guard usually traveled in pairs, and only rarely on horseback.

One of them wore sergeant's stripes, and it was he whom Brandt addressed as the four moved their horses into the middle of the street, blocking Brandt's progress.

"Is there a problem, officer?" Brandt growled through teeth he struggled to keep from knocking.

"You were swaying on your horse," the man explained, speaking the words thickly.

Was it that obvious? Perhaps he was sicker than he thought. The last thing he needed, though, was to be tossed into the drunks' cell overnight by some half-witted sergeant of the guard. Here, clearly, a judicious bribe would do a world of good. Brandt began to reach for his purse.

This seemed to be some sort of cue for the guards to reach for their swords.

One man in the open is never a match for four, Brandt knew, no matter what the epics say. At least, not when the one man was Brandt, and especially not when he was ill. As the guards' swords flashed from their sheaths, Brandt knew that he would soon be dead.

Unless he fought an entirely different battle.

He let his entire body go limp—not a difficult task at all, given the way he felt—and rolled out of the saddle. Even so, he was not quite fast enough; as he slipped from his horse, the tip of a blade ripped open his shirt sleeve and traced a bloody line across his triceps.

Bloody, but not deep, Brandt knew as he hit the cobbled ground, drawing a long dagger that he kept sheathed at his right hip. He rolled over quickly, reversing his grip on the dagger, and plunged it deep into the underbelly of the sergeant's horse. The wounded mount whinnied in pain and reared on its hind legs, seeking to escape the deadly sting. Brandt's arm was wrenched as he held onto the blade. It jerked out of the horse's intestines as the animal rose, and Brandt felt a spray of hot blood jet across his face and shoulders. He rolled away just before the horse's front hooves returned with a clatter to the cobbles where, only a moment ago, Brandt's head had been. But the horse had not been attacking Brandt with purpose. It was mad with pain, as Brandt had hoped, and it continued to buck and trumpet with terror. The sergeant was thrown violently to the cobblestones and lay there unmoving.

Beyond Brandt's wildest hopes, the other horses became panicked by the smell of blood and their companion's cries of distress. They shied away and bucked wildly, keeping their riders busy just to hang on. The city guard, Brandt knew, used warhorses, trained in battle to respond calmly and ignore blood. These mounts, obviously, were no warhorses. And neither, Brandt realized, were these men city guardsmen. Perhaps, he thought grimly, such knowledge might cost one or two of their lives.

Suddenly, it was no longer a matter of one man against four, out in the open.

One of the men had mastered his mount while the other two, sensing the futility of trying, jumped from their saddles and let their horses dash madly toward the center of the city.

Where was the *real* guard, Brandt wondered, now that he needed them? There was certainly noise enough to draw anyone's attention, and the mercantile district was usually well patrolled. But, as it seemed, if he waited for the guard to arrive, he would be waiting as a corpse. Already, his attackers were beginning to regroup. With a precise motion, he launched his dagger at the most immediate threat: the remaining mounted guard. The blade passed through the man's neck, just behind his voice box, and the sharp metal tip emerged from the other side. Brandt smiled grimly with satisfaction.

But his satisfaction was premature. In trying to avoid being trampled, he came closer to bringing exactly that to pass. The dead guard fell backward over the horse's rump, and the panicked beast shot off wildly down the street, exactly in Brandt's direction. He dived away almost in time, but felt a flying hoof glance against his thigh. There would be a tremendous bruise there for weeks, he thought ruefully.

Except, he reminded himself, that corpses didn't mind bruises, and he would be one soon unless he got back to his feet. The remaining two guards were advancing on him from either side, swords lifted for a deadly stroke.

In most circumstances, one man is no match for two in the open.

Fatalistically, Brandt rose to his feet and drew his sword, wondering which man he'd rather take with him if he had to die.

The cocky-looking jerk with the mustache, he decided. And he sprang at the man, his sword whistling through the air. From behind, he could hear the other guard launch into motion. He would have only a moment.

Brandt's blade struck his opponent's with a tremendous crash, showering the night with sparks. Brandt swiveled, lashing out with his foot. It caught the man in the ankle, making a sharp cracking noise. The guard's mustached mouth gaped with pain as he began to fall, but the pain wouldn't last long. The tip of Brandt's sword ripped open his throat long before he hit the ground.

It had been a quick kill, but not quick enough. As Brandt watched the man crumple, he tensed for the blow that he knew must be coming in a fraction of a second— the blow that would spill his brains or sever his head.

I've failed, he thought, imagining Carn lying in his bed, crippled and unavenged.

But the fatal blow never came.

He whirled around, the motion making his head spin, and saw the remaining guard a few feet behind him, his sword lying on the cobblestones. The man was on his knees, clutching something with both hands at the small of his back. Clutching a knife, Brandt realized. A very long knife, and it had been driven with apparent skill beneath the man's ribs, into his kidney. Such a wound produced shock almost immediately and was invariably fatal.

The stricken guard toppled onto his face, as if to prove the theory.

Now that the man had fallen, Brandt could see a figure that had been obscured behind him. It was a boy, no more than thirteen or fourteen and rather short for his age. He was ill-clad, and his dark brown hair looked unbrushed for a week, unwashed for many more.

The boy walked around to his victim and matter-of-factly jerked his dagger out of the corpse. He wiped it on the dead man's shirt, holding it up for inspection when he was done. Brandt could see the blade gleaming in the light of the waxing moon. At least the boy was fastidious about something.

Suddenly, Brandt's gut twisted into agonized knots and he fell onto all fours, spewing back his loaf of bread, with a lot of bile besides, onto the bloody cobblestones.

"Not used to seeing gore?" the kid asked calmly, as if the massacre had been an everyday event. "It'd sur-prise me, the way you handle that sword."

Brandt retched again and remained on his hands and knees, trembling, waiting for his stomach to settle.

"But you'll get used to the blood," the kid went on. There was an amused tone to his voice. He was clearly enjoying himself. Brandt recognized that tone only too well: the cynical, streetwise armor of a city orphan. And a tough one. Hell, at this kid's age, Brandt had been busy running from the city guard and their random beatings—not sticking knives in their backs. What, Brandt wondered, had the guard done to this poor kid to provoke him?

The knot in Brandt's middle untied, and he caught a clear breath. He wiped his mouth on his sleeve, noticing that the cloth was blood-soaked, and he remembered his wound.

"Sick," he grunted.

"I can see," the kid replied, "but, like I said—"

"Ill," Brandt went on emphatically.

"Oh, that kind of sick." He sounded disappointed. "Yeah, I hear it's going around."

Another wave of pain coursed through Brandt, sending white streamers streaking across his vision. But just then the sergeant moaned, beginning to recover from his fall from the saddle, and Brandt realized he could afford no more time to catch his breath. He struggled to his feet and stumbled across the street to the man. When Brandt sat down heavily on his former assailant's chest, it was less to immobilize the man than to disguise the fact that he lacked the strength to remain standing. The unfortunate sergeant opened his eyes to find a small dagger held to his throat.

"Who?" Brandt gasped, still unable to speak without pain. His throat burned as if a volcano, and not merely dinner, had spewed its way forth.

"My name is—"

Brandt pushed his dagger's point into the man's skin. It was an effective way of shutting him up.

The kid walked closer, watching with appreciation as a thin, dark bead of blood rose at the tip of Brandt's knife. The guy might have a weak stomach, the boy thought, but he also had technique. Enviable.

"I don't care who *you* are," Brandt growled to the sergeant. "Who *hired* you, idiot?"

The man's eyes were panicked, rolling wildly in their sockets as if they sought to escape his skull. Brandt let the dagger's tip play with the man's thick, creased skin. That got his attention, and Brandt repeated the question.

"I'm not saying nothing," the man answered haltingly.

"Then you die quiet."

Nervously, the fake sergeant swallowed. It was a mistake, raising his throat toward the blade. He felt the tip prick deeper through his skin. A few more drops of blood rose onto his neck.

"If I talk, do I walk away from here?"

"I make no promises but this," Brandt replied. "If you don't talk now, you never talk again. *Who hired you?*"

"Don't know," the sergeant gasped. "No one hired me directly. I work for Gratham. He's the one who cuts deals."

Brandt drew in a sharp breath and heard the boy do the same behind him. So the kid knew Gratham. Not surprising. Anyone who lived in the underbelly of Prandis did. Gratham was a mobster, a king of the toughs and thieves and extortionists that made their little fortunes exploiting the ripe city. Brandt had never had any dealings with Gratham, whom he considered a common thief—a man already far below his level when he and Carn had first ridden into Prandis, two very uncommon thieves indeed. Odd that Gratham would accept any job aimed at Brandt. The petty lord of the gutters should have known enough to stay away from Brandt. That meant that whoever had hired Gratham had either scared or impressed the man just as much. Or more.

"Did you see Gratham's client?"

The "sergeant" started to shake his head but, feeling the bite of the blade as he moved, stopped. "No, not clearly. Just a glimpse. I drove Gratham to an old road in Riverdell, a dead end behind the old charterhouse—"

Brandt nodded. He knew the place. It was, after all, his business to know every place in Prandis. And now, he also had his suspicions.

"There was a carriage waiting there. Black, two horses, curtains drawn. Gratham got in, got out a few minutes later with a case full of cash."

"And this glimpse of yours?"

"Couldn't see his face. Big man, though."

"Big?" Brandt asked. He twisted the blade a bit to add impetus to the question.

"Fat," the man replied.

And Brandt nodded. He had his answer. *Some people,* he reflected, *fall back too easily into old habits.* Brandt smiled at the thought of the secret files in his mansion and the many old habits they documented. He had read some of those files again very carefully since the murders began, and he knew every detail of the important ones. Even a detail as minor as the spot where a certain man, long ago and a hundred pounds slimmer, had once met his masters from Gathony. Odd, the compulsion that drove men back to the scenes of their crimes, even if it was only to commit fresh ones.

But a new thought ran through Brandt's head. Even if the ambush had succeeded, even if he had been killed, there remained the ruinous possibility of exposure. *He* was not the real danger, after all—it was the information in his files. The removal of Brandt merely meant that it would be Gratham who would blackmail Brandt's former client. Even Gratham was that smart: *Pay up or I tell Karrelian's partner who offed him, and that's the end of your career, dear minister.*

That possibility was simply too dangerous, and so there had to be more to the scheme.

"What else?" Brandt insisted.

"What do you mean?"

"Gratham was paid to do more than kill me. What else?" He was beginning to tremble again as the pain in his stomach returned. Much longer, and the sergeant might discover how weak he truly was. To speed things along, Brandt put a bit more weight on the knife, pushing the point farther into the man's flesh than he'd intended. A steady stream of blood began to trickle down the sergeant's neck, steaming as it hit the cobblestones.

"Fire," the man replied quickly. "Your house is being burned tonight."

Brandt nodded. Apparently, the fact that he kept his files in the mansion had become common knowledge. Or at least common enough to incite arson. What wasn't common knowledge were the two thick stone walls that entirely surrounded the storage room, separated by a buffering air space. Brandt's files would never burn.

Of course, that was no insurance for the rest of his house, for Carn or the servants. Perhaps they should make a show of moving the files somewhere, just to keep everyone guessing.

His stomach knotted in pain. A good enough signal to let the man go, Brandt thought, when one last idea occurred to him. This sudden illness of his was odd. Too odd, perhaps, to be a coincidence. There were wizards who could cast such spells. Of course, Brandt had spent a fortune on his own wizards, who had claimed to have protected him from every curse, hex, and blight known to all of collected wizardkind. Little good it seemed to have done him, he thought, reflecting bitterly on the wasted money. But, then again, he made a fortune approximately every other week. He had, on the other hand, only one life to spare . . . and it was quickly becoming clear that he wasn't a well-liked man.

"Wizards?" Brandt asked. He glanced about, but saw nothing. Odd, though. Now that he thought about it, he got the distinct impression of being watched. It wasn't the boy, who was fascinated by this rare show and stood quietly nearby, as if making mental notes for future use. The feeling was something else entirely, more ambiguous.

"What?" the sergeant asked.

"Did Gratham employ any wizards in the attack? Is there one here now?"

"I wish there was," the man replied. "You'd be dead."

"Respect," Brandt warned, widening the cut in the man's neck. "Remember, I've made you no promises."

"No wizards, man. No wizards. I swear. Gratham's afraid of them, never works with 'em."

Brandt nodded. He'd heard such rumors of Gratham, but if you paid a man well enough, he'd work with the devil himself. Brandt was satisfied, though, that he'd learned all he could from Gratham's lackey. This stomach pain was just some natural malady he'd have to endure. With one hand, he reached into his purse—that's how this had all begun, he remembered—and felt around for what he needed. A moment later, the fraudulent sergeant found a shiny gold capital resting on his forehead.

Brandt rolled off the man and took a step back.

"What's this for?" the thug asked as he picked up the coin and struggled warily to his feet.

"You give it to your boss," Brandt said with a wicked smile, "and tell him to open wide."

The sergeant nodded dumbly, neither understanding the message nor caring. It only mattered that he was alive, and that was more than he had expected a moment ago.

"No!" the boy cried.

Brandt turned around. It was the first thing he'd heard the boy say in minutes. No longer calm and wisecracking, the youth looked stricken. His eyes followed the retreating sergeant in panic.

"No! You're not going to let him go!"

Suddenly, the boy's dagger was in his hand and he sprang off after the departing killer. Brandt was directly in his path, however, and a well-placed foot sent the youth sprawling to the cobblestones. The sergeant rounded the nearest corner and disappeared.

"What's the matter with you?" Brandt asked, at the same time lifting a hand to his head. It had begun to throb. Probably it had been hurting the entire time, but now that the fighting and interrogations were over, he had relaxed enough to notice it.

"You can't let him go," the boy protested as he scrambled to his feet, an edge of panic in his voice. "Gratham'll kill me if he finds out I spoiled his job."

"Why *did* you spoil it?" Brandt asked, turning his full attention to the boy for the first time. There was a genuine look of fear in the boy's eyes. He lived in the streets, where Gratham was undisputed king, and Brandt did not doubt that Gratham would look for vengeance if he could trace the botched assassination to this street rat.

The kid shrugged and pointed to a bookshop across the way. "I was breaking into that store when I heard the fight—"

"A *bookshop*?" Brandt asked. There were jewelers, wine stores, and apothecaries along the block—much more sensible targets. "Can't pick a decent lock?" he guessed.

The kid's cocky attitude seemed to return.

"I can get in any one of these places."

"So . . . ?" Brandt prompted, glancing at the bookstore.

The boy's face screwed up with disgust.

"So I like to read. Want to make something of it?"

Brandt smiled and shook his head.

"Anyway, I heard the fight. I don't exactly like the

town guard, so I figured I'd help you. Anyone the guard wanted dead, I figured I'd probably like."

"Sorry to disappoint you," Brandt replied. Again, he wondered what kind of savage beatings the kid had suffered at the hands of the guards to foster such hatred. Worse, perhaps, than the split lips and cracked ribs Brandt had suffered, years ago, before Carn had rescued him from the streets.

"Well, I can't say yet whether I like you or not." There was a canny look in the kid's eyes. "Depends on whether you get me killed for this."

Brandt began to laugh, but pain cut him short. "The answer's no. Depend on it. Listen, I have a message for you to deliver."

"What's in it for me?"

Brandt shook his head, amazed. Worried for his life, but the kid was still ready to haggle.

"For one thing, once you deliver it, you won't have to worry about Gratham again."

"You *owe* me that one," the boy responded quickly. "I saved your life, you save mine."

Brandt grinned; that, thankfully, didn't hurt. This guttersnipe was better medicine than anything he'd find in the apothecary's shop. At least, a better distraction.

"What's your name?"

"Katham."

"Well, Katham, here's what's in it for you. You go to my house and you tell a man named Carn everything that happened here, especially about the arsonists, and you move your butt doing it. If my house is burned down, you won't be getting paid. Tell him I owe you. . . ."

There was a problem. He needed some quick sign that Katham was a legitimate messenger. "Tell him I'm giving you the Yojo."

"Not cash?"

"Better than cash. It's an ebony statuette. You'll find

it just past my front doors, on a pedestal. It's worth a small fortune. Also tell him that you can have any five books from my library. Lord knows I don't read them."

"And the cash?" the kid asked impatiently.

"I told you, the statuette—"

"You ever try to fence a statuette?" Katham asked, fists resting cockily on his hips.

"As a matter of fact—"

"Well, *I* haven't," Katham interrupted, sensing that Brandt's answer was about to steamroll over his minor attempt at extortion. "Takes time to fence anything at a decent price in this town. Speaking of time," the kid added slyly, "is that your house I smell burning?"

Brandt sighed. Katham had him over a barrel. "Fine. Tell him to give you fifty capitals, too. But this part is very important. This part you've got to memorize word for word."

The kid closed his eyes, as if the better to hear. "Okay, shoot."

Brandt considered a moment how best to phrase it. "It's time to slaughter our pig," he finally said, slowly and clearly, "and serve him on our best china."

Katham repeated it.

"Good," Brandt approved, preparing to send the boy off.

But what, he asked himself, had he really solved? Kordor might be dealt with, but the real problem was the files themselves, the cancerous mass of secrets that dwelt beneath the house, inciting Brandt's former clients to arson and murder.

Brandt doubled over, impaled on a lance of pain. He retched forth what little was left in his stomach, most of it bilious yellow. Momentarily, at least, he felt better— hollowed out, but clean.

And that was the answer. He had lived long enough with these secrets, protecting the treacherous Kordors of the world in exchange for the commissions on iniquity.

It was time for a purge, to clean the mansion out and make it new—to see if Carn, and perhaps Masya, could make something different of the place.

Brandt didn't care about the red or yellow files—the records of transient errors and misjudgments. Most of those people had done nothing that deserved their lives being brought down in ruins. Few, indeed, had done anything worse than Brandt himself. But the black files—Kordor and every snake like him who betrayed the principles they professed to believe. . . .

"There's something more," Brandt added, catching the boy by the arm. Judging by the kid's look, he realized he must be squeezing tighter than he intended.

"Tell him this, too," Brandt said, releasing Katham's arm. "Tell him: Fire burns yellow and red, leaving black ashes for all to see."

Katham furrowed his brow, more perplexed than before, but repeated the sentence without error. Brandt nodded his approval and gave the boy directions to the mansion. "Now get going."

Katham turned to leave.

"And one last thing," Brandt added. "Tell Carn to get you a bath."

"What?" Carn roared as Katham nonchalantly recounted the part about the arson. "Why didn't you tell me that immediately?"

Katham merely shrugged.

Carn's cries had brought Baley running into the room.

"Have the grounds scoured," Carn ordered. "Expect intruders tonight!"

In an instant, the servant was gone.

Carn took a long look at the disheveled boy before him and shook his head. "If Brandt knew you were going to make such a mess of delivering his messages, he'd never have agreed to pay you two hundred capitals."

Katham grinned. "And the ten books."

"And the ten books," Carn repeated wearily. He wondered how much Brandt had really consented to pay the boy, but a little petty fraud didn't bother Carn, not when Brandt's life had been saved. And small investments had an uncanny way of paying dividends later.

"If there's any danger," Masya said, "we can return to my flat. It's no mansion, but no one's tried to burn it down as long as I've lived there."

Carn looked up at her and laughed. "I've waited too long to lure you into this house to flee at the first sign of trouble. You and I are staying." He turned back to Katham. "And you may finish your tale."

The boy shrugged, explaining that there wasn't much to add. In a few minutes, he described what had happened after Brandt let the fake sergeant escape—at least, most of what had happened.

Breathless, Baley burst back into the room. "We found two men at the mansion walls, sir. They had rags and bottles of kerosene."

"And what did you do?" Carn asked.

The guardsman's face screwed up in confusion. "Nothing."

"*Nothing?*" Carn thundered. "What do you mean—"

"There was nothing to do," Baley amended hastily. "That is, they were already dead. They'd both been stabbed."

Baley lifted his finger and pointed to the small of his back, directly above his left kidney.

Katham was grinning like a demon.

Dividends and dividends, Carn thought.

"Very good. Now show Katham to his room for the night."

Still grinning, Katham began to retreat toward the door.

"But before you do," Masya added, staring disapprovingly at the unkempt youth, "show him to a bath. And find him some decent clothes."

And, suddenly, the grin was gone.

While **K**atham grumbled about all the hot water he saw filling the marble tub—he'd been *sure* not to mention that part of Brandt's instructions—Brandt himself finally approached the huge gates that marked the city's official limits. A cold, steady rain had begun, sending the guards scurrying into the gatehouse where they huddled over their coffee and cigarettes. One guard remained at his post by the window, but he did nothing more than look strangely at the traveler who rode hunched over his saddle, a keen spike of pain twisting in his gut.

Brandt wondered what it would be like tomorrow, when the secrets began to emerge, flying from their basement prison, desperate for the light; when respected financiers were led through the streets in shackles; when politicians, hearing the knock of the city guard at the door, would choose a knife or a vial instead; when corpses would begin to bob like buoys upon the River Mirth, each carried along on a tide of vengeance long deferred.

Brandt wondered whether Carn would really destroy the rest of the files by fire. Quite a bonfire it would be, the flames licking skyward as the ashes wafted away on the breeze. And when each of those files was gone, when the basement vault lay empty, there would be no sign remaining that Brandt had ever been there at all.

Yes, all the secrets would emerge tomorrow. Solan would tell Carn the true meaning of the papers they had signed, transferring irrevocably the ownership of Brandt's enterprises into Carn's sole possession. Brandt's business associates might be briefly puzzled by the change in ownership and his disappearance, but Carn would manage the business more ably than he ever had. And soon enough, his name would be forgotten—whether Brandt Karrelian or Galatine Hazard.

A moment more and he passed the guardhouse, leaving the cobbled streets of Prandis behind. Before him, through a burning mist that veiled his eyes, Brandt could see the hardpack road stretching west into the night, stretching toward Belfar, the city of his youth.

Stretching toward a killer named Hain.

And, beyond that, stretching perhaps to freedom.